STRAWBERRIES

IN THE SEA

by Elisabeth Ogilvie

Down East Books / Camden, Maine

Strawberries in the Sea

Copyright © 1973, by Elisabeth Ogilvie. All rights in this book are reserved. Reprinted 1999 by arrangement with the McGraw-Hill Book Company, Inc.

Jacket illustration © 1999 by R.B. Dance
ISBN 0-89272-466-8
Printed and bound at Capital City Press, Burlington, Vermont

5   4   3   2   1

Down East Books
P.O. Box 679
Camden, ME 04843
BOOK ORDERS: 1-800-685-7962

Library of Congress Cataloging-in-Publication Data

Ogilvie, Elisabeth, 1917–
      Strawberries in the sea / Elisabeth Ogilvie.
         p.   cm. — (Bennett's Island saga ; 6)
      ISBN 0-89272-466-8 (pbk.)
         1. Islands—Maine—Fiction. 2. Women—Maine—Fiction. I. Title.
II. Series: Ogilvie, Elisabeth, 1917–   Bennett's Island saga ; 6.
PS3529.G39S77   1999
813'.52—dc21   99-17862
                                         CIP

The man in the wilderness asked me,
How many strawberries grow in the sea?
I answered him, as I thought good,
As many as red herrings grow in the wood.

Old nursery rhyme

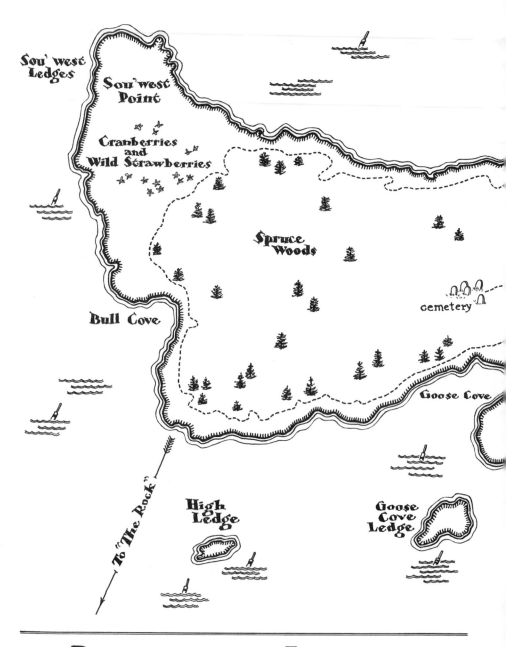

Sou'west Ledges

Sou'west Point

Cranberries and Wild Strawberries

Spruce Woods

cemetery

Bull Cove

Goose Cove

"To The Rock"

High Ledge

Goose Cove Ledge

❧ BENNETT'S · ISLAND ❧

2½ miles from Sou'west Point to Eastern End Cove

Harbor Ledges

To Brigport

Western Harbor Point

Barque
Cove

Big Wharf

Eastern
Harbor
Point

① Clubhouse
② The Well

Paths ------

① Nils
and
Joanna ②

Harbor Beach

Long Cove

The Homestead

Schoolhouse

School-
house
Cove

Ice pond
Barn

Woods

Pudding
Island

Windward
Point

Eastern
End Cove

To Tenpound Island

W
N
S
E

Shag Ledge

What isn't woods is ledge (all around shores) and field.

Map by A.B. Venti

I

She thought the pain was going to burst out of her in a groan or a cry there on the dingy staircase. Half-blinded with tears and with a sensation like that of a knife in her throat, she reached the vestibule and stood back against the wall, holding her big handbag up to her chest like a shield. The doors stood open and Main Street was a blurry glare of motion with the people passing by and the flashes of light from moving cars. The cheerful din seemed to be rising to some fearful climax.

Trying to press herself into the wall and become invisible, and knowing that was impossible for a hundred and seventy pounds in wine-and-turquoise knit, she fought the silent fight so familiar from the days when she tried not to cry in school. In the early grades she used to lose the battle quite often, in a noisy, blubbering surrender that delighted the rest of the class and made her loathe them. But only until the next day, or even until just after school the same day; she was a compulsive optimist who would rather be friendly than not.

Even now, in a panic for fear someone who knew her might glance in and see her wallowing in the mire of lost pride, she was not angry with Con for being the cause of it. Instead she was grief-stricken, as if she had just made arrangements for his funeral. When she'd told the lawyer where the papers could be served, it had been like telling the funeral director where the family plot was.

If she was mad at anybody, it was at the Seal Pointers who'd been waiting to see just how long she could hold Con. They'd never really believed in their marriage. How could a Conall Fleming fall in love with a Rosa McKinnon? Sure, she was a good girl, a great housekeeper, handy in a boat, and strong. If a man wanted a helper, he wouldn't have to pay twenty per cent out of each haul. But a girl like that for Con Fleming?

No. Rosa McKinnon had property, that's what it was. The old man should have left it tied up. He hadn't been gone a year before Con had the boat, the gear, the shore privilege, the whole works. That was all good old Rosie had for Con Fleming.

Rosa knew what they said, because some of the older ones had tried to warn her. She believed their doubts had ill-wished the marriage from the start, and at this moment, in the stuffy vestibule of the Hanchett Block, her rage was like the dash of icy water tossed in her face when she was three and used to hold her breath. She gasped, the flood receded, and she groped in her bag for one of her father's big handkerchiefs; tissues were no good, they were too small and frail. She wiped her face vigorously, remembering too late that she'd worn powder and lipstick today and experimented with eyeshadow as a kind of armor.

Oh, the hell with it, she thought, and blew her nose. Then she stepped out into the sidewalk traffic, and moaned softly with a purely physical pain. Her feet had swollen since she'd gotten them into high-heeled pumps this morning. Dampened with perspiration, her girdle had tightened into a ribbing of iron. She fixed her eyes on the pickup truck parked down the street in front of the First Baptist Church. To get home and free her flesh to cool air, and then howl for hours in a locked room until she couldn't wring out another sound, was the biggest bliss she could imagine at the moment.

The sidewalk ahead of her shimmered and billowed like an ocean swell under the sun. When she stepped off the curb, one of the high heels turned and she pitched toward the pavement. There was a car coming, but she was not allowed to plunge beneath its wheels. Arms went around her waist like a vise.

"Con?" The name came before she could hold it back, twisting to look into a stranger's face; young eyes laughing at her shock and astonishment, but not maliciously, out of a wilderness of hair and beard.

"Sorry I'm not," he said, still holding her.

"Never mind," she muttered, burning hot. "Thanks, I guess I was about to break my neck." He·let her go. He had a friend, John the Baptist with dark glasses and bedroll. At least they didn't know her, she was nothing to them, not Con's fool or anyone's. For this she could smile and say again, "Thanks. It's these damned high heels. I should've stuck to my rubber boots."

They laughed, and she felt a small triumph. She lifted her hand jauntily. "Goodbye."

One of them said, "Don't blow your cool, sis." He sounded kind. She set off blindly and rapidly, and in a few yards bumped into someone else, who called her by name.

"Rosa! Hi, Rose! Where you bound for?"

Her mother's cousin Jude Webster stood in her way. His face gradually grew clear to her, so narrow the features seemed sharpened like an ax blade, graying hair springing back from high temples, his eyes set deep in creases behind his glasses.

"Come on and have a cup of coffee," he said. He pulled her arm through his; he was very strong for such a thin man. When they went into the coffee shop he said, "You better go wash your face. I'll get a booth."

She started to object, until two young girls approached her, hastily looked away, and giggled after they'd passed by. She plunged toward the door marked Ladies and locked herself in. The mirror gave back her face shiny with damp, streaked and blotched with lipstick and the green eyeshadow.

3

Why green? she wondered dispassionately. Those boys had been damned mannerly not to hoot out loud. She soaked a paper towel and sprinkled it with liquid soap, and scrubbed her face until the skin was pink and stinging. She had a square chin with the big McKinnon dimple in it, and wide cheekbones, lightly freckled. As she looked back at herself to see if she was presentable and wouldn't disgrace Jude, her gray eyes were at once timid and eager, staring into the glass as they'd gazed into mirrors all her life, watching for whatever it was that watched *her* from behind those eyes.

The doorknob rattled impatiently, and she called, "Just a minute!", hastily combing her hair. She'd chopped it off one day in rage and frustration when she didn't have the guts to cut her throat but wanted to do something violent. She'd looked foolish with long hair anyway; just another of Con's jokes on her. *I love your hair, I want it long enough to tangle my hands in.*

She unlocked the door and went out, smiling steadily at the woman and the jiggling child. She smiled the same way at Jude, who looked relieved.

"Now I recognize you. What was that green stuff around your eyes?"

"Eyeshadow. I was just wondering why I thought it had to be green."

"I thought you'd come down with some new disease, like Irish measles. . . . I ordered you an eclair. I know how crazy you are about that stuff."

"Stay me with eclairs and comfort me with cream puffs," she said. "I've been stayed and comforted for so long that if it was all liquor I'd be rolling in the gutter by now."

"Better food than rum anytime, girl."

"Ayuh. If you're lonesome, just put on twenty-five more pounds. Create your own group." She slapped her belly, and Jude flinched slightly but forebore to glance around.

"Look, Jude, let's get this over with," she said. "I'll need two witnesses. Will you be one? I can get Leona Pierce for the other."

4

"Sure," he said. "Anything to help you get rid of that critter."

She kept her mouth shut. When the waitress came she took the coffee but refused the eclair. "Look, will you put that and five more in a box for me? Thanks. . . . For Lucy, if you don't want any, Jude," she said. "She can stand it, but I've got to stop eating sometime."

"Now don't go to the other extreme and starve yourself." He went on in a more hushed voice, bearing out the funeral *motif*. "I guess I don't need to ask what you're doing in town today, all dressed up and so forth. I'm sorry, Ro."

"Don't be," she said briskly. "The way I see it, I'm lucky to've had three years, and I wouldn't give that up, no matter what—" Her throat grew tight and she sipped coffee.

"Well, if that's the way you look at it, it's your business," said Jude, but his tone scorched her and she thought, You think I'm a fool as much as Con ever did. . . . Even to think Con's name swamped her in the adoration and ache for something so glitteringly beautiful that without it she had no life whatever. As the wave retreated she had hardly the energy to hold her cup, yet she had to keep drinking, her eyes downcast to avoid Jude's.

"What about the place?" he was asking. "He signed off yet?"

"Yes."

"Good!" Jude slapped a palm down. "Of course he wouldn't mind that much, not with what he's stepping into. Now what about *Sea Star?*"

"Oh, we're going to sell her, but he's using her till the new one's ready."

Jude wagged a long bony forefinger at her. "You make sure that you handle the sale, my girl. If he does, you'll never see the money." When she didn't answer, but kept staring at the other people, he asked softly, "You letting him have it all?"

"Well, he's a man, Jude, he has to have more, and where he's starting out with a family on the way——"

"Oh, my God, now I've heard everything." Jude pushed

5

away his pie and sat back, shaking his head, looking over his glasses at her and then shaking his head again. She thought, You haven't heard everything, Jude. You haven't heard that I made him a present of the boat the first Christmas, not just the gear and Papa's colors.

Jude said, "You sell some shore property so he can have a forty-footer built with every damn gadget but an elevator, and then he tells you he's got a woman in the family way so he has to have a divorce. And now you're about to stand fairy godmother to the three of them. My God, Ro, where's your wits? Where's your pride?"

"Maybe I've got neither left," she said thickly, "but, like you said a while back, Jude, it's my business." She started to get up.

"Oh, sit still. I guess you got a right to run things your own way. No use saying anything, you've got that stubborn McKinnon streak."

"Well, the Webster strain don't help any." They grinned at each other and she sat down again. "But you see, Jude," she began placatingly, "I knew Con had a roving eye. He was born with it, and he can't help it any more than he can help his red hair. I knew that when I married him, and you can say what you like about the property and all, he had plenty of other chances, and he wouldn't have tied himself down to one woman if he hadn't had good intentions."

"Good intentions for *him*. And he didn't tie himself down none."

She ignored that. "And maybe if we'd had a baby right off he'd never have gone wandering. A man wants a son. Papa was good to me, but I know how it must've hurt him, never having a boy to carry on the name." She kept turning her spoon over and over, watching the reflection of the pink lights on the stainless steel. She'd wanted a red-haired baby so bad, boy or girl didn't matter, so bad it was as if she'd had it and it died.

"You've got two boys, Jude, so you can't know what it's

6

like to want them and see the time going by and yourself getting older without them."

He didn't answer, and, though she'd have resented almost anything he said, she resented his silence even more. "He needed an anchor," she said. "A family would have been that. And after a while he wouldn't have run around any more."

When she stopped she heard the echo of the words in their falseness. Bitterly she said to the spoon, "Women wouldn't leave him alone. While he was on the loose it was like they all had a chance, even the married ones who wouldn't step out of their own dough dish, nossir, but they'd *dream* about it plenty. And they couldn't stand thinking he'd picked somebody like me to marry. It put them down, you see. They just couldn't get over it. Now they're all—they're all—"

She shut her teeth down on her lower lip and picked up her cup, which slopped as her hand shook. Jude said with a humiliating gentleness, "If you've got it all reasoned out, why, that's about all anybody can do. I hope you've done some reasoning about your future."

"I've got the place and most of the land except that piece on Back Cove I sold. And I've got the boat," she lied. "I've kept up my lobster license too. Never told him, the way he felt about women lobstering, but I paid up every year just in case he got an infected hand from a bream bone or a kink in his back, and needed help aboard the boat. So I can always make a living, as long as they don't make a law saying women can't run a string of gear."

Jude laughed, and she demanded, "You think that's what puts men off me? They want something frail and womanly, instead?"

"My God, Ro, there's plenty of men would look at you if you'd give 'em a chance. You're all woman, and you can't hide the fact."

"Why, Jude, how you talk," she teased him. "And you looking like a minister. . . . And I sure can't hide the fact that there's quite a lot of woman to squeeze into dungarees."

7

But he was serious. "They knew you were around, all right, but all you saw was Con. He showed up like the one new penny in a handful of change. Some of that could have been fifty-cent pieces or even silver dollars, but all you saw was that one penny shined up enough to put your eye out. You ain't the first woman to do so, nor the last."

She wanted to ask what she could ask no one: could she help it for coveting the coppery dazzle above everything else? And was she sorry now? If she said loudly, "*No*," Jude would be shocked. She almost said it anyway, to stuff his sermons back down his throat. Instead she said airily, "Jude, are those Wileys still renting your place out on Bennett's? I heard something on the short wave the other day, fellers talking back and forth while they hauled, and it made me wonder if they'd moved off."

"Ayuh, they moved off a couple of weeks ago. Soon as school finished out there. The youngest boy finished the eighth grade and he'll be going to high school in the fall, and his folks don't want to board him out over here, they're scared of all this drug business and fast cars and so forth. The old man's going lobstering in the bay, out of Limerock."

"So the house is empty?"

He was still innocent. "Yes. An older boy works for Owen Bennett, so he lives with them."

"I sh'd think you'd rent your place to summer people."

"It'd need some fixing up and a lot fancier toilet than it's got now, if I can mention the fact at the table." They both laughed. "No, some fisherman'll come along and want it. I guess we'll sell it this time. My kids are all away from home except Edwin, and he's no lobsterman."

"Sell it to me," said Rosa. "How much do you want for an option?" She was opening her bag and taking out her billfold. "Fifty, a hundred, two hundred?" She began counting out bills between the coffee cups.

"Good God, put that stuff away!" He shoved the money

back at her, his face red and his eyes jumping behind his glasses as if she'd started taking her clothes off in public. She looked purposely stupid and amazed, and he said rapidly, "Now listen, Ro, I'm not letting you do anything foolish while you're still in shock. What do you want with a place way to hell and gone over the horizon? Home's home, and you'll feel better about it after you get the stink of Con out of it. You belong in Seal Point, and he's the foreigner. Our folks settled there before the Revolution, and roots count. Without 'em you're a vessel without ballast."

"Next thing you'll be telling me I ought to join the D.A.R. so's to take up my mind," she said. "Sure I'm in shock. I've got to divorce my husband. I've got a couple of months to get through first, and I'll be damned if I spend 'em in Seal Point with everybody clacking and staring and oozing pity like pork fat when they're not snickering."

"All right!" His mouth snapped tight on the words. "Go on out there and use the house for the summer, if you want to, and welcome to it."

"Take fifty dollars for an option to buy, just to humor me?"

He wasn't amused. "Twenty-five, and you'll get it back when you move back in here. And it's just to humor you."

She smiled at him in genuine affection. "Thank you, Jude."

The rigidity went out of his face. "You always were the damndest little mutt," he said. "If you smiled more often like that, you'd find out something.... Look, the Wileys were clean enough, but he was no hand to fix things up. I sent out shingles to patch the roof, but he never put them on, and there might be some windows need puttying."

"I can camp out somehow. I'll go out on the mailboat next Monday."

"I'll get the keys to you before then," Jude said.

She wished she could go now, launching herself like a gull from a roof on Main Street straight out over the broad blue wind-wrinkled plain of the bay; to be transmuted into everything that she was not and could never be, and never come back to Seal Point or be seen again as Rosa Fleming.

2

Driving the pickup home barefoot, she was of half a mind to throw the shoes into the first alder swamp she passed outside Limerock. She never wanted to wear them again, or any of the clothes she wore today, as she'd never worn again the clothes she'd bought for Papa's funeral. But they were practically new, and it would be a criminal waste for nobody to have the use of them, just because the sight and feel of them turned her stomach. She would do with them what she'd done with the funeral apparel: put everything in a carton and leave it just outside the entrance to the town dump. The carton would be gone in an hour, and some defeated soul from the Quarry Road would be trying the clothes on and feeling fancy and gay for a change.

I'll throw in all the make-up too, she thought cynically. That green eyeshadow ought to make some hovel into a happy home.

A vision of Bennett's Island lying on the sea was superimposed on the familiar view ahead of road and spruce woods. It was a place where Con had never been and where nobody would know about him and her. She had gone there often in the years when her father had run a lobster smack to the outside islands. Awkward with her height and puppy fat, she'd been too bashful to go onto the island itself; she used to sit on a nailkeg in a dim corner of the store on the wharf, licking an ice cream cone or drinking pop, and watch the island people come and go. All of them, even the children, were as mysterious to her as the island itself with its unknown fields and woods. *Anything* could lie beyond the visible part of the village; *anything* could go on in the heads and behind the eyes of these island people who moved as casually in their exotic ambience as ordinary people did back at Seal Point.

She'd been around sixteen her last trip out there, and Papa was beginning to fret about making a boy of her. She'd just gotten up enough courage to promise herself that next time she was going to walk around the harbor and across the island to the other side and see what was there when he gave up smacking, saying the run was too long and too tough for a rheumaticky man. But later he made a few trips with *Sea Star* in the first year of the boat's life and the last of his, taking out bait and bringing back lobsters as a favor to his successor when the younger man was having engine trouble.

"It's a favor to myself too," he told Rosa, "and even more to the boat. She gets tired of slogging around that string of traps every day. She says, 'That why you had a new boat built, Cap'n? To go round in circles, day in, day out?' No, she'd like a chance to spread her wings and head out to sea and just *go*."

"Well, so would I," said Rosa. "How about me going next time?"

He shook his head. "No, no. You and I, we'll take a sail out some pretty Sunday, but when it's a business trip it's no place for a woman."

It was no sense arguing that a weekday trip would be better than a Sundayfied one. "All right, just as long as we get our sail."

"We will, we will. That's a promise, Punkin."

By then he wasn't even happy about her helping him with

his traps, as if he thought he was cheating her out of a girl's life; he seemed to think that when she wasn't in school she ought to prefer to cook, to garden, to make new curtains, and spend happy afternoons doing fancywork for church fairs. Somehow all these activities would magically turn her into the kind of girl who was taken to movies and dances and was eventually married in the Seal Point Baptist Church, with everyone there.

About once a week she assured Papa that while she didn't mind cooking for him and her, and raising vegetables in summer, she didn't want to do anything else but be on the water in *Sea Star*, with maybe some mackereling and clamming on the side. This always made him look worried.

When she and Con were married she thought, I hope Papa knows, and he's happy that everything turned out all right; better than all right, even if we were married by a justice of the peace in Belfast and not by Mr. Murray in church with everyone there.

Now tears squeezed slowly into her eyes, not for Papa but for her own incredulous happiness that night in Belfast. She kept her vision clear for the last mile into town by blinking furiously, but when she turned in under the cold shade of the maples in the driveway, the open barn doors shimmered before her and salt drops began to run down her cheeks.

A good long bawl, that's what you need, she thought. Get it over with and then start packing.

She went in the side door between the eave-high white lilacs, handbag under her arm, shoes in her hand, stockings trailing. We never did make that special trip, she thought. There never was a pretty Sunday all that summer, and in the fall Papa was dead. He hadn't expected that.

She dropped her shoes in the short hall and went into the kitchen unbuttoning her dress.

Con was there. He sat on a stool at the counter drinking coffee, eating pie, and reading *The Down-East Fisherman*.

He looked around with mischievous appreciation and she began struggling to button her dress again, but her fingers had no strength.

"Why all the modesty?" Con asked. "We're still married."

"Damn you!" she said. "You've got one hell of a nerve! That's the cherry pie for the Brownies' cooked-food sale!"

He had a soft, surreptitious, snorting laugh that always used to make her laugh just to hear it. It maddened her now. She went across the kitchen into her room and shut the door, remembering not to slam it as that would only amuse him further. She stripped off her clothes, hurling the damp girdle viciously across the room, and went into the bathroom and took a cool shower. She returned to her room and put on fresh underwear and a cotton dress, and went back to the kitchen in her bare feet.

"Coffee, love?" Con invited. "Or how about a cold beer?" He went toward the refrigerator. The new penny, Jude called him, and that was the color of his hair, crisp and glittering on his tanned neck.

"Never mind the beer," she said. "What are you here for?"

He turned, hands outspread in innocent surprise. "I came in to load that last batch of traps to set out tomorrow morning, if it doesn't come in thick of fog. You knew I was coming." He was hushed with hurt.

"What are you doing in my house? That's what I mean. Walking in here as if you still had rights. And cutting into that pie."

"The best cherry pie I ever ate, by God. Listen, love, you wouldn't take me on as a boarder, would you? Strictly business? Geneva Rowland's the worst cook in three counties."

She went to the cupboards and began assembling materials for a new pie. She had to form an image of each item and say the word to herself. *Yellow bowl. Shortening.* . . . "It's all under way," she addressed the flour can. "They'll serve

13

the papers on you at Geneva's. Sometime in August you'll be off the hook. Goodbye, and I mean it."

"Ah, Rosie, don't be so bitter," he said in a low voice, close behind her. "You've never once talked to me like a human being since that day."

"There was nothing to say. There's nothing now." She opened cupboard doors, glared blindly inside, slammed them shut. "You said it all."

"Not all." He put his hands on her shoulders and turned her around. She could have resisted, and was ashamed because she didn't. His face was close to hers, tenderly earnest. "Don't hate me, darlin'. I can't stand having you hate me, after what we've been to each other for three years. You gave me my first real family, my first real home. You think I'm happy about this, but I'm not. Somebody should've knocked my brains out with a club before I ever got that close to Phyl!"

She lifted first one of his hands off and then the other, gingerly, as if they were repellent to the touch. "But you *love* her," she said, making her eyes big. "You can't live without her, remember? You couldn't help yourself. And didn't I want you to be happy? If I really *loved* you, I'd want you to be happy, no matter what. And besides, there was the little feller, he had to have a name. Could I take it out on an innocent child?"

"Sure, I said all that because I was half out of my mind! You know what hell is? It's not what somebody does to you, it's the day when your own foolishness catches up with you. Goddam my wandering eye, you're enough woman for any man."

"Will you go now?" she asked stolidly. "I've got another pie to make."

"Oh, to hell with the pie!" he shouted. He was red. "I still love you, Rosie, that never stopped! Sure, I'll admit she turns my guts inside out by just looking at me, but so do you in your own way, despising me with that cold eye, you that was always so warm."

"I love little Rosie, her heart is so warm, and if I butter her up enough she'll do me no harm." She laughed loudly. "It wasn't only your eye that wandered, was it?" She turned her back on him, reaching for the two-cup measure. "Look, you better stop using this wharf and fishhouse. I thought for a while it'd be all right, but I've changed my mind. She's got a decent wharf over there in Birch Harbor."

"I can't start tying up there till I'm married to her!" He sounded actually shocked.

This time her laughter almost got away from her in wildly spiraling hoots. "With every fisherman in Seal Point seeing you tied up there when you were supposed to be hauling, with everybody from here to Limerock knowing she was in the family way before I did? Oh, go away, Con!" she gasped. "Get out and don't bother me any more."

His arms enwrapped her from behind, his fingers pressing into her breasts. His lips brushed her nape. "Listen, Rosie, if it wasn't for the kid I'd call it off in a minute, I swear it."

She wrenched his arms apart and moved away from him with a twisting thrust of her shoulder. "What do you want me to do for you? Tell you it's all right, I know you can't help it so go along with my blessing? Salve your conscience for you? Well, I won't."

His head jerked and his eyes widened as if she had slapped him, and she grinned maliciously. "You mean it, don't you? You can't stand to have anybody mad with you. It *does* kill you if anybody gives you a hard eye, no matter what you've done to deserve it. Has everybody got to love Conall Fleming? So he'll feel safe and happy?" She remembered the weight and warmth of his head against her breast in the long winter nights. "Now go on. You're through with the wharf and fishhouse, remember. I'm not having you run in and out as if you still had a right to, and I don't think she'd care for it either, not that I give a hoot in hell what she likes."

"You want to watch it, you're turning sour, Rosie," he said sorrowfully. "You'll be spending the rest of your life alone, and there's no need of that. Even if you've got no more use for me, there's other men in the world."

"When did you come to that conclusion? Put the boat back on the mooring when you go down to the fishhouse to pick up your stuff."

"What's the harm in leaving her at the wharf for the night? I won't come near you in the morning."

"I don't trust that promise, and I don't want you within a half mile of me. It could upset the divorce and I don't want to take any chances on that. I can hardly wait to get shed of you."

He turned abruptly and walked away. At the sight of his back going out the door she felt his name rise in her throat like something to be compulsively spewed out, and she put her hand over her mouth to hold it in.

She half-turned toward the sink window to watch him going down to the wharf, but instead she bolted for the back stairs, and was up in the attic chamber pulling bags out when the diesel engine started up. She stood staring up at the familiar shreds of bark left on the old hand-hewn beams but not seeing them, listening to *Sea Star*'s progress among the moorings until the soft pulse was drowned out by a nearer outboard motor.

3

By now she was beyond tears, she felt parched and barren, and in this desert she made the new pie for the Brownies. While it was in the oven, she picked up some things to take away with her. This was Friday, and the mailboat wouldn't go again until Monday, but she wanted to pack so she would feel she was moving forward all the time. She had a sleeping bag, and clothes were no problem, just an assortment of shirts, slacks, sweaters, underwear, and a change of sneakers; her oilclothes in case she wanted to walk in the rain. She'd always liked that, but Con was like a cat about getting wet. At work was one thing, but for *pleasure?*

There'd be all those shores foreign to her, the gray seas rolling in and the scent of wet rocks and fresh-pulled kelp, the drenched woods on one side of her and nothing out there in the rain and the mist but the ocean. Papa was always quoting about the surf, *Break, break, break, on they cold grey stones, O sea,* from a poem he'd learned in school, but he never could remember anything more than that. But he'd said it so often that she always thought it when she was on the shore in certain weathers. Now it meant Bennett's Island in the rain, and it filled the house with storm-swept seas while the June day moved into burnished evening outside the windows. When the timer rang for the pie, she came back to the moment with a slight shock of disorientation.

She set the pie out on a bench in the back entry to cool, and called Leona Pierce to tell her where it was. Then she found a box for the clothes she had worn today, emptied her handbag of personal things, and put in all the make-up and the last bottle of perfume Con had given her—she'd always had a suspicion that Phyllis had picked it out—and put the bag in the box too. She loaded the trash and garbage containers into the back of the pickup, set the box of clothes beside her on the seat, and drove out through the village.

At the eastern end of steep Main Street the harbor was as blue as bachelor's-buttons, and the boats, wharves, and sheds were all coated with evening sunshine, thicker and richer than the morning kind. It was suppertime and hardly anyone was in sight. She drove up the hill toward the Civil War monument, the young soldier turned a burning bronze by the long rays of late sun, and followed a silent road past lawns and gardens where no one was. In the curious light and stillness it seemed like a place from which all humankind had been removed by some unspeakable catastrophe out of science fiction. The impression was so strong that when she met two boys on bicycles she was relieved; then she thought, Why should I care if everybody else but me disappears? At least nobody would be looking at me any more. And nobody'd have Con if I couldn't.

Her calm began to thin and waver like dissolving fog, and she braced her jaw and stepped harder on the gas. She took the turn-off by the Advent church and drove through the woods of the Glencoe section, where the dump was. There was no one else there at this hour, only gulls and crows, and she was glad of that. She didn't know which was worse, the concern of the older people who had watched her grow up and thought she'd been victimized by Con, or the greedy satisfaction of those who felt vindicated now, even if none of them was the one to get him. At least Phyllis was a pretty little thing; of course he'd just latched onto Rosa so he'd be set up in lobstering for free, except for the cost of the marriage license.

Ah well, at Bennett's the people would be indifferent to her, not caring why she had come, and indifference would be the balm laid on the blistering burn.

She left the garbage and trash inside the wired enclosure, and the box outside, the shoes perched on top to attract attention. Just as she was getting back into the pickup, a sagging station wagon came cautiously up the hill from the Quarry Road. Children's ragged heads poked out of the windows.

"Mama!" someone shrieked. "Lookit them shoes!"

Feeling slightly cheered, Rosa drove back home.

There was a car in the driveway and it wasn't Leona Pierce's. She swore softly, and was of a mind to drive straight by, but as she hesitated a man came from the shadows of the barn and stood in the doorway looking out at her. It was Jude Webster's son Edwin. She turned into the driveway, grudgingly, not wanting to be civil to anyone. She wanted to hold on to what peace she had left.

As she got out Edwin came toward her, his thin height casting a shadow that seemed as long as a telephone pole. Solemnly he dangled a key ring overhead like a sprig of mistletoe. She remembered suddenly, and made an excited grab for them, and Edwin raised them out of her reach, then relented.

She held the ring tightly in her fist. "Come on in," she said. "I've got part of a cherry pie." She was very hungry all at once.

His male presence exorcised Con's for the time being. He slouched comfortably in the armless rocker, smoking his pipe, one foot up on the other knee, gazing around the kitchen as if he were tranquilly glad to be there.

He was thirty-one, two years older than Rosa. They each

had light brown hair, fine and thick, and the straight Webster nose. Otherwise they looked nothing alike. Edwin had a long head and a thin but meticulously shaped mouth that seemed sardonic in repose, as if the irony of his situation had become an integral physical part of him. Until he smiled, the mouth discouraged or actually repulsed advances, like the odd-colored eyes; a yellowish tawny that could have been unpleasant or even sinister. But the color became attractive and entirely fitting when one came to know him, as essentially Edwin as his smile or the expressiveness of his hands; just as his enforced silence seemed more profound and significant than the silences of ordinary people.

He wore his clothes well and was always immaculate even in working gear; she suspected it was his chief, or perhaps his only, vanity.

He and Rosa talked while they ate, Edwin reading her lips part of the time, and she reading what he scribbled on the notepad he carried. This wasn't always necessary, because they were so used to each other that she could understand many of his gestures and some of his most subtle shifts of expression. Once during the evening he wrote swiftly, "Stop reading my mind," and she laughed; the sound astonished her, it was as if they'd forgotten propriety and laughed at a funeral.

Con was always made uncomfortable by their conversations, and could never talk easily to Edwin. His poise and nonchalance would be shaken, he was no longer the dancer on the high wire delighting all with his nimble grace, and soon he would leave. Edwin had never showed any reaction to this, but after a while he came very seldom, so it had been a long time since he had been here.

Her precarious peace shivered. She asked desperately, "What's your new job?"

He wrote about the old house he was restoring for some summer people. Money was no object, he was given a free hand. The woman was planting a colonial garden, so she was there sometimes, but she left him to himself.

"They know it's no sense trying to bend my ear," he wrote. "So they make big circles around me. The mad genius. I might blow up, who knows?"

"What about if you need a helper?"

"He'll have to be a mind-reader, unless I can get my father, but he's got a camp to build this summer. How about you? I forgot, you're leaving."

She shrugged and sat looking down at her cup, lost in Con again. Edwin left the table, and she didn't know where he went or how long he was gone until he came back from the sitting room with her guitar. He handed it to her, and gestured with his head at the low rocker, then pulled his sketchbook from his jacket pocket.

She sat woodenly with the guitar across her knees. "No!" she burst out. "I can't stand to touch the thing. I'll never play it again, never! I'll kick it into kindling first."

He gave her a narrow, cold glance, then wrote on the pad and held it up before her eyes. "Don't be so goddam sorry for yourself."

"If I'm not sorry for myself, who the hell's going to be?" she demanded. "No, everybody either thinks it is good enough for me, or else now I'm over the measles so everything's fine!"

Impassively Edwin watched her digging around for a handkerchief, and then gave her his. Of course it had to be linen, fresh, and folded in crisply ironed creases. "You make me feel like a slob," she said indignantly.

She blew her nose, put the guitar on the table, and went over to the sink. She ran cold water into the basin and plunged her face into it, opening her eyes under the surface to flush and cool them. When she felt for a towel, it was put into her hands.

When she had finished drying, Edwin was smoking a

21

cigarette at the back door. The harbor was invisible in the dusk. A scent of lilacs and grass came through the screen, and a faint, damp, easterly breath that could mean fog.

She stamped her foot to get Edwin's attention, then picked up the guitar and sat down in the rocker. He walked around, looking down at her from several angles and then sitting on his heels to gaze up at her. She was used to it and concentrated on tuning the guitar, reacting with a slight but genuine pleasure to familiar motions and sounds. Presently she began to play and sing softly to herself.

Literature studied in her high-school English classes had meant nothing to her as literature. She had simply realized that some things made good songs, and thus they had become her own, some of them more private than others. So tonight she sang scraps of Shelley — *"Many a green isle needs must be In the deep wide sea of misery,"* and the descriptive passages of *The Forsaken Merman* — *"Now the wild white horses play, Champ and chafe and toss in the spray."*

Once a young teacher in love with the language used to chalk daily messages on the blackboard in the hope of seducing his students into the same passion. A passage from Meredith had accomplished it with Rosa, though the teacher had never discovered what lay behind the calm, stolid face. And no one else ever heard her tune, because it was not the sort called for at sing-alongs.

Now, safely unheard by Edwin, she sang it for herself.

> " 'Let us breathe the air of the Enchanted island.
> Golden lie the meadows; golden run the streams;
> Red gold is on the pine stems.
> The sun is coming down to earth
> And walks the fields and waters.
> The sun is coming down to earth,
> And the fields and the waters
> Shouts to him golden shouts.' "

As she sang it Bennett's Island rose on the horizon like an island in a myth, and her consciousness flew toward it like the gull she had wished this morning to become.

At the end of the song she found herself back in the kitchen, suddenly aware of the incredible events of her life, remembering that this morning the divorce had begun. Her heart was beating hard. She ached to do something wild and terrible in screaming defiance of everybody.

Edwin sat at the table, drinking more coffee and eating more pie. He was always neat and composed in his motions, he looked thoughtful in a particularly tidy way, as if his thoughts would never get away from him into jungle territory. The sight of him there shedding tranquillity like light returned her to herself. She put the guitar down, stood up and stretched, poured coffee, and reached for the sketchbook.

He had her in a few merciless lines, the extra flesh piled on by weeks of compulsive eating, but also the apartness of the singer lost in the song.

"Gone away," he had written under the sketch. She realized she couldn't even remember when he had finally begun to draw. He was watching her, both wary and quizzical, and she half-smiled and pushed the sketchbook back at him.

When he was ready to go she gave him the spare set of keys to the place, and a carton of frozen food from the refrigerator.

"The eider ducklings will be out now," he wrote. Then he added, "We had a path behind the house to the cove."

He hadn't been there since he was eleven years old. She looked into his eyes as she said, "I'll look for it," wondering what he was trying to tell her; if he felt homesickness or indifference. She walked out to the car with him. The fog was coming in, still only in pale smokelike shreds. Edwin put his arm around her and hugged her, and kissed her cheek. She knew by the tightness of the embrace that he was concerned for her and wished her well.

When he had gone she lingered outside, absentmindedly drawing down a branch of lilac to smell the damp blossoms, listening to the foghorns beginning. Seal Point Light sounded close enough to be just off her wharf, Ram's Head was muffled by distance, others were still farther away. When she shut her eyes her head reeled. The day had been so long that now it seemed as if her appointment with the lawyer must have been a week ago instead of early afternoon. She would have to sleep tonight, from sheer weight of fatigue.

She had moved downstairs, away from the bed she and Con had shared, to the big room off the kitchen and living room that had been her parents'. It hadn't been much help, but it had been handy for making all the cups of tea and coffee and cocoa she'd drunk at midnight or at two in the morning through the recent weeks.

In bed tonight she couldn't sleep after all. She could only go over and over the visit to the lawyer's office. It was as if she had attended her own hanging and her ghost was still anxiously loitering about the scene of her violent death because it didn't know yet it was dead. But Con still lived, he was solidly of this earth, involved with life, wound up in it, making love and begetting children, moving from one bed to another as if it were no more than changing his socks.

She shivered and her teeth chattered, she pulled extra covers up tightly around her and lay staring into the foglight waiting for the spasm to subside.

Lilacs and fog came in at the windows, the foghorns, a dog barking. Poor Con, no wonder he'd looked stunned and sick when he walked out today, with her screeching after him like a harpy. He was caught in a cleft stick, all right, and she was squeezing it together on him.

Oh, poor Con, she thought, growing voluptuously warm with pity. She understood. She of all people knew what it meant when he said, "She turns my guts inside out just by looking at me." All right, so it was another woman he was talking about, and no amount of moaning and whining was going to change that. But, if that was the way he felt about Phyllis, he was no more to blame than if he'd come down with pneumonia. She knew; it was the way she felt about *him*.

So, if she wasn't going to be around this summer, what was the harm in his using the wharf and fishhouse? Besides, to leave them unused would be pure spite, like throwing those perfectly good shoes into an alder swamp.

She got out of bed and went into the kitchen without putting on any lights till she got to the corner where the telephone was. Then she switched on the pin-up lamp so she could see to dial. But as she lifted the telephone her own excitement repelled her. Sure you just don't want to hear his voice again? she jeered. Sure you don't want him rampsing in here tomorrow morning and hugging you up?

She put the telephone down. Con wouldn't be back at his boarding house for the night yet, anyway. He'd be at Birch Harbor. She'd have to give the message to Sam or Geneva Rowland.

And, if you're willing to talk to one of them, especially Geneva, she thought, that proves—what? Only that you do want Con to come here tomorrow. You don't care how or why, as long as he comes and you can eat him up with your eyes. And you won't go away if he's using the wharf, because you know he'll come into the house each time till he gets you where he wants you. . . . And you're such a damn soft custard of a woman you'd take anything you could get.

She shut her eyes, folded her arms and pressed them against her breasts until they hurt. After a few moments she put off the light and went back to bed.

4

She was overtaken by sleep like a blow on the head and woke up just as suddenly, as if someone had called her or shaken the bed. The light was paler; you couldn't call it brighter, it had the dead quality of dense fog. It was almost four by her watch.

She went out into the kitchen and put the tea kettle on the gas stove, then went through the entry and out onto the back walk in her bare feet. The weathered planks were velvety under her soles, and the mild wet air cooled her hot eyes. She could see the fishhouse and wharf down the slope, and to the end of the wharf. Its one gull on his favorite corner spiling stood like an ink drawing against space. The harbor had disappeared. Something startled the gull, and he raised his wings and took off, and vanished. Anything else that went down that wharf and over the end would also vanish. It would continue to exist in its own world beyond the wall, but for the watcher here it would have ceased to exist.

It would be so simple.

She hurried back into the house. The tea kettle was boiling and she made a pot of coffee and then dressed in jeans and a warm shirt, with wool socks under her sneakers. She carried a mug of coffee around with her as she worked; she made her bed, she stowed away her toilet articles, she brought in a carton from the entry and loaded it with food from the bread box, the pantry shelves, and the refrigerator. She poured the rest of the coffee into a thermos bottle and wrapped bread and butter sandwiches in waxed paper.

She wheeled one load down to the end of the wharf, and came back. This time she added her rubber boots. She hadn't worn them for a long time, since Con had eased her out of lobstering a year ago, saying the new hydraulic hauler did so much of the work that he didn't need someone to plug lobsters and keep the bait irons filled. Besides, he told her tenderly, his fingers in her hair, he liked to think of her at home. She had accepted this humbly, ashamed that he'd had to tell her what should have been obvious: a man wanted to be alone sometimes, his work should be his own. Nobody else's wife went.

Her only rebellion had been silent. She renewed her lobster license, because she'd had one ever since Papa had given her the dory and ten traps when she was twelve years old, and she felt as incomplete without one as without a driver's license.

The new boat was to be eight feet longer than *Sea Star*, and he planned to go farther offshore and try for lobsters and rig up for shrimping in the winters. Rosa had been proud and happy to sell the shore lot at Back Cove so he could have the boat of his dreams. "Tell you what," he told her in bed. "You're going with that boat too, you'd better believe it. We'll have her fixed up so in the slack time next summer we can go cruising along the coast. Poke into all the gunkholes, go slumming at Bar Harbor—how about *that?*"

"Oh Con," she said. "You make life so much fun! I don't know anybody that has as much fun as we do."

"And we'll have more instead of less," he promised.

In late spring, with the new boat half built, he told her about Phyllis. Rosa was probably the last person in Seal Point to know how long he'd been seeing Adam Crowell's young widow. Adam had been a prosperous seiner, and had eventually bought the sardine factory that gave work to a good

27

part of both villages. When he dropped dead aboard a carrier one summer evening, he left his wife well provided for. However, he did not leave her pregnant, and, as Con told Rosa, it wouldn't have been possible to make anyone believe it. "Adam's been dead just a dite too long," he said.

She hadn't been able to answer; she'd been barely able to think. In shock she was looking back on the months of believing Con's reasons for being so late in from hauling, and his accounts of poker games at the firehouse, and long talk sessions in someone's fishhouse.

Stupefied by pain but not stupefied enough, she heard him say, "You'll be a good sport about it, won't you? I told her you would. I told her you've got the greatest heart in the world. . . . Well, I'll just go tell her you know. She'll be relieved. She's been some sick and nervous, poor kid."

She stood listening to the pickup back out.

She could not now, a month later, remember anything more of that night.

She took one final tour of the house. It was five now and the day was taking on a faint tint from the sunrise. She checked doors and windows, and at the last minute she decided to take her guitar. She hadn't wanted to, but she couldn't make herself leave it.

"All *right*," she muttered with a sullen, harassed glance, and rummaged around in the closet under the front stairs until she found the canvas case. She put the guitar into it like an exasperated mother stuffing her child into a snowsuit.

When she had everything on the wharf, she went into the fishhouse and looked around. Con hadn't taken his tools, of course. He'd been too mad yesterday, he'd just put the boat off on the mooring.

"Too bad, Cap'n Fleming," she said flippantly. "You'll have to see the Websters about getting anything of yours out of here."

Her dory was there, full of buoys and rope now. She gave her a pat and then went out and padlocked the door, and walked away without looking back. The gull had returned to the spiling. He regarded the wharf as his own, and his favorite corner was littered with crab bodies, broken mussel shells, and white droppings. He stood on one leg watching her with yellow eyes while she transported her dunnage from the wharf to the float. The tide was moderately high and she could stand on a lobster crate on the float and take her belongings off the edge of the wharf.

A green skiff lay motionless beside the float on the pale satiny water. She was broad and high-sided enough to take everything in one load.

Occasionally as she worked her glance met the gull's. It was like an exchange between equals who never speak but who nonetheless respect each other's existence. When she finally had everything balanced fore and aft, she stepped into the skiff and put the oars in the oarlocks. The gull watched her row away. When she was fifty feet or so from the wharf, it and the gull disappeared. Therefore she had succeeded in becoming invisible. At once she felt more free, and slowed her rowing to a steady, leisurely stroke.

Soon the moored boats began to show, first as gigantic shadows and then as familiar sterns and sides. She moved among them, at ease and safe, if not happy. On the land a rooster crowed like the last signal from a sinking continent. There was a slow flap of wings over her head as a gull took off from a canopy and made an unalarmed circle back to his perch.

Eastward the fog became suffused with pink and gold. Finally when she looked over her shoulder she saw a familiar dark bulk in the fog, seeming as high as a house, and with a few strokes of the oars she came alongside *Sea Star*. The boat returned to her normal size. She was Nova Scotia–built, high in the bow and broad in the beam. Dry clean traps were stacked across her wide stern and along the port washboard well up toward the bow. Each had its coiled warp and yellow and blue buoy tucked inside. She knew where Con planned to set these; she had taught him the rounds. She permitted herself a small, malicious grin.

"Won't you be surprised when the fog lifts, Cap'n Fleming?" she asked. It wasn't much help but it was better than bawling.

She stood up and began loading her things over the starboard side by the wheel and hauler. The fog was dazzling now with sunrise, and the warmth increasing. She shed her jacket and worked fast. Once everything was stowed in the cabin, she checked the gas tanks and found them full.

"Thank you, Cap'n Fleming," she said. "You're a mighty obliging gent."

She started the engine, and while it was warming up she got out the roll of charts from the locker and found the one on which her father had marked the course and the running time for a foggy trip to Bennett's Island. His old boat had been slower than *Sea Star* so he had had to re-time the trip. Reading the figures now put him aboard the boat with her; she saw the ballpoint pen tiny in his big fist, his seamed and rosy face under the brim of the old Swampscott sou'wester bent in concentration over the chart.

"Twenty-one minutes from Seal Point Light to Ram's Head." She could hear him. "By Gorry, that's ten minutes better than the old lady could do, bless her just the same." Then the incandescent grin. "And doesn't that diesel sing some pretty song!"

She climbed up forward onto the high bow to cast off the mooring and fasten the skiff, then ran aft, jumped down into the cockpit, and put the engine in gear. Her hand on the wheel started the boat in her slow circle out around some other boats toward the harbor mouth. The compass swung in the binnacle, needle quivering constantly. When Rosa was small she used to think the compass was alive.

The skiff was Con's, and she left it behind on the mooring, dancing a little in the bubbling wake. *Sea Star* went out past the granite hump of Seal Point, where the tower was hardly visible in the fog. Rosa heard the horn above the engine and the wash, and looked at her watch. Now she would run her twenty-one minutes to Ram's Head with eyes, ears, and all pores open for the ledges that made the approach to Seal Point Harbor a horror story for a stranger. She had learned them in childhood, drifting over them and around them at low tide in dead-calm weather while she hung head down over the side of the dory to see everything there was to see. Later, with her first outboard motor, she'd deepened the acquaintance by miscalculating her depth often enough to break at least a half-dozen shearpins.

She saw the fog-swell slither silently over Whaleback to port, and a little farther along the slight turbulence at the edge of the fog to starboard was the Tar Kettle. Glancing at the trembling needle, watching for pot buoys through an open pane in the windshield, feeling the response of the boat to her lightest touch on the wheel, she shed every other concern.

Ram's Head was where it should be in twenty-one minutes; she heard its powerful blare overhead, and got a glimpse of the red rock cliff through a veil of mist, then she was past and the fog closed in behind her. She let her breath go out in a long loud whistle, and realized her neck and shoulders were stiff.

She set her course southeast; it would be so all the way now. She was crossing a lane where the small tankers and cargo ships passed, heading for the mouth of the Penobscot. They picked up their pilots at Monhegan or Mosquito Island, so it would be local men in command now, but that would do *Sea Star* no good in the fog. She was too low on the water to show up on the radar screens. The vessels would be blowing all the way, but when you were listening hard you heard all manner of sounds through the pulse of the engine and the hypnotic hiss of water along the sides.

But it was a narrow lane, she'd be across it in a short time. The circle of sea upon which she moved within the moving wall of fog had become a milky blue with silvery glints from the diffused sun. Back inland, away from the shore, it would burn off to a clear hot day.

Great swells rolled up through the southerly wall of fog and billowed toward the boat, slid under her and coasted away to the north. New ones always came, lustrous and silent. But even with the load of forty traps aboard, *Sea Star* rode with the smooth grace of a whale.

She was away from the shipping lane now and out in the bay, with an hour and a half to run before she picked up her next mark, which should be Harbor Ledge buoy outside the harbor of Bennett's Island.

The fog was so dazzling with sunlight that she wished she had dark glasses. She was hungrier than she had been for weeks, and she ate bread and butter and drank coffee without neglecting her navigation. Bennett's Island was a small target, and she could easily overshoot it. Everybody in Seal Point would have a new laugh if she had to drop anchor somewhere and send out a distress call.

There had been no pot buoys for a long time now, nothing else but herself and the boat, and the endless swells rising up ahead and sliding away behind. The bay in fog bore no relation to the bay in clear weather. If she hadn't trusted her watch she'd have thought she'd been trapped for a day in the circle of white glare. She began to wish she'd meet another boat, some islander coming to the mainland, but none of them would be the fool that Rosa Fleming was, starting out in thick of fog.

Then a gull appeared and circled the boat. She threw out a piece of bread. He swooped and picked it up, then followed her, taking whatever she tossed to him. When she had nothing more he came down to perch on the stack of traps on the stern, and rode with her for a while. She couldn't talk to him because he was behind her, but she liked knowing he was there.

She knew when he took off because he flew up past the canopy, and she hastily averted her eyes so as not to watch him out of sight and put bad luck on him. Now she felt an exhausting wave of loneliness that went into her hands so that one came down too heavily on the wheel, and she had to get back on course. She was excruciatingly homesick for a sight of the other gull, the one who thought he owned her wharf. She saw the kitchen with the sun coming into it now as the fog burned off, the windows full of the harbor's sparkle that danced on wall and ceiling; the catbird exploding with song in the lilacs; Con's red head coming around the door. Maybe he'd throw his cap in first. And, if she smiled at him, or at least looked placid and kind, and said, "Hello, Con," wouldn't that have been all right? It wouldn't mean she wanted him to put his arms around her again, or that she wanted to go to bed with him; or that she'd have been willing to be one of his two women and be grateful for the chance.

"Oh yes, it would!" she shouted suddenly. "Yes, it would, you're as soft as a turd!" But even in her self-disgust she saw Con rowing out to the mooring and finding the boat gone, and thinking she'd gone crazily headlong out into the fog, maybe in the middle of night and by now had wrecked and drowned herself. Poor Con, what a terrible thing to do to him. . . . "Poor Con, hell," she yelled. "He's probably *hoping* it's so. No divorce, and he'll inherit the place!"

The sound of her shout was like the alcoholic's first drink. She dragged out words that made her cringe, and used them with savage joy; she insulted and damned half of Seal Point by name, whooping like an Indian. Finally—hoarsely—she settled down to sing in rhythm with *Sea Star's* motion.

> " *'With the Loorgeen, o hee*
> *With the Loorgeen, o ho,*
> *Light as a seagull will she*
> *O'er the heaving waves go!' "*

She'd learned the odd minor-keyed song in a Nova Scotia harbor one summer when her father was buying lobsters and smacking them to Boston. The man who had taught it to her, skipper of a herring seiner, told her it had been brought from Scotland by his grandfather, who sang it in Gaelic. As she sang it now, it seemed to her that the swells rising and falling beneath the boat belonged to another sea entirely, as if she had crossed an ocean this morning and was now approaching a foreign land.

She looked at her watch and stopped the engine to listen. After a moment she heard the bell buoy off the southern end of Bennett's. A warm wind blew across the unseen island, bringing her the scent of spruce and grass. She started the engine again and went on singing.

> " 'Billows lashing, o hee
> Waters crashing, o ho
> Without blenching we see
> There be stout hearts on board.' "

The red spar buoy reared up ahead of her as if it had that instant shot up from the sea. Her heart too seemed to shoot up; she felt half-drunk and trembly, her mouth smiling foolishly by itself. That was the Harbor Ledge buoy.

She went well to the starboard of it and then made a turn to the east, and there, rising above her like a hill of gold in the sunlight, were the high yellow rocks of the western point of Bennett's Island harbor.

5

Rounding the beacon on the end of the breakwater she re-
duced speed and went slowly into the harbor. At once it was
very hot and still, the motionless water throwing up an eye-
burning shimmer, the village and spruce woods very clear and
bright against the blue-white glare of fog beyond. It was only
a little past seven and she felt as if it should be seven the next
morning, her awaking, packing, and hidden departure seemed
so far away.

A boat passed her, going out. The man at the wheel stared
at her, then waved hastily as if he'd just remembered his manners. All but two of the moorings were empty except for
skiffs, showing that almost everyone had gone out in the ex-
pectation of the fog burning off. It was too early for the
children to be playing, and she was glad of the emptiness, and
hoped it would last until she got into the house.

She wondered which was Jude's wharf, and if she could
get into it. The tide had been going and was fairly low now.
Then she saw the big wharf where her father used to load
lobsters, and headed toward it. The harbor was so much
smaller than Seal Point that she felt as if she were maneuver-
ing on a chalk line among the skiffs, and she went very slowly,
getting out of her wool shirt with one hand while sweat soaked
the hair on her forehead and the back of her neck.

As she approached one of the boats left behind, she saw a

man's bare blond head just showing over the washboard. The cant of it was familiar; for all her life she had seen men on their knees beside recalcitrant engines. She idled hers and got her gaff ready to keep the boats from rubbing; his paint looked glassy with newness.

"Hello!" she called as *Sea Star* slid alongside. His head came around fast and he looked across the washboard at her with blue eyes, not the greenish-blue sparkling color of Con's. These were a dark and quiet blue under eyebrows lighter than his skin.

"Will you please tell me which is Jude Webster's wharf?" she asked.

He stood up and she saw that he was bigger and older than she'd thought. Still with no discernible expression he said, "Jude sold out?"

"He's thinking about it," she said. His hair was sun-bleached almost silver. A cold color, like the way he looked at her. She thought of hair red enough so that the sight of it warmed your hands. Her eyes felt scalded from staring so long into the fog, she felt their sick staring and was sure he felt it, but she couldn't stop it; and she was homesick enough to die.

"Thinking about it," she repeated dully, wondering who was thinking about what.

"Where's your husband? Down below? Coming in another boat?"

"Which is Jude's wharf?"

"You people figuring on fishing those traps out here?"

She hadn't. The traps were just there when she took the boat. But she rose to his bleak challenge.

"What's it to you?"

"How come Jude let you come out here cold? Why didn't he write or call up to see if it was all right to let another fisherman in here? Forgot his obligations, didn't he?"

He didn't raise his voice, which made it worse. She'd been lacerated to begin with, now she was suffering from homesickness and the inevitable let-down after the pride and exhilaration of her perfectly navigated trip. She was astonished by her impulse to strike with the gaff at his stolid face.

She said stiffly, "Maybe he reckoned forty traps wasn't going to put anybody out of business, everybody's so rich on Bennett's Island."

It got a reaction; at least something flickered across his face, and then he said, "Only forty traps and a boat that size. It doesn't add up."

"While you check your arithmetic, I could be tying up at Jude's wharf, if I knew where it was."

"Oh, it's over there," he said indifferently, pointing to a cluster of wharves halfway around the harbor's curve. "The second one in, with the fishhouse that needs paint."

"Thank *you*." She unhooked her gaff. "I'm much obliged."

"If I was your husband, whenever he gets here, I wouldn't rush to set 'em, only forty or no. People don't just come on here and start lobstering as simple as that."

"So I can see," she said. "Especially if you meet them all in the harbor. They must be a year older before they ever set foot on shore. You forgot to ask for my passport, and I'm glad of that because I'm traveling with forged papers."

He turned his back on her abruptly. She reversed *Sea Star* away from his boat and headed toward the wharves. There was deep water off the outer ends, and space between the wharves if she wanted to run *Sea Star* up inside. For the time being she tied the boat bow and stern off the end, and got her gear onto the wharf still blessedly unobserved, unless it was from some of the houses across the harbor. With everything landed, she stood on the wharf a few minutes to realize that she was actually on Bennett's Island.

The light and the silence and the space were as she had imagined it, the gulls' cries small from the uninterrupted sky. A group of female eiders shepherded their large flock of ducklings among the harbor ledges. The infants made tiny

37

excited sounds and upended ardently in the floating rock-weed, the mothers kept up their warnings and their watch on a blackback gull paddling greedily back and forth.

"The eider ducklings will be out now," Edwin had written, and she wondered how many times as a little boy he had stood here, not hearing, but seeing everything.

From the wharves there came the sweetish reek of grassed-over traps brought in to dry out. There was a double rank of them on the Webster wharf, and she carried her things up a narrow aisle.

The shabby fishhouse was unlocked. It seemed to be full of cultch of one kind or another, and at first glance nothing looked like anything except the wheelbarrow, which she took out. She put her food and her sleeping bag on it, stowed the other things in the building and wheeled onto the sand and coarse turf. A rough track ran around the harbor behind the fishhouses, and once she had crossed it she wasn't sure where to go. The houses were set haphazard, some back from the water and against the spruce woods, some less than a hundred feet from the wharves. She could hear a radio from behind the kitchen screen door of the nearest one, a woman's voice, children, yet she could not make herself go to the door and ask directions. The encounter in the harbor had shaken her more than she realized; the business with Con had scraped her raw in spots.

And she was tired. The ground rose and fell under her feet in swells like the sea. She blinked, trying to steady either her head or the view, whichever was going out of focus, and with dumb resignation she heard a dog coming at her.

His roaring charge stopped short at the wheelbarrow, where he began amiably sniffing at the load, and then lifted his leg at the wheel. He was only a small red shaggy dog after all, but through her blurred eyes he'd seemed as big as a chow.

"Come back here, you chump!" a man called from the screen door. He came out and clumped down over the lawn in his rubber boots, a round-faced man with a little belly out over his belt. "Kids call him Tiger, he figgers he has to live up to his name." His smile was shy but friendly. "Saw you coming in. Awful thick chance, warn't it?"

"Pretty thick." She tried to smile back. "Can you tell me the way to Jude Webster's house?"

"Go right up across the field there by the well, then you go through that clump of spruces and across the path and you'll see it." He turned around, pointing. "Not that one out in the open there, that's Percys'. You can't see Jude's from here, it's grown up some thick around it."

Which suits me, she thought.

"Thanks," she said, reaching down for the wheelbarrow handles.

"I'll go down and give your man a hand," he said.

"He's not there," she said quickly. "I mean . . . I'm alone."

"*You* brought that boat out alone, blind?" He marveled, and she felt a slight glimmer of pride. "Well, I'll be cussed. You musta been around the water all your life then."

"Just about."

From behind the screen door a young woman's voice called, "I thought you was having a long confab with Tiger out here, Rob." She came out onto the doorstep, two little girls crowding behind her.

"Somebody for Jude's place, Maggie."

The wife was skinny and sandy in coloring but she was as ardent as a child in her candid and expectant curiosity. "Oh! Isn't that *nice!* Pleased to meet you. We're the Dinsmores, Rob and Maggie and Tammy and Diane."

"Hello." Rosa ducked her head. "I'm Rosa Fleming, Jude's cousin." Good God, this could go on forever. "Well, my butter's probably melting. Is that the village well, or——"

"Oh sure, that's for everybody," Rob said. "Never goes dry."

"Real good water," Maggie said. "If you haven't got a decent pail, I can lend you one."

39

"Thanks, I'll take you up on the offer if I need to," Rosa said. The ground had stopped heaving and the wave of weariness had receded. She began wheeling again along the path that passed the Dinsmore house and cut diagonally across the field by the well. When she passed into the cool wet shade of the spruces and went onto another path, full of small birds flashing back and forth, relief gave her the impetus to shove the heavy wheelbarrow up the ledgy little track among the trees to the Webster house. She went around to the back door through tall grass and daisies, and then the house was between her and the place next door, between her and the whole village. Otherwise she was surrounded by woods.

There were unpruned lilacs under the kitchen windows, an enormous thicket of them bent down with heavy purple blooms; the yard was full of their scent, something of home and yet not of home. She unlocked the entry door and went in.

The paint was shabby, the paper peeling in spots, the house smelled mousy, spiders lived in all the corners. Sunshine sliced through the emptiness. It was the emptiness that she cherished, like the pocket wilderness outside. When she walked through to the other side of the house, she found that more spruces diminished the house next door to a glimpse of white clapboards and a glimmer of windows through sweeping boughs.

The place was clean except for dust and insects. A pair of galvanized pails had been left upside down beside the sink; it was a black sink, and rusty, but she could soon fix that with kerosene. She took one of the pails and went down to the well. She didn't worry about eyes now. She was excited about her house and could only think of getting back to it.

There were two lamps under paper bags, and odds and ends of dishes in the cupboards, a few battered pots and pans under the counter. A little wood had been left in the wood-box and she built a fire to heat water. There was a gas stove and refrigerator, but no gas. She didn't care. She opened the cellar bulkhead and an earthy coldness came up to her. There were no wild animals here bigger than mice to take a cellar over. She could keep her food cool down here, all right.

When the water was hot she made tea and took her lunch out onto the back doorstep, and ate gazing into the woods and watching the birds that lived out their lives without caring how she lived hers. Gulls circled far over head in wide leisurely arcs. She could hear the bell buoy clanging desultorily to the southwest of her.

Gradually she became aware of the wash along the shores somewhere beyond the belt of spruces, perhaps breaking in the cove Edwin had mentioned. She wanted to walk out there and see, but she could not move. She leaned her head back against the scaly clapboards and looked up at the circling gulls. Her hands and feet were too heavy to move, and her eyes kept closing.

She staggered up finally and went into the kitchen, undid her sleeping bag with slack, fumbling fingers, and spread it on the dry floor where the sun had been. She took off her sneakers and outer clothes and zipped herself in. For a few minutes as she lay there with her eyes closed she heard the wind beginning to blow through the trees, chickadees loud and strong just outside a window, a fly buzzing against a pane, a mysterious ticking, creaks in the house, a little scurrying somewhere... Good thing I'm not scared of mice, she thought drunkenly, and slept.

6

She woke to darkness and silence, and lay stiffly still, fearfully seeking something familiar, and finding only alien forms: the gray oblongs of the windows too far above her, the hardness beneath her, the foreign hush—no clocks, no harbor or road sounds. This, as if she had suddenly gone as deaf as Edwin, panicked her.

"Con," she said with the thick, labored utterance of nightmare.

As if his name were a signal for her brain to wake completely, she knew at once where she was. Then she heard through the night the strange foghorn, and close at hand a faint fine dripping from the lilac leaves outside the windows, and inside the little creakings and tickings of the house.

She unzipped the sleeping bag and sat up groggily, her mouth dry, her back and hips lame from the floor. Quarter of ten. The tiny illuminated face of her watch was friendly and reassuring. At least it could have been, but she felt anything but befriended and reassured. She crawled around on her hands and knees, feeling through her scattered dunnage for her flashlight.

She went up to the little toilet discreetly set among spruces. The door was hanging off the hinges, and the place needed a good sweeping down and cleaning out, but it wasn't foul. Afterwards she didn't want to go back into the house, so she walked along the edge of the woods flashing her light among the wet black trunks. It picked up a well-beaten path winding away from her in the general direction of the fog-horn.

She followed its serpentine curves around ledges and past thickets of alder and wild rose whose leaves gleamed like wet green enamel in the ray of light. There was a strong perfume among the herbal and spruce scents, coming from a kind of wild honeysuckle that twined wherever it could. At first the fog floated in among thick old spruce trunks like the artificial streamers of mist in bad horror movies, but soon it grew thicker and smelled of salt and iodine, of beach debris and fresh rockweed blotting out the sweetness of the wild honey-suckle.

All at once she was out of the woods and at the brink of space, standing on the edge of a cliff. It was as jolting as her awakening had been, until she flashed the light downward and saw the gradual fall of rosy rock sloping away from her feet, crevices dark with mossy and prickly growth, and then, far below, water glimmering through the shifting thick-nesses of fog. The tide was very low, and so quiet around the weed-grown boulders that the dripping in the woods and the horn five miles out were the only sounds.

She put off her light. The very deadness of the fog and the low tide made her feel worse; it was like the deadness in herself, to which she had wakened. A crash of surf and rattle of great rocks down there, wind beating against her face so she could hardly keep her eyes open to it, the woods creaking and thrashing behind her—that would be proof that the planet hadn't died while she slept, to become one mon-strous black and silent swamp.

She was eager to get back to the house now, to make a light and a fire. Her clothes were coated with moisture, her face and hair wet. When she got back to the yard she saw through the spruce boughs a misty light next door, and at the same time someone down toward the shore whistled to a dog.

Tiger. And that recalled the man with the round face and shy smile, the wheelbarrow, the wharf. The boat. Dear God, the boat. Tied up at a strange wharf and forgotten for more than twelve hours. Low tide.

She was alive now, frightened, furious with herself. She ran down the path and across the field past the well. If that wharf was out at dead low water, and *Sea Star* had fallen over on her side onto the rocks—loaded with traps—she wanted to sob in rage and panic, and averted it by calling herself profane names in a choked whisper as she ran.

She'd never forgotten the boat before, even with Con around; the boat was always *there,* a part of her like an identical twin.

At the end of the wharf the light showed damp sand and ledge, and the boat was gone.

Con? Borrowed a boat and followed her out here? How did he know? Did he have a friend out here? What about the Dinsmore man? Was the grin sly rather than shy? What about the one who'd challenged her before she'd ever set foot on the shore? She flashed the light around, knowing it was futile; she was positive that Con had come and taken the boat as she slept this afternoon, and by now Seal Point was rocking with the joke.

By God, she'd call off the divorce and let him whistle, and then see who was the laughingstock. She swept the beam rapidly back and forth, uselessly, ready to cry with rage. It picked up as if through gauze the moorings closest to the wharf. The familiar shape of *Sea Star* took gradual if unsubstantial form.

A sound of relief and joy burst from her throat. Then she blushed. What must they have thought of her, coming out alone in the fog and then disappearing like this and never giving her boat another thought?

She hurried back to the house as if it were midday and the village teeming with people to be astonished or shocked by her behavior, or, in the case of the blue-eyed frontier guard, contemptuous.

She lit a lamp, built a fire, fried bacon and eggs and toasted some bread. The house became her cave, with a camp-fire to keep the beasts away. With dry socks on her feet and food in her stomach, she thought expansively, Poor Con, what awful things I thought about him! As if he'd do anything like that.

No, except where women were concerned, Con was straight as a spar spruce, and he was a lot more honest about women than some men were. He was like Edwin not being ashamed of his deafness, just saying to the world, *This is the way I am.*

She took down her guitar and sat on the floor with her back comfortably in the corner and sang for a while. She sang none of the love songs that the kids always asked for; she would never sing those again. She went through a variety of sea and fishing songs, her own tunes and others, and then, growing tired she finished off with a few little short verses for which she had made up tunes when she was quite small. She used to sing herself to sleep with them, and they amused her now and lulled her.

She sang *Monday's child is fair of face,* and *When the wind is in the east,* then four lines which had attracted her for the words in them and not for any sense they made.

> " '*The man in the wilderness asked me,*
> *How many strawberries grow in the sea?*
> *I answered him, as I thought good.*
> *As many as red herrings grow in the wood.*' "

The tune was a minor one, and if you sang the song quietly enough, with the right chords, it seemed to have some poignant significance; it asked far different questions from the nonsensical ones about strawberries and red herrings. For instance, who was the man in the wilderness? She always saw him, or rather the mysterious form of him, standing alone in a clearing in a wilderness that was like nothing she had ever seen outside dreams and books.

She hung the guitar from a handy nail, blew out the lamp, and took her sleeping bag upstairs to a room that faced the invisible harbor. There was an iron bed here with a clean dry mattress, and she spread the bag on it. She pried up the window and held it open with a piece of lath that must have been used for the same purpose by the Wylies.

She made herself think of the wilderness until she was lost in the glories of the word, and fell asleep.

She woke in a chilly, clear dawn and at once thought of the boat. From the window there was a clear view between two big spruces over the fishhouse roofs to the harbor and beyond. *Sea Star* was there all right, and so were all the other boats. This puzzled her for a moment until she remembered that it was Sunday.

At the Percy house a door slammed and someone came around the corner whistling *Soldier's Joy;* the spruces hid the whistler but didn't dull the whistle, then she saw him for a moment before he crossed the lane at the foot of his lawn. He was a stocky man with a brisk walk. When he was out of sight the whistle came back sharp and merry in the early hush.

She looked back at *Sea Star.* The boat seemed perfectly at home out there, with one gull standing atop the traps, and another walking around on the bow deck.

She went downstairs and built a fire, put water on for coffee, then stripped for the first time since she'd gone to bed at home two nights ago, and washed in cold water, standing before the open oven door.

"Get rid of all that blubber, girl," she said, mercilessly scrubbing with a rough washcloth and then with a coarse towel. "If you wanted to kill yourself, why didn't you pick out something faster than food?"

She dug into a duffle bag for clean underwear, jeans, and shirt, and brushed her hair in front of a wavy mirror on the wall between the two front windows. She propped her sneakers, wet from last night, on the oven hearth, and carried her suitcases upstairs to the room where she had slept.

After she washed her breakfast dishes in the rusty sink, which would have to wait until she got some kerosene to clean it with, she dusted and swept the kitchen, scrubbed the counters on either side of the sink, and washed the refrigerator and gas stove. But all at once she'd had enough of indoor chores, and anguish was threatening like the first signal of a recurring pain.

She went out fast, but grabbed the broom on the way, and picked up a broken bushel basket from the clutter between bulkhead and back steps. She propped the toilet door wide open; rehanging it wouldn't be much of a job if she could get hold of some tools. She wished she'd brought some from home. Inside, she ripped down the tattered and rain-stained pictures tacked on the walls, and removed a stack of mildewed paperbacks. All this went into the basket for burning. Then she swept the ceiling and down the walls, as vigorously as she could when she had to work around nails.

"Why didn't you have the sense to bring a hammer?" she muttered. "God, if you had any more brains you'd be a half-wit."

When she finished sweeping she brought out water and a piece of old flannel shirt she'd found in the entry. With this and a thin slab of yellow soap she scrubbed the seat and the small window high up on one wall.

Then she went around behind the building to see about digging a trench. Alders and bay, wound through with the wild honeysuckle, were crowding in, and she longed for a

47

machete or an ax, but she did the best she could with her jackknife and by breaking down and ripping off thicker branches that got in her way. Now there was room for a trench but she had nothing to dig with. She sat down on a rock, puffing, itching from twigs down her neck, and wondered if there was anything in the fishhouse she could use. She'd be damned if she'd borrow; she'd come out here to be left alone, and that worked both ways.

7

Lying by her feet was a spray of wild honeysuckle, its fragile blossoms pale yellow and ivory. She took it into the house and put it in a broken-nosed pitcher. This used up her water, and she was just about to go to the well for more when she heard voices and saw movement past the kitchen's side windows. Before she could escape, someone was knocking gently at the back door.

At least this time she didn't expect Con, she thought with an attempt at cynicism. "Come in!" she called.

Instantly the place filled up with young girls, all looking exactly alike with streaming hair, shorts, long legs, and bare feet. After a confused moment the throng shook down to three. She felt enormous. She made a weak gesture with the pail. "I was just——"

A tall girl with yellow hair said, "There's a telephone call for you. For you to call back, I mean. He called up yesterday." She frowned, and it made her look familiar in some way. "No, last night, really."

Another girl had thick black bangs and round dark eyes, like a Shetland pony, and a pony's way of moving head and feet. "Young Mark came up to tell you, but there was no light and he was too bashful to knock. He wanted to get the first look at the new lady."

"I'm sorry I disappointed him," said Rosa, and they laughed with relief, so she wondered if she'd looked grim, wild-eyed, or vacant. Then there was a self-conscious silence, a shifting of bare feet and of eyes, and Rosa's mind was quite blank of anything except Con waiting for her to call. She started to say, "Well, thank you for——"

The blond girl said at the same time, "Well, we'd better be going——"

There was another little burst of nervous laughter, a general movement toward the door, when the third girl stopped and said, "Is that your guitar?"

"Yes," said Rosa, so anxious to get them out that she began to sweat.

"It looks as if it's been played a lot." She had sharp, freckled features and elbows to match. She had a brusque, choppy manner except when she reached out and touched the guitar delicately with one finger.

"That one's been played for about ten years," Rosa said, trying to get them in motion again.

"Gosh, you must really know how to play, then."

"I'm pretty good," Rosa admitted.

"Vic's a pretty good piano player," offered the blond girl, smiling affectionately at her friend.

"Vic for Victoria?"

The freckled girl, diverted from the guitar, became jerky and self-conscious again. "Isn't it awful for somebody who looks like me?"

"Rosa's just as awful, especially when you're hefty," said Rosa. "It makes people think of baby elephants, for some reason." She was amusing them, and she felt better. "What's your name?" she asked the blond girl.

"Linnea Sorensen, and this is my cousin Holly Bennett" —the Shetland pony—"and my friend from school who's spending the summer with me. Vic Marchant. I mean Victoria Imogene Marchant."

"How'd you like to pick this out of your eye?" Vic doubled a fist. All three burst into laughter.

How easy they were, luxuriously foolish, spendthrift with summer. She didn't resent that; they were children, and hard times came soon enough, not only to the fat ones and the fidgety ones with awkward elbows. Look at Phyllis, pretty as a money kitten; she must have put in some sick hours knowing she couldn't pass the baby off as Adam's and scared that Rosa wouldn't divorce Con in time.

Well, she's safe enough now, Rosa thought, or will be by August.

"... Mrs. Fleming?" It was the blond girl, serious and polite. "Are you all *right?*"

"Of course," she said crossly. "Is there a short cut to the store or do I have to go down across the field?"

They were all in a hurry to tell her about the lane turning into a path to the store. She felt she'd upset them and was sorry. None of them was Phyllis, even if she turned out to be a Phyllis in time.

"Thanks very much," she said to them at the foot of the overgrown lawn.

"Oh, that's all right," young Holly assured her handsomely.

Almost to the store Rosa realized she hadn't had a chance to wash up after her work, or even comb the twigs and leaves out of her hair. Well, too late now.

Only Mark Bennett was in the store, a solid dark man with graying temples. He was working at his desk in the post office section, and looked out at her with a peroccupied stare.

"Jude Webster wants you to call him. You know his number?"

"Yes." Not Con. Still hoping for miracles, she jeered.

"Dial one first," Bennett said. He tapped his pencil, still gazing at her through the little window, but as if he were thinking of something else.

Thirty-five miles away the telephone was ringing in Jude's kitchen. Jude answered, grave and moderate, and when she said, "Hi, Jude," Bennett's swivel chair creaked. He walked through the store and went outside and down the wharf. She could see him going away through the long shed and then out into the sunlight, where he disappeared down the ladder to the lobster car.

"Now whatever possessed you to do a fool thing like that, Ro?" Jude asked with asperity.

"Like *what?* . . . Damn it, I just felt like it, that's all! Everybody else is doing what they feel like, so I thought I'd try it for a change."

"Well, it was a fool thing——"

"You've already said that. Funny, whenever *I* do anything it's always a fool thing. Maybe I should sit in a closet with my face to the wall for the rest of my life, so I don't do any more fool things."

"Now hold on, Ro," Jude said. "Come on down off your high horse. This is costing you money, so stop talking and listen. Con called me up yesterday morning all in a sweat because you and the boat were both gone in thick o' fog. He thought maybe Edwin might know something, when he saw the car there the night before."

So he'd driven by, maybe intending to come in till he saw Edwin was there.

"Are you still there, Ro? You hear what I said?"

"Sure!" she said belligerently.

"No, you didn't. Anybody mentions that feller's name,

you go into a trance. Listen, I had to tell him where you are. I couldn't do anything different, he was all for getting the Coast Guard out."

"Well, I'm here, anyway. I came out through fog thick as dungeon and hit the Harbor Ledge buoy bang on the nose. What do you think of that for navigation?"

"You're a chip off the old block. How is everything?"

She tried for enthusiasm. "The house is nice and dry, Jude. And it's so quiet out here I've been sleeping like a pig and trying not to eat like one." Her chuckle was fairly successful. "I think I'm going to have a great summer. Oh, I started cleaning the toilet this morning. The Wylies left everything pretty good, but I don't think they ever shoveled that place out. What are you snickering at?"

"Nothing, Ro, nothing at all. Well, I dunno what'll happen about the boat. You told me yourself it was still his to use, and you've gone and taken her and a load of traps besides. He was some mad. He sounded feather-white."

"Probably he was, to think I wasn't drowned and the boat wrecked, and him having all that insurance to play with. That reminds me, I'd better change the beneficiary on my life insurance. If anything happens to me I don't want to be paying for the honeymoon."

"Don't talk like that, Ro."

"It's better than bawling, isn't it? And it's being practical, isn't it? Well, I've got to get back to my digging, if I can locate a spade." She snorted. "See, I've reached the point where I can call a spade a spade. — Jude. Thanks for telling me the news. I'm sorry if I've made a mess for you."

"Good Lord, girl, you haven't made a mess for *me*. Be careful now. When Con comes for the boat, don't fight with him. Let him take her, and then you settle down and enjoy the place and get over him. He's not worth the powder to blow him up State Street."

"So long, Jude. Give my love to Lucy and the boys. And thanks for calling."

She was trembling after she hung up, and leaned against the wall in the dim, empty store looking out at the bright harbor beginning to flash under a northwest wind. *Sea Star* was steady at her mooring. So Con's coming for you, she thought. Why didn't I ask Jude *when*, so I wouldn't have to see him? But she wouldn't call Jude back and ask, she couldn't be sure of keeping the shakiness out of her voice.

She walked to the end of the wharf and looked down. Mark Bennett stood on the lobster car smoking his pipe, and watching two small boys who lay on their bellies with their arms overboard.

"I'm through," Rosa called down. "How much do I owe you?"

"I'll let you know when the bill comes in."

He came up the ladder, and as he reached the top and stepped onto the wharf he gave her a surprisingly warm and youthful smile. "I know who you are now. Jude told me. True McKinnon's girl, used to sit on a nail keg in the corner and eat ice cream, too bashful to move."

"That was me, all right." She nodded at the boys, "What are they doing?"

"Manufacturing excitement. Trying to catch pollock by hand. Stevie's been reading about tickling salmon."

"*Really* tickling?"

"So he claims. So far they haven't found a pollock who likes his belly tickled." They began to walk back up the wharf.

"Who put my boat off?" she asked. What else had Jude told him? She tried to decide if he was being exceptionally kind, as to a child or a mental patient. "I meant to come see to her, but I was so dead tired I overslept."

"One of my nephews, I'm pretty sure. Seems like I heard his father say something about it."

"I'm much obliged. I want to thank him."

"You'll see him around. They've got the fishhouse this side of yours." They came out of the shed and stopped, looking

53

across at *Sea Star*. "She's a great boat. I remember when True first came out here with her. He was like a kid, he was so happy."

"Yes, he loved her. He had one good year with her, anyway." She was herself again; it was only Con, or speaking of Con, that could shake her up. "How can I order a couple of cylinders of gas?"

"I always keep some extra on hand, they use a lot of it out here. When Ralph Percy comes in from setting traps I'll get him to haul up two with his tractor, and hitch them up for you."

"He must be the only atheist if he's out working on Sunday."

Mark laughed. "Nope, he's just making up for the time he lost last week when he drove his wife and kids to Vermont to visit her folks."

In the store she ordered a bag of lime for the toilet, paint for the seat, cleaning and washing supplies, and what groceries she could think of without a shopping list. Then she was embarrassed because she'd come without money, but he told her she could pay later, and he would send the heavy stuff up with the gas.

She thought she might be able to borrow tools from him, but she wouldn't ask unless she knew beyond a doubt that she couldn't make do; she hadn't been through the fishhouse yet.

Just as she was leaving, two women came round the corner. There were startled but friendly greetings, she flung back her responses at random and kept on going. She was perspiringly aware of her rear view in the tight jeans, but there was nothing to do but keep going and for God's sake remember to put a dress on if she came down to the store again for anything, which she would have to do if she didn't intend to live on shore greens and mussels.

In the noon quiet, when Sunday dinner occurred on Bennett's Island just as it did everywhere else, she took the wheelbarrow and went down to the fishhouse for the rest of her belongings. The building was so crowded with the debris of years that she wondered how the Wylies had ever had room to work in here. Even the workbench was loaded. She cleared a path through a tangle of old rope, rotten laths, empty paint cans, used shingles saved for kindling in the almost-buried oil-drum stove, cardboard cartons, buoys, broken furniture, and finally reached the ladder to the loft.

After the mess downstairs, the space under the roof seemed extravagant. It hadn't been too handy to throw junk up a ladder.

It was lighted by two gable windows, one giving on the harbor and the other on the island. The light was dimmed through dusty and cobwebbed glass, but she could make out the big pile of soft black nets in one corner, a long-handled dipnet, a flounder trap, and in another corner an old wooden fish box full of glass balls.

She felt something like an upsurge of joy, a faint one to be sure, a mere ghost of the old stab of rapture at finding some unexpected treasure, but the sensation set up a chain reaction so that when she knelt beside the box she was simultaneously discovering mayflowers for the first time in her life; she was carrying into the kitchen a stray kitten found crying on the doorstep; she was finding a small punt on the beach after a hurricane, entwined in kelp, half full of sand and rock-weed, but perfectly whole; and seeing her first guitar under the Christmas tree.

No one else had ever found her mayflower patch, she'd been allowed to keep the kitten, the advertisments about the punt had never been answered so it became hers, and the guitar had become her second voice. There had been other discoveries and other gifts, but these had gone deepest in a way to become bone of her bone, so that now, as she knelt by the box, sights, sounds, smells, and textures overlaid each other; mayflower fragrance and cold wet leaves, kitten fur under her chin and the small heart beating under her fingers, the drenched pungence of the storm-torn shore and the long cannonade of surf; the lustrous curves of polished wood reflecting Christmas lights, the smell of fir, and with it the pain in her fingertips from the tight wire strings, so that they almost stung now as they touched the cool dusty surface of the glass ball floats.

The last ones she'd seen had been old Chet Parkin's toggles, and they had belonged first to his uncle. He'd had to take them all up finally and use bottles, because some boys began stealing them, cutting them off the warps in their twine bags, and selling them to an antique dealer out of town.

Here there must be twenty-five or more. They were amber, faint amethyst, and the palest blues and greens; even the clear ones had a tint. She held them up to the light and saw her fingers change color. They were treasure found in a cave, or magic fruit in a forest. She could have made a song about them, but it would have to be sung to herself alone, you couldn't say the word *balls* out loud without someone cackling.

Where had they come from? Did Jude know about them? If so, why had he left them behind? If she bought the place, would they be hers? She hovered protectively over them, until suddenly her elation died. She got up from her knees and bumped her head on a rafter. The pain and surprise put tears in her eyes, and they became tears for something else. *Where your heart is, there is your treasure also,* the Bible said.

What did that leave you?

She blew her nose and wiped her eyes and went down the ladder. Angrily she saw that someone was working on the Sorensen wharf to her left, out of sight behind the barrier of drying traps. It was high tide, and they had brought a boat in and were loading traps on her for tomorrow. Logical, reasonable, part of a lobsterman's work. Only why'd they have to be around right now? And why had she ever believed she'd have privacy?

She remembered what Mark Bennett had told her, that the nephew who had put her boat off had that fishhouse and wharf, and she supposed that she should go around and thank him.

But not while she looked and felt like this, dammit.

She worked doggedly, starting a heap of burnable trash in one corner and sinkable junk in another. Buried under the debris she found a good spade. When she thought the red had gone away from her eyes and nose, she put the spade across her gear on the wheelbarrow and went home.

8

While she was starting to dig the trench behind the toilet, trying to break through the tough turf, she heard the girls' voices, and froze, but they went by the house and up the lane. She caught a glimpse of them through a gap in the trees, a swirl of hair, a profile clear for an instant against dark spruce. There were more than three this time, some younger; a baby rode on someone's hip. They flowed through the gap like a school of bright fish flashing through a sunray. Their voices were still heard, laughing and calling from further up the lane.

At their various ages she'd been happy too, as long as she could be aboard a boat. Too bad I didn't run away to sea while I was young, she thought dryly. With the right shape I could have disguised myself as a cabin boy.

The spade cut down through roots at last, and with a certain satisfaction she turned the first sod.

When Con walked into the yard, she had no warning. She was hot, and had come out from behind the building to let the breeze strike her, and there he was, grinning at her. He was wearing green bellbottoms, and a green-and-gold striped knit shirt. Phyllis's choice, no doubt.

The first reaction was the hope that he'd identified himself as Rosa Fleming's husband where enough people could hear him and thus be astonished that anything like her had acquired anything like him. However, a swift recognition of her own idiocy was helpful. She said calmly, "Well, Con?"

He looked her over deliberately: twigs and leaves in her hair, her face flushed and sweating, her shirt pulled out, her jeans powdered with dirt. It was as if he were savoring the contrast with his own dapper perfection.

"What do you think you're doing out here, Rosie?" he asked indulgently.

"Digging a hole behind the toilet to shovel the shit into," she said.

"You would be!" he said in amused exasperation. "Who but you? My God, Rosie, why in hell——"

"Because I got tired of shoveling my way through the Fleming variety," she said. "At least this is a change. It wasn't thrown at me in the first place."

"Don't give me that." His amusement was as thin as her poise. "What's the idea of pulling this crazy stunt? Scaring the guts out of me and leaving me with no boat and five hundred traps to haul?"

"I want a drink of water," she said, and walked by him into the house. She took a drink, then brushed the spills out of her hair, put more cold water in the basin and washed her face. When she straightened up and was drying herself, he was sitting on the edge of the table, smoking a cigarette.

"Come on back with me, honey," he said. "We can start back just as soon as you get your stuff together. Todd brought me out, and I'll go down to the shore now and tell him not to wait."

For an instant she thought it was all over with Phyllis, and it was happening as it happened in books; that, when he believed she was dead, he knew what he'd lost. Her face felt weak and unmanageable.

"I need the boat till the new one's ready," he went on, "and you ought to be in your own home. You made your gesture, you ran off and upset everybody——"

"Everybody meaning *you*," she interrupted. No, it wasn't happening as it happened in books.

"Don't you think I've got feelings?" he asked indignantly. "You were always so sensible. When you tore off like this in thick of fog, it wasn't like you——"

"How do you know whether it's like me or not? If I did it, it must be like me. After all, what you do is like you, isn't it? And I didn't run off or tear off, whatever you want to call it. I've moved, that's all. I'm renting this place for the summer with an option to buy. You should be happy to have me out of sight, out of mind." Insolently she flapped hands like wings.

He reddened. "Well, Jesus, do you think I like knowing I've run you out of your own town? I may be a son-of-a-bitch but I'm not that bad."

"Oh, you mean you want your mind put at rest again? I thought we had that all out the other day. I don't care what you like knowing or hate knowing, Con. I'm here and I'm staying here." She looked speculatively around the kitchen. "There's enough work to keep me busy for weeks. After I finish the toilet I'll start puttying the windows, and then patch up the roof, and after that——"

He stood up. His face was drawn so tight he seemed to have no lips at all. "All right. You've had your fun. Speaking of shit, you've sure rubbed my nose in it. Now start picking up your gear."

She sat down, linked her hands between her knees, and gazed at him stolidly. "Go away, Con. Go back with Todd."

He came and stood over her. She smelled cologne; Phyllis's

choice again. She had to tilt her head to look at him, but she fixed her stare so it wouldn't waver.

"Let me take the boat and you come in on the mailboat when you're ready. Maybe the little change out here will do you good."

"I'll never be ready," she said, "and you can't have the boat. If you help yourself to her, Con, I'll be all right. I'll be back to call off the divorce."

It was almost as if his breathing stopped. Then he put his hands in his pockets and moved away from her, sidewise, lightly, as if in a dance step. "I didn't want to tell you this, sweetie," he said, "but everybody's either laughing or shaking their heads over what you did. A grown woman taking off like a kid in a tantrum, taking a chance on losing herself, the boat, everything." He overdid the amazement. "I've covered up for you the best I could. Said I knew you were going, it was something you wanted to do, and if you come back with me they'll figger I was telling the truth. See?"

"You mean they're laughing at *you*," she said gently. "Oh, I don't doubt some are snickering at me, the same ones who always did. They're tickled to death because I was conned. Hey, that's a good one, Con. Get it?" She grinned at him. "But they all know that fog or clear I can find my way anywhere with a chart and a compass, so if I took off in thick fog it was for my own reasons and no tantrum. No, it's you everybody's laughing at, isn't it? That's what you think, and it's made you sick enough to puke."

He turned and walked out the back door and she went behind him. The sun slanting down over the spruces made his hair shine, and she looked away and went over to the lilacs. With her nose in a purple plume she said, "And of course you've got no way to haul those five hundred traps. Didn't Adam leave a couple of boats? I thought you were marrying a rich widow, Con."

"Damn you, *damn you*. You're nothing but a harpy after

all." He was so upset he had a hard time lighting a cigarette, and he was very pale. She was shaken because he was, and was about to say, *Take the boat but get out of my sight.* Only he spoke first.

"You know that was theft, running off with the boat and traps like that. I could press charges and make 'em stick. That'd look fine in the *Patriot*, wouldn't it? Your father'd turn over in his grave."

"He's been turning over in his grave ever since I married you, Conall Fleming," she said. "Now you get off my property, and you just try coming out here with the sheriff or a U.S. Marshal and see what you get!"

He left. She knew she could have called him back, before he went by the trees in the lane, but she put her fist against her mouth and let him go. Then she tried to pick up the spade, but the yard was too full of him, and the house was no refuge, now that he'd been in the kitchen. She turned toward the path to the cove.

She had been here only late at night, in the fog and at low tide. This was high tide in the early afternoon, and the cove brimmed with shimmering, shifting blues. She went along the uneven bluff until she found a clear space of turf on a sort of prow out over the mouth of the cove. She lay on the warm, tough grass, her head in her arms, wondering how she was going to survive. It was no help to remember how many times she'd wondered the same thing since she'd first found out about Phyllis, and was still living. Always before, she had wanted to go on living, if she could only be rid of this intolerable pain. But now, like a person with a fatal illness, she was tired of being revived after each sinking spell; she wanted only to be done with it.

In a little while she heard an engine from the vicinity of the breakwater, and she sat up, her eyes blurry from all the brilliant light after the darkness inside her arms. As they cleared she recognized the Seal Point boat, with two men in the cockpit. One of them walked toward the stern and seemed to be looking back at the island. She wouldn't have known him from this distance except for the bare red head.

If only she hadn't run away from the house. He might have come back to try again with her, and she could have taken back the things she said. Oh, why had she said them anyway? Couldn't they be friends? Wasn't it better than nothing, better than this agony which was far from nothing?

She squeezed her eyes shut to hide the sight of the boat leaving. It mightn't last with Phyllis, in fact it probably wouldn't. Easy come, easy go. If she'd fallen into bed with Con so fast when she was still Adam's wife, what wouldn't she do when she was Con's wife and he was off seining?

Some women were like that. They didn't care who the man was. Con had been trapped, really. If he wasn't so inno-cent—because he *was* innocent, falling in love all over the place like a teen-age boy—he wouldn't have got caught like this. He'd have made damn sure Phyllis couldn't get pregnant by him. He was decent, so he wanted to make the baby legiti-mate. But, when that was accomplished, or maybe before, he'd see the entrapment. Maybe he saw it already, but pride kept him from telling her. If she'd given him half a chance . . .

She lay down again. Between the sun on her back and the sound of the water just below her, she was beguiled into a cozy dream wherein Con headed home to her as soon as the baby was named. In an even better version, Phyllis became mad about somebody else and wanted nothing more from Con, not even his baby, so he came back to Rosa with the baby in his arms.

It would make no difference to her that Phyllis was the physical mother. It would be Con's baby, and that was what mattered. Then it would become Con's and hers: she sighed now with longing for the small weight in her arms and her hand cupped over a tiny bottom.

9

The dream was deepening into the insulated refuge of sleep when a gull spoke distinctly into her ear. "You come away from that water, Johnny Campion!"

Johnny Campion was a funny name for a gull's child to have, and it was even funnier that he should have to stay away from the water. She rolled over and sat up. The gulls were making noises like gulls, but a small band of children were coming around the rocks from Western Harbor Point, accompanied by Tiger and a larger dog who ranged much farther in long ardent leaps over the juniper and daisies. Johnny Campion was easily identified as a small boy who was reluctantly ascending a long slant of rock from the water, while a girl with hair like a dandelion blossom scolded him in piercing tones; she was the talking gull.

The big dog would discover Rosa long before the children did, and she had a great respect for large dogs accompanying children. When they all dipped out of sight in a gully, she got up and went back along the top of the bluff to the woods. She walked quickly, for fear the dogs might follow and catch up before she reached the house.

The urgency of the escape shook the dream loose. It was still there, but its reality now was no more than that of a bright pebble picked up on the beach and carried in the pocket. One could take it out and look at it, return it to the pocket or throw it away.

She had thrown it away by the time she saw the house through the spruces. She was wide awake and seeing Con with a clarity that was cruel, not to him but to her, because it took away any hope. The man who had come and gone today hadn't felt humble or trapped. Annoyed, yes, because she'd humiliated him, and he'd have to rent or borrow a boat till he got *Sea Star* back. Even Phyllis was no good to him there. The boats were all in use, and Adam's son by his first wife had the say of them anyway.

Con should have *Sea Star*, and she was being just plain sadistic. And I like it, she thought ferociously.

There was a metallic clinking from her yard. When she came around the last twist in the path the stocky man from next door was hitching up two hundred-pound gas cylinders to the fittings on the outside wall by the kitchen windows. He had rust-colored hair, nothing like Con's.

As she approached, he looked around and called, "Hi, there!" He stepped back with a flourish of his wrench. "There, that'll do you for a while."

"I'm much obliged," she said. "What do you charge?"

He blew that away with a gesture. "Don't talk so foolish. I grab any excuse to play trucks." He gestured at the little tractor and cart. "Besides, I owe you wharfage. Those are my traps on your wharf. I'll get them right off."

"I'm not using the space, you might as well wait till you'd be taking them off anyway."

"Well, thanks!" He shot out a thick hand. "I'm Ralph Percy. My wife would have been over before this with an invite to supper or something, but she and the kids are away."

"I haven't been much in the mood for socializing," said Rosa. "I've been so busy I just crawl under the kelp at sundown, and that's it."

"That's it for everybody at this time of year, I guess. I'll light your refrigerator up now and check the stove. That oven pilot's a hell of a thing. Gracie Wylie was always coming for me to light it. She never trusted Arnold, thought he'd blow his head off."

"I can do it——"

But he was already tramping in past her, talking the whole time and not missing a thing. "Hey, you've done some slicking up in here. You buying, or did I hear wrong?"

"No, you heard right."

"Finest kind! An empty house right next door bothers me. The Wylies were good neighbors, and I remember when Jude lived out here too. He was always good. Great carpenter, too. Of course I was a kid then." He opened the oven of the gas stove. "Got a wooden match?"

Silently she presented the box to him, and he hunkered before the oven. "Now you turn her on full and press in the button while I hold the match. . . . Your old man's got the right idea. Let the woman come ahead and get things ready. I suppose he'll be out to set that load of gear and take the boat in for some more . . . There she goes. Keep holding down that button for a minute more."

"We haven't been up before the board yet," Rosa said.

"Huh?" He cocked his head up at her. "What board?"

"Whoever says we can fish here or not."

"Oh hell, you're buying, aren't you? And Jude wouldn't send out any outlaw. At least I don't think he would."

"Still, it's probably safest to take soundings before we do anything," Rosa said.

"Go ask Mark if it'll make you any happier. He'll be the one to buy your lobsters, and damn sure nobody's going to buck him. Okay, let go the button. She'll do." He flopped down on his belly to light the refrigerator. "Got it clean as a whistle under here, I see." He held another match in place. "You play that guitar up there?"

"Uh-huh." Rosa leaned against the counter with her arms folded.

"We'll have to get together. I scrape away on the fiddle

some, and Pierre Bennett plays the accordion." There was a small popping retort from the mechanism and he echoed it with a grunt of satisfaction. "There she is."

He rolled over and sat up. "From Seal Point, huh? At least that's what the boat says."

"She says right."

"You know the Bartons out here? They're from Seal Point."

It was like a knife slash across her midriff. She pressed her folded arms in on the pain and tried to keep her face straight. She couldn't think. Barton. Barton. All she could remember was old Chad Barton who'd died a few years ago, and he'd lived alone. Ralph, lighting a cigarette, was still talking.

". . . hadn't lived in Seal Point for a long time before they came out here. Years, I guess. Barry just mentioned it once, that's all."

The pain eased away. If she didn't know them, it was likely they didn't know her. They might have known her father; who wouldn't know True McKinnon? But Rosa Fleming should mean nothing to them.

"Well," he said reluctantly, "I'd better push off. I called my wife last night and told her we had neighbors, she was real pleased." He rolled up lightly onto his feet. "Folks around here are friendly, but they won't shove in till you give the high sign."

"That's what I've always heard," Rosa said. "Thank you for your help. Bringing up the gas and lighting pilots and everything."

"I was happy to do it. And, like I said, I owe you wharf rent. Look, I'll carry that bag of lime up to the toilet. Where do you want the kerosene, in the entry?"

Afterwards he drove the tractor around behind the house and into his own yard, whistling *Garryowen*. She contemplated the silver cylinders of gas; they set a seal upon her occupancy.

66

I can live out of forty traps, she thought, and not touch what I've got in the bank unless I want something special. *Something special.* The words echoed and jangled.

You've had that, she thought dryly. Oh boy, have you had it. Now go on in and get yourself something to eat and get back to work.

By sundown the toilet had been cleaned and thoroughly limed. In the house she had washed the cupboards and the storage spaces under the counters and sink. She had cleared the rust from the sink with kerosene. When she was through for the day she sat down on the floor in the corner again with her guitar, and played and sang until she was ready to fall asleep.

She was awake at daylight with the gulls, and the boats going out. While she drank her coffee she wrote a note to Edwin on a lined pad she'd found in a bureau drawer. She asked him to pick up some towels and bedding at the house— her sleeping bag had been almost too warm last night—and to get certain tools from the fishhouse. If he would put everything in a carton and send it out on the mailboat, she'd be much obliged.

"Your path is still there," she added. "And there's a yellow million eider ducklings."

Then she made a grocery list, and when she thought the store was open she took the wheelbarrow down to the big wharf. A small dark-eyed boy was solemnly arranging cans of fruit on lower shelves, and a large gray-and-white cat who acted like the real owner of the place came to greet her with a flourish of his tail.

She bought a stamped envelope and addressed it to Edwin. "Do you have putty or shall I get somebody to send me some?" she asked Mark Bennett. "My windows are in tough shape."

"I've got everything you need for fixing windows," he said. "On this place somebody's forever having to put in a pane of glass."

She sealed her letter and dropped it in the box, and then began on her grocery list. This morning she felt at least all of a piece, if not happy. She had more to do than muddle around in her own misery.

When the wheelbarrow was loaded, she gave Bennett a check for everything she'd gotten so far. Then, before she could change her mind, she said quickly, "I don't know if Jude told you, Mr. Bennett, but my husband isn't coming out to stay, and I'm not going back. I'd like to set out those forty traps. I'm buying the place from Jude, so does that give me the right to fish out here? Will anybody object?"

Sitting on the counter, he listened, his dark face without expression. The cat jumped up beside him and his big hand kept slowly stroking the broad head. The child leaned against his father's leg and looked at her the way his father did. Between the two pairs of dark eyes she began to feel uncomfortable, but she finished out.

Mark rubbed his jaw, looked out at the harbor, and said, "You're right up and down like a high board fence, and I like that, so I'll try to be the same with you. I don't know who'd object to your fishing that handful of traps. We try to keep down to a dozen fishermen here, and we've only got ten now. We don't count the kids who have traps out for the summer. . . . We've got another rule amongst ourselves, and that is, when everybody starts fishing short warps around the island in the summer nobody fishes more than two hundred pots. Outside—" He shrugged. "No matter. But inshore, we try to keep limits, or it could just be plain hell, everybody fouling warps. Tempers get mean when you have to be clearing snarls all the time."

"I'd keep out of everybody's way——"

"Putting forty pots overboard isn't plastering the place. No, I don't guess anybody'd object."

"Someone already has," she said, "before I had a chance to ask."

"Who was it?"

"I don't know his name. He was tinkering with his engine when I came into the harbor. He's got yellow hair."

Mark grinned. "That's the feller who put your boat off the other night. Jamie Sorensen, my sister's boy. Tried to scare you, did he?"

"I don't scare," said Rosa.

"I can see that. Well, you go along and set your traps, just don't drop 'em on top of anybody else. Got any bait?"

"Yes, thanks." She wanted to get out of there, but something held her to the spot, uncomfortable under all the eyes—the cat was now fascinated with her, for some reason. Finally, reddening and clearing her throat, she said, "I wouldn't want anybody to think I took it for granted about setting traps out here. I mean I didn't have any idea. I mean—" The red was pure fire. "The traps just happened to be on the boat when I started out."

He nodded in a kind of massive calm, and she burned to think that Jude must have told him something of the truth. But at least the child didn't know what they were talking about.

"Do you think I could rent that mooring my boat's on?" she asked.

"No need. That's Jude's mooring. He paid for it. It's in good shape too. The Wylies put a new pennant on it last year."

"Then that's that," she said, out of the fire now, everything concentrated on the boat. "This is my last question, I promise. Do you know where I can rent a skiff?"

"I've got one tied up at the car you can use." Humor narrowed his eyes. "Jamie's got one for sale, but you and he may not want to do business."

She shrugged. "It's up to him. Does he just naturally have a chip on his shoulder, or what?"

"Hard telling about Jamie. Nothing ever seems to get under his father's skin, but his mother's pretty quick off the mark. Calmed down some through the years. Mellowed, Nils

69

says." His amusement deepened. "Jamie favors her some days, other times it's his father. Depends on which side of the bed he gets out of."

"Like all the rest of us," she admitted. "Maybe his engine had him all fussed up that day. How much rent do you want for your skiff?"

He raised and then flattened one hand in a negative gesture. "It's a spare. Young Mark has his own. Let's see how long you use it before we talk rent."

She felt easy enough with him now to put a lot more into her thanks, though she never could be lavish even if she were melting with gratitude inside.

"I appreciate everything, and I don't plan to be a nuisance."

Again the slow gesture of the hand. "Anything for True McKinnon's girl," he said with a smile. "You'd be so cussid solemn, working away at that ice cream. Nobody could pry you off that nail keg."

"I was some bashful. And you know what? I can't stand ice cream now. You just can't imagine that, can you?" she asked the astonished child. His father laughed, and she went out feeling quite pleased with herself.

Wheeling her load home through the early morning with only the birds out, she experienced for the first time the peace she hoped to find here. She returned to her dooryard with a tinge of proprietory affection; this was the first home she had ever obtained for herself, and it set her apart from everything she had ever been and everybody she had ever known. She was a person alone, neither True McKinnon's daughter nor Conall Fleming's wife.

10

She put the plastic billfold holding her lobster license in her hip pocket, took her oil jacket, and was on her way. Setting traps didn't call for rubber boots or oil pants, and there were work gloves aboard the boat.

When she walked by the store someone was inside talking with Mark. She went into the shed, which smelled exactly as she remembered it, damp and pungent with the hogsheads of bait along one side. The planks underfoot never dried out, and gave off the rich moist bouquet of the years. When she came out into the sunny open, Young Mark and the cat were on the car, lying in wait for her; brown eyes and green eyes never missed a motion as she went down the ladder. Young Mark's skiff was obviously the five-footer with the name "Louis" painted in large, wobbly, red letters across the stern. But she asked him, anyway.

"Which one is yours?"

He pointed.

"Who's she named after? Or maybe I should say who's *he* named after?"

Young Mark pointed to the cat.

"Oh. . . . He got your tongue?"

"No," said Young Mark with great dignity. Rosa grinned.

"For a minute you had me scared." She untied her skiff, and suddenly he was under her elbow, kneeling on the car to hold the skiff steady while she stepped in. He was manfully braced, expecting God knew what from somebody her size. She always felt lithe as a willow when she boarded a boat; the skiff hardly bobbed, and she was proud of that and Young Mark's relieved approval.

"Thanks," she said to him as she rowed away, and he gave her a gesture so much like his father's that she wanted to laugh.

There was a light northwest breeze skimming across the harbor and riffling the surface in dark blue patches. The skiff sped toward *Sea Star*. For a moment she was conscious of village windows but not concerned, then she forgot them altogether when she reached the boat. She reached up and patted the side. "How do you like it out here, old girl?" she asked. "The other ones speaking to you? Or are they stuck-up? Hey, what about that Sorensen putting you off the other night? I hope you were a credit to me." She swung herself aboard. "Well, here we are. Let's have fun."

She took the boat across the harbor to gas up. Mark had seen her coming and was down on the car with the hose. "Watch the bottom, now," he advised paternally.

"I've got my chart, plus the fathometer."

Even when you knew the grounds, setting traps was always an adventure in gambling and hope, but this time she was in foreign territory and not about to dump pots just anywhere. Once she was past the breakwater and heading down the west side, she had that sensation of having crossed an ocean instead of a bay to get to this place. With her chart at hand, she set out on a voyage of exploration.

The island was high on this end, and still in its morning shade it looked even higher, the woods almost black against the early blue-white radiance of the sky. Past Barque Cove with its one pink wall, the rocky shore turned black and brown, sometimes streaked with dull rusty red; even in sunshine, it would soak up light rather than give it. It was broken at intervals by steep little coves with stony beaches, submerged in the shadow of the heights, the brown eiders and ducklings almost invisible. In one cove toward Sou'west Point a boy was hauling from a double-ender, as close to the rocks as the birds could get. His fluorescent orange buoys caught the eye like flashes of fire.

The boy waved as *Sea Star* cruised slowly by. Up on the ridge the forest thinned out to a few stunted, wind-wrung individuals. Gulls stood on the cliffs, breasts to the wind, or circled high above the ledges in their tireless aerial circus. The place looked wild and barren even with its sunny green slopes, and she could hardly wait to walk to it.

But the water excited her more; the blue-green combers advancing, rearing, breaking white over the long black reefs that tailed off the point, then the glassy slide of seas in retreat, and the return in a powerful and deliberate rhythm of attack.

Someone was hauling on the outer edge of the turbulence, and she went well outside him. There were two men aboard, or rather a man and a boy, and they both waved. She returned the salute, but was not taken in; new fishermen had been greeted like this in other places, including Seal Point, but on their first time out to haul they had found never a trap. She was not naturally suspicious, and she knew Mark Bennett could be telling the truth. But she knew also that she was as alien in this place as it was alien to her.

Around the Point and going up the south side, she was in a hot lee of flat shining water and sunny woods that bore no relation to the dark forest on the other shore. Outside the lee the seas were breaking on ledges and islets she identified on her chart; boats worked around them, rolling in the swells. Another boat was hauling along this shore of the island, just a little ahead of her. But she was dawdling, and at last the boat disappeared around a point that she found on the chart as Schooner Head.

She was glad of that. She wanted to be alone while she was finding her way. Buoys were a spatter of color every-

73

where, like exotic seabirds. She noticed a string of green-and-white buoys, and knew she'd set nowhere near these and give Sorensen an excuse to say she'd set on top of him.

She passed the long, deep bite of Goose Cove, with the Bennett Homestead at its head, crossed Schoolhouse Cove and Windward Point, and around into Pump Cove.

There were a few traps in this cove, but no green-and-white buoys. She set *Sea Star* to moving slowly in a circle, and took the lid off the bait box. The herring had a clean, acrid, nose-prickling scent that meant it had been freshly corned just before she came out here. Forty of the nylon twine bags she'd knit for Con had been filled. Not by her. She used to bag up for him before the break-up, but now he hired some youngster to do it, and the kid sure hated to stuff a bag. About one herring apiece, it looked like; well, never mind for this time. The bait was just about perfect, nothing like the bream cuttings that were nothing more than garbage after they had been standing around a few days.

She slid a trap along the washboard and took out the coiled warp, toggle, and buoy. These traps had bricks for ballast, built right into them. They were not the heavy traps that Con had built in the winter, and they would need some loose ballast to hold them on bottom. She picked two roundish rocks out of a lobster crate that Con had filled the same day he had piled the traps on board, and laid them in the bottom of the trap, speared a filled bag with the bait-iron and threaded it onto the baitline. She fastened down the door by twisting the baitline around the cleat on the top of the trap. Spitting on the trap for luck she said, "Get in there and do me proud, baby."

She slid the trap overboard, watching it become indistinct through sun-shot green depths as she paid out the line. As it disappeared completely she tossed over the gin-bottle toggle and the blue-and-yellow buoy.

"There we are," she said to the boat. "Now we'll find out about these famous Bennett's Island lobsters."

She began to get another trap ready. As the boat swung in a leisurely arc, she caught motion from the corner of her eye. Bait-iron in her hand she watched the boat come full tilt across the cove. She didn't recognize it from the direct head-on view, until she saw the green-and-white buoy mounted on the canopy roof.

Captain Goldilocks. Head of the Bennett's Island Gestapo. . . . She went on baiting the trap. Just as she slid it overboard, he slid alongside, gaff out to keep the boats close but not touching; his paint job was so new it looked like fine white china.

I'll bet he's nasty-neat, she thought. She tossed over the buoy and turned to him with a broad, dazzing smile. "*Good* morning, Skipper! I want to thank you for putting my boat off the other night."

"That's a nice boat," he said coldly. "I'd hate to see anything happen to her. I don't know what you've got at Seal Point, but around here you just can't leave a boat tied up at a wharf and forget all about her, especially with low green tides."

"I wouldn't have forgotten her, ordinarily, but I—" She stopped herself. What the hell business is it of yours? she thought. She slid another trap into place and began taking out the warp and buoy, conscious of his eyes. They had the pure almost dazzling blue of shadows on fresh snow. They made her defiant and flourishy in her motions.

"When's your man coming with the rest of his gear?" he asked.

"He's been and gone, Herr Kapitan. Don't tell me you never noticed."

He ignored that so well she wondered if she'd said it aloud. "How many more traps will you be setting after these?"

"Your uncle told me there'd be no objection."

"My uncle isn't a lobster fisherman, he just buys our lobsters. He doesn't speak for everybody."

She rested her hands on the top of the trap and looked at him. "I take it you're registering an objection here and now."

"Maybe not to these forty traps, if that's all, though they could be a hell of a nuisance. Did he tell you about our limits?"

Her neck was as stiff as his. "He did. No more than two hundred traps apiece in to the rocks. Listen, I'm reasonable. I'll go by the rules. Right now I've got only these, and you won't find any of them near yours."

"Thanks," he said. There was a faint change in his face, she couldn't tell whether it was amusement or anger. In any case, it couldn't get by the ice. *What if your face froze that way?* they used to say when she was small and pulled her mouth around in a sulk or a squawk.

"By the way," she said breezily, "your uncle says you've got a skiff for sale. How much do you want for her?"

"If I sell her, fifty bucks."

"*If* you sell her, will you sell her to me?"

"I suppose your money's as good as anybody's."

"You never can tell. I might have printed it up in my cellar just last week." She felt like telling him what he could do with the skiff, but he must have known what she was thinking. She waited while he gazed off toward shore, and finally she looked too. The two boats were being carried on the tide gently but inexorably toward the steep inner bank of the cove. The girls were descending a long flight of wooden steps to the pebble beach. The long fair hair; Linnea Sorensen. Of course.

"You can have her," Jamie said abruptly.

Nearly killed you, didn't it? she thought.

"I'll bring a check to your fishhouse when I see you're in this afternoon. Okay?"

He nodded, turned back to his wheel, and put his engine in gear. He slid past *Sea Star*'s stern and spun away in a wide circle toward the mouth of the cove. He didn't look back. "Adios, muchacho!" she called after him.

She baited and set the trap, but forgot to spit on it. "Oh well," she said, "Our Leader has given you his blessing. What more do you expect?"

The girls shed shirts, appeared in bikinis, and arranged themselves on the rocks. Some younger children began to wade. Someone saw Rosa, and everyone waved. She waved back, but left the cove looking for more deserted spots in which to set gear. Now she could see why hermits became hermits. Alone, you were all to yourself in one concentrated package. With other people you were scattered around in bits, no two pieces the same. Whatever anyone's image of you was, even in the most casual context, it was something stolen from you. Given enough people, there'd be none of you left; you could disappear after all, leaving only your name.

She went back along the southeastern side the way she had come, and set a few here, a few there, wherever she saw other buoys (except Jamie Sorensen's) but not near enough to be in the way. Then she cruised around the outside islets where gulls and shags had their rookeries, ran halfway to Matinicus Rock to feel the deep-water motion under her, and jogged back admiring the island from afar.

She returned to the harbor by way of the Eastern End, sailing under the Head where there must always be a surge as there was at the other end of the island. When she came along Long Cove she met the mailboat leaving the harbor. There were a few passengers, who waved, and the captain swung his arm out the wheelhouse window. She felt almost like a native, and came into the harbor singing, until she saw the scattering of women and children around the wharf and the store. Silently she went to her mooring, made fast, and rowed to her own wharf. She was still under the spell of the morning. Nothing had been real out there but herself, the boat, the gear, and the sea. Con had become insubstantial, a fog-phantom burning up in the sunlight. This was going to be easy, she thought. She could hardly believe it, but she'd had the proof.

She started to walk home with the proof intact, and Maggie Dinsmore sang out from a kitchen window, "Hello, there! How've you been?"

"Oh, fine!" She kept on walking but Maggie came out to her, Tiger ahead and the little girls hurrying so as not to miss anything. They stood staring up at Rosa with hardly a blink between them.

"Would you come down to supper tonight?" Maggie asked. "I wanted to ask you before but I haven't seen you, except once when you were to the well and I was doing something I couldn't leave."

How could you fall so far and still be standing in one place? She was too hot, too tired, too depressed, and too stupid. "Well, I—could I come another time?" she asked, stumblingly. "I'd enjoy it more. I'm so tired at night right now."

"Oh, sure, sure," the other soothed her. "Of course! I know how it is. It's so different out here, I always say it's another world, another *planet* really. Like something on that TV show *Star Trek*. You know?" She laughed heartily at that, and Rosa joined her; it was easy, she was so relieved.

"Mama knew you were coming," one of the children said suddenly. "She saw you in her teacup."

"It must have been an awful big teacup," said Rosa. The child put her hand over her mouth and giggled. Maggie let out a robust guffaw.

"In the leaves," she explained. "I read the tea leaves. Sometimes I hit things right," she added modestly. "I've got second sight, you know. It runs in the family. My aunt was a medium. I'll read for you sometime, if you like," she offered.

"That would be fun," said Rosa untruthfully, determined

never to go near the Dinsmore house or even approach a teacup if Maggie were in its vicinity. "So long," she said to the children, and winked solemnly at the smaller one, who was convulsed with joyful surprise.

In her own yard she sank down on the cellar bulkhead and put her head in her hands. Oh Con, she thought wearily, what in hell am I doing out here, away from you?

Now that she had actually set the traps, everything she had done so far seemed incredible. She was stuck in the glue of a dream that wouldn't release her, and she could partially move within its tiny radius, able to make only feeble, crippled motions and never escape again.

She couldn't endure it. Dearest Jesus, she prayed with the fervor she'd had as a religious child, what's happening to me? I can't die, but I can't live either. Help me.

There was no answer, either in herself or from the kindly big brother she'd imagined Jesus to be in those hero-worshiping days. And she was ashamed of her appeal. It was so conceited and trivial and selfish to pray for salvation from her own foolishness when at this very moment people were dying of famine, war, and fire, and some child was being murdered by its own parents.

The gruesome image bounced her up off the bulkhead and into the house, where she washed up with cold water and a lot of spirited splashing, and began to get a noon meal ready.

II

A large damp patch on the ceiling in the front bedroom upstairs showed where the roof needed patching. Reluctantly she conceded that she might have to borrow a ladder for that. She had her heart set on puttying windows, but a soaking rain could bring this ceiling down.—What she really wanted, of all things, was to be out aboard again. If there was one place in this world where she could escape Con, it was with the boat, and that was a funny thing when you considered how much time she and Con had spent aboard *Sea Star* at the first of their marriage. She'd been some happy, and she knew now that he'd been just putting up with it.

With a grimace rather than a sigh, she sat down on a scarred old sea chest under the windows and looked out across the village. At least it wasn't Seal Point. Nobody out here gave a hoot in hell about her and Con; the women taking in their washing, hovering over their gardens, setting out for walks or calls; the children playing around the long harbor beach, small ones climbing over a couple of beached seine dories, older ones rowing out to fish; the men working on gear on their wharves or socializing in fishhouse doorways.

Some little girls were trundling doll carriages across the marshy field past the schoolhouse that faced out to sea across Schoolhouse Cove. They helped each other get the carriages over the tumbled rocks and tide rubble left on the brow of the beach by the last flood tide, and disappeared toward the water. At the far end of the long curve, Windward Point thrust out toward the open Atlantic. She remembered how it looked from the water when she was setting her first traps on the other side of it, which brought her inevitably to Jamie Sorensen.

His boat was on the mooring now, so she wrote out a check to him and walked down to the fishhouse. Maggie wasn't around to hail her this time, but a dark-haired woman at the well called, "Hello!" She seemed about to make more of it, but was diverted when the dark collie with her started to lift his leg against the wellcurb. While she was scolding him, Rosa kept on going.

Someone was building traps in the fishhouse. The door was open and a radio was tuned low to the ball game in Boston. The man who was lathing trap bottoms at the bench wasn't Jamie; braced for meeting him, she started to back away before the stranger could notice her, but as if he had eyes in the back of his fair head he said without looking around, "Don't run off."

He put down his hammer and turned around to her, his hand out. "I'm Nils Sorensen. I knew your father. Welcome to Bennett's Island."

They shook hands. With him the blue eyes were a different matter, neither cold nor suspicious. This was a man, not an arrogant kid. "Your son's selling me a skiff," she said. "I came down to pay him."

"Jamie's catching up on his sleep right now, they'll be out looking for herring tonight. The skiff's tied to your ladder."

"Well, would you give him the check?" She took it out.

"Don't you want to look at her before you pay for her?"

"If she'll get me to the mooring and back, that's all I care."

"Come see her anyway."

The skiff floated in the shadowy rectangle between the

wharves. Her buff paint was clean, and the oars were tucked neatly under the seats. The bottom looked dry.

"She looks solid enough," Rosa said. "And big enough. I need something a little more than a sardine tin."

"She's eleven foot, and solid, all right. Jamie built her himself."

"I shouldn't think he'd want to part with such a good piece of work."

"Because he likes his new one better. This one's a little too flat-bottomed to suit him. She was an experiment, more or less. The new one's faster."

"Well, she'll suit me," said Rosa. "I don't think I'll be rowing in any races."

"You can't tell what you're likely to get into out here." There was an aura of kindness about him, and she wondered if he were speaking to True McKinnon's fat little motherless girl. Well, that was a change from being Con Flemming's deluded fool of a wife.

"Maybe Maggie Dinsmore can find out in her tea leaves," she said.

"Maggie's a great addition to the place. We never knew what we'd been missing till she showed up. But just don't believe that Ouija board of hers. Thing's an unprincipled liar." They both laughed, and it was a good time to leave.

"Well, I'd better row Mr. Bennett's skiff back to the car," she said. "Will you give this to your son, please?"

"I shall do so." He put the check in his shirt pocket. "Thank you."

Nobody was on the lobster car when she tied up there, but there was conversation in the store so she walked quickly by, and turned off onto the lane, wondering if she could borrow a ladder from Ralph. The trouble was, he'd probably want to patch the roof for her, unless she was lucky and he had no head for heights. Con couldn't even stand getting onto the shed roof at home. Poor Con. . . . Poor Con *hell*.

There was an aluminum extension ladder out behind Ralph's shed, but no sign of Ralph. She went home and painted the toilet seat with gray deck paint. The door needed re-hanging but that wasn't an emergency. She decided to putty the front downstairs windows instead, and she could reach most of their upper sashes by standing on a lobster crate. She worked through sunset, when she suddenly realized she was hungry. After a can of soup for supper it was easy to fall into bed and drift off to sleep.

In the morning everything was too wet with dew for her to go back to puttying, and the traps would have to soak for a few days. So she began tackling some of the darker corners of the house, beginning with the back entry. Everything went out into the yard, to be inspected for potential worth or destruction. There were some tattered flannel shirts that would make good cleaning rags, and a couple of earthenware crocks. One of these held the shrunken remains of mackerel salted so long ago there was not even a smell left. And behind the crocks, under a rickety shelf (which Jude had never built), she discovered what every house should have.

"Well, we are certainly off to a good start today," she said, hauling it out into the open. It was a dust-furred, mouse-visited wooden box bearing the dim words Common Crackers.

It held a lavish jumble of nuts, bolts, screws, nails ranging from threepenny fines to wharf spikes; hooks and eyes; washers; twists of wire, little balls of twine; a faucet for an oil drum; padlocks and keys, rusty drills, unmatched hinges, parts of door latches. There were also a hacksaw, wrenches of different kinds, half a folding rule, several chisels, a hammer, and a screwdriver. Treasure indeed.

She remembered seeing a shelf of empty preserve jars in the cellar, and she opened the bulkheads to the sun and brought up an armful of jars. With a mug of coffee beside her on the doorstep she spent an absorbed hour sorting out the

83

small hardware into containers. She was able to match up some of the keys and padlocks. Anything rusty but still good went into a jar of kerosene to soak.

She swept the entry clean of cobwebs and mouse dirt, washed the small window, reinforced the shelf, and arranged her jars on it. She washed a thick pelt of dust from the cracker box and put the tools back into it, and anything else that was too big for the jars but which might come in handy.

With that done, satisfactory as it had been, she felt one of those wild, restless, forlorn spells coming on, that incredulous waking up to the facts. So she went out to Barque Cove and down onto the beach with an idea of going all the way to Sou'west Point, driving the devils away by a strenuous hike, if that was the only thing that worked.

She'd been so busy until now that she hadn't even been down on the beach yet. It was a narrow, steep, stony stretch between the pink eastern wall and the black western side where the rocks were like a flow of petrified lava. Wild rose-bushes and beach peas grew up through the tidal detritus at the top of the beach, and in a wet, tussocky area behind it blue flag grew in thick sheaves, boneset, swamp candles, snow bedstraw, bindweed. The beach was so cluttered with drift-wood that she had to pick her way, and the first whole board stopped her.

She carried everything good back to the foot of the track and then up to the top of the pink wall. The sun was hot down here, it dazzled off the pale smooth stones, and drew up a moist enervating air from the ground. If she wanted exhaustion she'd found it. After she'd struggled up the track with a fifteen-foot hardwood plank, still partly water-soaked, she collapsed panting in a hollow full of buttercups and lay supine until she realized she was sharing the hollow with ants as well as buttercups.

Groaning, she got up and looked at her loot without much enthusiasm. The thought that every beach along the west side must have held an abundance of driftwood only filled her with fatigue. Being a compulsive beachcomber could be as bad as being a compulsive eater, except that it wouldn't add weight.

Well, there it was, and like everything she'd sorted through this morning, it might come in handy. My motto, she thought sourly. Is that what I thought about Con?

She loaded up with what she could carry and went slowly and awkwardly home along the winding path. At least it was cool in the woods. She wished for a pail of fresh cold water at the end of the trail, but she'd have to get it for herself.

She came into the yard and could have sworn aloud. There were four girls this time, just coming across what should have been her lawn. The Sorensen girl was ahead, carrying a plate wrapped in a dish towel.

What in hell do they think I *am?* Rosa cried silently. Some kind of *freak?*

The girls seemed startled at the sight of her. Linnie's "Hi" was a little breathless. Rosa dropped her load with a crash and said, "All I need is a good long trunk and then I could be my own work elephant."

They giggled and became ordinary kids again, not young sadists come to stare at a woman who couldn't keep a man. "I *love* beach-combing," the Shetland pony said fervently. "We've lugged home so much stuff the barn's getting full and Daddy keeps threatening the biggest bonfire we ever saw."

"Did you ever look for ambergris," Linnie asked Rosa, "and keep thinking how rich you'd be, and what you'd do with all your money?"

"I used to get all fussed up trying to decide how to spend it," said Rosa. "I'd have exploded if I ever found any. But I was always looking."

"Now I bet it isn't worth anything," the new girl said, sounding cheated. "They do everything with chemicals." She had a strong resemblance to Holly Bennett, the Shetland pony, except that her hair was cut short like a black lamb's fleece. Linnie introduced her as a cousin, Betsey Bennett. Holly had gone back out of sight around the corner.

Linnie held out the plate. "Yeast rolls. My mother's baking bread today. She says she won't call till you want callers, but this is a kind of hello."

"Hello," Rosa said to the towel. She breathed deeply of the scented steam and said, "Gorgeous. Thank your mother."

Holly appeared carrying a guitar. "We were wondering——"

"You mean *you* were," said Vic. Holly was flustered but persistent.

"All right, me. I was wondering if you'd show me a little about it. I can play some, but not much."

"Well now, listen, I'm not so hot," said Rosa.

"But you've been playing so long, you must know an awful lot more about it than we do."

"I can't think of anything," Rosa stalled, "until I have a drink. I'm dryer than a cork leg and there's no fresh water in the house."

"I'll go!" Holly pushed the guitar at her cousin. "Where's the pail?"

Rosa went in and got it, pouring the stale water into the wash basin. Holly went off at a run, swinging the pail. Rosa sat down on the doorstep, and Betsey sat on the bulkhead, cuddling the guitar. Vic was always in motion, hands fidgeting, bare toes wiggling. Now she was loudly inhaling lilac scent. But Linnie, standing perfectly still, had a quality of concentrating her entire being on one object, and right now it was Rosa.

"Jamie Sorensen must be your brother," she said.

"The Golden Fleece," said Vic. "I could eat him. I keep wearing my sexy perfume I got for Christmas, but he doesn't even look at me unless I can make him trip over me."

"I told you how Jamie was," Linnie said.

"Sure, but I believed all those stories my mother told me about movie stars making it with freckles and buck teeth, so

I was brainwashed into thinking I'd knock him dead when I stepped off the boat."

"You haven't got buck teeth," Linnie objected.

"Oh yeah? Well, I've got an awfully short upper lip, then. That's great, if a man's crazy about rabbits." She burst out laughing and so did Linnie, but Rosa wondered what Vic's self-ridicule really covered. She reached for the guitar and began to tune it. Linnie sat down crosslegged, graceful and erect. Vic fell down like a gangly pup, all elbows.

"When I get to college," she said, lying on her back and pointing a leg at the sky, "I'll probably turn into a real sexpot. Then he'll go mad with desire and I'll laugh in his face. 'Burn, little Jamie, smoulder smoulder,'" she sang to *Glow Worm*. "'You'll really burn before you're older—'"

Rosa played along with her. Vic sat up, grinning in surprise and delight, but couldn't think of anything more to sing, filled out with *dah-de-dah* and a finish of great power if not melody; "Darn it, I've gone blank!"

They all applauded, and Linnie shouted, "Bravo, bravo!"

Holly arrived with the water pail, hardly out of breath though she seemed to have run all the way. The large collie who had tried to desecrate the wellcurb came behind her, switching his stern happily at the sounds of good fellowship. He went to Linnie and she took his head in her hands and they gazed into each other's eyes.

"Thanks, Holly," Rosa said, taking the pail. "Anybody want a cold drink?" Nobody did. She took the pail into the house, had a drink, and came out again. Linnie was still holding communion of souls with the dog. Vic was now doing push-ups, Betsey chewed grass, Holly played chords and sang to herself some vaguely familiar country-western song.

All those long bare legs, how Con would love it, Rosa thought dryly. And if he should walk into the yard right now, they wouldn't even know I was alive any more. Nor I them.... She took the guitar that Holly pushed at her, hunched over it and shut her eyes, shut out the girls. Without singing, she played *Moonlight Cocktail* to limber up, and was transported to the back doorstep at Seal Point, Con lying on the lawn with a cold can of beer beside him, the resident gull on his corner of the wharf, and beyond him the tame harbor cross-stitched with summer's noisy runabouts.

Con liked her music, she could at least say that, though the minute she did she could see how pathetic it was.... Applause returned her to Bennett's Island, and she blinked at the girls, playing her part of good-natured simpleton. Holly was on her knees, as close as she could get. She moaned, "I can never, *never* do that. How do you do it?"

"My brother does something like that, but he'd never show us how," said Betsey.

"Male chauvinist pig," said Vic. "That's what they all are, besides being absolutely adorable."

"It's easy," Rosa told the younger girls. "Like drumming your fingers on the table. See?" She demonstrated on the step and then across the strings. Holly and Betsey tried and were frustrated, Betsey silently scowling. Holly made dramatic gestures of despair.

"Play something else," she begged. Rosa couldn't resist the admiration. At least it wasn't the sweetness that put weight on. Better than eclairs, wasn't it? Or alcohol? She played and sang a few short simple songs, then gathered the girls in on *The Tavern in the Town*, which they sang with a good deal of energy.

"There," she said at the end. "That enough?"

Holly asked her about popular songs, and she shook her head. "You can get that stuff on records. Some of it's nice, I'll grant that, but most of it's not for me. I do my own thing."

"What kind of love songs do you like?" Linnie asked.

"Love?" Rosa made her eyes round. "What's that? I just know about the grass growing, and the birds singing, and the fish swimming."

"Sing just one thing more," Vic urged. "How come you aren't out being a folk singer?"

"I thought you had to have long hair and a beard for that," said Rosa. "Okay, one more and then I have to go back to work." She sang *Strawberries in the Sea*, and they were very quiet. When she finished Vic said, "That's a nursery rhyme but you sing it like blues. I've got gooseflesh."

"I love it, but it's not long enough," said Betsey. "Can't you write some more verses?"

"Oh, no, it's perfect the way it is," Vic objected. "It leaves you wondering all kinds of things."

Linnie, using the dog for a pillow, said, "Jamie should hear it. Anything that mentions herring sends him."

"I knew someone once named Marilyn Herring," said Vic. "If I was Victoria Herring Jamie would be at my feet."

"He sure would," said Linnie kindly. "He's so crazy about herring he couldn't resist the temptation to marry one."

"Is he a seiner?" Rosa asked.

"Sort of. A stop-twiner, really. He's got a crew and they stop off the island coves. They were out last night looking for fish, and I wanted Vic and me to go, but the *Centurion* and a carrier were on their way out, and Jamie kept saying there might be trouble. If you ask me he's *hoping* for trouble. My father says he's a Viking throwback."

"I've seen *Centurion* in the harbor at home," Rosa said. "The stop-twiners in there aren't too fond of the purse-seiners, either."

"No, they break up the big schools or divert them before they get into the coves. And the carriers slice off pot buoys like crazy with their propellers, if they don't have cages, and most of them don't. I don't mean they do it on purpose, but how can they help it, when everybody's set in so close to the island in summertime?" She stood up and stretched; her hair in the sun was more golden than her brother's. "Anyway, there wasn't trouble, but then Jamie never found any herring either."

"So, he should have taken us for luck," said Vic. "I could inspire him."

"To more swearwords," said Linnie. "Come on, kids, Rosa's got things she wants to do."

"Lin's hard as nails," Vic complained, getting up. "Because she was never in love, that's why. What *I* could do with that hair and those eyes. All wasted on *her*."

The younger girls considered this wildly funny. Vic's primly sour expression was comic enough, but Rosa wondered what lay beneath the clowning. At seventeen—or at twenty-nine—you could agonize over yourself, not just your looks but the whole clumsy, hateful, hopeless parcel.

Linnie said, "But I love Rory Mor, don't I?" she leaned down to pat the dog, who pranced stiffly around her.

"There's something seriously wrong with that family," Vic said to Rosa. "She loves her dog and her brother worships herring."

"I love Rory Mor as a son," said Linnie with dignity. "After all, I became his mother when he was seven weeks old. I can't explain my brother except that maybe he's metamorphosing into a seal, the way that Kafka character turned into a cockroach."

"*What?*" asked Holly.

"Come *on*. Thanks an awful lot, Rosa." The others added their thanks. Rosa almost said, "Come again." She'd enjoyed them after all.

12

She had been sleeping very heavily every night until this one, which was full of busy dreams. Half the time she dreamed she was awake and fretting about not being able to sleep. Toward morning she woke up in reality. It was still dark, and she heard an engine in the harbor. It was running in little muted purrs, with rhythmic stops as if for breath. She would not have heard it if there had been any breeze stirring the spruce boughs or making a run on the shore.

She lay there listening, at first too involved with the last dream to be curious about the engine. There had been a confrontation with Phyllis, whom she had not seen in life since a church supper in the winter when they had all three sat together, and she'd thought how very brave and cheerful Phyllis was, after losing a man like Adam Crowell.

And all the time Phyllis had Con. Rosa had already lost him, and the other two knew it. The memory of that night had been burned into Rosa's brain as if with the branding iron they used to burn license numbers on traps and buoys. After a while she had succeeded in not consciously brooding over it, but it had sometimes returned in her dreams. It had been one of the things she hoped to leave back in Seal Point. But here it was, polluting this house.

In the dream they were at the church supper, but everyone else except Rosa and Phyllis was invisible, though present.

Con was there, unseen, but close. Phyllis wore the same wine dress with the round frilly collar that set off the delicate, wide-eyed-waif face.

"This time I *know*," Rosa said to her. "I know what you are and what he is. But he's still mine. Whatever he is, he's still mine."

She knew suddenly that a terrible power was hers to use if she dared, and she dared anything to keep Con. She had only to keep her eyes steadily on Phyllis's, never glance away or even blink.... And it worked. The face wavered, dissolved, and vanished under the strength of Rosa's gaze.

With an exaltation unlike anything she'd ever known, she cried out to all the unseen presences; "Now Con is mine forever!"

It was her own voice that woke her, the sound of Con's name on her lips. Then she heard the engine. She lay there clutching to herself the anguish of knowing how her dream had deceived her, while the boat crossing the harbor softly breathed, paused, breathed again.

Stealthy. Sneaking in or out? Con, coming out to steal *Sea Star* back?

She got out of bed and went to the window. The lights were moving very slowly along the far side of the harbor shore, well away from *Sea Star*'s mooring. Then the engine stopped altogether and the lights went out, or else the boat had glided on her own momentum out of sight beyond the fishhouses.

The herring crew coming in.

She sagged and at once became conscious of the pre-dawn chill. She went back into her sleeping bag. The dream had become worse than ridiculous; it was disgusting that she could make such a fool of herself even in her sleep. She tried to think about the men out looking for herring, the boat cruising slowly across the quiet seas of a summer night, the long shimmering streaks of reflected starlight in the slick places, the black shapes of land and ledge, the cold salt smell, the bow wave and the wake glowing with white fire. But it was no escape; it only made her wish with a grinding envy that she were a man, free to choose and then to act, free to hunt and then to take, and not only herring.

She had chosen to come here, she had acted, but it was not to hunt and take, it was to escape. She'd run away, but not from herself. She was stuck with someone who was nothing but a fool and the others were right to despise her.

It wasn't conducive to sleep. She went downstairs and built a fire, made coffee and toasted yeast rolls on a fork over the flames, then sat before the open oven door with her feet on the hearth while she ate and drank.

Suppose it had been Con out there in the harbor? At least for a few hours of the night he wouldn't have been sleeping in Phyllis's arms. Officially he was a boarder at the Rowlands', but that was a fiction and everybody knew it.

For a long time it had been physically impossible for her to imagine them together. She used to feel that her head wanted to burst and her heart race itself to death. Now she had become used to it, though sometimes it could still surprise her. She took her coffee mug out to the back doorstep and saw the light growing over the eastern trees, and heard the first tentative voices of the dawn chorus. The daisies and buttercups on the uncut lawn glimmered like stars. A rooster crowed from the Sorensen barn.

She could get ready now to go to haul, but the traps should soak for another day. She could start puttying again as soon as the dew dried off, but from now till then what in hell could she do? Her head began to ache.

Finally she took two aspirins and went back to bed. She half-feared the room would be haunted by her dream, but daylight and the warming-up of engines promised safety of a kind, and she fell asleep.

When she woke up it was after nine o'clock, and her first conscious thought was that the windows on the sunny side should be dry enough for her to work on. If only Edwin

93

had sent along the other things. I suppose this is how a drunk feels, praying for another bottle to get him through the day, she thought with grim humor.

She was standing on her lobster crate puttying the small panes in the upper sash of a kitchen window when the boat whistle blew outside Eastern Harbor Point. When the boat had left and the people had gone home, she'd go down to see if Edwin had sent her what she asked for. Close by her the bees worked around the heavy curled heads of lilac. She felt companionable with them, and the sun was pleasantly hot on her head and back.

I wish I was the only person alive, she thought. She imagined herself wandering alone and free on this place, with Con and Phyllis no longer existing; not dead, she could never endure to think of Con dead, but vanished as the girl's face had vanished in her dream. No bodies to lie close and warm, nothing left to ache for the loss as she ached.

Meanwhile she went on puttying; the small panes reflected her frown of concentration. They also reflected spruces, sky, the bright yellow flash of a warbler, and then, as she shifted her position, a man came into the mirror world.

It was Edwin.

The crate teetered under her as she turned and jumped down. They embraced hard, laughing, then he held her off with his hands splayed out over her sides, fingers digging brutally for her ribs.

She tried to grip his wrists and get free, but he was too strong. "Yes, I've lost some," she protested, "but I haven't been here a week yet. Give me time! Or did you just come out to check on my diet?"

He grinned, and nodded at what he had carried up from the boat, zipper satchel, bedroll, and paintbox.

"For how long?" she demanded.

He held up three fingers, four, and shrugged.

"Are you through with your job this soon?"

He took out his pad and wrote, "Waiting for the thumb

latches and hinges. Hand-forged on order. Takes time." He picked up the wheelbarrow and started away with it. She carried his things into the house, deciding to let Edwin live in the new and private world she'd been creating.

When he came back he had two big cartons holding all that she had asked for. He had also brought his tool carrier, a box of paperbacks, and food; steaks, salad makings, a large wedge of store cheese, honey, the black cherries she liked, French bread. There was also a dozen fresh doughnuts.

"Fried at six this morning," he wrote. "My mother thinks food will cure anything."

"Well, it won't," Rosa said. "I've tried it. But Lucy's doughnuts are something else." She put some in the oven to warm, and made coffee. They took the food out into the yard, and while they ate he gave her what news there was. She kept waiting for him to mention Con. When it didn't happen she was irritated with him, whether he had kept Con out of it from consideration or from indifference. At the same time she was relieved that he'd given her nothing new to chew on. She had enough to poison her now.

He got up finally and went to the entrance of the path, and stood looking into the woods. After a moment he beckoned to her. He led the way out to the cove, looking around him without having to watch where he put his feet, his hands in his pockets. Walking behind him Rosa contemplated with admiration the poise of his head and the ease of his shoulders, remembering how when he was small he carried his head very stiffly, his shoulders hunched almost to his ears sometimes, his elbows crooked but pressed in tight to his sides, his fists doubled in perpetual readiness to meet an attack.

Rosa had always been in awe of him in those days, afraid of his strange cries and explosions of temper. Their friendship hadn't begun until he was in his early teens and had come to terms with his deafness. Or rather, the world had come to terms with it, and had begun to reach him.

They went down to the beach, and stopped, she thought,

to watch the ducklings diving amid the floating rockweed. But his face was wiped clean of expression, as if his vision were somehow turned inward; he was not only deaf to the outer world, but blind also. When he was like this he was a stranger, and it always gave her a pang of both awe and loss. Their comradeship then seemed to be pure delusion on her part, a kindly humoring on his, and she would feel awkward with him, even timid. She moved slowly away as if lost in her own thoughts, pretending to be interested in a pink-and-white striped stone, a big mussel shell, the name on half a styrofoam buoy split by a propeller.

When she looked around again Edwin was sitting on a bleached log, filling his pipe. He still seemed very much in his own world. She sat down at the other end of the log, wondering what old memories crowded and jostled him now. It was on Bennett's Island that his mother teetered on the edge of insanity, denying his deafness because she thought it was a disgrace, a punishment for mysterious crimes that nobody knew about, not even herself. Jude had been too gentle, too helpless. The children ran like wild goats on these shores. Rosa remembered when Lucy had been brought off and taken to Bangor, but she had been a child then herself, and knew nothing of the circumstances.

It was his sisters who had told her later how it had been with them on the island until a new teacher corralled the little flock and found out that Edwin was deaf. When the family left the island, Edwin had been tutored by a teacher in Limerock and then sent to a school for the deaf in Portland. Knowing Lucy today as a cheerful, busy, middle-aged woman and Edwin as a talented and independent man, Rosa found it impossible to view their past as anything but a hazy nightmare dreamed long ago. But what of those who had actually lived through it, and returned now to its setting?

Timorously she kept glancing at Edwin's aloof profile, and was afraid he would not stay. Suddenly he turned to her with a smile that made him hers again, and took hold of her knee and shook it. Then he tipped his head back toward the path.

They took the mattress off the bed in the small downstairs bedroom behind the living room, and carried it out to sun on a ledge that showed among the daisies of the lawn. She pried open the window, and swept and dusted the room. Edwin went to work re-hanging the toilet door, building a new frame for it from her salvaged lumber, and she returned to puttying windows. She whistled now while she worked. She felt almost completely contented, and wished no one out of existence, though she didn't single Con and Phyllis out for consideration one way or another.

After their noon meal of steak and salad, Edwin took the wheelbarrow and went off to the fishhouse to get the shingles. She saw a sketchbook in his hip pocket as he left, and knew he wouldn't be back right away. She unpacked the cartons he had brought her, and put away the contents; then she turned the mattress in the sun on the ledge and lay down on it, watching the daisies and red clover tremble against the sky, and fell asleep.

She woke up chilly because the shade of the house had moved over her, but happy with the immediate consciousness of Edwin's presence on the island. Her first impulse was to go to the store for the makings of one of those high, thick-frosted chocolate cakes they both liked but, hands on her flattening belly, she resisted with a kind of holy ferocity. She dragged the mattress into the bedroom and put Edwin's sleeping bag on it, and two pillows with fresh cases. Upstairs in the front bedroom there were some extension screens, a few of them not too far gone with rust to be used, and she brought one down for Edwin's window. The only furniture left in the living room was a wicker rocking chair and a couple of small stands, unless you counted the gaudy linoleum square on the floor. She put a stand beside Edwin's bed, with one of the clean dish towels from home for a cover. This called for a filled lamp and a newly washed chimney.

While she was working in his room, he went past the

window and across into the Percy yard, and came back with the aluminum extension ladder. He went to work on the roof and she finished the windows. So the first day moved quietly toward night, and she could not remember when she had last been so happy on land. She hoped Edwin was as happy up there on the sunny roof. She could not understand this euphoria when she knew she was really miserable, but suspected it was self-hypnosis, willing herself back into the days before she began worrying about boys liking her.

Queer to think that somewhere Con had been a cocky little redheaded kid, everybody's pet (to hear him tell it) and never dreaming that she existed. Well, they'd met, and they'd parted, and he was fine and she was wretched. So was it *meant* or not? And if it was meant—what for? She'd have liked to discuss the theory with Edwin, but she had never willingly discussed Con with anyone, and she never would. Yet it angered her for people to avoid mentioning him to her, as if he were some unnameable disease that had almost killed her; or, as she suspected with Edwin, he was simply an element that had come and gone and was of no account whatever.

Yet because of Edwin's presence, signified by the sound of his hammer from the roof and an occasional glimpse of his neat narrow head against the sky, she was able to think objectively about Con and his influence.

Con acted and I reacted, she thought. But when I came out here, I acted. Then he reacted. It was funny, in a grim way; she supposed the battle could go on forever if she'd let it, and sometimes she wanted to; while she still meant something to him he could not forget her, she was a stone bruise on his heel. Cutting the last tie, even one so vexatious, had the finality of death.

After supper Edwin wanted more sketches of her with her guitar. He had a painting in mind, and she jeered at the idea of using up so much paint on her. "It won't be a portrait of you," he told her coldly. "You're just part of the design."

"Be sure you make it good and abstract. Give the guitar

hands and me strings. The guitar can play *me*. How's that?"

Austerely he ignored it. "I may use spruces for the background instead of the kitchen at Seal Point."

"Be sure to get the toilet in. The door looks absolutely elegant."

He herded her outside again and pointed to the cellar bulkhead. She sat with her back against the house and he sat on one of the sawhorses he'd made that afternoon. The western sky was saffron barred with violet behind tar-black spruces. Unseen from the yard a ball game went on in the well-field, but heard: shouts, applause, praise, insult, and dogs barking. Also unseen but heard, the seiners left the harbor on the nightly search.

" 'Three fishers went sailing out into the west,' " Rosa sang to herself, " 'Out into the west as the sun went down—' " She stopped; as a child the song had horrified her, as if it had been from the home harbor that the boat went out, and the bodies washed up on her own beach. She slid into *Take Me Out to the Ball Game,* with so much gusto that Edwin's gaze froze her into sobriety again. She was supposed to be remote.

She shut her eyes and visualized the school songbook they'd used in the eighth grade, and selected *The Meeting of the Waters* as proper for the mood. Ralph came around the corner of the house and sat down on the back steps. When she finished, he applauded softly. "My God, I don't know if it's that tune or the way you sing it, but I'm about ready to go down and call my wife and tell her to get ready to come home. . . . Hey, blat some more, as the old feller used to say."

"What old feller?"

"I dunno, I just made him up." Edwin went on sketching without looking up. "One thing about him," Ralph said, "you can't disturb him unless you hit him. . . . Unless he's got ESP about all these long legs coming." He gazed with candid appreciation at the approaching girls. "Times like these when I wish I was eighteen and single."

The girls came up from the darkening lane in single file,

Linnie ahead as she always was, her pale hair catching the last brightness from the western sky.

"Hi, Rosa!" she called, then stopped dramatically short. "I'm *sorry!* I didn't know you had company!" She looked at Edwin who, glancing up at his model, briefly noticed the girls and returned to his work.

"Now isn't that strange, love," Ralph said. "I could have sworn you all went by dragging your feet and staring your eyes out while Edwin was shaking hands with half the population down at the harbor this afternoon."

Linnie said haughtily, "It just so happens we came up to ask Rosa something. Of course we could wait until Mr. Webster"—she nodded at the oblivious Edwin in a stately manner—"went away, but that might not be for a long time."

"True, true," agreed Ralph. "Have you thought up yet what you're going to ask?"

Holly and Betsey gave up the struggle to keep from giggling. Vic gazed glassily at a treetop. Linnie began to blush, and stood even straighter than usual, and said her words very distinctly, "It just so happens that this is a legitimate errand, Ralph Percy."

"You mean it's no little come-by-chance?"

Betsey and Holly collapsed on the ground, Vic's mouth was trembling. Linnie put her twitching hands in her pockets and refused to blink. Edwin gave the sky a cursory glance. As the light was almost gone, he put away his sketchbook, and looked inscrutably at the rest, as if the previous conversation would have meant absolutely nothing to him even if he'd heard it. Linnie, your curiosity's about to bounce back at you off a high brick wall, Rosa thought.

"This is Edwin Webster, my cousin," she said formally to the girls. "They were too young to know you in the old days," she said to Edwin. He stood up, bowing slightly as Rosa pronounced each name. The girls were self-conscious, not knowing whether to speak or not, but Vic nodded back at him and said conversationally, "Do you read lips?"

"*Vic!*" Linnie was horrified.

"Why shouldn't I ask? I want to know. I've never known anybody who could do that."

Edwin looked tolerant. Rosa said, "Yes, he reads lips, so nobody has to shout at him, and that wouldn't do any good anyway. You can always write things down, too."

"He wrote me a message today," said Ralph. "He says, 'For God's sake don't split your gullet yelling at me.'"

He laughed enormously, and the girls laughed too, and moved in closer. They were remembering their manners, trying not to single Edwin out with stares, but they kept giving him quick glances. The Bennett girls began talking vivaciously with Ralph, giggling loudly at frequent intervals. Rosa guessed that Vic was anxious to try conversation with Edwin, but she couldn't think of anything to say and she was too intelligent to speak to him as if to a small child or a simpleton. Linnie slumped on the bottom step, broodingly chewing a stalk of grass, her hair falling forward to hide her face. Even if Edwin's deafness hadn't been the disturbing and exciting element here, his whole atmosphere would have put them down. Sitting on the sawhorse again, holding the ankle propped across the other knee, he had what his mother called his "pawky look": slightly sardonic, slightly amused, and altogether superior.

"What was it you wanted to ask me?" Rosa asked Linnie's sheaf of hair.

Linnie didn't move or speak, and Vic gave her a poke in the ribs. "Wake up, Rapunzel," she said.

"What, is it time to let down my hair?" Linnie threw it back and looked around at Rosa with her usual smile, which tonight reminded Rosa of Mr. Sorensen's; she didn't believe Jamie could smile. "Will you be in our show this summer? We like to do something to raise money for the Seacoast Mission, and we have a supper and a show and a dance."

"What would you want me to do, and when?" She didn't have to do it, but no harm in talking about it.

"Sing some songs, and it won't be till late July or August,

when they have a lot of summer people on Brigport, and there are more yachts around."

"All right," said Rosa, feeling gracious and generous; it was the evening and its mood. Tomorrow she could wake up feeling rotten, as if today had been one long drunk.

"O.K.," said Vic, "let's go."

"We're going over and wash Ralph's dishes for him," Holly said. "Come on, Bets. Night, Rosa." They looked at Edwin, said "Good night" loudly, and went off across the back yard to Ralph's. He followed them, whistling *Garryowen* again.

Vic said very precisely to Edwin, "I'm glad to have met you." Edwin's nod of acknowledgment had been fined down by the years to a regal gesture, and Linnie gazed at him as if the sawhorse were an impromtu throne for a ruler in exile.

The girls left, and Rosa went into the house and lit a lamp. Edwin followed her, took the empty water pail, and went out. She stood looking around the kitchen, yawning and relaxed. It had been a good day. She had hardly thought of Con since her four o'clock waking except in this detached way, of which she was immensely proud; she hadn't believed herself capable of it. Through watering eyes she saw with sleepy pleasure Edwin's jacket slung over a chair back, and his pipe in a scallop-shell ashtray on the table.

When he came back with water he was smiling to himself. "You ham," she said. "You had those girls wondering if they ought to curtsy and kiss your hand."

He brushed that off like a Don Juan bored with his own powers, and went into his room. When she finished brushing her teeth he was just returning. He put a cribbage board and an unopened bottle of Jim Beam on the table.

"I'm dead on my feet!" she protested. "I couldn't even see the cards!"

He held up one finger.

"All right, but no more than one. And I don't want a drink." But he was already reaching into the cupboard for glasses, and didn't see her refusal. He poured out a small drink for her, a larger one for himself, and began to shuffle the cards. She stifled her yawns, but her eyes watered in streams, and she had to keep wiping them. Edwin seemed to be entertained by her discomfort.

When he sat down he had taken the sketchbook out of his hip pocket and put it on the table. Determined to come awake for at least the one game, Rosa reached for the book, but with his eyes brightly fixed on hers he slid the book out of her reach.

"What's that for?" she demanded, laughing. "What have you got in there besides me? Bare nekkid women?"

He smiled and began to deal. Like his silence and because of it, his smiles were always enigmatic, even when one knew they expressed simple, uncomplex human reactions. This time she wasn't sure of that, but she was too sleepy to try to solve a secret which she had no chance of ever finding out. She arranged her hand and tried to focus on it, ignoring her drink. His was already gone, and she hadn't even seen him swallow it.

He was not an habitual drinker, and she realized now that the sight of the bottle had already jarred her, even before he moved the sketchbook out of her reach.

All right, Sunny Jim, she thought, just for that I'll skunk you.

Five games later she hadn't skunked him. She was groggy. Edwin had taken her drink and poured two more for himself. There was a flush along his cheekbones deeper than the day's sunburn, and his skin looked unusually tight over his bones. The brightness of his eyes had become a glitter like that of fever; their color was that of the lamp flame. He had been speeded up rather than drugged by the liquor, his gestures over-precise, and the poise of his head was exaggeratedly alert, as if he were listening hard for something. His triumph whenever he won seemed to be over something more than a card game.

Rosa's uneasiness became real discomfort. Finally, at the end of a game, she dropped her cards and stood up. "No more," she said emphatically, with a sidewise slash of her hand. "I'm done. I'm going to bed."

He tilted back in his chair and looked up at her with a kind of luminous hilarity, and she shook her head. "Stay up all night and play solitaire! And get drunk! I don't give a damn!"

She went out to the toilet. The night was quiet except for the rote and the irregular clanging of the bell buoy beyond Sou'west Point. When she went in again, the kitchen seemed too warm, smelling too much of liquor. Edwin still sat at the table but turned away from it, hunched forward, elbows on knees and his hands hanging loosely clasped between. He gazed into space with the same blind preoccupation she had noticed this morning at the cove, only it was more intense now. The effect was of complete and desolate solitude, and it punched her in the stomach.

She went to him and put her hand on his shoulder. He didn't move, he felt like heated stone under her palm. She took the pad from his shirt pocket and wrote on it, "Why did you really come out here?"

She held it in front of his face so that he had to move his head back. He read it, then knocked it out of her hand. He stood up and threw the pack of cards with a flip of his wrist that scattered them across the kitchen; he threw the cribbage board next, and it hit and dented the wall between two windows. His hand came for the bottle next, but she grabbed that and the lamp.

He brushed past her, heading for the back door; he staggered slightly, enough to hit the doorframe with one shoulder and throw him a little off balance as he went out. Her heart was beating so hard she still felt sick to her stomach and she couldn't stop thinking of his face drawn tight in dreadful immobility, with only the tawny eyes alive.

Rage or something else? Awed, frightened, and anxious, she went out onto the doorstep and listened. Again she heard nothing but the rote and the bell. Well, he had run all over this island at night in the past, and he wasn't falling-down drunk, she assured herself. She went inside and picked up the cards and the cribbage board. The sketchbook wasn't around, he must have done something with it while she was out to the toilet.

She left the bottle on the counter by the sink and blew the lamp out, and went to bed.

13

She lay awake for a while, not worried about his being out but about his mood. She had known of at least five suicides in the last few years, and, in the case of the one at Seal Point, nobody could believe that the girl was the type to kill herself. So it could happen with Edwin, who surely must sometimes find his deafness unbearable. She was frightened, but she didn't know where to search for him.

All at once she was sure that he was safe, at least physically. He might have come to the island because he felt a low coming on and thought he could work it off out here, away from the over-sensitive eyes of his parents.

In that case, she was no friend if she kept harassing him. Why had she herself come to the island? ... She slid down into her covers and went to sleep.

When she woke up it was coming morning, there was a cool wind blowing in on her, and a robin was singing the same song over and over from one of the spruces just outside her windows. *Giddyup, giddyup, hurryup, hurryup, giddyup, giddyup* . . . She shut the window on it and got shiveringly into her clothes.

Downstairs she looked into Edwin's room. He was a long narrow bundle in his sleeping bag, just the crown of his head showing. There were faint fumes of Jim Beam.

She didn't bother to build a fire. She made her coffee on the gas stove and drank it with the last of Mrs. Sorensen's yeast rolls; she filled her thermos with more black coffee to take out with her, and successfully won a little struggle about taking some doughnuts too. She left them behind, and the decision made her feel pounds thinner.

It was warmer outside than it had been in the kitchen, but it was cloudy and smelled of rain. In the lustrous gray-and-green harbor the gulls were washing themselves with silver splashings. Men were rowing out to their moorings and two boats were already leaving the harbor, racing abreast; one was Jamie Sorensen's *Valkyrie*, the other Matt Fennell's *Peregrine*.

Ralph Percy and Rob Dinsmore were talking on the wharf on the other side of Rosa's. On the wharf beyond that, Philip Bennett and his young helper were loading traps aboard *Liza*. From the next wharf someone was whistling with great virtuosity.

"Gonna rain for sure," Ralph said. "Turd birds are whistling."

"Beats me how he's got the pucker for it this early in the morning," Rob said.

"It's not early for him, he probably hasn't been to bed yet," said Ralph. "He's courting over to Brigport, I heard."

"I thought they were out chasing herring again last night."

"Chasing women is more like it." Ralph gave Rosa a burlesque wink. She was just going down the ladder to her skiff. "Oh hell," Ralph said, "I suppose I better get moving and not let a woman shame me."

Outside there was a southwest swell, gray as a gull's wings, and the horizon was obscured by a silvery smoke of mist. *Sea Star* was at her best in this kind of water, working with wind and tide as if with an intelligence of her own. Rosa found all her buoys, though some were just spindling in the fast-running tide. The traps had not been molested.

The gear fished well; she estimated around seventy-five pounds in the crate when she had hauled the last trap of the forty, which held three counters, four little ones, and a V-notched female to be thrown back with the shorts. "You'll pay your way, old girl," she told *Sea Star*. The boat rode homeward through seas beginning to cap with crests that sparkled in the intermittent gleams of sunlight. As usual Rosa had been completely happy, everything else forgotten, even Edwin's disturbing behavior. She sang, "Oh, *swift* goes my *boat* like a *bird* on the *billow*," and the song took her all the way up the west side and into the harbor.

Mark congratulated her on her haul and paid her one hundred and eight dollars and seventy-five cents. She was modestly proud of her gear. "It may be the way the heads are set," she told him. "My father never set his heads like anyone else in Seal Point and we—I've always done it the same way since."

She filled up with diesel fuel for the next day and took the boat back to the mooring, where she sluiced down the washboards and swept the cockpit with a wet broom. Hers was the only boat back in, and the wharves were empty except for gulls. She remembered her first morning here, the heat, the fog, the silence, and her misery. She was still miserable but there were times when she was less so; it was as if the basic and fatal disease remained but at intervals the pain could be beaten down by drugs.

She hung her oilclothes in the fishhouse and changed her rubber boots for sneakers. She had saved out five lobsters; Edwin liked them, and she hoped that would take the edge off their first meeting since last night. He was likely to be in a rotten mood for having made a fool of himself. Of course the cause would still be there, and maybe it wasn't too bright of her to think the lobsters would make a difference. Edwin had never seen fit to eat his way through difficulties the way she'd tried to do.

She felt hot and cranky now, imprisoned on the land after the freedom of the water. She resented Edwin for being a worry to her instead of the comfort she'd expected him to be, and found herself composing angry attacks on his self-pity. But the trouble was that everything could be turned against herself, and by the time she reached the lane she was arguing with some faceless antagonist.

Well, why is self-pity such a great sin, such a big crime? Maybe deafness isn't the worst thing in the world, maybe losing Con isn't, but for Edwin and me they are the worst things right now, and it doesn't make them hurt a goddam bit less because we haven't lost a leg or our eyesight or something.

She was glad everybody was inside eating dinner; in this mood she'd have been hard put to shout cheery greetings. And when she reached the house Edwin wasn't there. She felt a sharp thrill of anxiety and irritation. Then she saw that there were two full pails of water on the counter beside the sink, and the dishes had been washed, so he couldn't have been in too foul a mood. The whiskey bottle had disappeared. Taken it with him to finish it off?

On the table there was something new, an old glass mustard jar turned pale lavender by exposure, holding a twig of wild rose buds and a spray of wild honeysuckle. A note was propped against it.

I've gone to Sou'west Point to paint surf. Come on down and bring some grub. Don't forget the beer. Yours faithfully, Gauguin.

She was at once restored, laughing aloud in the silent house, and suddenly she was starved; she could hardly wait to consume warm lobster, bread and butter, and cold beer on the cliffs of Sou'west Point. She felt as if she could run all the way, light as a sand-peep.

She put on water to boil for the lobsters, then got out of her workclothes and washed up, and dressed in clean faded-blue jeans and a new shirt that had been too snug. It wasn't now, and she could take up three extra holes on her belt.

While she was waiting for the lobsters to cook, she went looking for the box of paperbacks Edwin had brought. She'd been too busy until now to go over them, but she anticipated carrying a stack of them up to her room for night reading.

The box was on the floor beside the chest of drawers in his room. As she leaned down to pick it up, she saw the sketchbook lying on the chest, and she wondered mildly why he hadn't wanted her to see it last night. Mischief, most likely; trying to needle her by being unexpected. Well, I can be unexpected too, Old Smart Alec, she thought. Sneaky. How about *that?*

She flipped open the book. It was the same one he'd had at Seal Point last week; she recognized the finely detailed drawings of an ornamental cornice, a newel post, and a corner cupboard. There was Jude's basset-beagle sprawled in sleep, and herself with the guitar from several angles. All these she had seen before. Then he'd done sketches coming out on the mailboat yesterday, and around the harbor in the afternoon; boats, ledges, ducks, and gulls, kids in a dory, men lugging traps. From last night, there was herself on the bulkhead, and a comic little impression of Ralph. The girls; he'd gotten the girls in while they all thought he was still working on Rosa. He hadn't missed the legs, which would be a relief to Ralph.

Now blank pages. So why hadn't he wanted her to see it? Simply to tease or even irk her, because that was the way he felt last night? ... She leafed through the blank pages, not expecting to find anything more, and came to a drawing of a woman who knelt by a flat of seedlings, lifting out a plant.

She wore slacks and a shirt open deeply at the throat. Her long hair was swept around her head and fell in one long thick tress by her left cheek and down onto her breast. Her eyes were downcast, her face smoothed of all expression; she could have been praying, or blind.

The next page showed her in a sidewise pose, sitting on a stone wall. She was laughing, her head thrown back in complete abandonment to whatever was so funny. On the following page she wore a sleeveless blouse or dress and was pinning her hair up on top of her head. She was serious about it, but not blank-faced, there was the impression of a very faint smile but Rosa couldn't find it either around the eyes or the mouth. Still, the atmosphere of intimacy remained, as if she had known that Edwin was sketching her.

Nothing in the three drawings was closely detailed, yet in the grace of the lifted arms, the long throat, the shuttered face bent over the plants, the laughing one and the secretive one, Edwin had set down what he did not want Rosa to see.

She was both ashamed and shaken. The pure, fresh, almost childish joy with which she'd welcomed the picnic with Edwin had gone, leaving her excited in a different, depressing way. She laid the sketchbook back just as she'd found it, and left the room without touching the paperbacks. Five minutes to wait for the lobsters. She sat down at the kitchen table with her chin in her hands.

It had to be the woman for whom he was restoring the house. She and her husband were renting a place nearby. The man was away during the week, but she came on good days to work on her colonial garden. . . . And on Edwin? Attracted, as some women were, by a handicap? Finding him mysterious, or simply male and vulnerable?

Maybe she didn't know anything about it. But Edwin was in love with her.

"Oh God," Rosa muttered. "Why does it have to be someone he can't ever *have?*"

The instant she said it, she thought of Con. And the lobsters boiled over.

She took the kettle outside and drained it over a thistle

plant that had been pricking everybody's bare feet, and wrapped the lobsters in newspapers to keep them warm. At least she wouldn't have to make conversation, and if Edwin sensed anything gloomy or distracted about her, he would blame it on Con.

But Edwin satisfied with a morning's work was hardly the frustrated love-sick man who'd accompanied her all the way to Sou'west Point. She almost doubted that one's existence after a while, and began thinking she'd seen the sketches through her own love-sickness. Edwin could have been drunk and foul-tempered the night before for any number of reasons besides this woman or any woman.

The threat of rain had passed over, sun flashed off the sea and warmed the sheltered rock shelf where they ate above the surf. Afterwards Edwin went back to work, making studies of gulls in flight or walking around amid the litter of sea urchin and mussel shells. She wandered by herself, almost as liberated out here as she had been on the water. Back on a green and sheltered slope she found a few sprays of ripe wild strawberries, with plenty of green and white ones. Everywhere there were great thickets of wild roses all heavily in bud, and each clump seemed to have its resident sparrows. On the side toward open sea daisies danced in a wind that should have destroyed them, and the precipitous shores dropped away in falls of rock to the surf. On the leeside there were pools of icy calm and a dazzling heat.

It was nearly suppertime when they started home. Rosa had piled up salvage, not in the hope of getting it all for herself but because she was a compulsive beach-comber. She carried everything she could but was forced to shed some of it by the way. Edwin refused to carry anything more than his paintbox and the lunch basket. He managed to look both indulgent and supercilious when she couldn't let a lone oar drift out to sea again, and sloshed around in wet rockweed untangling a length of good yellow nylon warp.

There was one lobster left, and she made Edwin a sand-

111

wich for supper, and had sardines and crackers herself. Her feet vibrated from tiredness and her eyelids were heavy. The memory of the sketchbook had become so faint it was transparent, if not actually invisible; Edwin drinking coffee across the table from her was nobody's victim, and his composure was contagious.

She mopped her wet eyes after a series of yawns to find Edwin's notepad before her. "Come on for a walk up around the orchard and the cemetery and out to Goose Cove."

"How late did you sleep this morning?" she wrote indignantly. "I was awake at the crack of dawn, for heaven's sake, and I've been moving ever since."

He laughed and got up. Except for some new sunburn over his tan, he looked absolutely fresh. She said, "Go ahead, have a good walk, I'm going to bed and read."

It dawned on her that he might not want to be trapped by the girls again; they'd been so fascinated last night, especially Linnie, that they could very well be gathering now. She hurried to clear off the table, and brushed her teeth. Then she went boldly into Edwin's room without a glance toward the sketchbook, took the first half-dozen books off the top of the box, and went upstairs.

14

The smell of bacon and coffee aroused her in the morning. Edwin, washed and shaved and with the table set, looked as if he'd never had a problem in his life; or, if he had, he'd solved it. He insisted on serving her breakfast, and for some reason this made her feel very guilty about the sketches. But why guilt, if he had nothing to hide? She hadn't discovered a profoundly personal secret, just a new model, and a good one, certainly a change from her own familiar and unglamorous geography.

She asked him if he wanted to go to haul with her, but he preferred to finish repairing the roof and then go back to Sou'west Point to try some watercolors. He walked down to the wharf with her in the sunrise. The sky had the porcelain-fine translucent blush of a weather-breeder.

When she was putting on her boots and oilpants, Edwin stood contemplating the cultch in the fishhouse. She took his arm and shook her head at him. "Don't touch it. Go ahead and paint. When you're famous I can say I helped."

He smiled and lightly squeezed the nape of her neck.

There was no one else out yet on this side of the harbor, but across on the other side Barry Barton and Terence Campion were talking as they rowed side by side to their moorings. By hurrying she got out of the harbor first, and headed around Eastern Harbor Point up Long Cove, singing as the sun rose above the woods. Going to work this way was pure indulgence, giving herself an extra sail, since most of her gear was well down along the southern side. The swell had subsided since yesterday, except for the boisterous play around the ledges and the constant rough action below the Head. *Sea Star* took them with insolent grace.

When Rosa finished hauling in Pump Cove and came out around Windward Point, Owen Bennett's *White Lady* was just leaving Schoolhouse Cove. He was at the wheel, a big man without fat like all the Bennetts, but the darkest she'd seen so far. He waved, smiling. His young son wildly swung both arms. The helper, who had a long bob and neat bangs, was more moderate in his salutations.

Goose Cove was shut off by a line of bright orange net floats across its narrow mouth. No wonder the boys were late starting out this morning. Amiably she wished them well. She had three traps in Goose Cove but they could wait. She went on toward Schooner Head, still the only boat out here. She anchored to her next trap and had a cup of coffee. There were just gentle swells now; the light surf broke without hostility on the rocks, withdrew and returned the way a cat's paws worked on a hospitable thigh as he purred himself to sleep.

She tested herself by imagining Seal Point at this hour. It was clear enough but with only one dimension; something seen on film, nothing to touch her or be touched by her. Con had been able to rent a boat to go hauling in, Edwin had told her, but since she didn't know the boat she couldn't visualize Con working. Daringly she summoned up the picture that had always threatened to split her brain in two: Con and Phyllis in bed together. But she lost her daring when she felt the sweat starting out on her neck and forehead and a faint squeamishness in her gut.

You're not clear yet, you chump, she told herself contemptuously. You never will be. Admit it.

She had her last ten traps to the west of the bell off the southern tip of the island, and she was hauling there when she saw Jamie Sorensen heading for her, smashing through the surge and throwing white water like a breaking ledge. He slowed a little distance from her, but still came on fast enough, with his gaff out to fend her off.

"What's the matter, warden?" she called across to him. "You want to underrun my gear?"

"Feeling pretty damn good, aren't you? Moved right in and settled down." He gave her the hard blue stare she had come to expect from him.

"Look," she said reasonably, "I never crossed your net this morning and bothered your herring. And you can't be jealous of what I'm making out of forty traps."

"I couldn't care less about your traps. The first good blow you're likely to lose the whole gang anyway. They're too light for out here."

"Well, look happier about it," she urged. "Rejoice." She reached out to unhook his gaff from the guard rail, and he said menacingly, "Wait a minute! Just look up there by the Devil's Den." He pointed with his free hand toward the island.

She looked too, but not very hard. "I don't know where the Devil's Den is from here. Is Old Nick up there in person, doing a jig?"

"You can see two people on the skyline, can't you?" he snapped.

Edwin was unmistakeable. She'd know his long silhouette anywhere. He stood with his hands in his pockets at the very brink of the rock. Linnea was a little distance behind him. From this distance her long hair looked almost white. Rosa waved energetically but neither responded, and she realized they were looking toward Matinicus Rock.

She turned back to Jamie. He was staring up at the two on the cliffs, and she was astonished by the passionate rage he couldn't, or wouldn't, hide. "What are you so mad about?" she asked in wonder.

"Does he know she's only seventeen? And she's so damned impressionable—she doesn't *fall*, she *crashes*. What in hell is he up to?" he demanded. "Ever since he's been on the island she's been crazy as a coot. She's been pretty cute about hiding it, but last night she gave herself away. Matt Fennell came in and just mentioned that Webster went by their house on the way to the cemetery, and in about two minutes flat *she* was out the back door and taking the short cut. Left her friend behind."

"You mean she was chasing *Edwin?*" Rosa played up her incredulity. "How do you know? Did Vic tell you? Or did you see them together last night?"

"Nobody told me anything, and I didn't see anything. I went out to look for herring."

"How many do you think you've got?" she asked chattily.

"I'm not talking about herring this morning. I'm talking

about *that*." He looked again, squinting as if the sight seared his eyeballs like the sun.

"What is there to talk about besides the fact that they're standing about twenty-five feet apart on the tip end of Bennett's Island?"

"That's twenty-five feet too close. Now, either they made a date last night, or she chased him down here, and I don't like it."

She made a genuine attempt to reassure him. "Look, I don't believe they made a date. Edwin never has been interested in young girls, and, besides, he's got a lot of things on his mind right now."

"I'll bet he has."

She ignored that. "And if she did follow him down there, or met him by accident, she couldn't be any safer unless she was at home with Big Brother. He's probably ignoring her like mad, and that's pretty easy for a deaf man to do."

"Listen. I know a little something about men, being one myself. And I haven't lived all my life on this island, in case you think Seal Point is the Big World. I was four years in the Navy."

"And saw the world."

"Yeah, I did," he said belligerently. "A hell of a lot of it, too. But I didn't have to go into the Navy to know that most guys who have something the matter with them, well, they think they've been cheated, they've been done dirty somehow, and it makes them—" He tapped his temple.

She felt her anger beginning and tried for a pressure point. She spoke gently. "You mean because Edwin's deaf he's not right in the head?" Then it slipped out. "What's *your* excuse?"

"You know what I mean, goddamit! I remember him from way back. He used to get these rages. He's your cousin, you ought to know." He stared accusingly at her.

"He hasn't had one of those rages for a long time," she said. "It was because he was so frustrated—he couldn't communicate, and nobody could reach him. That's ancient history now." She remembered the other night's rage, but ignored it. "You ought to know, one of your aunts was the teacher who found out what was the matter with him. And he was only a little boy then."

"Yeah? Well, he's a grown man now, and she's a school-kid. I haven't chased a schoolkid since I was one myself!"

"I thought you said *she* was chasing him."

"She wouldn't without encouragement."

"You don't know much about girls, do you? Lots about herring, but very little about women."

His blush deepened, which she hadn't thought possible. His ears were fiery. He seemed beyond words.

"Look," she said severely. "I like Linnie. I like the other girls too. But I didn't ask them to my house in the first place. Now if you don't want your sister having any contact with my cousin, why don't you tell your folks to keep her on a leash until Edwin leaves? He'll appreciate that, if she's being a nuisance. Which she probably is."

She turned from him and put her engine in gear. "You'd better let go," she called back to him, "unless you want to be towed straight at the bell."

He took back his gaff. This time she was the first one away, giving *Sea Star* her head and leaving Jamie in the wash. She ran directly east toward the surf piling on Sou'west Point. As she turned to go up the west side toward the harbor, she saw Jamie going off toward the south, as usual not favoring the boat. On Sou'west Point nothing human now stood against the sky. There were only the gulls circling like skaters at an ice rink.

She was shaky with delayed rage, but by the time she reached the harbor she had calmed down. She was still indignant about Jamie's view of Edwin, but Jamie as an over-protective and domineering older brother would have been upset no matter who the man was.

He had a hard life ahead of him, she thought patronizingly. If there wasn't a war on when he woke up in the morning, he went out and started one.

The mailboat had left, but there were still some children around the wharf when she sold her lobsters. Vic and Holly were alongside the car in a skiff, fishing for pollack.

"Where's your sidekick this morning?" Rosa asked Vic.

"She went off somewhere to get a start on her summer reading list." Vic leaned so far over the side of the skiff her nose almost touched the water. "Are those sea anemones under the float? Opening and closing like that?"

"Ayuh." Holly was busy chopping up a corned herring for bait. Vic continued to be so fascinated by the sea anemones that she couldn't converse face to face with Rosa. Her muffled voice came up. "Are they really animals, I wonder?"

Maybe Linnie *was* chasing Edwin. Well, she was safe enough, and before long she'd get tired of being ignored. There must be boys over at Brigport, even if she was related to most of those on Bennett's.

At home, eating a hard-boiled egg and drinking non-fat milk, Rosa achieved an objective irony. Her relatives had worried about her being entrapped by Con; she suffered because Con lost his head about Phyllis. There was the woman in Edwin's sketchbook to give her cause to worry about *him*, and Jamie Sorensen was running scared about his kid sister hurling herself at Edwin. But who was concerned about Jamie?

Maybe he's the brightest one of us all, she thought. Chasing herring.

Edwin came home in mid-afternoon with a good collection of sketches and watercolor studies. In one of them a girl crouched over a tide pool; it was hardly more than a few lines, but the long flowing hair indicated Linnie.

"Did you have company down there, or was that a hallucination?" she wrote.

"Real enough," he wrote back. "But maybe I'm a hallucination to *her*. Her family all talk so much she can't believe in a man who doesn't."

They both laughed. She was tempted to tell him about Jamie, but instinct warned her off; he mightn't find it so funny after all. She hadn't, at the first of it.

They took a walk to the Eastern End in the final exquisite hours of daylight to see Mrs. Steve Bennett, who had discovered Edwin's deafness and arranged his first training. That night they played cribbage without liquor on the table. Linnie and Vic came to the house during the evening; Vic was even more fidgety than usual, and Linnie had an air of silent defiance.

"I don't suppose you'll be playing and singing tonight," Vic said tentatively.

"If I don't give Edwin a chance to skunk me, he'll cut my throat."

Vic laughed, but Linnie's face didn't change. She had done her hair up on top of her head, which brought out the faintly oblique set of her eyes and gave her a strongly Scandinavian look. She seemed taller and older, but it was like a child going from five to six; she was still a child. She kept her eyes fixed on Edwin as if she didn't care who noticed. Rosa was as uncomfortable as Vic, but Edwin serenely played cribbage as if no one were in the room but him and Rosa. After a while Linnie got up and walked out.

"Good night," Vic said with a little nervous laugh, and went after her. Rosa followed to the door. She felt guilty of rudeness, even though she hadn't asked them to come.

"Another night we'll sing," she said. "I was too tired tonight anyway."

"Everybody's tired, including me." There was an odd dullness about Vic. "Maybe we need a couple of rainy days. Everything's so beautiful I'm worn out."

Beautiful, including Jamie? Rosa almost asked it. Instead she said, "Linnie's disappeared."

"That's all right, I can find my way. She's feeling grim.

She had a scrap with Gorgeous George tonight. Out in the barn, in loud hisses. I don't know what it was about," she added, probably untruthfully. "Night, Rosa. See you."

15

The rain came in the night, and in the morning there was no wind and the air was warm; the showers had become so light they were hardly felt on the face and hands, softly dampening hair and silvering the nap of sweaters as they silvered the grass. Edwin wheeled trash from the house out to Barque Cove, and they burned it down on the wet dark stones at low tide. After the weather-breeder's prismatic colors, today's sea was dead gray to the horizon, and in the preternatural stillness the ducklings whispered and whistled. The air smelled of warm beach stones in the rain, and wet rockweed.

Against the pewter sea and black ledges, the fire transmuted rubbish into glory. Edwin stood leaning on a pole gazing into the flames, whose red light fluttered and shivered across his face. The voice of the fire drowned out the ducklings' sounds. Watching a fountain of sparks, Rosa remembered the saying about man being born to trouble as the sparks fly upward, and she saw again the woman in the sketchbook.

As if he felt the weight of her thinking, he stared back at her. They were both serious, even somber. She broke away first and went to gather mussels and goose-tongue greens for their supper.

In the afternoon they went down to the fishhouse and worked. They carried the trash out to the wharf, to be taken down and burned that night on the rocks at low tide. They stored potentially useful articles up in the loft, and here she showed Edwin the box of glass balls. He didn't know anything about them, but was as pleased as she had been; he took some downstairs and arranged them on the workbench for a possible still life.

"Hi!" Linnie appeared in the doorway, breezy today, her hair down again, her jeans disreputable. She gave Edwin one fast glance, and concentrated on Rosa. "Vic's baking. Can I help clean the fishhouse?"

"How'd you like to sort out that box of nails?" Rosa suggested, waiting for the refusal. But Linnie smiled with innocent happiness and carried the box to the bench where Edwin would have to walk around her. He nodded at her, and when he did he saw the branding iron hanging beside the long window over the bench. He reached past her head for it, and laid it beside the glass balls. She said brightly to Rosa, "I never knew an artist before. It's so *interesting*."

"Mm," said Rosa. She picked up a sagging carton of debris and carried it down the wharf. It was high tide now, still without wind. The faint precipitation darkened fishhouse shingles, made buoys shine, and misted the harbor like breath on glass. Woodsmoke blew down from Philip Bennett's fishhouse; where his young helper built trap bottoms just inside the open doorway with his transistor radio for company, mercifully turned low. Rosa could barely hear it, and then it was drowned completely as distant engines grew louder along the west side, and Matt Fennell and Jamie came roaring abreast around the breakwater.

Rosa admired the boats in action until they slowed down to cross the harbor, then went back to the fishhouse. Edwin had given up his arrangement for the time being and was using a broken shovel to scoop up old shingles into a tar-stained washtub. Linnie sat on the bench, legs hanging, sorting nails, and looking actually radiant about it. Lucky kid; it was enough for her merely to be in The Presence.

About ten minutes later Jamie appeared without warning in the open doorway. Rosa, coiling old pot warp, saw him first. She started to greet him, but austerely he avoided her, ignored Edwin, and spoke to Linnie in a low voice.

"Come on."

"I'm busy." She kept her eyes on what she was doing, but color began in her throat and swept upward.

His voice was still low, and heavier. "I said, Come *on.*"

"What for?"

"You're wanted at home, that's what for."

"You haven't had time to get home and find out," Linnie said. She gave Rosa a furtive and desperate glance. Edwin went on scooping up shingles as if no one else were there, though he had obviously seen Jamie by now.

"Thanks for helping out with the nails, Linnie," Rosa said. "I hate that job."

"I do most of the time, but today I love it," Linnie said fiercely. "But some people can't stand to see other people doing something as—as harmless and helpful as sorting nails. Doing something *neighborly.* They don't know what the word *means.*"

Impervious as stone, Jamie waited. She slid down off the bench and he moved aside so she could pass stiffly by him and out to the road.

"Saved in the nick of time," Rosa murmured. "In another minute, *rape.*"

Jamie ignored her and followed his sister. Edwin straightened up and gave Rosa an inquiring look. She shrugged and shook her head. She was more amused than annoyed by Jamie now. No wonder he didn't have time for a girl of his own.

Sunday came off fine. Rosa and Edwin went on a leisurely

cruise in *Sea Star* to see the seals on their ledges, and out around Matinicus Rock light to get a glimpse of the puffins and medricks. They circled Pirate Island and the outlying islets of Brigport, then they went around the big island itself, jogging slowly past coves and beaches and identifying ledges from the chart. Finally they went into Brigport Harbor, which was as busy with small-boat activity as a mainland harbor, even though Sunday wasn't a working day for the fishermen. The *Ella Vye* had brought out a crowd for a day excursion, a cruise schooner lay at the harbor mouth, two big herring carriers and a broad-beamed seiner, *Centurion*, took up a good deal of space. Because of all the extra people the store was open, and Rosa and Edwin bought bread, salami, and cold soft drinks, and walked over to the broad white sand beach that was one of the island's glories. There were other picnickers there and a few brave swimmers, but the space was great enough to give everyone a sense of solitude.

The mainland hills were blue as hyacinths in the north. One could not see to the west where Seal Point was, so there was nothing here to blemish the hour. Rosa felt that given a choice she would still choose to be here, as long as she didn't examine the question too closely. The real choice would have been Con, before Phyllis, and with no Phyllis to be. Con, herself, and a baby son.

But the way things were now—no, she couldn't ask for anything better than this, she assured the invisible donor of choices.

But as usual she couldn't leave well enough alone. She had to wonder what Edwin was thinking as he gazed out from under half-closed lids at the glittering blues and greens. The colors, maybe? The never-repeated patterns of water breaking and swirling over the white sand? Something as simple as that and not of a woman with a long throat and a head thrown back in laughter? Now why did she have to keep coming back to *that*?

When they came home in the late afternoon, Bennett's seemed unnaturally quiet after the activity at Brigport. The children had all gone across the island to Schoolhouse Cove. Philip Bennett and his wife were on their front porch when Rosa and Edwin came up from the fishhouse, and Philip called to them to come and have a drink.

Rosa was still under the influence of her day, moving as effortlessly through the atmosphere as a fish through water; she was conscious of this, enjoyed it, and hoped it would last. At least it kept her from being wretchedly self-conscious with Mrs. Philip in the porch swing while the men sat on the steps. She could even stand off and admire the progress she'd made in less than two weeks from a horribly solid lump of snuffling anguish to this slightly thinner and outwardly poised creature, sipping a Tom Collins and discussing puffins and medricks like a charter member of the Audubon Society. For some reason, perhaps the drink, she wanted to laugh out loud at herself.

Ralph was mowing his lawn when they got home, and expansively she invited him to supper without knowing what it was going to be. She told him that and he said solemnly, "Lady, if you was to cook up a mess of grass and put it before me, it'd taste good because somebody else fixed it."

"I can do a little better than grass. I think. Or do you mean something else by grass?"

"You mean you actually got your own little marijuana patch? Is that why you won't let Edwin mow your lawn?"

"No, I'm saving the daisies. I eat the centers, and, boy, do they turn me on."

When she set oven-browned corned beef hash on the table, with sliced tomatoes and cucumbers on the side, he said, "Hey, where's the stewed daisies? I can't get high on this stuff."

"Have you ever tried chewing dried peas?" Edwin wrote. "You get great visions, all colored green, along with broken teeth."

She thought that the whole day had been one of the best

124

in her life, because for so long she had expected never to be even halfway happy again. It was like waking up after a bad accident to your eyes to find out you weren't blind after all. Broken in places, bruised all over, but the slash across the eyes hadn't destroyed them.

"I'm sorry, I haven't got dessert," she said to Ralph.

"Sing me a song, then."

She felt gracious and generous, taking down her guitar, "What do you want?"

"Your choice. Something not too sad."

She laughed, thinking how before she lost Con she'd liked the melancholy old ballads. Now she couldn't even stand *Careless Love* or *Old Smokey*.

They went out into the sunset light both quieted and emphasized by the screen of trees. Edwin sat on the railing of the back doorstep, Ralph sat on the top step, and Rosa went to the bulkhead where she could put her back against the still-warm clapboards and be surrounded by the lilac scent. Without thinking she started to play *Green Grow the Lilacs*, but that wouldn't do. She switched to *The Ocean Child* and her own tune. While she was singing, the girls filed quietly up from the lane, trailed by some smaller girls who kept staring around the yard with awe and curiosity, not able to choose between her and Edwin for chief oddity.

The older girls sank down crosslegged in the grass, and the little ones imitated them, politely silent, trying not to giggle when Ralph winked at them. Linnie sat holding her ankles, head bent, her hair hiding her face.

Rosa finished the song and was applauded. One of the younger ones, now recognized as Dinsmores, asked bashfully if Rosa knew *Old Dog Tray*.

"No," Rosa lied. "How's it go? Come on over and sing it for me." The child came up on the bulkhead and began singing the song in a husky but true little voice, and Rosa picked out the chords. Halfway through, she saw Linnie's head come up and slowly turn, her eyes large and solemn, her mouth pathetically drooping. She glanced in the direction of Linnie's gaze and saw that Edwin had disappeared from the railing.

She and Tammie finished the song together, and Ralph and the others clapped strenuously. Tammie, stiff with pride, marched back to her place; Linnie arose like a sleepwalker, crossed the yard, and went into the path. Vic sat up alertly and called, "Hey!"

Linnie gave no sign of hearing. Her pale hair and long legs glimmered for an instant in the leafy twilight of the path before it twisted out of sight. Holly and Betsey whispered, laughing secretly behind their hands. Ralph said candidly, "Well, there's no harm in trying."

"There's no sense in throwing away your pride, either," Vic said in a dry, harsh voice.

Rosa said to the other Dinsmore child, "Don't *you* have a song to teach me?"

"*The Bluebells of Scotland?*"

As the evening began to dampen and darken, Rosa had to take the guitar indoors. She invited the others in for manners' sake, not really wanting them. The Bennett girls were eager, but Vic said in her new lifeless fashion, "These little kids should be home, they're out on their feet. I'll bet you're tired too, aren't you, Rosa?"

"Frankly, yes."

The others gave up. They went off into the dusk, trying to teach the Dinsmore children to sing *Row, Row, Row Your Boat*. Vic thanked Rosa, looked once toward the dark tunnel of the path, and then walked away through the ghostly floating moons of the last daisies.

"Want some coffee, Ralph, or some cold beer?" Rosa asked. "I'm dry."

"I wouldn't mind a beer, but I don't want to keep you up."

"Oh, come on."

She lit a lamp and got out the beer. They sat at the table talking about lobstering, Bennett's Island, Rosa's father, Ralph's family. On the surface it was a pleasant interlude.

Ralph was easy to be with; he didn't seem to take her either as a renegade woman or an imitation male, but simply as a human being.

But beneath the superficial peace of the moment she was both anxious and irritated. She didn't care how hawsed-up Jamie Sorensen got about his sister; it was good enough for him, he was a born troublemaker. But she wished Edwin would come back. Sometimes it jolted her to realize he was a stranger in so many ways. Bad enough for Con to astonish you like a violent fall that knocked the breath out of your lungs. But Edwin—as reliable and familiar as your own two hands— Well, nobody really knows all about anyone else, she argued under cover of the desultory talk. Look how little anyone, even Edwin, knows about *me*. But I don't like him being out there with Linnie. And who says he's with her? She may be home by now. Took a roundabout way up from Barque Cove past the Fennell house. He could be—

"Here's the man now," said Ralph, and as Edwin came in she jumped as if awakened roughly from sleep. He leaned against the counter, arms folded, frowning against the lamplight. She got up and went to the refrigerator, but he put out an arm to bar her and shook his head.

"Coffee then?"

He refused that. Ralph finished his beer and stood up. "Time for me to be crawling under the kelp," he said. "Back to work tomorrow morning. Thanks, Rosa."

"Any time. Come again, and bring your fiddle."

"I'll do that." On the way out he touched Edwin's shoulder and said, "Good night." Edwin gave him a curt nod. He came over to the table and sat down to write. Rosa watched, wondering if her stomach were roiling from the cold beer or something else. Edwin would never lay a finger on Linnie. Never. She was just a kid. No. She was a tall seventeen, and she was asking for it. Edwin was not a monk, Edwin was a healthy male. He hadn't wanted her to see the sketches and now she wasn't sure it was just out of mischief. The impact of her first impression had repeated itself again and again, and was always as strong as the first time. In some frightening way it had gotten all tied up with Linnie, Linnie following him, silent and determined.

Darned kid. Cussid kid. Tramping through a mine field in ski boots. But Edwin would never. Would never *what?*... And the whole miserable, worrying argument began again.

He was waiting for her to read.

"Leaving tomorrow. Been here too long. Have to get back to work."

She was ashamed of her relief, and grief-stricken, not at his going, but because she wanted him to go. She put up a token protest. "Your hardware hasn't come yet. Nobody's called or written."

"I've got other things to do."

She shrugged angrily and went to bed. Afterwards she wanted to go down and make up; she wasn't mad with *him.* She went down the stairs halfway, but by then his light was out. What good would it do, anyway? He would never tell her anything. And, as long as she didn't know, she could be-lieve—almost—that nothing had happened tonight to precipi-tate his departure.

16

They were so meticulously natural with each other the next morning that they were extremely unnatural. She packed the few of Lucy's old dishes that had survived the Wylie boys, and an ancient Seth Thomas clock that didn't go, but which Jude wanted to tinker with. They wheeled and carried everything to the wharf in a bright, sharp-edged morning. The northwest breeze was not strong enough to keep the boats in, and she looked longingly at *Sea Star*, knowing that to be with the boat was the only help for her.

The mail had been given out, shopping done, and nobody was left around the wharf but the small boys who were dedicated to catching and casting off lines. Edwin went aboard the mailboat and she handed his things down to him. He stowed everything away in the passenger cabin, came onto the wharf again, and stood beside her smoking his pipe until Mark and the captain came down through the sheds with the mailbags. Then he put an arm around her, took his pipe out of his mouth and kissed her, and went down the ladder.

Her eyes filled with tears. She didn't wait for the boat to go, but went quickly around the harbor to the fishhouse and got ready to haul. She was rowing out to the mooring when the *Ella Vye*'s whistle blew, and the big boat backed slowly away from the wharf and turned her bow toward Eastern Harbor Point and the return stop at Brigport. Rosa did not look over her shoulder for a glimpse of Edwin.

The wind kept freshening in quick hard gusts, so that the tops of crests blew off like smoke. Rosa's traps were in the lee of the island, but she had to round Sou'west Point to get there, and here the seas seemed to rush from all directions at once. To circle this wide area of tumbling white water, calculating wind and tide, took all Rosa's concentration. When at last she glided into the warm lee she felt a reviving pride of accomplishment. She looked around for her thermos of coffee, but she'd left in such a hurry this morning she'd forgotten it. This recalled Edwin's departure and the massive weight of her depression; but out here, heading for her first buoy off Bull Cove, she could not carry the burden for long, even knowing she would assume it again when she stepped ashore.

The wind gusted down over the trees and slapped at her,

but the island broke its force. Outside the lee the chop began again, and jets of surf blew high over the ledges. Someone was hauling almost out of sight behind the Seal Rocks, a bright red jigger sail helping to hold the boat into the wind. She spotted others here and there, but it was difficult in the confusing dazzle. This was nothing to them, she supposed; or at least, not much out of the ordinary. But she wondered how they could even see their buoys out there, between the motion of the boats and the action of the water, with the sunlight flashing off it into their eyes.

She had three traps at the edge of the turbulence off Schooner Head, just enough of a challenge to keep up her exhilaration. There were some long steady squalls now, roaring in the high woods like hurricane surf; she could hear that and the breakers on the nearest ledges above the pulse of the diesel as she came up into the wind and gaffed a buoy.

In fact she could hear it all too clearly. The land was moving rapidly away from her as *Sea Star* began to drift powerless before the wind.

The engine had stopped, and it was as if her own heart had stopped. For an instant disbelief held her motionless and staring. Then she began the automatic motions to start the engine again, all the time thinking with an icy foreknowledge, She won't start.

She was right. There was not even a token of life. Now *Sea Star* was clear of the island's shelter and drifting out fast, rocking with a deceptive gentleness, toward the uneven barrier of ledges where breaking seas kept firing off like depth charges at staggered intervals.

She snapped on her radio, took down her microphone, and pressed the button. "*Sea Star* calling anyone," she said calmly. "I'm broken down and heading for the big ledge off Schooner Head, not much more than five minutes to go."

It would take more than five minutes for anyone to reach her. She looked back at the island. If she could fight her way through to the lee she'd be all right, but she gave herself no chances at all in that stretch of cold and rough water. She glanced into the cabin and saw the big anchor lying on the port locker, its attached rode line coiled beside it. She knew that by the time she got the anchor out and overboard, and the line paid out, she would be in the surf, the anchor useless.

She repeated her words into the microphone, and hung it up.

The gleaming crags of the ledge loomed high above the rushing breakers, and behind the surf she could see the water running off the rockweed in miniature cataracts. She ducked into the cabin for a life jacket, and when she came out again there was a boat bearing down on her from around the eastern side of the ledge, throwing water over her bow in glittering showers, jigger sail blood-red. She rode in close to *Sea Star*, rolling in the troughs.

It was Jamie Sorensen. He had a line ready and it snaked across to her; she caught it, and he made his end fast around the cleat on the stern deck. With a swiftness born of fear she went forward on hands and knees to the *Sea Star*'s bow and fastened her end of the line around the pawl-post.

Valkyrie surged toward the land with all her power. Rosa flattened herself out on the deck, clasping the pawl-post. For a moment it didn't seem as if the other boat could move *Sea Star*. The line snapped out taut and *Valkyrie* strained without making headway, and then gradually *Sea Star*'s bow came around and she began to follow.

In Bull Cove, Jamie shut off his engine and stood ready to fend off *Sea Star* as she rode ahead on momentum. Rosa came down from the deck as the two boats gently nudged each other.

He took down his microphone and said, "Everything's all right, we're in Bull Cove. *Sea Star* and *Valkyrie* out." He hung the microphone up and looked around at her with one eyebrow lifted. "Out of fuel?"

"I couldn't be!"

"Go look."

She *was* out of fuel. Humiliated and blushing, she drove her hands hard into her pockets and turned her back on his gratified smile. "My God, I never did that before in my *life!*"

"Well, there's a first time for everything. You wouldn't want to be perfect now, would you?"

"I wouldn't mind having a shot at it," she muttered.

"Cheer up," he said. "I did the same thing in the same place once, and my uncle snagged me out of the breakers. Just be glad I'm not your uncle, or I'd say the same thing he said to me."

"I deserve it, I guess. I suppose I should thank you for not saying it," she said, staring desolately at her feet.

"Look, I'll run around to the harbor and get some fuel for you," he offered. "Better anchor, we're getting out in the wind again."

"I hate to interrupt your hauling," she said.

"You planning to sit here till somebody brings you a can on the way out to haul tomorrow? Throw that anchor overboard and just sit tight. I'll be right back."

He pushed off and was on his way before she could say anything more. Feeling like a small child doing an adult's bidding she got the anchor and dropped it overboard, holding the line till it caught on the bottom. Then she fastened it to the cleat in the stern deck and sat down on an empty crate to wait for his return.

When he was out of sight, he was out of hearing, the engine sound killed by the tumult in the trees and the cannonading of surf. She slumped on the empty lobster crate till all at once she had to vomit over the side of the boat. After the spasms subsided her head was clearer, and she realized that not only the boat would have been lost through her carelessness but herself. It was unpardonable to have allowed herself to be so distracted by anything else that she'd forgotten to fuel up. It would be a long time before she got over it. At least if she were dead now, beaten and smothered in the surf, she'd be free of shame; she and the boat gone together, twinned in death.

She was sick again, and this time she didn't make it over the side of the boat. She had to sluice down the washboard with buckets of water, and she had just finished when Jamie came back.

She was still shaky but hoped he wouldn't notice. At least through his takeover she was spared trying to lift the heavy can to pour the fuel into the tank, weak as she felt.

"Now start her," he ordered, "and if she doesn't go I'll tow you in. Maybe Terence or Foss can find out what ails her, besides being dry. They've got diesels."

"You have to be patient with her," Rosa said, back in charge. "She was never the kind of engine you could swear at."

"Some different from mine, then." He watched with his head cocked like an aggressive terrier. After a few tries the engine coughed into life, and then took on a firm rhythm. Jamie and Rosa looked at each other and laughed in spontaneous satisfaction.

"Look, what can I do to pay you for this?" she asked. "I could have drowned." She began to stammer. "N-n-not to mention the b——"

He looked fixedly at her, as Linnie did. "I know what you can do. Knit me a hundred baitbags. I'll supply the twine."

"Just knitting isn't enough," she said. "I'll supply the twine."

"You don't know what kind I use. So just hold up till I get it. *Now.*" He climbed back aboard his own boat and went into the cabin, and came out with a thermos bottle and a lunchbox. "How's about shutting her off and joining me in the mug-up I was about to have when you yelled for help? How about some coffee?" He put two thermos cups on *Sea Star*'s washboard and poured coffee. She'd been drinking hers black for a long time now, and this had sugar and cream in it; real cream, she could tell by the texture. Hot and rich, it soothed her empty stomach. He shoved the lunchbox toward her. "Sandwich or gingerbread?"

"This coffee's enough," she said. "It's wonderful."

"Have some more."

"Nope. That's got to do you for the day."

"Oh, go on, live a little. I've got water aboard if I dry out." He filled her cup again and pushed a crusty square of gingerbread at her. "*Eat it*," he said sternly. "Listen, we've kind of got off on the wrong foot. I guess I took too much on myself, what I said when you came into the harbor that day." He was busy capping the bottle, scowling at it, but that was no help to her. He knew now what her story was.

"And the other thing—" he continued. "Hey, you don't intend to make it easy for a guy, do you?"

"Making what easy?" She was surprised into looking at him.

"Apologizing. Jesus, it's sticking in my throat enough now."

"What are you apologizing for?" she asked, mild with innocence.

"Jumping on you about your cousin! You couldn't do anything about him any more than I could about that fool kid. But I was so mad I had to light into somebody."

"And there I was," she said, "and you thought, If *she* wasn't here he wouldn't be, either. Well, he's gone now. He went in on the mailboat. So you don't have to worry. Not about *him*, anyway. But there'll be somebody along, and then somebody else, and then somebody else——"

"There's no doubt of that," he said glumly. "You ought to hear her and that buddy of hers, reading love poetry to each other, and to my mother."

"What does she say?"

"She says they're normal."

"Well, since she was a seventeen-year-old girl and you never were and never will be, why don't you take her word for it?"

"Oh, I do. But I don't happen to think it's anything cute

or funny or sweet or anything like that. Those two could be picked off the way I've seen blackback gulls pick up new ducklings. Well, maybe not Vic so fast, she's tougher."

Not where you're concerned, Goldilocks, Rosa thought.

"What's so funny?"

"Vic. I get a big kick out of her."

"Yeah. But Linnie . . . well, she just wants to be in love. She doesn't care who it is."

"Then you're lucky she lit on Edwin this time."

"I don't see it that way. I'm damn glad he's gone."

"Edwin has a girl on the mainland," she said, taking liberties with the truth. "He's also a man, not a kid. I mean a real man, who doesn't take advantage of a youngster."

"All right, you have your opinion and I have mine. He's your cousin, so I'll shut up. But damn it, I worry about the kid," he said angrily. "Maybe because I'm closer to her, or something. My mother and father—" He brushed them off, baffled and annoyed. "We have an older sister and she always kept her cool, no matter what. They think Linnie's like Ellen. But I know better. . . . Listen, what kind of a kid would be fascinated by a man who's deaf?"

"Who's also good-looking and smart and talented and . . . Oh, skip it!" She laughed. "I'm prejudiced and so are you."

"Stalemate," he said with a grin. They were silent for a few moments. The lee was warm and peaceful, and outside the wind seemed to be dropping down. The whitecaps were fewer, although the surf still broke on the ledges.

"Well, I've got to get back to work," he said finally. "Start her up again, so I'll be sure."

The diesel began without difficulty. "See?" Rosa said with pride. "She always does her best as long as I don't forget to feed her."

He started up his own engine, and she untied the line that held the two boats together. "Thanks again," she called, but he was on his way out, fast, and he didn't look back.

17

There was something to be said for nearly getting drowned. It had knocked everything else out of her mind. She hadn't thought of Con at all this morning, and, even while she and Jamie had been talking about Edwin, he seemed as distant as if she had made a great journey away from him, in time as well as space.

At the wharf Mark Bennett filled her tanks and said, "Well, you're initiated now. You're one of the club."

"Are you the uncle that got Jamie out there one time?" she asked. She wasn't self-conscious now; people ought to have narrow escapes quite often, it flooded away a lot of the junk like a spring tide cleaning off the beaches.

"It was Owen," said Mark. "Like to burned the boy's ears off. Blistered them, anyway. I guess Jamie thought a stormy death would've been kinder."

"Anybody who forgets to gas up ought to get their ears blistered," said Rosa.

"He blister yours?"

"Nope, he was very restrained. He gave me coffee and gingerbread."

"Jamie's a good boy. He probably knew you were suffering enough without him rubbing salt into the wounds."

She bought a couple bushels of bait, and Young Mark and the cat closely supervised the bailing of herring from hogshead to her buckets. As she was getting back aboard the boat the boy said suddenly, "Do you like to bag up?"

"I love to. Always did. Do you?"

"When I get the chance," he said grumpily.

"Mark's looking for a job," his father said. "Trouble is, his legs aren't long enough and his hands aren't big enough yet."

"I had that trouble once myself," Rosa told the boy. "But it's something you grow out of, believe me." She was swaddled in contentment, everything a part of it; the sun, the gentle motion of the boat, the solemn child, the man standing by the scales smiling, the cat washing up, the good acrid scent of herring; and being alive. Yes, that was it, being alive.

Back at her mooring she spent an hour filling bags. Mark had offered both herring and bream, both fresh; the bait boat had been out yesterday. She would always take herring over bream, her father's personal preference from the days before the radfish plant opened in Limerock, when the men seined or torched herring for their bait, salting away a whole season's supply in hogsheads in their baitsheds. Even now her toes could curl in ecstatic memory of how those damp cool planks had felt under bare feet when she, like Young Mark, had longed to get into the herring and was still too small.

She stuffed bags without hurrying, now and then tossing a herring to a gull that hovered hopefully near the boat. It was tranquilizing work. She could hear the surf along the windward side of the island and on the outside of the breakwater, she heard the tide rip hissing by the harbor mouth, but the boat hardly moved. The fast-growing eider ducklings paddled and up-ended in the floating rockweed around the ledges, too big now for the blackbacks to grab—she remembered Jamie's analogy—and the herring gulls sat on spilings and fishhouse ridgepoles with their breasts to the wind. Children were playing among the rocks on the Campions' shore, and most of the women had taken advantage of the drying wind to get washings out.

When she finished bagging up, she cleaned up the boat

and scrubbed her arms with salt-water soap, and rowed ashore. Her yard was scented by the hot wind-stirred spruces. From beyond the woods she could hear the water crashing into Barque Cove and the stones being tumbled about in the surf.

As she'd have been tumbled. She felt a qualm but it didn't last. She was safe now. Alone but not lonely, because she had her life for company. . . . She felt a different qualm when she went inside and saw one of Edwin's pipes in the scallop-shell ashtray, and in his room his dented pillows and the book he'd been reading.

Oh never *mind!* she thought. You can't do a damn thing about it. We all have to dree our own weird. . . . Even Con. Now why did I think that? Because everything's fine for him. Of the three of us, he has exactly what he wants, just the way he wants it.

She got out of her hauling clothes and into clean slacks and shirt, and made up a packaged soup for her lunch, which she ate out on the back doorstep. Her daisies were going by; maybe she'd borrow Ralph's lawn mower and wrassle that around the place, but should she take a scythe to it first? . . . No hurry, she thought. I've got nothing to hurry about. After this morning, it was not bitter knowledge.

Linnie came up from the lane, Vic slouching gracelessly along behind her with her hands in the rear pockets of her jeans. She gave the impression of being unwillingly in tow. When she caught Rosa's glance she sucked in one cheek and opened her eyes to saucers.

Linnie spoke with a hard clarity. "Did Edwin go back to the mainland or just to Brigport?"

"Back to the main." To soften it she added, "He had to get back to work."

Vic sat down in the midst of the daisies and picked one. "He loves me, he loves me not," she recited. Linnie gave her a sad if not martyred look. "Wasn't it awfully sudden?" she asked Rosa. "I mean, did you get a telephone call for him, or something?"

"No, but when he came he only intended to stay three or four days."

"Oh." Linnie collapsed bonelessly on the grass. She studied something there with intense interest. Vic said, "Do you know any love songs, Rosa?"

"Not today," said Rosa.

"I know a lot of good things you could set to music. 'When I am dead, my dearest, sing no sad songs for me——' "

"I am going to burn that book," said Linnie, "if you don't stop quoting from it."

"*Victorian Love Poems*," Vic said to Rosa. "We found it in the attic. And, you know, it's really great in spots! I guess people have always felt the same about love. There's not much difference between some of those poems and a lot of the pop songs now."

"I wouldn't know," said Rosa. "I'm no expert on love."

"Who is?" Vic sounded elderly. "Maybe it's all made up anyway. You read the poems and sing the songs and watch the movies, and you think, This is how it's supposed to be. But maybe it's not that way at all. It's all a big put-on."

Linnie got up very neatly without touching her hands to the ground for balance and walked to the path as if she were carrying a book on her head. Vic and Rosa watched her go. Vic twisted a thick strand of hair around her neck. "I could die sometimes when I see Jamie," she said suddenly. "When I don't expect to, or when I know he's coming, either way, the minute I see him—wow." She pressed a fist against her chest. "It's almost enough to make me sick. But I wouldn't have it any other way. Oh, sure, I'd like to have him feel the same way about me. But maybe I couldn't stand it. I'd probably burn to a crisp like a moth in a lamp." She made a monstrous face, cross-eyed and slack-jawed. "But if this is all it's going to be, well, I'd rather have this than nothing."

"Why?" Rosa asked.

"Because I like being in love, I guess. It changes everything you see and hear. You've never been so alive in your whole

139

life . . . and maybe not having Jamie makes it even better. We might start fighting right off. Or get all torn up about being separated. Or even—you know"— She colored a little—"go all the way, and then the bloom's off and the whole thing gets to be one big pain or it turns ugly."

"How old did you say you were? A hundred and ten?"

"Three hundred and ten, and I'm really the reincarnation of just about any gorgeous female you can name. See, I've had more than my share of being a great sex symbol, so for this life I have to be the kind that men never notice except to ask if they've got the notes from the last Ancient and Medieval History class."

"Seems as if you ought to remember some of the tricks from the old days."

"That's against the rules," Vic said seriously. "You can't remember a thing from the past unless there's a cosmic accident where something breaks through like a dream."

"Do you *believe* all this?" Rosa asked. "You sound it."

"Nope, but it's a great line at parties. I'm going to study palmistry this fall, and that'll give me a chance to hold hands with all the boys." She got up. "Well, I suppose I'd better track down Linnie."

"Maybe she wants to be alone."

"Not for too long. I mean, it's not that kind of suffering. It's like what I just said. It's the state of being in love."

She looked down at Rosa. "We'll all recover, I expect," she said, almost as if she were including Rosa.

When Ralph came in from hauling, Rosa borrowed his scythe and hand lawnmower, and was working in the yard when the girls came back in late afternoon. They had been eating wild strawberries and their lips and fingertips were red. They were both in high spirits. Linnie gave Rosa a small plastic container full of berries, all hulled. "I washed it out in salt water, so it's clean," she said. "Oh, it was just gorgeous out there this afternoon. I've got so much spray in my hair I've got to go home and wash it, and my shorts are soaked. I'm covered with salt."

"We forgot to tell you something when we went through before," Vic said. "We were so emotionally disturbed and so forth. Weren't we, Lin?"

"Oh, shut up," said Linnie amiably. "Look, they're having a big supper and dance at Brigport the Fourth and almost everybody's going that can crawl. Jamie's taking a bunch, so how would you like to go with us? It's going to be moonlight on the way back, and everything."

"If it's stormy or foggy I'll die," said Vic. "You know something? Siegfried can't avoid dancing with me. I mean, he'll be there, so of course he'll dance with me. At least once, anyway, just for good manners."

"Now Vic," Linnie said kindly, "remember what I told you. He might just take it into his head to stand outside the hall all evening. There's always a bunch that does that."

"I'm thinking positive," said Vic. "I can't let that evening go to waste. I may ask *him*."

"Listen, you'll be too busy dancing with everybody else. If you can move a foot you'll never sit out a square dance."

"I was thinking of something wildly sexy like a waltz," said Vic. "You said they do waltzes at these dances. I'm glad my mama sent me to dancing school."

"But I never said *Jamie* waltzed! My goodness, he'd think he was compromised!"

They left, hilariously arm in arm.

18

They had taken it for granted that she was going with them. Late in the morning of the Fourth, when she came in from hauling they were waiting for her. The hour was hot and still. Cloud reflections lay nearly motionless on shining waters all the way across to Brigport. The Bennett girls fished dreamily from a dory in the harbor, and the two older girls, with younger children circulating around them like small bright-colored fish, sat on the end of the Sorensen wharf in their bikinis, brushing and combing their newly washed hair. Farther around the shore young boys played in an inviolate masculine world.

"We're leaving at five, Rosa," Linnie called.

"Oh gosh," said Rosa. "Look. I appreciate you asking me and everything, but I couldn't last out an evening. I wake up so early, I'm out on my feet by dark."

"You don't have to stay all evening," Linnie argued. "You can go over with us and come back with my father and mother. They're going to the supper, and some of my uncles and aunts are going with them."

"And so are her cousins and her uncles and her aunts," sang Vic. "Her uncles and her cousins whom she reckons by the dozens——"

"They'll stay for some of the dance but not too late," Linnie said. "The people with little kids come home early too.

Oh, come *on*, Rosa. You're young! Don't you want some fun? You like to dance, don't you?" She looked disappointed. "Maybe you don't. You never said."

"I do like it, and I like square dances best," Rosa assured her. "But honestly, I don't want to go tonight. Don't worry, I won't weasel out of your show when the time comes."

A little girl patted Linnie's arm. "Hey, Linnie, what are us kids going to do in the show this time? I can say the piece I did for Memorial Day. You weren't here then. It goes like this—" Linnie was surrounded, and probably deafened, by the rest.

Rosa changed from boots to sneakers in the fishhouse, which by now was almost tidy, at least more roomy. Every time she looked at the clean bench she was tempted to start building traps, but the forty were doing well enough for her, and they were enough for her to manage alone. She walked home thinking of her lunch, and of painting the house. She hardly ever thought of noon at Seal Point when she was going home like this. Sometimes the memory of the high-ceilinged rooms, cool and shady after the summer glare outside, passed through her mind, and the scent of fresh-cut grass here always evoked the thick lush lawns of home, but never homesickness. Crossing the well-field, she smelled the hot noon scent of the new-mown hay in the Sorensen field, and instantly recalled the barn at home, though it had been a long time since the loft had held hay.

But she was not nostalgic. Perhaps it was because she would not allow herself to be. To dwell on the house at Seal Point would be to arrive inevitably at the months and years spent in it with Con, and she could not trust herself to that. She was pleasantly anesthetized here, moving at a cautious, unjarring pace from one project to the other. The important thing was not to run out of projects.

After lunch she went to work scraping and painting on the outside of the house. High on Ralph's ladder she whistled softly as she worked. Marjorie Percy, who had come home last boat-day, was working around a flower bed below her porch. "I wish I could hire you!" she called. "Ralph fusses over painting his boat as if he was Rembrandt, but he never has time to do the house."

"Sure, I'll do it," said Rosa.

"Heavens, I was just kidding!" Marjorie came over to the foot of the ladder. "But are you serious?"

"Why not?"

"Gosh, I may just take you up on it. . . . When you're feeling dry, come on over for a cup of tea. The kids are all at Schoolhouse Cove and I can hear myself think for a change." She went back across the path; from the back she looked like a teen-ager, and she was as limber as one. She had plain features redeemed by a kind of humorous sweetness. From the moment of meeting she had behaved as if Rosa had always lived next door. This afternoon they drank mugs of tea on the porch, talking like neighbors who had nothing new to discover about each other, and then Rosa went back to her stint.

In the late afternoon five boatloads of islanders left for the celebration at Brigport. Silence took over a deserted village. No evening ballgame, no generators started up for television. She had no intention of wasting this luxurious solitude. In the amber light of sunset, with her shadow long before her, she set out to walk across the island to watch the moon rise out of the sea.

The Sorensen dog barked desultorily behind the gate, and Tiger picked it up from inside his house. Otherwise everything was coated by the golden quiet that seemed to drip from eaves and branches in soundless showers. But when she was passing the harbor beach, she heard an engine. The splendor was shattered as the bow of the still-invisible boat was shattering the chrysoprase sea on which this gilded island lay.

One instinct was to hurry across the flowering marsh and be out of sight before the transient dragger or haker came into the harbor. The other, equally strong, was to stay and see what sort of boat it was. While she was standing there, wanting to run but still wondering why the engine sounded familiar, the boat came in around Eastern Harbor Point with a rushing and ruffling of waters.

It was *Valkyrie*.

Rosa still could have disappeared, but she had waited a moment too long. Jamie saw her and waved energetically, whistling. Her heart began to beat in a heavy cadence and her throat seemed to be paralyzed. He had a message for her; nobody was in the store here to answer the telephone, because Mark's family had gone to the celebration, so someone had called Brigport. About what?

She turned to walk back to the wharves, and she could hardly move her legs. Something had happened to Con. He was still her husband, so of course they'd call her. She'd have to take charge. He'd been drowned, or it was some terrible road accident. Last year a woman had been beheaded. . . . Con's head. Red curls an aunt used to twine around her fingers.

By the time she turned in between her fishhouse and the Sorensens, her legs wanted to give away and salt water was running in her mouth. She heard the clatter of oars, dimly saw Jamie's fair head in the cold shadow between the wharves, and then he was coming up the ladder.

"Hi!" he called. "Were you going or coming when I whistled?"

Trying to think of a way to break the news. She said quietly, because she hadn't the strength for vehemence, "Did you have a message for me?"

"Nope. Why? Oh, you mean the whistling. Hell, I was just trying to get your attention. Did, didn't I?"

The bloody picture of Con vanished, leaving her lightheaded. She braced herself as if on a tilting deck. "What did you want me for, then? What did you come back for?"

"What are *you* doing?"

"I was just going for a walk to watch the moon rise."

"Then that's what I came back for," he said. "Come on, let's go."

145

"Wait a minute——"

"What's the matter?" He barred her way. "You scared to walk with me? I wasn't planning to make a pass at you, if that's what you think."

"No, I didn't think *that!*" He made her feel ridiculous, as if she were afraid to be alone with a man. "I don't know why I said it, to be frank. I just object on general principles. It was born in me, the way it's born in you to make a legal case out of everything."

"Not quite everything," he said.

"No, you didn't when you hauled me out of the breakers, and you could have skun me good." She smiled. "Let's go, then."

He wasn't a glib talker. He gave her some island history as they went along, but she had to keep priming him with questions, and wished she had the courage to let silence take over. After all, he'd barged in on her walk and it wasn't up to her to act like some fancy hostess who had to keep the conversation lively. What the hell did he think, that because he'd given her a tow he'd made some kind of link between them? Or did he think because she was apart from her husband and waiting for a divorce that she wanted company or comforting? The way some men came honeying around . . . Except that you couldn't very well call it honeying around, the way he did it. He'd just taken over her walk, told her Fern Cliff was better than Windward Point, showed her the way off the Eastern End path through ferns and juniper, all but told her where to roost, and now sat with his folded arms resting on his hauled-up knees, staring at the red-gold moon rising out of the sea. He slapped a mosquito on his neck without taking his eyes from the scene.

"I read somewhere that the Japanese have moon-watching platforms," she said. "They aren't too comfortable, because you're not supposed to be taking it easy. I suppose that's why we have mosquitoes."

That got no response. She felt like laughing, and wondered if he'd think she was crazy. She might try it. . . . She decided against it. The gold was fading now to silver. The quiet was as immense as the ocean, and the sense of the almost unoccupied island behind them was as strong as a presence.

At the most distant rim of the silence she heard an engine. "That wouldn't be a seiner tonight," she said. "Not with moonlight."

"Likely somebody coming home from Brigport," he said.

"When I first came out here, I heard there was a war on with the purse-seiners. Was that just talk? Because I know the stop-twiners and purse-seiners tangle sometimes at home."

"Always will, I guess. Yeah, the war's going on. It's been quiet around here for a week or so because *Centurion*'s been seining off Pirate Island, but I expect 'em all back here next dark of the moon." She had uncorked the right bottle. "I've seen as many as five purse-seiners out here at once, with that many carriers standing by to take out the fish. So they don't only break up the big schools before they can get into the coves, but they also ram right through the gear and slice off buoys left and right. Goddamit, this is our own island and they come down on us like vultures."

"It seems funny that you all can't get together and talk," she said.

"Talk's been tried, with the men themselves. Look, they're not all bad. Most of the skippers honestly try not to cut off buoys. But Purvis, on the *Triton*—she tends out on *Centurion*—he's just plain mean. Sure, the sardine companies are backing the seiners, and they've got to get fish. But there's other places besides Bennett's Island, and the others do go somewhere else sometimes. But I figure *Centurion* keeps coming back here just to raise hell with us; just trying to prove that nobody, but *nobody*, is going to keep them out of any place they want to go. They're a bunch of pirates. . . . Well, there's a special way to deal with them."

"And somebody ends up in jail," she said skeptically.

"Only if they can name names. Who can prove who ran through their nets with an outboard, if they didn't catch him in the act? Who can prove somebody was firing over their heads? If they can't show bullet holes in a boat, how can they say anyone was trying to sink 'em?"

"Well, I don't blame you for being mad," she said.

"Mad? I'm so sore all the time it's a wonder I don't get ulcers. We could get thousands of bushels of herring without leaving home. Plenty for bait and to sell. But these guys come from somewhere else and we don't have the freedom of our own waters."

"And it's one of those things that's so unfair and so damned hard to fight," said Rosa, "unless you do it your own way."

Suddenly he reached out an arm, pulled her toward him, and kissed her briefly but hard on the mouth. She was more astonished than anything else. "What's that for?" she asked, bracing back.

"For not preaching at me." He was grinning. "For not telling me not to take the law into my own hands. You know, the older generation on here keeps talking about working within the law. Well, they made their own law out here once. They just don't like remembering."

"Or else they think you can't manage as well as they did. They never think we're as smart as they were, and, besides, the wardens take to planes these days, remember."

"At night?" He took her by the shoulders and kissed her again, this time with more obvious enjoyment. He let her go before she had time to object. "That may look like a pass to you," he said, "but, if it is, I didn't plan on it, so I wasn't lying."

"Either you're telling the truth or you've got a damned good line," she said. She got up. "Well, I've seen the moon rise."

He stood up too, and she wondered if he'd follow up the kiss, but he didn't offer to touch her. "I've got to go back for the kids later, around eleven. Come on with me. A moonlight sail around Tenpound is quite a sight."

The habitual negative was already in her mouth, but surprising herself she thought, Why not?

"All right," she said. "Meet you at the wharf at eleven, then. What'll the kids think? They asked me to come, but I said I couldn't stay awake that late."

"Anybody has a right to change their mind, or maybe have insomnia." They both laughed. On the way back to the harbor in the moonlight they talked more, and not just about herring, which for a while she had believed to be the only subject that fired him up. The second kiss had proved something different, and though he would never be an easy or fast talker he was entertaining on his family and local history. They swapped anecdotes about themselves as children, and by the time they reached the harbor beach, and she heard herself laughing out loud, she realized that for a little while she'd been feeling like the old Rosa; Rosa B.C., she thought cynically. Before Con.

Several boats had returned, and Terence Campion was just coming in, the bow wave sparkling in the moonlight. They stood watching, both hypnotized by the sight of a boat in motion. The boat slowed down and moved on spangles toward her home wharf; children's excited voices piped clear of the muted engine. Behind her in the harbor she had left flakes and ripples of light, and each moored boat touched by the wake rocked in quick-dying bursts of radiance.

Tiger recognized his children's voices among those across the harbor, and he began to bark. The Sorensen collie joined in. From out of sight up at the Homestead another dog picked it up.

"Ten o'clock news broadcast," said Rosa. "The place is coming to life. For a little while there was nobody on it but us."

"When I was a kid," Jamie said, "and I'd get mad with everybody, I'd want to tilt the island up on end and slide everybody off. Everybody but the animals, I never got mad with *them*. I'd live here with them like Robinson Crusoe, and keep the Brigporters off with a shotgun."

"Are you still that antisocial? I thought you were, the day I came."

"Don't sound so worried. I'm not going to turn into one of those mad snipers. I know I sound antisocial sometimes, but grousing and growling and cussing is as far as it goes."

"Except for purse-seiners."

"Except *Centurion* and *Triton*," he corrected her. "The rest we can live with." But he was still good-natured, as if the grievance didn't go too deep after all; at least it didn't obsess all his waking hours. "Come on up to the house and have a mug-up with my folks. You'd just get home and have to come out again, anyway."

It was like somebody not being able to refuse to drink, she thought. She should call off the whole thing now, say she'd changed her mind; anybody had a right to, he'd said it himself.

Behind the Sorensen gate the collie whined and moaned in ardent greeting.

"Hello, Rory Mor," she said to him to hide a sudden attack of embarrassment. Jamie was ahead, singing out, "Ahoy the house! Got company!" She lingered outside with the dog, fiery, wondering what they'd think of Jamie fetching her home like this. But the dog wanted to go in too, and the voices were welcoming.

Joanna and Nils made little fuss over her. Their hospitality was obviously a part of themselves, nothing assumed for the occasion. It was pleasantly deflating to realize they were used to setting out extra cups and plates innumerable times a day. They had known her father and the Websters; whatever they knew or had heard about her married life, it was her identity as McKinnon's daughter and Edwin's cousin that influenced their interest in her and what she was doing here.

Jamie was alert but not edgy; he seemed at ease as the son of the house. He was like his father in the shape of his mouth, the curve of nostril, the modeling of eyelids and of the bone around the eye-hollows, the silver-fair eyebrows. But the quick smile taking one by surprise came from his mother's line. Rosa had seen it already in almost every Bennett she'd met, down to Young Mark, in whom it shone all the brighter for coming so seldom.

"All the girls talk about nowadays is your singing and playing," Joanna said to her. "I gather they're going to unveil you at their show."

"Hey, how about a sneak preview?" Jamie said. "I guess I'll come up around there some of these nights."

"I hope they're planning on something else besides me," said Rosa.

"Oh, they ring in everybody they can," Nils said. "Last year they even had somebody playing the spoons. Haker, staying here in the harbor. His partner played the harmonica. Pretty good, too."

"They smelled to high heaven," said Joanna reminiscently. "They'd been sleeping aboard that boat for weeks, and I think they lived on fried hake. But they were happy, and everybody clapped like mad. Somebody even yelled for an encore."

"Which went on for five minutes," said Jamie. "You see, Rosa? Any real talent'll be wasted. They clap for anybody with the guts to get up there in front of them, no matter if he doesn't do anything but recite the alphabet backwards."

"I'd clap for that," said Rosa. "The only way I can do it frontward is to sing it. Can *you* recite it backwards?"

"Now that you mention it, no." He looked at his watch. "Come on.... You want to ride over with us?" he asked his mother.

"If I said yes, what would you do? No, thanks, I've had one moonlight sail tonight, and after *Hull's Victory* and *Lady of the Lake* with thirty couples up, I feel as if I'd been in the Boston marathon."

"You're not admitting to age, are you?" Jamie asked.

"Only to tired feet. After all, when I was a young thing

I used to sit out a few dances now and then, under a spruce tree somewhere." Her husband listened, half-smiling. They both told Rosa to come again. Walking down to the wharf with Jamie she said, inadequately, "They're nice."

"Ayuh, times when I think I did pretty well for myself."

"You didn't want to tip them into the ocean along with everybody else, did you?"

"Sure, when I was mad with 'em. Didn't you ever get that mad with your old man?"

She considered. "I guess so. Yes, and with my mother too. When I was real small."

"Well, I was real small too. When you're little you don't actually want people to die, if you know what death means when you're that age. You just want your own way and everybody out of it. When you get older you try to figure a way around people."

And do you manage as well as Con does? she wondered. She thought not. He was too blunt and too impatient. She imagined him walking away from a capricious girl, saying, The hell with *you*, sister.

But not away from *Centurion*, to hear him talk. He wasn't walking away there. Herring again. "Rory, Rory, get the dory," she sang softly so as not to rouse Tiger, "There's herring in the bay."

"*What?*" said Jamie, and she laughed out loud.

19

The moonlight was so bright they could see the sheep on
Tenpound. The water slid back from the base of the steep
shores in long, polished swells, and she had to admit that
Valkyrie took them almost as well as *Sea Star*. The tide was
high, and they went into Brigport Harbor through the Gut, a
narrow passage between guardian hills of granite. They passed
silent wharves and fishhouses and into the upper harbor, where
there were three times the work boats that Bennett's had, and
a windjammer at rest like a specter from the past. *Valkyrie*
moved almost silently toward the float at the end of a wharf.
When the engine stopped they heard voices and laughter from
a dory rowing among the moorings.

"I told them to be down here at quarter past twelve,"
Jamie said.

"Do you think they'll make it?" She wondered what sort
of evening Vic had had.

"They'd damn well better." He brought out a couple of
buoyant cushions from the cabin and put them on the stern.
"Here, everything's wet with dew. Or do you want to go
ashore and walk around? Up to the lily pond, over to the
sand beach?"

"Right here is all right."

There was a whoop from out in the harbor. "Somebody'll

be overboard next," he said cynically. "What are you thinking about?" He sounded genuinely curious.

"Once when I was a kid I believed what they used to say about the moonlight making you crazy. I guess I believed it for all one summer, and I kept my shades pulled right down, and I wouldn't go out in it without a hat. My folks thought I was crazy already."

He said, "What about Fern Cliff?"

"What about it?" She was mystified. Then she remembered. "Oh. Well, yes," she said diplomatically.

"It didn't mean anything more to you than a mosquito bite, did it?"

"Nicer," she said. "Mosquitoes poison me sometimes." But she was ashamed of joking and not remembering the kiss, painfully aware of male pride, and thoroughly annoyed. After all, she hadn't asked him to kiss her, so why should she feel to blame about it?

"Look, Jamie," she began, gently enough.

"I know, you're still in love with your husband," he said. "Nobody else exists."

"Anyway, I thought that was just supposed to be appreciation or something, like a hearty handshake. And that's how I took it."

"Well, hell, I wouldn't have kissed you if a handshake would have done just as well," he said indignantly. "But it wouldn't for what I had in mind."

"If you kissed me because you thought I was an attractive woman, I'm more than flattered," she said. "I'm honored. And that's the truth."

"But you still don't know there's another man around besides the son-of-a-bitch you're married to. Excuse my language, but that's what he is. I've found out all about him."

And about me, she thought. So I should be grateful for anything, is that it? She felt like someone jolted awake far from home and bed and the safe dark. She shivered involuntarily. Jamie said in a low voice, "I'm sorry. I didn't have any right to say that. . . . Seems as if I'm always apologizing to you about something."

"You'll be sick of the sight of me pretty soon. Don't you wish I'd stayed home in Seal Point?"

"No." He groped for her hand and gave it a violent squeeze. "Look, the guy must have something, for you to feel that way about him. But I'll be damned if I let him scare me off. I'm going to hang in there, Rosa. I'll have my day."

She was shaken because he was, and for something else. "But why *me?*"

"If you don't know, you're probably the most innocent female I ever met. And if you do know, but you're acting, that makes you more like the rest. Either way, you're not shaking me loose. I don't intend to make passes——"

"That's what you said earlier."

"Intentions are one thing. You never know what an occasion is going to call for."

"And you never know what reaction you'll get, either. Is that understood?"

"*Understood.*" He snapped off the word. She laughed and then he did. They were interrupted by what sounded like a stampede of talking horses on the wharf. The herd sorted itself out into the Bennett's Island teen-agers and Brigport companions. The night echoed with incomprehensible merriment and uproarious good-fellowship. "They sound drunk as coots, all of 'em," said Jamie. "Just on lemonade and dancing."

"Don't forget midnight and moonlight," said Rosa. She hoped Vic's evening had turned out to be a spectacular without Jamie. She tried to find her in the milling group. Linnie was easy; her head shone like silver in the moonlight. A lanky boy with long hair and an Indian headband had his arm draped over her shoulders and was talking earnestly to her.

"Hippy!" muttered Jamie. "Come on, come on!" he

called. Young Richard Bennett jumped from the wharf onto the float. "Come on, Holly!" he yelled back at his sister.

It wasn't Holly who came running down the ramp, but Vic. Her eagerly smiling face showed plainly as she crossed the float; she looked slight and graceful in her short dress, a stranger in the moonlight. When she saw Rosa she stopped. Her astonishment was as obvious as a shout. Grace deserted her, suddenly sharpened elbows pressed into her sides, her face became dulled. Rosa wished at once that she hadn't come.

"Don't say it," she said in a loud bantering voice which she hated. "I know I said I couldn't stay awake. . . . Well, I couldn't have spent the evening dancing, I know that much."

The girl said colorlessly, "Sure." Her eyes went to the two cushions on the stern deck. The others came rowdily down the ramp, greeting Jamie variously as Captain Bligh, Cap'n Ahab, and the Flying Dutchman. Linnie came down last, accompanied by the insistent boy with the headband. She seemed both entertained and absorbed by what he was saying.

While the others got aboard, Vic stood on the float fumbling with her raincoat. Her wedge-shaped face had a stony pallor.

Suddenly Linnie saw Rosa. "Oh, *hi*," she said in a penetratingly clear voice. "I see you stayed awake after all."

"Only because I wouldn't let her go home and go to bed," said Jamie. "Come on, get aboard."

"And if you can't get aboard, get a plank!" shouted Richard. An older boy obligingly groaned. Richard, giggling, ran up on the bow and settled himself crosslegged behind the pawl-post.

"You get back down here, Richard Bennett," Holly commanded. When he didn't move she appealed to Jamie, who said, "*Richard*," and cleared his throat. Richard returned to the cockpit. Linnie slipped her arm through Vic's.

"Night, Fritz," she said offhandedly to the boy. "Come on over if you want to. We'll be around. Bring Ken."

She and Vic stayed astern all the way home, facing back over the wake toward Brigport. The rest clustered under the canopy, the boys close to Jamie in purely masculine formation, the girls with arms wrapped around each other for balance and singing appropriate songs. *Moonlight Bay, Santa Lucia, Over the Summer Sea.*—"Come on, Rosa," Betsey urged, "sing with us."

"Got laryngitis." She faked a strained whisper. She was unhappily conscious of the two in the stern. Of course they had it figured for a put-up job; she refusing to go, Jamie refusing to stay. The disappointment for Vic must have been agony, but she had looked forward all evening to the sail home; anything could happen between Brigport harbor and the home gate, especially with Linnie's connivance. Jamie might, all at once, *see* her. She might hit upon the exact thing to say to make him wonder why he hadn't noticed her before.

How well Rosa knew. She'd been through it. And there was nothing she could say to Vic that wouldn't sound patronizing or insulting.

Back in the harbor of Bennett's, she said good night and thanks to Jamie and was the first one up the ladder, well away from the wharf before anyone else. She thought she heard Jamie call "Rosa!" and then whistle, but she kept on going and didn't stop until she reached her kitchen. Then she went quickly up to bed without lighting a lamp.

For a while she lay awake thinking about Vic. Maybe she was putting too much of herself into it because of Con; a new burn can't endure to be near heat. Vic was a realist, she'd known a long time that Jamie wouldn't notice her; she was too young, for one thing. But she was also too young to be a realist for long. At seventeen you hoped for the miracle. At seventeen? At twenty-nine, too. He was always going to change his mind. . . . He was always about to appear in a magic cloud of smoke. . . . He was always going to say, *Dear Heart, it had to be you.*

It's all a big put-on, Vic said. The songs and the stories say this is how it is. So you keep waiting for it to happen.— I know, Vic, she thought, sighing heavily. I know. . . . Tonight seemed so much worse too because it was such a waste. Vic didn't get her dance with Jamie and she'd be forever wondering what that dance might have gained her. Jamie's kiss and his statement of intentions meant nothing to Rosa, not even as a nuisance. She was simply beyond either joy or rage with any man but Con, and for the first time she saw her state as poverty. It had not been that at first; it had been an arrogant contempt for second or third best. She had been proud to believe that, having known Con, she would never again be stirred by another man. . . . Now she thought tiredly it would be nice to feel *something* so you'd know you were still alive.

The house was haunted by moonlight and sliding silver hills of water. She got up finally and pulled down all the shades, and then she could fall asleep.

20

The Bennett girls came, wanting more help with their guitars, and younger children strung along behind them; sometimes even the boys came, but never Linnie and Vic. She saw them sometimes going up the lane, rowing, crossing the island toward Schoolhouse Cove or disappearing past the Eastern End gate. They always seemed to be far away from her, and it irritated her to suspect they were avoiding her on purpose. The minute things went wrong for them, they turned on her. And she'd liked them, Vic especially. . . . Hard, self-centered little cusses. Showed what they were, all right.—She put herself out for the younger children, reinforced by their admiration.

"When do you start getting ready for the show?" she asked Holly, who gestured wild bewilderment. "We don't know! We can't seem to get hold of Linnie and Vic. They're always too busy."

Betsey said angrily, "They're trying to avoid us. They talked it up like mad and now they don't give a darn. Well, I bet Holly and I can do something."

"I bet you can too," said Rosa.

One day when she went down to the harbor the two girls were just rowing ashore, and she went quickly out onto the Sorensen wharf and waited by the ladder.

Vic started up first. When she looked up and saw Rosa leaning against the hoisting mast, she stopped halfway on the ladder the way she had stopped on the float that night, and Rosa felt as if she'd hit a bird or a chipmunk on the highway. Then Vic assumed the climb. As she reached the top, Rosa said bluntly, "I've missed you two."

Vic was not purposely rude, she could not bring herself to it. Her smile was a weak, sickly flutter, worse than a scowl would have been. "We've been busy," she murmured. She called back, "I'm going right home, Lin. I'm so thirsty."

"All right." Linnie came up one-handed, carrying a plastic bucket with cleaned flounder and fishlines in it. She gave Rosa a glassy-bright stare, and brushed past her to attend to the haul-off lines. While she was pulling the skiff out Rosa said, "Look here, is this all because I rode over with your brother that night?" Linnie's chin went visibly out and up, but she didn't look around. "Come on, Linnie, be grown-up and tell me what's biting you two."

"All *right!*" Linnie said passionately. She made a couple of half-hitches around the spiling, yanking hard on the line. Her eyes were brilliant with tears. "You made Edwin go because Jamie told you to. And then you got Jamie when you *knew* how Vic felt about him! You got her to confide in you and everything. And all the time you—I'll bet you laughed about her with him, didn't you?"

"My God," said Rosa quietly. "How wrong can you *be?* I never made Edwin go. He's a grown man—I couldn't make him do anything, and I wouldn't dare try. I was as surprised as anybody. And certainly your brother couldn't ever tell *me* what to do. And I haven't *got* him, whatever that means."

"I don't believe you." Linnie's mouth was trembling.

"Are you calling me a liar?" Rosa asked quietly.

"No—" Linnie stumbled and backtracked. "Only Jamie was making such a fuss about Edwin, and then all at once you and he are real friends——"

"Because he hauled me out of the breakers when my engine stopped one day, that's why. And Vic's name has never been mentioned between us except in normal conversation. I don't know how *you* operate, Linnie, but I don't pass on confidences to somebody else. Now you tell Vic I'm sorry about the night of the Fourth. When Jamie asked me if I wanted to ride over to pick you up, I didn't know I was committing any great sin."

"You and Jamie had a date. That's why he didn't stay to the dance."

"And Vic was counting on it, I know. I'm sorry he didn't stay. But we had no date."

"Well, it doesn't make any difference," Linnie said unsteadily. "You're his age and all, and you're *here.*"

"In other words, if I weren't here Vic would have a chance."

"Yes," Linnie said defiantly. "There's a lot more of

summer. But he's always over in your fishhouse talking, or going up to your house, and he took you out to set his mackerel net, not us. What about Ralph and Marjorie asking you and Jamie to supper the other night, when you and Ralph played jigs and reels all evening, and then you and Jamie took a walk out on the west side?"

"Do you have your own private detectives?" Rosa asked.

"The Percy kids told me. I didn't ask them, I'm no sneak. Anyway, Vic feels just awful and she wants to go away. Our whole summer's ruined." *All because of you* was on her lips, though she didn't say it aloud.

"Linnie, I'm sorry," Rosa said. "Believe me. But I haven't done anything on purpose to hurt Vic. Jamie just talks to me like—like one fisherman to another." It wasn't true, but it might help. She even laughed. "We discuss herring a lot. You don't think there's any hanky-panky going on, do you? With *me*?"

"What's the matter with you?" Linnie asked grudgingly. "I mean, you're thinner now, and you're good-looking——"

"And I'm also a married woman, which means plenty to me even if I'm not living with my husband. Well, tell Vic I enjoyed knowing her. When's she going?"

"Friday, and I am, too. We're going to visit her aunt in Connecticut. She has horses, and it's on the Sound too, lots of yachting and stuff." She glared past Rosa at the blazing harbor. "It ought to be fun." Her tone said nothing could be less fun.

"What about the show?"

"Who cares about that now?" Linnie kept staring at the harbor, apparently trying to will tears back. Having been in the same box herself at times, Rosa walked away up the wharf without saying anything more. At another time in her life it would have been both comic and enjoyable to be considered a dangerously powerful and attractive woman by a couple of lissome teen-agers. Maybe it was comic anyway, but she couldn't stand off and see it that way. It was all bound up with Con somehow, causing her alternate twinges of pain and anger; she could feel *with* Vic and in the next instant or even at the same time resent the fact that a few years from now the girls could look back reminiscently on this summer, laughing and shaking their heads, groaning at their choices. Their lives would go on flowering in spite of this year, but she had experienced her own shattering finish as a woman.

She was out hauling on Friday when the boat came and went. She was relieved; she'd been having to brush the girls off her mind like black flies off her arms.

She had a long letter from Leona Pierce, full of everything that had happened in Seal Point since Rosa left it. At the end she mentioned Con without writing his name. "Nobody sees much of *him* around town. He's still boarding with the Rowlands, but he's hardly ever there. I don't know who he thinks he's fooling . . . *I* think she's sickly. Of course a third of Adam Crowell's estate is quite a lot, maybe it'll be worth getting stuck with an ailing wife. I only hope the baby's healthy. Be a shame if the poor little thing's got allergies or something worse."

Leona meant only to comfort her, but she was surprised at the personal anguish she felt at the thought of the child being defective in some way. She'd seen it for too long as a second Con, springy and indestructible. She couldn't take any satisfaction from the prospect of Con's being burdened with a languid, anemic wife; not if the baby was going to suffer too.

This was when she decided to start repainting the inside of the house. She had finished the outside and until now she had been in no hurry to start on the inside. But suddenly she couldn't endure it, and began scraping the last old paint off the kitchen cupboards; she lay awake thinking of colors, and wrote to Edwin describing the exact shades she wanted, "Something paler than a robin's egg, not too pale, but not too bright either. . . . Yellow more creamy than yoke-yellow but not ivory. . . ." She borrowed the Percys' mail order catalogues to study floor coverings and curtain materials with a febrile attention she'd never before bestowed on household furnishings.

Who knows, she thought, this may turn me into one of those wonderful housekeepers who always keep their stoves wiped off and the teakettle polished. I might even sink to scalloped shelf paper and embroidered bureau scarves.

When she wrote something of the sort to Edwin he wrote back, "Stop dramatizing yourself. It's just the normal nesting instinct." She couldn't think of any answer which he couldn't demolish with a better one. He went on to write in detail about the work on the house, with illustrations in the margins. He did not mention the garden or the woman who was planting it.

In turn she never mentioned Jamie. He'd walked her all over the island on the evenings when he wasn't seining, often dropping in at one house or another until she became fairly casual about that. If they hadn't stopped in somewhere else, sometimes she gave him a cup of coffee and cookies in her own kitchen, but she would never sing for him when they were alone. It was as if it would bring him too close; she had seen the way his eyes changed when she sang at the Percys'.

On the next dark of the moon she saw less of him. Chasing herring at night and hauling traps by day left little time for courting. Some purse-seiners were in the area, but none came close to Bennetts'. When she called across the wharf to Jamie one afternoon that the war seemed to be over, he said curtly, "*Centurion*'s being overhauled. The engine went all to hell. They'll be back."

"They can't be in every place at once. Didn't you ever get herring in the harbor when they were at Bull Cove?"

He aimed a finger at her like a gun. "Don't let me hear

that from *you*. The point is, we don't want any purse-seiners around here *anywhere*. The point also is we might sometimes want to stop off at Bull Cove and the harbor, both the same night—we've got the twine for it—and we've got a right to. Hell, we've got the right to shut off the whole damn island. Moral right if not legal. The others don't come now, just that McGraw bunch and Purvis right behind them, sailing high, wide and handsome down through the lobster gear and cutting off buoys left and right. It's a duel now. And for me there's no such thing as compromise. That means surrender in my book. They'd win, don't you see?" He was at once impatient and disappointed with her.

"But I do see." She understood compromise, all right; someone was always the defeated. She might have saved her dignity but she'd still lost Con. Jamie could tell by her expression that she'd given in, though not why, and he laughed jubilantly. Heads turned toward them from the other wharves, in amused disbelief: "Jamie's caught, by God," someone said loudly.

"I knew I could count on you," Jamie said to Rosa. "*You* know it's personal, don't you? Between them and me?" He leaned his folded arms on a stack of traps and his chin on his wrists and his eyes moved to take in all of the island that he could see, harbor and land. No one else but Rosa knew what he was saying; let them think he was a man bemused by love; and he was, but not the way they thought. "Jamie Bennett came over here from Brigport in 1827. He built a log cabin in the woods at Schooner Head and lived in it till he finished the first part of the Homestead. He paid a hundred dollars for the island, but it was everything he'd saved and could borrow, and it was as big as maybe fifty thousand now ... at least to *him*, earned handlining from a wherry year in, year out, come day, go day, God send Sunday. There's a direct line from him to me, and I'm not about to let *Centurion* catch herring anywhere around this island.

What's in our waters belongs to *us*." He grinned suddenly. "Thought I was going to say *me*, didn't you? Well, I'm not that much of an egomaniac, though there's some who could give you a good argument on that. A few right in my own family."

"Well, cheer up," said Rosa, "My relatives don't think much of my actions, either."

Still leaning on the traps, he was smiling and mellowed. "I'd like to be lying under a tree with you in the woods on the west side," he said. "Where we could see the water so blue between the trunks, but we'd be in the shade, and the tops would be just moving in the little breeze. That would be the only sound. Except maybe for a little wash on the shore."

She said, "Did you ever take time to lie under a tree?"

"Never could see any point to it . . . alone. If I came up to your house some hot afternoon, would you go with me?" He made it sound like a dare or a joke, but he didn't take his eyes from her face, and she felt a prickle of sweat on her forehead under her hair, and on her back. It was the kind of encounter she'd avoided so far by refusing to sing; there was something particularly disturbing about having it happen out in this sunny open, with his father working in the fish-house and a couple of his uncles only two wharves over. She looked away from him, oddly flustered for one who was past even indifference. But what did her answer matter to *her?* If it put him off, or falsely encouraged him, that was his risk, wasn't it. Not hers.

She said finally, "I'd even supply the cold beer."

"The two ding-dongs we had around here would start quoting something about a book of verse and a jug of wine. A guitar and beer sounds better to me."

At that moment Ralph Percy came out on his wharf with his two sons in tow like a dory and skiff behind a beamy, rolling seiner. "Hey," he called over, "when can I make a deal for a hogshead of herring?"

"You'd be safe enough," Jamie said to Rosa. "If I sat still for five minutes I'd fall asleep." He left his wharf to go around the Webster fishhouse and out to Ralph's.

The show petered out with the death of organizational fervor on the part of Betsey and Holly; a yacht carrying six boys and two counselors from a sailing camp down east put in and was fogbound for ten days. The younger children consoled themselves by playing "show" daily in one dooryard or another, with the resident mother supplying drinks and cookies.

Rosa sang for herself nowadays, not often, and no longer on the kitchen floor with her back in a corner, but upstairs in a little room facing out over the woods so that no one on the village side might hear her.

21

She had not consciously forgotten the divorce, but as long as no one mentioned it—and no one did, even in letters, as if they were avoiding the name of cancer or death—it seemed to have no immediacy. It passed through her mind occasionally like a bird flying past her face, but with less substance than a bird had. She had exchanged one world for another, and the exchange could only be valid as long as she refused to recognize the existence of the other.

On a foggy, blowy Monday morning she went early and

eagerly for her mail, expecting an order from Montgomery Ward; new curtains and a large braided cotton rug for the living room floor. Bit by bit the house was becoming a home, rather than a shelter for a fugitive squatter who simply rolled up each night in a sleeping bag.

"Do you like to walk in the fog?" Joanna Sorensen asked her in the store. "Come down to the Eastern End with me this afternoon."

Rosa agreed; after all, Joanna had sent her by Jamie some odd pieces of furniture from the Sorensen attic; a couple of comfortable old rocking chairs which needed only fresh paint, and a small sturdy table that would hold books and a lamp.

Mark spoke her name, and she went to get her packages and one letter. When she saw the list of names austerely printed on the flap of the envelope, she felt the seismic shock of her two worlds colliding.

She walked outside, seeing nothing or no one on the way. Busy with their own mail, the others seemed not to notice a strangeness about her.

"You all right?" Jamie startled her. She hadn't heard him coming through from the shed. "You're feather-white."

"I'm all right." She crushed the envelope in her hand and started to walk away from him. "It's nothing."

"It's something," he said grimly. "What in hell's so bad about that envelope that you're ready to pass out even before you open it?"

"I never passed out in my life." But she had neither the energy nor the inclination to snap at him. "It's from my lawyer. It has to be about the divorce."

"Oh!" At once he was cheerful. "Now you can get it over with. About time, isn't it?"

"I suppose," she said, artificially vague. "I'd better go home and read it." Maybe Con had changed his mind.

"I'll see you later, then," Jamie said, but she heard him as if from a distance, and didn't answer.

Young Mr. Chatham wrote that her divorce was scheduled for next Monday. He requested that she and her witnesses come to see him at two on this Thursday afternoon, if possible. She took aspirin with hot tea and tried to pin her erratic thoughts down to practical considerations. She should haul and double-bait her traps before she left on the mailboat Wednesday; she wouldn't take a chance on going ashore in *Sea Star*, for fear of Con seizing the boat. She would have to get in touch with Jude and Leona the instant she got in, she would have to go over her clothes. And she should make a list of what she wanted to bring back with her. When she thought of returning, the pressure of the squeeze between the two worlds loosened until she could breathe better.

But she couldn't stand the house, and she couldn't go out in this fog and wind to tend to her gear. She went along the dripping path to Barque Cove, remembering how she had come out there her first night and stood in the dark and the fog in total desolation. It came back to her now, as bitter as it had been then. Nothing in between had diluted it to a tolerable mixture.

Jamie found her hunched on the old log at the brow of the beach, her face and hair wet with fog, her sweater misted with it. Water brown and white with rockweed and foam swirled noisily a few yards from her soaking sneakers. Jamie sat down beside her and said severely, "You know it's almost two o'clock? And you never had any dinner, did you? I've been in the house and there weren't any dirty dishes. Look, you wanted this divorce, didn't you? To get rid of the bastard once and for all and start living your own life? So what are you sitting here for, all bunched up like a broody hen?"

"I'm worrying about dressing up for court," she said. "Wearing a girdle, if I have to tell you the indelicate facts to shut you up."

"You don't need a girdle. How many pounds have you dropped since you came out here in June?"

"About eighteen," she said with a faint stir of satisfaction. Such vanity seemed indecent when you were about to attend your own funeral. But you might as well get something out of it... *She looked real handsome. They did a good job on her.*

"Come on," Jamie urged. "Let's get you something to eat and then go down to the Eastern End."

She'd forgotten all about his mother's invitation. I can't, she protested silently. I just can't. "*Let's?* I thought it was a hen party."

"I just decided to go. I may buy some traps from Uncle Steve. Come on." He put an arm around her and gave her a boost. "Or by God I'll stay right here and stare at you all afternoon."

He was capable of it, so she got up. "All right, I'll do it to get rid of you."

When she came downstairs in dry clothes, he had water hot for tea and wanted to fry eggs for her. She refused that and made a peanut butter sandwich.

"You look good," Jamie told her. "The fog makes your hair curl. My mother said today that she considered you a damn good-looking woman."

"Did she say *damn?*"

"Nope."

Joanna didn't know that Rosa was disturbed about anything, which made it easier to hide the fact. At the Eastern End Jamie left the women and went down to the fishhouse where his uncle and his helper Willy were working. The children were in and out of the house with two dogs, and there were a cat and kittens behind the kitchen stove, so there was never any time for Rosa to be ambushed by her own thoughts. By the time the men came up from the shore, and Willy's wife came across the yard from her house, Rosa felt almost peaceful for the first time since the letter had come. She was hungry; her mouth watered for the Scotch scones with honey or home-made jam. She had never tasted such wonderful tea. Deliberately she recollected the escape from the breakers and thought, No matter what, life is best.

After all, the island had done what she had wanted it to do; the divorce was only an interruption. When she came back, she would pick up her new existence on the other side of the interruption.

She felt eyes on her, willing her to look up and around. Jamie's eyes, across the kitchen table, penetrating in their determination to read, to *know*. Con never tried to see that deep; he used his eyes as magic or a weapon. She gave Jamie a small one-sided grimace, almost a wink, and his face smoothed out unconsciously into relief and pleasure.

For the rest of the day she kept a truce with herself. She went to bed before dark, afraid that Jamie would come up and one way or another the fragile armistice would be broken. Sympathy would be deadly at this point.

He did come, and knocked softly. After a moment or two, he went away. She read a spy story that meant nothing to her, tried a Gothic and threw it across the room, blew out the lamp and lay awake. It was a terrible night, with a graveyard hush after the wind dropped. The fog lifted, so she didn't even have the horn at the Rock for company. She went over the whole thing with Phyllis and Con from the first, she composed long, exhausting, pointless conversations with them both, and it was all rather like being lost on a desert and scorched beyond the relief of tears. She didn't fall asleep till nearly daylight, and was awakened around seven by the Percy boys having a fight between the houses.

Her clothes felt damp, she shivered at their clammy touch, but didn't bother to build a fire this morning; she warmed herself by the open gas oven while she drank several cups of coffee. When she went out to haul everybody else had gone, so there was no need to dispense sunny greetings here and there.

Being aboard the boat did nothing for her. The best one could say for the day was that it wasn't windy, rainy, or foggy. But its very calm was enervating, the flattened sea was a sad gray, the wood black against a dead-white sky, and even the rocks looked bleached to an ugly pallor. Rosa was cold as she hauled her traps and baited them, but the chill seemed to come from inside her, and spread numbingly outward into her limbs. Even if the sun had been shining she would have been cold.

She put extra bait on her traps to take them through the next week. Because she was late getting out, she didn't meet anyone or even come within signaling distance as she usually did, and that suited her. Once she saw Jamie well outside Goose Cove Ledge, alongside his friend Matt Fennell. She hoped they'd go seining again tonight, to keep Jamie away.

When she got back to the wharf a lobster smack was tied up beside the car. She recognized her, an old-timer in the bay exotically called *Zuleika*. The skipper had been a friend of her father's, and he was a Birch Harbor man, so he would know all about Con. She swerved toward her own wharf, and then decided that if she got rid of her lobsters now she could go home and burrow in like a woodchuck in her den and perhaps get this rotten freeze out of her belly if she had to drink up Edwin's liquor to do it. She'd found the rest of the Jim Beam under the sink; it gleamed now like a lighthouse in blackest night.

She eased *Sea Star* in to the car, bracing herself to be True McKinnon's robust tomboy daughter. But it wasn't Aldric Thomson with Mark after all. The new captain was a young man with brawny shoulders and a broad fresh-colored face, constantly and lazily smiling. His thick dark sideburns and the hair curling out from under his cap in the back made him look old-fashioned, like a steamboat captain. His deckhand and engineer was a chubby boy with even longer hair, and immense sunglasses in spite of the gray day.

Rosa realized when Mark introduced them that her name meant nothing to either man. The captain showed an indulgent and patronizing interest in her and the boat, and made the usual jokes about Woman's Lib. It was easy enough to take; anything was easy from someone who didn't know about Con. Watching Mark weigh her crate, she heard the engineer say something about taking his wife to the movies that night, and she said to the captain, "Are you going to Limerock from here?"

"Straight as a gull flies. Want to go?"

"Yes," she said, and he laughed with surprise.

"Can you be ready in"—he looked at his watch—"half, three-quarters of an hour?"

"You'd better believe it." She cast off the line that held her to the car.

"Here, don't forget your money!" Mark passed her some bills and the slip across the washboard.

"Somebody must be waiting on the pier for her," said the captain.

"Ayuh, and he's just crazy about me in oilpants," said Rosa. "Really turns him on."

She left them laughing and went across the harbor to her mooring. When she walked up by the Binnacle, Maggie came out. "Come on in and have a mug-up with Kathy and me. We're going to read the tea leaves. We've got to do something desprit on a day like this."

Kathy, Terence Campion's wife, called from inside the screen door, "Come on and get your fortune told, special bargain rates on Tuesdays."

"Gosh, I hate to miss that," Rosa said, "but I'm going in on the smack."

"Oh *boy!*" said Kathy. "If I didn't have kids I'd run off myself, and go to the movies, eat a pizza, and come out on the mailboat tomorrow."

"Have a good time, Rosa," Maggie said, knowing nothing of the divorce.

Rosa washed up at the sink and changed into fresh clothes. She packed a bag, checked the gas stove to be sure everything was off, and took her list from under the sugar bowl on the kitchen table. As *Zuleika* cleared the harbor, with a couple of goodbye toots of the whistle, Rosa remembered that she hadn't locked any doors. It didn't matter; no doors, locked or unlocked, had kept her from losing what she had already lost. Besides, she cared only about her guitar out of all the things in the house, and the island wasn't a thieving light-fingered place.

She could have left a note for Jamie, though. She was ashamed at not having thought of it or of him either. But this all slipped rapidly through her mind like the foam on *Zuleika*'s bow wave, lost forever in the boat's wake. She stood bundled in her loden coat with her back braced against the wheelhouse and watched the steel-blue waves of the mainland hills come inexorably toward her.

At first the skipper turned the wheel over to the engineer, and stayed on deck trying to make conversation with her. She should have been flattered, she thought dryly; but she felt unable to make any sort of response, let alone the kind he expected. She told him she didn't feel well, that was why she was going ashore.

"If you want to lie down, there's bunks up in the *foke* and the blankets are passably clean," he said. He was a good loser, though he must have had so many women ashore that this encounter wouldn't even count as a loss.

"Thanks, but I need the air," she said. "I'm afraid I'll get seasick."

He went back to the wheel, and the engineer came out with a couple of life jackets for her to sit on. She thanked him, he disappeared down the companionway, and then rose again silently holding up a steaming mug. It seemed rude to refuse all their attentions, and maybe if she accepted one they'd leave off. She took the mug of coffee, which was too sweet and had too much milk in it, but she nodded and smiled at the boy, who then vanished for quite some time.

From the wheelhouse behind her she could hear the crackle of voices from the radio transmitter. Now and then the skipper talked with another boat. They all sounded so carefree, with their jokes and quips; she felt envy like a grinding stomachache, and it was no good telling herself that they had their problems. Never mind what anyone else had or didn't have, for her there could be no agony, not even in a physical sense, worse than losing Con.

22

At the lobster company wharf in Limerock the skipper told her he'd be glad to drive her down to Seal Point if she wanted to wait until the lobsters were unloaded. His persistency was a compliment, and briefly she considered the effect on Seal Point's more malicious gossipers if she were seen driving through the village in an Italian sports car. But she was tempted for only a moment, then shook her head.

"I've got to get home just as fast as possible," she said. She remembered she wasn't supposed to be feeling well. "Maybe I can get an appointment this afternoon," she added. He was charmingly sympathetic and called a taxi for her from the office.

In the gray day and the thick dark shade of the maples, her house looked gloomy and cold. One of Leona's boys had been mowing the lawn; this mainland grass seemed almost too rich and thick after the wind-burned turf of the island slopes. The delphiniums were blooming all for themselves, the peonies had gone by. The catbirds were noisy and exuberant all about the place.

Inside, the house felt as chilly as it had looked from the outside, in spite of the thermostat having been left at sixty. She turned it up, wiped a film of dust out of the bathtub, and ran a hot bath. She soaked in it for a long time. Sometimes the telephone rang but it was never her ring, because nobody knew she was here yet. The taxi driver had taken the back way into town, and she had the same expansive sense of invisibility as when she ran away from here in the fog.

By the time she was dried and dressed in pajamas and a winter bathrobe, the chill was off the house. She made a lunch of whatever she could find in the cupboard; cocoa, crackers, a potted meat spread, and canned fruit. After she ate she walked through the rooms. She stood for a long time in the big bedroom upstairs that had been hers and Con's. She remembered the unbelieving joy of those early nights in the marriage, and how she had been positive that nothing could be more perfect. She was still certain that there could never be anything else in her life even remotely like it. That was why so much more than a marriage was finished.

Gazing at the smoothly tucked coverlet handwoven by a great-great-grandmother and the winey dark polish of the pineapples on the posts, she was separated from the past by lack of sleep, the morning's hard work, the long trip on the boat, the bath, and food. She felt herself swaying where she stood. She went downstairs yawning, but the sight of the telephone reminded her of business.

She called Leona, who squawked with happy surprise and commanded her to come at once to supper.

"Thanks, but I've just eaten something and I'm going to bed," Rosa said. "It's been a long day. Look, it's coming up next Monday. Are you still one of my witnesses?"

"Am I! I'd love to tell a whole courtroom what I think of *some people*."

"Simmer down," said Rosa. "It'll be in the judge's chambers." Mr. Chatham had promised her that much privacy.

"Oh, I know I'll only be able to give yes-and-no answers," Leona was saying, "but I'll do it with real conviction."

"We have to see the lawyer Thursday at two. Can you do that? If you can't I'll ask him to change it."

"I can if Scott's dental appointment goes through on time. In fact, I could leave him there. Yes, I can make it." She sounded jubilant. "We'll expect you at supper tomorrow night. Had any corned hake lately?"

"Nope. I'll be there."

She called Jude next and told him. "I'm sorry it'll mean taking time off from your work," she said.

"I'm not," Jude said. "We're just scared foolish you'll back out at the last minute, thinking he might come back if you held on long enough."

"Thanks for your high opinion of my intelligence."

"You mean you don't *want* him back?"

"I mean I don't expect him back."

If Jude caught the difference, he let it pass. "Hold the line a minute, Lucy's wig-wagging." She heard Lucy's clear high voice, and knew what Jude was going to repeat. "Lucy says you come and stay with us. She doesn't think you ought to be alone."

Rosa laughed. "I'm not going to go to pieces down here and hang myself in the barn or something. I've got too much to do. Thank her for me and tell her I'm fine." The prospect of being tiptoed around as if she were a deathbed made her itch.

"Oh, say." Jude was carefully nonchalant. "Edwin won first prize at the museum. For the best portrait, that is. So you and he are kind of famous."

Rosa whooped. "Hooray for Edwin! I ought to send him one of those horseshoes all made of carnations. And imagine *me* as a prize-winning subject."

"You look good in it," Jude reproved her.

"I can hardly wait to see it," she said ironically.

The Pierces had collected her second-class and junk mail at the postoffice several times a week and left it in the back entry. There were two issues of *Down-East Fisherman*, and she took them to read in bed.

She was completely unprepared for the story about Con's new boat. It was like walking into the edge of an open door in the dark. The cruel surprise is everything for a few moments; the outraged astonishment at being tricked. Then she wondered how many people on Bennett's had read this article, but had never mentioned it to her. Jamie must have seen it; there'd been issues in a rack in the Sorensen house.

She read the article with reluctance, yet she couldn't ignore it. There was a good photograph of Con and the builder standing under the lovely sheer of the bow. Con was laughing like a boy. His hair was longer than it had been, maybe Phyllis wanted him to let it grow so she could curl it on her fingers as his aunt had done. He was wearing the Fair Isle sweater Rosa had given him last Christmas.

The author frequently mentioned Con's "infectious high spirits," his buoyancy, and the way he behaved as if an aura of good fortune surrounded both him and his boat.

"Oh, it surrounds him all right," Rosa muttered. "Thanks to various parties who shall be nameless." There was no hint that he'd ever been married, in fact was still married at the time of writing; it was an account of his upward struggles, his progress from boat to boat until he'd finally attained this splendid craft which was almost ready to be launched.

" 'And she's not the end,' Conall Flemming assured me. 'There'll be others. Oh, I'm in love with her all right, I've been in love since I saw her on the drawing board. I'm always in love with boats. I was crazy about my first peapod.' His contagious grin flashed anew, his blue eyes sparkled like the sea that is his life. 'But I'm always looking for the next one. I'm a kind of Don Juan, I guess. Or maybe Casanova.' He laughed at himself, a truly happy man."

177

"I wonder how many people threw up when they got to that part," Rosa said aloud. She read the name of the writer again, to be sure it was a man. "If I was his wife I'd worry about him. He's more taken with Con than with the boat. All he left out was 'roguishly tossing his red curls.'"

The story finished with the line, "When asked for whom the boat was named he smiled mysteriously and shook his head."

Rosa threw the paper across the room, but it fell apart and scattered en route. She was far from sleep now. She heard every car that passed and there seemed to be more than she'd ever remembered, even in midsummer. The telephone was also abnormally busy. After the silence of the island house her ears were too sensitive to the electric pump and the refrigerator's subdued mechanism. Finally she got up and wheeled the television into her room, and from bed she watched an old science-fiction movie that put her to sleep. She woke up later in the midst of a hospital drama, drunkenly turned it off, and fell back into sleep until morning.

She was rested, hungry, and the sun was shining. As if her mind had been busy organizing her while she slept, she awoke full of plans to make the time go rapidly until she could return to the island. She looked out of the window at the harbor beyond the wharf and fishhouse, and remembered the days when she used to think she would die of homesickness if she ever left it. Now she was homesick for the sight of *Sea Star* in the small harbor of Bennett's Island; she wondered if Jamie were out to haul already or if they'd gotten herring last night and were sleeping late. What if *Centurion* came back? The seiner was a powerful obsession with Jamie. Obsessions could be dangerous. She knew.

"Snap out of it!" she said loudly. "Get to work!"

When she tidied her room, and picked up the scattered sections of *Fisherman*, she wouldn't look at Con's picture, but put the whole thing in the box of old newspapers in the back entry. Then she went up to the attic. She was not consciously considering selling the house, but if and when she did everything up here would have to be gone through, sorted, and disposed of.

She worked in this static and yet alive world of the past until the sun began to penetrate the screen of leaves and make itself felt under the roof. When she went downstairs, it was a return to the present and its unlovely sounds. Were there that many outboards in the harbor last summer? she wondered as one cut by the wharf with a piercing whine.

She looked over her clothes. Now she could get comfortably into those she had worn before this year's compulsive stuffing. She picked out a shirtwaist dress in a light, silky raspberry-colored chambray. Her legs looked good once more, and were tanned because of the cut-off dungarees she'd been wearing around the yard at the island, so she didn't need stockings if it was hot, and she remembered Jamie telling her she didn't need a girdle.

"My, what a romantic conversationalist you are, Mr. Sorensen," she said aloud. "And pretty forward, if you ask me."

Sandals, no make-up, a comb through her hair, and she was ready; she recalled with a painful pity the creature stuffed into tight clothes and torturing shoes and trying to make herself brave with inexpert make-up.

She was locking the pickup in the museum parking area when they opened at ten. Before the tourists began coming in to see the permanent Wyeth collection, the galleries echoed with a cool emptiness. The open show occupied the north gallery, and the girl with a guitar faced Rosa as she entered. She walked straight across the wide room to the painting. She had a weird sensation of meeting herself in a dream and of seeing a complete stranger there at the same time.

Edwin had done away with the rocking chair; the girl sat on the slanting bulkhead doors, her back to the clapboards, her head tilted back to rest against them; past the corner of the house the spruce woods were black against a faintly sunset-colored sky. Toward the viewer the hand and wrist were curled loosely around the neck of the guitar, yet conveyed tension in the fingers so Rosa could feel the strings pressing into her fingertips; profile and throat clearly outlined against the dark woods, eyes half-shut, lips parted. A big woman but not a stout one, absorbed in some half-painful, half-pleasant revery, singing to herself.

There was a card beside it identifying it as the first prize-winner in the portrait group. Another card titled it: *Strawberries in the Sea.* By Edwin Webster.

"I wonder what that means," someone said beside her. It was a short woman with blue-gray hair, peering at the type over her glasses.

"I think it's the name of the song she's singing," Rosa said.

"Oh." The woman was frowning and discontented. "I think that picture of the children, with the apple trees, should have got it. It's a lot prettier, all that pink and white, and the blue sky and sunshine. But everything's hippies nowadays. Even in Maine." She went away scowling. Her feet hurt, you could tell by her walk. Hello, you hippy, Rosa said to the painting.

More people were coming in now, and she left, feeling as if she'd gotten out of the frame and were walking invisibly away. It was being in a fairy tale, and presently she would meet a come-to-life scarecrow who would turn out to be a prince. Only for me it would be the other way around, she thought. I'd better not take any chances, or I'll end up with a bunch of old cornstalks dressed in overalls.

She drove to the supermarket at the north end of Limerock and bought enough food to take her through the time she'd be spending on the mainland. She still shrank from shopping at Seal Point; she couldn't forget all the times she'd gone into the store or post office when the rest of the people standing around had known about Con and Phyllis, and she hadn't. They must have started talking about it the instant the door closed behind her.

She drove back to Seal Point and spent the afternoon going through the contents of the fishhouse. She had supper at the Pierces', and went early to bed.

The next afternoon Mr. Chatham commented with pleased surprise on her appearance. "Almost anything would be an improvement over the last time," she told him. He was young enough to blush slightly and stumble over his protests.

"No, but you look great! I mean, uh—well, that place must agree with you."

"She's a darn sight handsomer than what he swapped her for," said Leona. "You see her portrait in the museum? *His* son painted it." She nodded at Jude, who smiled modestly.

"Really? *Your* son?—And you're the girl with the guitar?" he asked Rosa. "Of course! I can see it now! Tell me what the title means."

"It's a song," she said briefly. "That's all."

"She made up the tune," said Jude. "She makes up plenty of music."

"I'm beginning to think this is a mighty talented family," said the lawyer.

"Oh, they *are*," Leona assured him. "And it's my opinion that Con Fleming just couldn't stand it——"

"Mr. Chatham's got something he wants to talk to us about," Rosa said.

After he was through with the others she asked for a moment alone with him. "I'm not taking any money," she said. "I wouldn't take any before and I don't want any now."

"It's your right. I told you that before. You've helped him, set him up; this new boat is no small item."

"He was my husband, and I did it because I wanted to. What happened then is over, so I want to cut everything off. I can support myself, and he'll have a family. The only thing is, I want the other boat, *Sea Star*, made over to me."

Mr. Chatham seemed pleased by this evidence of self-interest. He made a note. "I'll call his lawyer right away." He walked into the outer room with her, where Jude sat reading, Leona having gone to pick up her son.

The lawyer shook hands with them both. "Enjoy your weekend and don't worry about Monday," he told Rosa.

"I have no intention of worrying," she said with deceptive placidity. She was afraid of Monday, or rather afraid of herself on Monday, of what unexpected action she might take at the moment when the divorce was granted; it would be like hearing a death sentence, or seeing an execution when a shout of protest or despair is wrenched from the watcher in spite of all controls.

"Good girl, that's fine." He was patting her on the shoulder. As young as herself, he managed to behave like a kind uncle. The other time must have been as rough on him as it was on her, and she almost told him so, but decided to leave the thing decently buried.

The instant they were outside the door Jude said, "Come on over and look at Edwin's picture."

He was so eager that she pretended she hadn't already seen it. She put her arm through his. "I'm dying to."

"Lucy's been in to see it about everyday, and I'm almost as bad," Jude said, as they turned off Main Street onto a quieter sidewalk. "When I think of him running around wild as a bobcat kitten, and then I see something like this ... Well, of course we've known for a long time that Edwin was all right. Better than all right, really. I mean, the boy's smart. He's *gifted*." Jude stopped and took off his glasses to wipe them. "Darn heat, steams 'em all up." But she saw his wet eyes before he put his glasses back on. "When you remember him way back then, and you walk into that million-dollar museum and see a painting signed Edwin Webster—well—even without winning a prize it's something great—" Jude ran out of words, but only until they were standing in front of the painting. She'd never heard him talk so fast, he was like a boy in his excitement. She was glad she'd come earlier by herself; now she could answer him, say *yes, yes* to everything he pointed out, smile or marvel with him, touch his arm in sympathy when he had to wipe his glasses again.

Yesterday she had been in some queer way disturbed by her image, and had had that sensation of escaping from the frame as if through a door left open by mistake. Today she saw the portrait differently. It was like, yet not like; a separate being with a separate life. All her worries, shames, and humiliations retained their inviolable privacy because the one who suffered them didn't exist for anyone else; the rest saw only what their own eyes let them see, a surface Rosa, a paper doll. Even Edwin saw her simply as a good model and a cousin whom he liked or even loved. Beyond that he could not go, any more than she could go past his façade.

No, what you have is your own, she thought. Good or bad. And if it isn't written on your face, nobody knows about it.

Jude was saying something. He seemed pleased that she'd been so absorbed by the picture that she hadn't heard him. "I said Edwin's only been in to see how they hung it, and never since, except when they gave him the check. He says he's too busy putting the finishing touches on the house."

"Are they happy with it? The people, I mean."

"Lucy and I drove around there one day, and the woman happened to be there. They've moved in by now, I guess. . . . She praised him to the skies, says he's a genius." Jude tried to deprecate, but one side of his mouth kept trying to curl. "She didn't know about this." He motioned to the picture. "So of course Lucy had to tell her all about it, and she said she'd come to see it." He gave up hiding his smile. "Edwin's funny. He never came near the whole time, he acted as if he didn't know us. He didn't need to stand over the painters *that* close. . . . She wanted to give us cold drinks, tea, or whatever, she couldn't have been nicer, but I figured Edwin would be a lot happier if we left. Not ashamed of us or anything," he explained, "but I think it was all this gushing, you might call it, going on between his mother and Mrs. Parnell."

"Probably," Rosa agreed vaguely.

23

She turned down an invitation to supper at the Websters', saying she wanted to get back to cleaning. This time she spent the rest of the afternoon out in the barn, trying to decide about one thing and another. She didn't accomplish much, but at least she was out of reach of the telephone, and could hardly hear car or boat engines. This saved her from anticipating Con's arrival either by land or water. She knew it was unlikely, but she would be looking for him just the same.

In the morning she went back to the attic, then to the fishhouse in the afternoon. Thus she used up the time, which on the island hadn't needed to be used up; it devoured itself. Sometimes the telephone caught her, other old friends besides Leona invited her to a meal, but she always had a good excuse and managed to sound so blithely busy that nobody could suspect her of hiding away. The truth was, she shrank from hearing talk of Con, and somebody would want to tell her, as Leona did each time they talked, how foolish Con was, how bad Phyllis looked, how everyone had laughed when Rosa took the boat, and how the men had plagued Con about it at the shore until he walked away in a rage.

They would tell her these things to comfort her and assure her of their loyalty; and she could not explain to them that it was no comfort at all, it only made her sorry for him and ashamed of her own vindictiveness.

Leona, being just next door, could trail her to attic, barn loft, or fishhouse, but she couldn't stay for long at a time. Usually a child came looking for her, or she had to transport five or six to a picnic. Once when she started in on Con with the usual gusto, Rosa said patiently, "Listen, Leona, I don't hate Con. I want things to work out for him, otherwise it's such a god-awful waste, what we've all been through, don't you see? It won't make me a bit happier if he has a hard time."

"It would make me real happy," said Leona. "But you're good-hearted, Rosa."

"And don't call me good-hearted. That's what they always say about a whore. Heart of gold. Because she can't say no to anybody, and that's why she's a whore."

"And because she likes it," said Leona. "At least anyone that *I* ever knew liked it, in spite of all this high-flown talk about loving their fathers too much or hating them, I can't remember which."

"How many have you known?" Rosa asked with interest. "Besides the amateurs we all know, right here in town?"

"Let me tell you, Maida Peal's no amateur!" They were off on a spirited conversation which took them far from Con.

Saturday morning she slept late because the morning was dark and rainy. She went to work in the attic again, and the water beat on the roof and splashed and gurgled in gutters and drain pipes, bounced off the glittering green leaves of the maples into which the attic windows looked. Going through old letters and photographs took her well into the afternoon, when she went downstairs to eat. Then she lay on her bed for a while, reading a book she'd brought from the attic. When she had finished it, she began looking over her clothes to decide what she would wear to court. She was pleased with the way she was managing; it wasn't going to be bad after all. To think she'd hunched desolately on that log in Barque Cove, when it was as simple as this.

The telephone rang. That would be Leona, hoping to take her by surprise. *The beans are ready to come out of the oven, and I'll bet you haven't had a blueberry pie yet this year.* She dropped a dress on the bed and ran to the kitchen and picked up the telephone.

"You don't have to tell me," she said. "I've been reading your mind. Do you have brown bread or johnny cake?"

There was a silence at the other end. She laughed. "Hey, did I stun you with that?"

"Rosie," said Con. "You sound like a million dollars! God, it's wonderful to hear you laugh again."

She stood like a statue, wanting to hang up yet unable to make her hand and arm obey.

"Look, can I come over and talk to you?" Con asked. "I'd like to apologize for the way I acted out there, and—oh hell, I'm not going to say it over the telephone. . . . Well?"

"I'm sorry," she said formally. "You must have the wrong number." She hung up, and still stood there, listening to his voice in her ears. After a moment the telephone rang again. She didn't touch it, but watched it with a mild wariness, as if it were a dog she didn't quite trust though it was behind a fence. It kept on ringing and finally she lifted it gently off the hook and laid it on the counter. She went back to her room and started to paw over the dresses strewn on the bed, but she didn't see what she touched. She found herself squeezing a sweater as if she were trying to kill it, and she flung it from her and squeezed her fingers together instead, fingers locked and aching with the pressure.

Little sounds rose in her throat but she tried to keep them down, knowing that to hear her own whimpers would be degrading. Almost as bad as hearing his voice; no, what was worst of all was that she wanted him to come. After everything, she wanted to see him come in the door, she would take any crumb of him that she could get.

She knew what he still wanted of her. "You could cut a man's throat, Conall Fleming," she said to him now, "and then say to him, 'No hard feelings? Promise me there's no hard feelings.' And hate him for being too busy bleeding to death to forgive you."

Raymie Pierce, Leona's oldest, took the turn into the driveway with a smoking screech of rubber, and bounded into the house with a speed that should have scorched his sneakers. "Marm says the beans are ready to come out of the oven, so come on."

"And she's got blueberry pie," said Rosa.

"How'd you know? She's been trying to get you on the telephone." He pointed. "You know you're off the hook?"

"Just how do you mean that, Raymie?" Rosa asked, re-placing the telephone. Raymie guffawed.

"That's pretty good! You will be off the hook, won't you?"

"Everybody will be. Wait till I get something on my feet."

She went to her room and he shouted after her, "Rosie, want to try my electric guitar? I just got it today. I've been all summer earning it." He went into an unintelligible list of components, which required no answer from her. When she returned to the kitchen he hadn't stopped talking. His bony young face radiated generous pleasure. "I thought of you right off, Rosie. You've never played an electric guitar, so here's your chance."

She'd never wanted to; she hated electric guitars. She said, "I'd love it, Raymie, if we can keep the sound down. Us old folks have mighty delicate ears." Hers still held the echoes of a voice. An evening in a house full of boys, dogs, drums, and an electric guitar might just possibly kill the echoes.

"Who's old?" Raymie was saying gallantly, holding the door of his 1950 Dodge for her. "When I get going to the Grange Hall dances I'll take you any time." He was very earnest about it. His Adam's apple move up and down.

"Thank you, Raymie," she said.

187

Leona and one of the dogs walked home with her toward midnight. Behind them a Pierce Saturday night was still going strong. It was audible even when the thick warm fog that had followed the rain blotted out the last trace of the lighted windows.

"My head's squeezing in and out like an accordion," said Leona, "but they'll all be grown up and out of the house too soon as it is. In a year or so we'll have to let Raymie go to the Saturday night dances."

"But you'll still have five at home, and by the time the youngest leaves the nest you'll be baby-sitting with Raymie's kids, Grammie."

"Not *this* Grammie, or Grampie either. We're planning to take in some dances ourselves." She sounded not complacent but comfortable. Rosa didn't envy her; it wasn't comfort she wanted at her age, at least not that sort. What she envied was Leona's bone-knowledge that she and Everett had always been in love. Having to get married at sixteen was exactly what they had wanted.

She had left the house locked in case Con took it upon himself to come in and wait for her. If he did, what would he tell Phyllis afterward? Was he already lying to her? No, he might really love her and the unborn child, and be tender with her when she felt sick. If he didn't tell her he wanted to talk with Rosa, it would be only to spare her feelings, if she felt ugly with her pregnancy, and oversensitive.

He wasn't in the driveway, of course. When she was still awake after one, she knew she was waiting for him to call again. She adjusted the bell to its softest and draped the whole instrument in a heavy blanket, then shut her bedroom door and watched the Late Late Movie.

One advantage of a thickly shrouded telephone was that it didn't wake her at four or so when someone called a friend to tell him it was a fine day to go deep-sea fishing. When she did rouse herself, a bediamonded world flashed and sparkled in sunlight, and an unharmonious chorus of engines almost drowned out the birds. There was no Sunday lobstering in summer, but the pleasure boats were starting out early, outboards speeding among the moorings taking a chance on not being identified by the harbormaster, deep-throated cabin cruisers warming up, sailing craft chugging out of the harbor under auxiliary power.

She had nothing overboard that she could row, and she didn't want to; she was homesick for Bennett's Island on such a fine morning, she wished it had kept on raining or stayed foggy. She was deeply depressed, dreading tomorrow. And what was the matter with Edwin that he hadn't gotten in touch with her? Never mind if she hadn't been to Jude's yet; if Edwin was such a good friend you'd think he'd be around to give her some moral support.

She worked up such a good head of indignation that when he walked in to the kitchen she gave him a hostile stare and almost said, "And *another* thing—"

He looked as if he knew it and was trying not to laugh. He leaned over her where she sat at the table, tilted up her face, and kissed her. Then he felt the coffee pot, got a mug from the cupboard and filled it, and sat down across from her.

"Good morning, Dapper Dan," she said, trying to hold onto her rotten mood. He lifted the mug as if in a toast, and drank. "I've been twice to see the painting," she said stiffly. "I like it."

He pulled out his note pad and wrote, "There must be something wrong with it then. People always hate their portraits."

"I didn't think it was supposed to be a portrait of me. It's a girl and a guitar, and spruces, and sunset."

He nodded approvingly and wrote, "Arrangement in opposing forms, tones, and textures. What are you doing today besides gaining back all the weight you've lost? Go get dressed."

189

"Why?" She sat defiantly heavier in her chair.

"I'm going to show you the house, and then we'll eat somewhere where they won't allow dungarees."

She was pleased but gave in slowly, with a sulky jerk of her shoulders. "I'll have to work at it to compete with you. Who chose that outfit for you? You must be dressing like an artist these days instead of a Yankee carpenter."

He really laughed this time.

He had a car new to him, a late-model Mercedes. Rosa admired it with restraint; if she'd gushed, Edwin would have either suspected her or made her feel foolish. She hadn't considered his job in terms of money, but now she realized that his fee must have been considerable. No wonder the Websters had a hard time believing in this Edwin when the other one had been both wound and terror for so long.

The restored house was in the hills behind Limerock. The roadside boundary was marked by a low stone wall along which the first black-eyed susans, goldenrod, and asters of the season bloomed lavishly. The house lay about two hundred yards in from the black road, settled among young trees and judiciously pruned old ones which must have been there almost as long as the building itself. From the back of the house the Fremont Mountains seemed very close in the morning sunlight. The lake below the steep and wooded hillsides was deep blue, and in the hush they could hear the fragile yodeling of loons. From the front of the house, Penobscot Bay filled half the visible world and the rest was sky.

The barn had been turned into a garage, with an apartment upstairs for the caretaker. He came to meet them, holding a German shepherd by the collar. At sight of Edwin, the dog's tail began to beat in a wide, wild arc, and the man let him go. Rosa held out a clenched fist and was given perfunctory but polite acceptance; Edwin was obviously a great friend.

The caretaker was a stout elderly man with a ruddy face

and thick white hair. He introduced himself and the dog to
Rosa.

"Your cousin's a master of his craft," he said reverently.
"A real master. Somebody ought to write him up. Maybe they
will when he finishes the Dudley place."

"Where's that?" Rosa asked. Edwin and the dog were
walking toward the side gate of the walled garden.

"You never heard of it?" Foster was delighted to tell her.
"Magnificent old place it was once, out behind Fremont. The
Dudleys owned all of Fremont once, before it *was* Fremont.
Right down to the harbor and their own shipyard.... The
new people paid a fortune for it. Friends of these folks." He
jerked his round head at the house. "Saw what Ed's done,
hired him on the spot."

"I didn't know," said Rosa. "He's too modest."

"All the great ones are," he said with a wink and a nod.
"Look, while you're here, I'm going to run down to the village and get my Sunday paper." He took out a key ring and
handed it to her. "I won't be long. There's lots to see, make
him show it all. The Parnells are in Massachusetts for the
weekend. Not that they'd mind," he assured her eagerly.
"Stay, Bruno," he called to the dog, who showed no intention of leaving Edwin.

There was a bicycle leaning against the side of the barn,
and with astonishing lightness Foster mounted it and rode off
around the house, ringing his bell. The sight of the merry old
man riding jauntily away to the spritely jangle unsealed an
unexpected spring of happiness in Rosa.

She went to Edwin waving the keys. "Dick Foster says
you should show me everything," she said. He opened the
gate and waved her into the garden.

They were just entering the house by the garden door
when Bruno began to bristle and growl; he shot in ahead of
them and down the shadowy hall that led past the staircase
through to the front door. "Bruno," a woman said. The dog

came to a skidding stop, rumpling up a rug, then went forward wagging his tail as the woman shut the screen door behind her.

"Well, hello!" the woman called to Edwin and Rosa; she sounded about to break into laughter. She was a tall, almost attenuated figure in narrow-legged slacks.

"Hello," Rosa responded unevenly. She felt like a trespasser or worse. As her eyes adjusted to the shade after the brilliance outside, and the woman came toward them, Rosa wondered whether she should explain or leave it to Edwin. She turned to him for help. Even allowing for the subdued light his color was bloodless, and his eyes were fixed on the woman with the cold amber gaze of the dog before he had recognized Edwin.

In spite of her passionate desire to be elsewhere, Rosa could still be intrigued by Edwin's reaction to the meeting. Yet she had a curious impulse to protect him. She walked forward, trying not to sound out of breath as she said, "I'm Rosa Fleming. Edwin brought me to see the house."

"I'm Laura Parnell." Still sounding amused the woman put out her hand. She had a good grip. Her eyes looked quizzically into Rosa's. They were a pale blue, with a curious dark rim to the iris. Rosa felt their question so strongly that she started to say *I'm Edwin's cousin*, but Edwin had come up noiselessly behind her, and took her arm; the pressure of his fingers inside her elbow hurt enough to startle her into silence.

"Good morning, Edwin!" Mrs. Parnell said. "Well, Miss Fleming, what do you think of it?"

"I haven't seen the house yet, but your garden is beautiful."

"It is, rather." She seemed pleased. "See here, this is my plan." She led Rosa down the hall toward a framed drawing on the wall, talking vivaciously. She was not as tall as she had seemed at first, but the fine, long bones were as Edwin had drawn them. Her skin was coarser than Rosa's and expert make-up couldn't hide that or the lines at the corners of her eyes and mouth. She was forty anyway, Rosa guessed, but she guessed also that it made no difference. Bemused by the voice, the manner, and by a delicate and probably expensive fragrance, Rosa studied without really seeing the plan of the garden of Martin Dunton, Esquire, in Ipswich in 1790. She felt caught in a tide-rip between the other two.

"We planned to be gone until tomorrow," Mrs. Parnell was saying. "But it was simply awful at my sister's. Visiting grandchildren not quite by the dozen, but it felt that way. So Bill and I got up at five this morning and folded our tents like the Arabs and silently stole away." She laughed. "Bill dropped me off at the gate and went on to the village to get his papers."

"So's Dick," Rosa said. "He went off on his bike, ringing his bell." It sounded to her like the proud statement of an eight-year-old wanting to converse with an adult.

"Dick's younger than I ever was," Mrs. Parnell said. "I'd love to ride a bike, but I always skin my elbows."

Edwin's fingers signaled Rosa. She said, "It's nice of you not to call us trespassers, Mrs. Parnell. We'll go along now."

"But you haven't seen the house yet! You haven't seen Edwin's beautiful corner cupboard, or his mouldings or mantels, or anything!" She sounded actually disappointed. "Let's have drinks, or coffee, or whatever you'd like—" She was talking to Edwin. Ignored, Rosa looked around at him, nervously, and was glad to see that now he looked perfectly composed as he shook his head.

"The immovable and inscrutable Edwin," said Mrs. Parnell. "Bill will be sorry to miss you. But if you must, you must." She shrugged them off, airily turning away; angry at the failure of her charm, her fragrance, her hand on his arm.

"Goodbye," Rosa said to her.

"Goodbye," she answered coldly. She was already on her way out the garden door. Edwin and Rosa went out the front way. At the car, Edwin made a signal to Bruno, who went back and sat on the wide brick doorstep.

On the way to the gate they met Dick cycling back, his

broad face smiling at the world, the breeze lifting his white hair. Edwin stopped the car and Rosa told him that the Parnells had come back.

"I saw him at the village," he said. "Showing some sense, I told him. Why anyone'd want to leave this place, I said to him . . . Well, it was nice meeting you, Miss. Tell Edwin to bring you around again and I'll give you a drink. You bring her again, Edwin," he ordered. "I'm glad to see you out with a good-looking girl."

Edwin glanced around at Rosa with his most pawky look, as if he hadn't really noticed her before, and nodded as if to say, *Oh, she's not bad.* Dick and Rosa laughed.

They drove for a long time in silence, up through Fremont and then off the main road onto the winding, narrow ones where houses were few and far between. The countryside simmered with August, giving off a moist, aromatic bouquet of earth and leaves. Edwin pulled off the road finally at a shady turn-around above a small lake. Across it there were two tents under the spruces, and a canoe pulled up on a scrap of sandy beach. A mountain of rock rose up behind the campsite, trees clinging to every crevice in the granite.

Edwin took out his notepad and gave her the choice of three places to eat. "Wait till I've been out behind a bush first," Rosa said. When she came back to the car he was standing beside it, hands in his pockets, watching the lake below. She took the pad and wrote, "Let's go to the least fancy place."

He nodded. She wrote again. "Did you have anything to do with her?"

His eyes widened slightly and lifted to hers. She held her ground, waiting for an icy put-down. Instead he wrote, straight-faced, "She wondered if deaf men did it differently."

"No!" Rosa said sharply.

"Couldn't have been any other reason."

"The reason could be that you're an attractive man within taking distance. So she took."

194

"So what does that make me?" His expression was sardonic. "A fool or a stud? No, she didn't *take*. I never went to bed with her. I wanted to."

"Why didn't you?" she wrote. "And call it an adventure? Men do it all the time, women too."

He seized the pad from her and wrote fast, bearing down hard. "Pride. Pure cussedness. Knowing she wanted to satisfy her curiosity. I'm a freak, so she expected me to be so damn grateful. . . . Lady Bountiful bringing a moment of beauty into my poor life. I'd never be able to forget it."

"Maybe it would have turned out to be the other way around. She might have been grateful, and never able to forget."

He grinned suddenly. "Well, we'll never know, will we?"

"She's still interested. I saw her look at you. And she was wondering who I was. I was flattered, but I could see it going through her head, *How can he prefer this horse to me?*"

He wrote across her words in big letters, "End of subject!" Then he opened the car door and motioned her in.

24

After all her fears, she felt nothing at all in court. It was over quickly. Outside the judge's chambers Mr. Chatham shook hands all around and went down the corridor with some other lawyers. Jude, Leona, and Rosa walked out into the morning. There was still a wet coolness in the shade, and the robins were singing in the courthouse elms. In the parking lot Lucy sat in Jude's car, knitting.

"There!" she said when she saw Rosa. She kissed her and said, "You look better already."

"Oh, she'll be fine now," Jude said, patting Rosa's shoulder.

"Yes, she can put it all behind her and forget that critter ever lived," said Leona. "What are you going to do to celebrate, Rosa?"

Everything that she had feared would happen back in the courthouse was threatening now. She saw the wave rearing up over her, about to drown her in a freezing smother of foam. She kept her slight, polite smile in place. "Well, if you don't have anything else to do uptown, Leona, I'd like to go home and shuck off my pantyhose. They're some hot."

Everybody laughed heartily, looking at her with admiration as if she were being incredibly gallant.

Rosa took Jude's hand in both hers and squeezed it. "Thanks for helping out, Jude."

"It was a pleasure," he said fervently.

"It certainly *was*," Leona said. "I'd just like to have said plenty more, that's all. And you letting him off without alimony, except that ten a week they insisted on. You won't even bother to collect that. *I'd* have skun him alive."

"I believe you would," said Rosa. "Everett better watch out."

"What do you suppose has kept him walking Spanish all these years?"

"Oh, come on before I melt," said Rosa. They said goodbye to the Websters and walked to Leona's car.

"I suppose he'll be rushing Phyllis to the preacher this afternoon," Leona said. "Roll down your window, it's hot in here. . . . No, he can't get married today, unless they do it at noon or so."

Will you stop talking about him? Rosa bit the inside of her lower lip to keep the words in.

196

"Because they're launching the boat today," Leona finished. On the last word she gasped, and there was instantly a clanging silence in the car. At least it seemed to clang horribly in Rosa's ears. She looked at Leona who, in the act of starting the car, had apparently been turned to salt. Staring through the windshield, fingers still on the key, she muttered, "I wasn't going to mention it. I could cut my throat."

"If you'll just drive back to Seal Point, that'll be sufficient," said Rosa.

"Tell me you knew it already and I'll feel better."

"No, I didn't know it, but I'm not surprised because she should be ready to launch by now. And if Phyllis is going to christen her, I sh'd think they would get married first, otherwise a very pregnant girlfriend is going to shock the pants off half the audience," said Rosa. "Stop looking as if you've been hit by gut cramps, or do you want me to drive?"

Leona straightened up with a long sigh, and started the car. "That's right, she's showing it awful. Maybe it's twins."

"Look, let's go back to where we left the courthouse and start in new. Talk about anything. Your kids, for instance."

"All right," Leona said. "Anything to redeem myself." She did well. All the way home her words made an opaque screen behind which Rosa was alone with herself. She made comments or explanations at the proper intervals, and was mildly surprised at her virtuosity in hearing what Leona said while she was watching in ruthless detail the christening and the launching of the boat.

At Seal Point she thanked Leona for helping her out, refused lunch, and went into the house still obsessed with the launching. For the first few months, the boat had been *Rosa Fleming*. But for how much of that time had she been secretly *Phyllis* to Con? The acute hurt of this had deadened somewhat with time, but she could remember it perfectly as she walked through the silent house, without self-pity but as if the revelation had been some terrible phenomenon of nature.

As the day moved on, she had the increasing sensation of being dismissed from life. But because she was still breathing and walking around instead of lying down dead, she had been obliged to attend to these legal technicalities so that the others could get on with their lives. Otherwise she didn't exist for them. She could have made them recognize her existence if she'd refused the divorce; they'd have called her wicked and spiteful, but they'd have known she was still around, all right. She could have asked for enough alimony to make Con feel the pinch. Back when he first told her about Phyllis, she could have done something about stopping funds for the new boat. But she hadn't.

So she had condemned herself to death as far as they were concerned. She had cooperated in causing her own nonexistence. But the weirdly comic thing was the way people kept telling her that the divorce would cut Con away from her like the core of a boil and she would be healed and begin to live.

With what? she asked. No. The best I can hope for is that it will stop hurting. Like when you die.

The tide was high at approximately four-ten this afternoon. Phyllis would break a bottle of champagne over *Phyllis*'s bow, and Con would stand with his arm around his wife and possibly a son (or two) and watch his boat slide down the ways. . . . Rosa looked up the number of the Limerock Airfield and asked what the chances were for a flight out to Bennett's Island around three this afternoon.

"Good, because I'm going out anyway to pick up a party on Brigport," the owner told her. "I'll have to land you there because there's no airstrip on Bennett's."

"I know that, and I'll find a way to get home."

She called Lucy and then Leona, telling them both that she had a chance to fly out this afternoon, and that she'd write. Leona began frantically juggling her schedule so she could drive Rosa to the airport, but Rosa stopped that by saying she'd already called a Limerock taxi. This wasn't strictly true, but at least she had the number written down.

At the small airfield, the little bright-colored planes were tethered in a semicircle, like butterflies on leashes. Over the Airport Lunch the wind sock stood straight out in the afternoon wind from the southwest. Rosa had never flown before; she had always suspected that the plane would develop a freak engine failure the instant she was a passenger, even if it had been completely overhauled just the day before. Something would have been left out, something would have reached its fracture point, or threads would have worn down to the fatal smoothness; the plane would suddenly plummet into the bay with only an oil slick to mark the end of Rosa Fleming.

But today fear was cast out by the necessity to get away. The pilot was chatty, and from up here the choppy water looked merely crinkled. In fifteen minutes, just about the time she had decided she was enjoying it, they touched down on the Brigport airstrip, a field that had once been pasture. There were no houses in sight, nothing but woods on three sides, and then the sea glittering to the horizon. While the pilot, still talking, was taking out her bags, an elderly Buick came lurching along a dirt road out of the woods, carrying the passengers for the return trip.

Rosa rode to the harbor with the boy who had driven his mother and sister to the plane. He was laconic but friendly. When he found that no one was meeting her, he offered to take her across to Bennett's. He had a big dory with a twenty-five-horse motor; another boy and two girls came too, the boy in jeans and rubber boots, the girls with long trailing hair, shorts, bare feet. They reminded her of Vic and Linnie, who seemed to have been removed from her by years, not weeks.

Centurion was anchored in the harbor with the seine boat and dories tailing astern. There was no one visible aboard; seiners slept whenever they could. Rosa wondered without any real curiosity if there'd been a confrontation yet. The

199

sight of the purse-seiner had recalled Jamie to her for almost the first time since she'd left the island last week. Con had obsessed her completely.

No more, Con, she promised him. No more. You've had enough of me. But she glanced at her watch. Almost tip-top high water.... The big dory left the moorings behind, the engine roaring, and they went out through the Gut and into the southwest chop. The dory smashed across it in bursting clouds of spray. Rosa, in the bow, was dry, but the girls shrieked and laughed as they were drenched, and the boys' faces streamed water. As the seas deepened in the full sweep from the southwest up between the islands the dory lurched, rose, dropped as if she'd never stop the downward plunge. The girls in their soaked and clinging clothes held tight to the gunnels, a little scared behind their screams of laughter.

At the moment when *Phyllis* slid down the ways, Rosa was hoping the dory's caulking would hold. This was followed by relief when they entered the harbor, and then she realized that the boat had been launched by now. She experienced a different sort of relief; a letting-go, a surrender at last.

They tied up at the lobster car. "Come on up to the house and I'll give you something hot," Rosa offered, but the girls, smoothing back their long wet hair like mermaids, said they weren't cold and their clothes were drip-dry. She thanked the boy, who refused pay but allowed her to buy soda all around. It was a quiet time at the wharf, most of the children had gone to Schoolhouse Cove. Mark Bennett wasn't around either, and his blond, quiet wife was tending store, sitting outside on the bench reading between customers. She said to Rosa, "You didn't come all the way from Limerock in that dory, I hope."

"Believe me, it felt like it, out there in the middle," Rosa said, and they both laughed. She bought a bottle of milk and a loaf of dark bread and walked home. No one was around the Percy house; Marjorie would be overseeing her children at the beach. Just as Rosa turned into her own dooryard the first boat came home, and the harbor began its gradual awakening to the life that always seemed suspended in sleep when the men were out and the children not visible.

With a catch of guilt she remembered not even glancing toward *Sea Star*. She ran upstairs and looked out her bedroom window. Of course the boat was all right. She'd been left for less than a week and there'd been no northerly storm to rake the harbor. Tomorrow they'd go to haul, but the prospect gave Rosa no lift. She sat on the edge of her bed, heavy-headed, squinting against the afternoon dazzle; she heard the wind and the rote muted by closed windows to an echo of the blood-sound in her ears.

It was over. And so what?

Jamie came up in the late afternoon, when she was lying on the grass in the yard trying to read but being constantly overcome with an unpleasant drowsiness. She sat up, blinking sandy eyes at him and running her hands through her hair. He stood looking down at her, his hands on his hips. He looked and smelled scrubbed, his sport shirt crisp and blue, his hair cropped since last week.

"Well," he said tersely. "You go through with it?"

"I did." She yawned.

"How do you feel?" He dropped down to his heels beside her, the better to look her in the eye; she was not to escape him. She yawned for camouflage and said, "Sleepy. It was noisy in there."

"You know what I mean. You relieved? Want to laugh, or cry, or swear, or hit somebody, or what?"

She considered, and then said, "What. That's it."

"*You*." He doubled a fist. "If I didn't know better I'd think you were drunk." He sat down beside her and hauled up his knees to rest his arms on them. "I suppose you're trying to tell me politely that it's none of my business."

201

"It's just—nothing." It was an effort to talk. "All the trouble was a long time ago. This was just a technicality. So, you see, it doesn't amount to anything."

"Yeah, but I read this stuff about divorce having a traumatic effect, even when you've been expecting it. So you shouldn't sit around by yourself and brood. Now I have to go out tonight, but——"

"*Centurion*'s back, I see," she interrupted.

"I know. But they set out by the Rock last night, and we did staving in Bull Cove. Might be they've got the message."

"You don't sound convinced."

"It never does to take anything for granted," he said. "I'd never take *you* for granted." He smiled for the first time. "Welcome back. And stay a while."

"I intend to."

He put his arm around her and took her chin in his hand, and kissed her. She neither responded nor rejected. He held her off a little and looked into her eyes as if he would never give up the search. "The first time I've kissed you as a single woman, and it's not going to be the last time, by God."

"Maybe so, Jamie," she said, "but for now . . . Look, I'm too tired to be anything but honest. I just don't feel anything about anybody. I'm beat. It's as if I'll never feel anything again."

"But you will," he insisted. "You're young and healthy. All the trouble is what you just said. You're tired, you're beat. But you'll bounce back higher than you were before."

"Thanks for that promise." She felt unexpectedly tearful.

"I know, see?" He held her face and kissed her on each cheekbone, on her nose, and on her mouth. "There. I'm not putting pressure on you. I won't even come near you till you give me the word. But if you want me, just whistle." He put two fingers in his mouth and demonstrated so well that Tiger and Rory Mor both began to bark. "Can you do that?"

"Bark or whistle?" She had to laugh and he was delighted that she could joke. "I'll practice," she promised, "I used to do it, but after I nearly blasted my mother's eardrums out she told me it wasn't very ladylike, so quit it. At least in the house."

"You must have been quite a kid. Hey, maybe if we'd grown up together you'd never have married that highbinder."

"Meaning I'd have married *you?*" She shook her head. "You'd probably have treated me like one of the boys. You only like me now because you saved me from a watery death."

"Listen," he began truculently, and then grinned. "I forgot. I'm not putting pressure on you."

"And I appreciate that." She walked down to the lane with him. "Good luck tonight or shouldn't I say it?"

"You can say it. The fish are out there, and they'll be in if nobody breaks 'em up. Want me to save you some? Most of us have got all the bait we can use, and we'll sell to the factory now, but I can keep some out for you."

"I'd like to salt down a hogshead full."

"I suppose this is treating you like one of the boys. I should be *giving* you herring, like roses or candy."

"I can see your crew putting up with that."

"Me too. Remember, I'll be around. Just put your head out the door and whistle."

He left. She knew he felt as sure of her as he was of driving away *Centurion* for good. What was his was his, and the whole world had better know it. He said he'd never take her for granted, but he was taking himself for granted, and of himself he had no doubts. So it added up to the same thing.

Still, he had helped, the conversation had been like an anchor thrown out to keep her mind from constantly drifting back toward the mainland and wondering how the new boat looked on the water and if Con felt the slightest twinge of guilt. Probably not; for him she was really dead and buried now.

What was it Vic had quoted, kidding Linnie? Something Rosa had seen in her own high-school books. *When I am dead, my dearest, sing no sad songs for me.* She'd tried it for music, but it didn't have the same appeal as the salt-water poems.

She took down her guitar and sat on the kitchen floor in the corner as she'd done in the early days here, and sang again *Let us breathe the air of the Enchanted island.*

She returned to her lobstering without joy. Something was lost between her and *Sea Star*, and she was saddened by her lack of spirit, or as saddened as she could be in this neutral zone she now inhabited. She salted away the fresh herring without the mouth-watering satisfaction the lobsterman usually takes in handling good bait. She drove herself to finish the scraping and painting in the house, but she felt so heavy and sleepy that sometimes she couldn't make the effort. Inasmuch as she could be glad of anything, she was glad that she had lost the urge for the compulsive eating which had fattened her in the spring.

Betsey and Holly came up to see her, bringing their guitars. The fog-bound boys had left, and the girls wanted to do some serious work before they went off to school on the mainland. But they found Rosa poor company. She begged off playing the guitar, saying she'd burned her finger that day. They volunteered the news that Vic and Linnie were having a good time sailing and playing tennis and going to summer theaters with men.

"That's fine," Rosa said. She was barely interested. The girls were like dream figures gliding transparently across dim landscapes. Sometimes she wondered through her narcosis if she were losing her mind. Could one simply sink deeper and deeper, like a lobster trap going down to the dark?

Aboard the boat she knew it wasn't so; she was neither dull nor forgetful in attending to both boat and gear. Ashore she carried on reasonable conversations with anyone she met. But the reassurance was cold comfort at best.

Jamie stayed away, and she didn't see much of him at the shore; between hauling and herring, he was always in motion when ne wasn't getting some sleep. Sometimes she heard him whistling. He was giving her time, but he was still positive.

She had begun walking out to Barque Cove every night at dusk, when there was no chance of meeting sunset viewers. She went without a light, and at first stubbed her toe, skidded on damp moss, once scraped her shin bloodily on a sharp edge of rock. But after a while she knew where all the hazards were. Being without a light, even when clouds obscured the stars, gave her that familiar sensation of invisibility.

Sometimes she became aware that she had been crouching for a long time in a turfy hollow staring toward the intermittent flash from Ram's Head Light, and she would not know what she had been thinking or if she had been thinking at all. This was always a little frightening, enough to stir up her senses and speed her heartbeat. But blankness was far better than the scarifying visions of Con and Phyllis making love.

The thing was always there, but as long as she didn't look directly at it she was safe. It was only in her sleep that she was vulnerable, so she tried to get on with as little sleep as possible. She stayed out late in the evenings if it wasn't too foggy or rainy. There was seiner activity to watch, the lighted carriers coming and going past the end of Brigport, lying off the shore over there waiting to load, or following the seiners that set outside Bennett's Island. The seiners jogged slowly by, their strings of dories like shadows behind them, wearing frills of phosphorus. She came to recognize engines. The *Triton* had a peculiar high note. *Centurion*'s overhaul had left her with a soft voice, unheard if there was any surge on the shore; she slipped silently by, keeping her distance, as if the furious words earlier had done away with the need for furious deeds.

Jamie's outfit was out and at work by sunset, standing off Bull Cove or Goose Cove as a warning to *Centurion* or any other boat. But sometimes Rosa saw and heard them coming home late, having given up for that night. *Valkyrie* sounded different in the dark, coming slowly up the west side to avoid hitting pot buoys. She could imagine the young men tired and yawning, without much to say.

She would wait until the sound and the wake died away, and then go home. It would be late, midnight perhaps, and she would set the alarm for five in the morning. She took naps in the afternoon, saved from sinking too deeply because of the children next door, and the dogs.

Marjorie Percy came over one day to ask if Tiger's barking bothered her. "Times when he drives me crazy. But he goes everywhere with Maggie's youngsters."

"I don't even hear him half the time," Rosa said.

"Come on back over with me and have a glass of iced tea. I've got lemon and mint in it. Gorgeous. Or *hot* tea. Beer. Rosé on the rocks?"

"Are you running a pub over there?"

"How about Kool-Aid? Home-made popsicles? I could even stir you up a jug of switchel. I just learned how, back in Vermont."

"Now that really grabs me. But I guess I'll pass it up."

Marjorie hesitated, her tongue touching her upper lip, as if she were trying to make up her mind. Finally she did.

"You don't look very good," she said. "I know it's none of my business, but most of us around here don't like to think of someone all alone and not feeling well. . . . If people thought you'd accept, you'd have plenty of invitations out."

"I know that," said Rosa, "and I've had some." She tried to sound grateful as well as civil. "But there are times when you just have to be alone to get over things." It was more than she wanted to say about herself, but Marjorie's nod of understanding was worth it. She didn't really understand, of course; she thought Rosa was trying to get over Con, and that was what she would pass around.

Had any of them here, Rosa wondered, ever tried to live with a dead self?

25

Sometimes now there was a crisp morning, and somebody at the shore was bound to say, "Feels fallish." Sometimes a quiet, windless chill moved in at sunset. The blackberries were ripening, and noon in the lane smelled of apples from the wild trees along there. There was a tree of yellow transparents in Rosa's woods, the windfalls rotting with a cidery fragrance and attracting bees and wasps; the apples still ripening on the trees glowed as irresistibly among the thick leaves as golden Christmas balls. Something out of childhood too poignant to be ignored was conjured by their sight and scent, and she would have to pick one just for the snap of the bite through the taut waxy skin and the first sweet-sour taste of the juice.

On the way to Barque Cove after sunset one night she picked an apple and walked along eating it. She threw the core overboard as she crossed the beach and climbed up the black rocks on the opposite side.

A sea lustrous as glass was darkening from blue through purple to a blurring gray, and under the slatey clouds in the west the last red light was fading. *Valkyrie* and her dories were anchored a little way offshore; there was just enough light for Rosa to recognize her. The cabin lights shone warm orange. Someone was rowing a double-ender, standing up and pushing on the oars, the strokes as soundless as if the oars were sheathed in velvet. She couldn't make out who it was, but she knew he was watching over the side for the movement of herring.

It was darkening so fast that the double-ender kept dissolving into the twilight. Out of habit she looked across to where Ram's Head Light should be, and saw the first visible spark of light. She wondered if Con were seining tonight, or if he and Phyllis were on the trip he and Rosa had planned out, visiting every harbor possible from here to Quoddy Head. The raging pain seemed to have died out long ago and taken everything else with it, except the taste of apples, and the chill creeping through her clothes to her skin. She turned around and went back to the house, sure-footed in the dusk.

She sat in a rocking chair with her feet on the stove hearth, reading one of those cold-war espionage novels with too many characters to keep straight even with your full attention. The only sounds in the kitchen were the creaks of the chair when she shifted her weight, the fire's small noises, the turn of a page. She stopped reading sometimes to listen.

The silence seemed to grow and surge in her ears, as if she were holding shells to them. It didn't make her nervous, but she thought of a dog's toenails or a cat's purring; some creature to talk to at these moments when you wondered what would happen if you spoke aloud, if your voice would come at all. You tried it, and it came too loud and you felt foolish and embarrassed and looked around quickly as if to catch sly watchers.

It was in one of these intervals that she heard from far off the shotgun. Almost instantaneously she was on her feet, the book bouncing away from her, the chair rocking wildly. She went out the back door and listened; the night had an autumnal cold scented with apples, the stars sparkled in the tops of the spruce trees. There was another shot, followed by shouts. She pulled her loden coat off the hook in the entry and went out to Barque Cove.

She was not so much excited by the shots as by the fact that she had reacted so quickly; it showed that she was still capable of being moved. *Centurion* must have come along while they were waiting for the herring to move in, and these were the warning shots, fired high to alarm and warn, not to do injury. She wished she had binoculars with coated lenses so she could see at night.

She crossed the beach at Barque Cove and climbed the other side to where she'd been earlier. All the way she could hear gabbled, fragmented shouting and it sounded like a riot. As she came over a rise the sight of the lighted carrier burst on her vision like an explosion of fireworks. The tall white vessel was illuminated from stem to stern, she could plainly see the men on her decks, and the low dark seiner alongside her. *Valkyrie* lay where she had been before. Spotlights from carrier and seiner swung erratically across the water between boats and shore; objects flashed into existence and disappeared as quickly. A gray dory, with glittering yellow oilskins in it, light glancing off wet oarblades; a face caught in mid-shout; orange net floats strung across water shiny as black oil. Reflections from the lighted carrier completed the dazzling confusion.

Were they fighting from *dories?* Swinging oars at each other? One voice rose breakingly high above the others. "Hey, look over there! Is that him?"

A dory shot forward, there was a groan. "Christ no, it's a log."

"Miff, you called the Coast Guard yet?" someone called.

"What in hell can they do that we aren't doing?" a man shouted back from the carrier. "Maybe he's crawled ashore somewhere. Row in close along the rocks."

A dory came Rosa's way, silhouetted in perfect detail against the blaze of the carrier. One man was rowing, standing up and pushing on the oars. Another stood up in the bow.

"*Jesus.*" Matt Fennell's quietly despairing voice came up to her. "How long can he stay up in hipboots?"

She turned around and returned to Barque Cove, thinking that when she was back in the kitchen, with the lights and the noise shut out, the whole scene would have ceased to exist. Someone had been shot, or had gone overboard and drowned, and there was nothing she could do about it. Maybe they hadn't seen him go, hadn't missed him until it was too late, and she couldn't bear to think of the man drowning in the dark, tangled in the net or rockweed, the salt water stopping his shouts. She had to get into the house and lock the doors, build up the fire, drink something hot to warm her, forget she'd been out there, forget what she'd heard and seen. She couldn't, of course; she wouldn't sleep tonight but maybe she'd get warm. She was shivering from the inside out.

As she crossed Barque Cove's beach, she heard a groaning sound, and something moved in the starlight, a long shape at the edge of the water. Once she had found a seal shot by seiners, and this was what she remembered now; her pity and horror for the drowned man merged with that for the dying animal, into a rage against all the men back there shouting and swearing.

She ran forward and knelt, thinking, Someone will have to come and put it out of its misery, it can't be left here to die like this. This is what people do, kill each other and all innocent things.

"Help me," the thing mumbled. "Help me."

She grabbed the man in her arms and dragged him up out of the water and entwining weed. "You're the *one!*" she said incredulously. "You're alive! I've got to tell them!" In her arms he shuddered as if he would fall apart just from the vibration. She laid him down and got out of her loden coat and wrapped him up in it. "I'll run now and tell them."

But he held onto her arms. "Don't go yet," he said between chattering teeth. "Get me warm first. I've never been so cold in my life. It'll kill me. *Please.*" His fingers tightened as if on existence itself. She couldn't get a hand free to loosen his grip. She had to humor him in order to move.

"All right, I'll get you to the house first. Come on. Can you walk?" With him hanging on to her, she got him onto his feet. He had no boots on, just heavy socks. Water ran off him, off his hair and his face, and he shivered in long convulsive crescendos. He could hardly walk, and she was glad he was not a big man, he felt about the size of Con through the bulky loden coat.

She pushed and hoisted him up the steep climb. The path through the woods was even worse, he tripped and fell several times, and once they fell together. She laughed the way one would to reassure a panicky child.

"Those cussid rocks. I'm black and blue from them myself. Almost there now. I hope you haven't broken a toe."

"I'm too numb . . . to feel it," he gasped.

She half-lifted him over the doorstep and into the house. In the warm dark his breath went out of him in a long, trembling sigh. She propped him against the wall.

"Lean there till I get a light," she commanded.

"You got a place where I can lie down?"

"As soon as you get the wet clothes off." She lit the lamp.

She saw a white face blood-smeared from scratches, long black hair plastered down over his forehead and into his eyes; lips so dark blue with cold they looked almost as dark as his hair. They were trembling and she could hear his teeth. She turned the gas on under the tea kettle, carried the lamp into Edwin's room, pulled the shades, and then came back to guide him to the bedroom.

"Start getting out of those clothes," she said. She got towels from the bottom drawer of the chest. "Rub yourself down hard with these."

She brought down her sleeping bag and laid it out on the bed. He was fumbling with his shirt buttons. "When you're undressed," she said, "and dried, crawl into that bag and I'll bring you something hot to drink. Somebody around here will supply you with dry clothes."

She started to leave the room, carrying the sodden loden coat, and he said, "I can't work my . . . goddam . . . fingers. They're still numb."

211

His hands were scraped and bloody, the fingertips cut by barnacles. "I'll help you," she said. "Here." She got his shirt off him and then a T-shirt. She heard the tea kettle begin to boil just as they'd reached his jeans, and she said briskly, "Everybody's modesty saved by the bell."

In the kitchen she took out Edwin's bottle and mixed a hot toddy. She could hear the man's grunts and whispers in the other room, and longed with exasperation to strip off the wet jeans as if he were a child and stuff him into the sleeping bag. Finally there was silence.

"All right?" she called.

He didn't answer. She went in with the hot drink and found him huddled in the bag. She wrapped his wet head in a towel and held the mug to his mouth. His teeth clattered on the rim, but he sipped and swallowed. When that was done she rubbed his head as dry as possible. It fell into thick damp waves. "This long hair is a nuisance," she said.

"It was even longer once," he said with feeble pride.

"I'll bet." She spread a dry towel on a pillow and put it under his head, zipped up the bag, then tucked a woolen blanket over it.

"I'll go let them know," she said. "Maybe someone's come around to the harbor." She went across the dark sitting room to the stair landing, and from the window there she saw lights in the Percy house, and Mark Bennett's wharf was illuminated. The carrier lay just inside the breakwater. "Yes, they're there," she called back. "I'll go down."

"*No!*"

The hysterical cry took her back to him. He was struggling to get out of the sleeping bag, his face contorted as if against torture. "Don't go! Listen—I'll tell you—" He freed his arms and got that death grip on her again in spite of sore hands. He was strong, muscled like a welterweight or an acrobat.

"I won't go yet," she said, "but get back into that bag."

"Do you promise you won't go?"

"I promise."

He lay down. The bed shook with the energy of his chills. "St-stay where I c-c-can see you," he commanded.

She sat on the side of the bed. He should drowse as he got warmer, and then she could go. She watched him in the grip of the tremors, wishing there were some quick way to warm him, and then watched him fight exhaustion in the quieter moments, trying to keep his eyelids up. She imagined what horrors he must see the instant the lamplit room and the comfort of another presence were shut off from him; the all-but-drowning in the dark, being carried along by the black water, reaching out frantically with fingers and toes for nothing; salt water washing into ears, eyes, nostrils, throat, and then something—maybe the big rock humped and shaggy like a bison in the mouth of Barque Cove—to hang onto while his vision cleared so that he saw the island rearing up over him, and a little distance away the white glimmer of the narrow beach.

She came back to the reality of the bedroom with relief. It seemed like a long time. He should be asleep, but he was watching her, his eyes a dull gleam under the lashes. The shivers were faint now, like the distant rumbles of a departing thunder storm.

"Listen," she said. "I've got to tell them. Maybe they've told your folks by now, or your wife. They should know the truth right away."

His teeth showed in a grin that was more a slow-motion snarl. "No folks. No wife. Nobody to worry about. I've got nobody but me."

"But the other men should know." He started to sit up and she said soothingly, "Look, I'll run over next door and tell the woman there. She can go down to the harbor and tell them, and I'll come right back. How's that?"

"No! *Please!*" The word came out in a gutteral explosion. His grip could have drowned a rescuer, if they'd been in the water. "There's time—there's time—they don't even know

I'm gone, it's somebody else they're looking for—" He became incoherent.

Finally he lay back, breathing hard, watching her with an intensity she found both frightening and moving; he was like a terrified animal that could harm her in its mindless terror.

She said, "Would you like another hot drink?"

"If you go for that you'll keep going right out the door." He spoke more carefully, piecing his words together, sweating with the effort to concentrate. "Don't give me up, please," he begged. "Let them think I'm dead. Then I can get away, see?"

"You're going to wring my arms right out of the sockets," she told him.

He wouldn't loosen. "I've got to keep you here. I think I killed a man back there. I clubbed him with an oar and he went overboard backward and didn't come up. I looked for him, believe me," he implored. "That's how I fell overboard and the dory got away from me. It was outside the cove. The guys with him saw me hit him. That's why they have to think I'm drowned, see? I got my boots off and tried swimming for the shore, but the tide kept carrying me. I didn't want to drown out there in the dark, I was going to come in somewhere different from where they all were, and hide in the woods till they gave up, and then go down to the harbor and steal a boat. They found him, I'm pretty sure, and they can see where I hit him."

"You don't know if you killed anybody. He could be ashore now and home all dry and safe."

"I know I killed him!" he said angrily. "I know what it sounded like when I hit him side of the head with that oar handle. Jesus! I didn't mean to, but they were lying in wait for us down there. One bunch came out fast from the shore with an outboard, and started going round and round us to break up the herring and keep us from putting the twine overboard, and somebody else was back there in the dark firing at us and the carrier. Christ, we weren't going to take that!"

"Was anybody shot?"

"No, they were firing high from the shore, but the damn

214

bastards, they said if we did put the twine over we'd never get it back in one piece. Well, they were spoiling for a fight, they been looking for it all summer, so by God they got it." He was suddenly exhausted and fell back. "Only I didn't mean to kill anybody. He shouldn't a got me so mad. Guy with real yellow hair. When I hit him I saw it in the light from the carrier."

"*No.*" She went slack under his grip.

"You know him?" he said hoarsely.

"Yes."

"I didn't mean to," he repeated. "You got to believe that. We were all like wild men down there."

"I believe you." She wanted to get away and vomit

"So you see why I want 'em to think I'm dead too." He was losing his voice. "Just let me rest and warm up, and I've got this friend who can come at night and take me off the shore where you found me. You can get a message to him. Write him a letter, and he'll come right away.... I do have this friend," he insisted, as if she'd challenged him.

"I believe you," she said again, automatically.

"And you hate my guts."

"No."

"If you give me up I'll kill myself. I mean that. I'll never go to jail."

"Look, I'm not going anywhere tonight except maybe out back to the toilet." The simple fact was that she could not walk away from this house tonight and down to the harbor and meet the announcement of Jamie's death. As long as she stayed here, there was a kind of nightmare unreality about the affair, even though this boy's panic and terror was convincing. Still, they were a part of the nightmare too, and they offered a hope of waking from it.

If only Jamie's face wouldn't keep coming up before her. The blue eyes, the quick belligerence and the sudden smile of triumph or capitulation. *But I'll be around. Just put your head out the door and whistle.*

She had to get out of the room, not to weep—which

215

would have been an easy release—but away from *him*, who had done it. Mean it or not, he had done it.

She said, "Let go. I told you I'm not going anywhere."

He released her. She could not look directly at him, but she sensed that he was staring at her with awe and fear. She could give him up and he would kill himself. They both knew.

"Do you want the lamp left?" she asked, standing up.

"Yeah. I hate the dark." He sounded chastened and weary. Without looking at him again she went upstairs, got herself a blanket, and lay down on her bed.

If only she had stayed home instead of going toward the shots. She'd be sleeping now, free from Con for a while, and for her at least Jamie would still be alive. In the morning when she met the news she'd be equal with everyone else.

In the morning, she thought coldly, I will have *that one* out of my house. She sat up, gazing out of the window. The Percy house was dark now, the lights had been turned off on the wharf, and the carrier was leaving. Taking Jamie's body and his parents to the mainland?

She abhorred the bed, she loathed her own skin and wished she could escape it. She went downstairs, and listened at the bedroom door. He was sleeping now, she could tell by his breathing. She was free to go and tell somebody about him. Nobody else would be sleeping much tonight, even if they'd put out the lights at last.

But *he* slept. His face was turned toward the lamp, not only drained of terror but of life. She could see it more clearly now than before when he had been so frantic. He was older than she had first thought, with aquiline, almost Italian features, the black brows and lashes like ink strokes on parchment.

She believed that he would kill himself in jail. These salt-water tramps were always around to fill in for someone on a seiner or a dragger, or to work as a lobsterman's helper, drinking up their earnings or losing them by gambling, never sticking at anything for long. Something in them, or lacking in them, turned them unpredictable. They were half-gull, but far less stable than a gull. It wasn't simply a hunger for change that drove them.

No, if he couldn't find a way to kill himself here, he could hang himself in his cell at the county jail. Such deaths occurred once or twice a year.

What he could do here, she thought, looking at the lamp, was burn up the house and himself along with it. She blew out the lamp and went back to her bed. Finally she fell into the restless state which sometimes passes for sleep. She woke from a dream in which Con was sobbing over the death of his child and she was crying too and trying to comfort him. It was a good dream in spite of its anguish, because Phyllis was nowhere in it, and Con leaned his head against her breast, and they mourned the baby together.

A man *was* sobbing. Still in the spell of the dream, without questioning what Con was doing here in this house, she sat up to go to him. With the motion, everything fell away. She remembered that it was Jamie who was dead.

26

The harsh, visceral sobbing went on. She went downstairs and found him crying in his sleep. And because it was in his sleep, when woe is so tearingly intense, she wanted out of simple compassion to wake him. But to what? The reality couldn't be much improvement on the dream.

217

Still, she could hardly bear to listen, and there'd be no rest for her, however broken. She spoke to him, even put her hand on his shoulder, but it didn't rouse him, he was too far away. She got her blanket and pillow and lay down on the bed, turned on her side and put her arm across the sleeping bag and held him firmly.

He began to quiet down. Occasionally he drew a long shuddery breath, but these became infrequent. Under her arm his body seemed to go boneless and flat. Her own body pressed heavier against the mattress. Her brain was spinning behind her closed eyes, and the whole bed began to swing like a boat at her mooring. It was rather restful. Everything external retreated to a great distance; she saw Con drawn rapidly away from her, becoming tinier and tinier until he disappeared. There was one flashing glimpse of Jamie, like the explosion of a setpiece in a night sky; the yellow head fell backwards in slow motion toward the water, but before she could cry out the scene died out in a train of sparks and left the night blacker than it was before.

There was really nothing, she thought. Cocooned in exhaustion, she slept.

Slowly surfacing in the morning, she thought it was Con in her arms, his breath against her throat, his hand on her breast. The small room was dim, but morning sunlight slanted in obliquely from the sitting room.

Last night came back to her like the big wave out of nowhere, she even tasted its salt in her mouth. She wanted to escape from the unconscious embrace, but she didn't want to wake him up and have to talk to him. She wished that he would mysteriously disappear without her having to tell anyone he was here. She inched cautiously out from under the naked shoulder and arm. For an instant he seemed to settle deeper against her, the hand slid off her breast to clasp her ribs, then he went slack, and she got away and out of the room without his waking.

She found she was holding her hand to her throat where

his face had been, she could still feel the heat of it; she remembered thinking it was Con, and was ashamed and disgusted. She snatched a towel and went out doors, taking long thirsty breaths of the cool air. She leaned over the rain barrel and splashed water vigorously over her face and throat. It was very cold. She kept at it, as if she could wash away the whole night if she just did it long enough. Nothing would, of course. She straightened up and dried herself.

Down at the Sorensens the rooster crowed over and over. She wondered if the parents were sleeping now, wherever they were. It was indecent to think of two people like that in grief. They should always be the way she had known them. *Jamie.* Oh dear God. And Linnie would have to be told today. Blue eyes scalded with hours of weeping. Blue eyes staring upward, blind blue glass.

She retched, without anything much to bring up. Jamie dead, and his murderer lying in her house like a beached fish at the edge of the tide. She wished something would save her from the appalling incredibility of it.

Heavily she went back into the house. She put water on to heat and went upstairs to change her clothes. He didn't move when she passed through the sitting room both times, but when she was sipping coffee in a patch of sun, trying to think beyond her misery, he suddenly appeared, wrapped in a blanket.

"Got any more of that?" he asked hoarsely.

"Yes. Sit down, and I'll get you some clothes." She put a mug of coffee and some canned milk on the table, and went upstairs to look at her clothes. She was in the habit of buying men's jeans because they fitted her flat rump better than women's sizes, so she picked out a pair, a flannel shirt, wool socks, and a pair of moccasins and took them down. But he was back in bed again, the coffee not touched.

She put the clothes on a chair and picked up the damp ones still in a heap from last night. "What's the matter?" she said.

"I'm sick. I think I'm going to die."

"Don't talk so foolish," she said angrily. She put her hand on his forehead and the dry heat startled her. When she started to take her hand away he held onto it and pressed the side of his face into it, and she remembered unwillingly the heat of his breath against her throat when she woke this morning. "See, I *am* sick," he muttered.

"Then you need to go ashore and be taken care of," she said.

"You mean give myself up, don't you?" He pulled her by the wrist till she had to sit on the side of the bed. "Well, I won't. I can't. I told you what would happen."

"Look, if it was the way you said, it was an accident. Everybody was milling around in boats. They'd probably call it manslaughter, if they went that far. Not murder."

"But I'd be locked up, wouldn't I?" His eyes were wild. "Listen, do *you* call me murderer?"

She looked away from the mad stare. "I don't think you meant to kill, no. If it's the way you said."

"Locking me up—driving me out of my skull—making me kill myself—that would be murder, wouldn't it?" When she didn't answer he jerked on her wrist. "Wouldn't it? And it wouldn't bring the guy back."

I'll be around. Just put your head out the door and whistle.

"No," she said, looking past him with yearning at the green yard outside and the inviting shadows of the woods.

"Then promise you won't turn me in." He tightened his grip. "Just hide me a little while, till my friend comes. You'll have to write the letter, my hands are too sore. I'll tell you what to say. When's the boat come again?"

"Tomorrow." It was like saying *next year*, the minutes were so excruciatingly long.

"He'll come as soon as he gets the letter. It'll be all over then. You won't even have to think about me again." He stopped, listening, his black eyes glazed, and she thought he was delirious until she heard the heavy rhythm of a helicopter.

"Coast Guard," he whispered. "Well, here's one body that'll never show. When I get ashore I'll split for Canada. No, down South. Somewhere good and warm this winter." He shivered. "Christ, that water was so cold last night it's still in my bones. How the hell can anybody burn and freeze at the same time?"

His hand had fallen away from her wrist, and she started to get up, but he seized her again. "You haven't promised me yet."

She looked down at him wearily, her mind refusing to think. Suddenly he sat up, wrapped his arms around her and pressed his face into her breast. "Promise," he said against her flesh. "You got to. I haven't got anybody else.... I don't even know if he'll come. Maybe he isn't even there any more."

After her dream, the familiarity of a male head and bare torso pressed against her caused a purely instinctive response. She wanted to thrust him away in revulsion, yet she could not refuse or deny the strong impulse to shelter and comfort. She both despised and pitied. With dismay at her own actions she put her arms around him and said, "All right, I promise."

The helicopter went low over the house, she felt its vibrations and it set up another vibration in him, from far inside, and his embrace was like a vise. Without thinking she put her face down to his hair and murmured, "It's all right.... It's all right."

His name was Quint Learoyd. For some unknown reason that filled him with disgust he'd been named Quintus. Rambling, making no sense, he told her no more than that. She moved him upstairs into a little room whose only window opened onto the woods toward the cove. Nobody could glance up at that window unless it was someone in the yard, and she expected no one to be there today. She would surely be forgotten.

But she pulled the shade anyway, in case Marjorie Percy

or Maggie Dinsmore should come up to tell her the tragic news. Quint was groggy and weak. She had to help him up the stairs. She gave him some aspirin and left him already half asleep in the clean sheets.

She hung the sleeping bag as the sun grew hot and strong, and rinsed the salt water out of his clothes with water from the rain barrel. She spread them out to dry over the bushes behind the toilet, well away from the paths. She rinsed her loden coat too, but hung that on a hanger in the open; she could always say she'd just decided to wash it.

While Quint slept, she spent most of the day in the yard, to head off any callers. She felt as if she were mired in the quicksands of a dream. The helicopter came and went; each time it passed above the house she wondered if the crew could feel the emanations of guilt rising up from her. It seemed particularly sinful to let their useless search go on and on. Boats left the harbor and returned, the air pulsed with engines. Nobody would be hauling, she was positive; they too would be hunting. A different, heavier engine drew her to the stairway window, and she saw a Coast Guard launch tied up at the big wharf, a cluster of men talking gravely on the car. Most of the island children stood respectfully on the wharf.

Next door Marjorie Percy didn't sing as she usually did at her chores, and when the children were home they were extraordinarily quiet, as if they too were awed and oppressed by the presence of death.

Quint slept on and on. She washed the floor where he had dripped, forever stopping to look out the windows so she wouldn't be taken unaware. His clothing dried and she brought it in and draped it over chairs upstairs to air. By mid-afternoon she felt as if the day had been a year long and relentlessly bright the whole time. Her eyes ached with tiredness, and she had gotten too stale for grief. With cruel slowness the cold shade began to creep out from the woods.

She lay in it with her hands over her eyes, thinking longingly of night.

A footfall on the ground brought her up with a startled gasp. Quint stood there smiling at her surprise. It was a weak and weary smile and he was not altogether steady. He wore his own jeans, no shirt, and was barefoot. He was the color of a gypsy.

"What are you doing out here?" she demanded in a low fierce voice.

"I'm only human. Man has to take a leak once in a while."

"Then be quick about it!"

She thought he'd never get to the toilet. Once he was there, she heard a screen door slam at the Percys', and was sure that either Marjorie or Ralph was on the way across. But Ralph was going to the well instead, and Marjorie called after him to collect the children from across the harbor. She'd be getting supper, then. The pressure around Rosa's lungs loosened, but she felt as weak as Quint looked.

Walking carefully, he returned to the house, and sat down to rest in the kitchen. She wanted him to go back to bed, but he insisted on washing up at the sink. Then he borrowed a comb and looked in the mirror; he shook his head, and swore to himself.

"I sure look like hell when I need a shave," he complained.

"This is a hell of a time for vanity," she said, despising the way he fooled with his hair. Jamie's hair was cropped short. This time yesterday he might have been running a hand through it as he talked. Who was combing his hair now for the funeral?

"You wouldn't have a razor, I suppose." Quint squinted at himself with distaste.

Edwin had left a spare shaving kit, and she had an extra toothbrush. She went and got them. "Go back upstairs," she said. "I'll bring the water up." His fingers were too stiff to unwrap a new razor blade and she had to do it for him. "If I cut my throat with that, it would solve everything, wouldn't it?" he said, watching her.

"Except what I'd do with the body and all that blood," she said, handing him the razor. She went downstairs and fixed a meal of scrambled eggs and toast, which she carried up to him on a cookie sheet as a tray. She set it on the small stand beside his bed and went back for coffee.

He had managed to shave, after a fashion, and smelled of Edwin's lotion. "Stay," he said. "Please?" His normal voice was soft and husky. His smile was tentative. "I know I'm asking a hell of a lot from you, and you probably figger I don't deserve any conversation but——"

"Maybe we'd better write that letter to your friend."

"Sure! Okay. Anything you say." He was eager. "You promised you'd help. I promise you won't be sorry."

"Eat while it's hot."

"I shouldn't be hungry, but I am." His smile deepened. He had long dimples like slashes in his cheeks, and she suspected that he knew it. She did not smile back. She went downstairs for a note pad, pen, and envelope, and took her time about it. He had finished eating when she returned, and was reclining on the bed with pillows behind him, drinking coffee.

"Good thing I don't smoke," he said cheerfully, "or I'd be nuts by now. I smoked when I was a little kid, but then I got the idea I was going to be this great fighter, see, and I started taking care of my wind."

She said impassively, "What do you want to say in this letter?"

"Oh, yeah. I got it all written in my mind." He began to dictate as if he had indeed memorized it. " 'Dear Danny, come to Bennett's Island and get me. It will have to be at night because nobody knows I'm on here except the girl who is writing this letter for me. I'm in some trouble, so don't talk about this, huh? I'll start looking for you as soon as I think you've got this. Lay off—' What's the name of your cove?" he asked Rosa.

"Barque. It's on the charts."

"Good. Tell him to lay off there around midnight, and bring a skiff so he can row in. If any of these wild men around here come along and ask him what he's up to, say he's got engine trouble.... Got that?"

She nodded. He signed his name awkwardly, and she addressed the envelope to a waterfront street in Limerock. When she looked up he was gazing thoughtfully at her. "You're good, you know that? I don't know when anybody's been so good to me."

"Since your mother," she said sarcastically. The liquefying compassion she'd felt earlier had dried up in the light of this endless day which Jamie had never seen.

"*Her!*" He spat the word. "If I knew where she was buried I'd go piss on her grave. She and her boyfriend used to beat me up for kicks. The neighbors were always complaining, so we'd keep moving just ahead of the welfare people." He lay back and folded his arms under his head and stared at the ceiling. "And if I ever came across *him* again, it wouldn't be an accident this time. It'd be murder in the first degree. Premeditated since I was four years old."

She was affected in spite of herself. She said, "I wouldn't blame you. But where was your father?"

His sly smile mocked her innocence. "I never had one. She found me in a cup of tea.... Naw, even she didn't know who he was. Maybe he was two marines from Galveston, like the old joke."

"What became of her?"

"When I came to one day that I could go to the police and talk for myself, and show 'em the marks his belt buckle made, and the cigarette burns—" He saw her involuntary wince, and gave her that mocking grin again. "Nasty, isn't it? . . . I told 'em that's what I was going to do, and he'd have strangled me then to shut me up, except I had the carving knife in my hand. I was about eleven." He chuckled. "I can see them now. She had eyes like green gooseberries. They were practically out on sticks she was so scared. He was a big guy and a great kicker. I used to go sailing across the room and end up against the wall. I was reading that nowadays the hospitals get real suspicious about babies coming in with broken bones, but back in those days they used to take my mother's word it was an accident, she was such a good cryer. Could drown the place in salt water and you didn't have to drop a hat, just me."

He spoke with a dry lack of self-pity, almost as if he were amused by the whole squalid picture, or by her horrified reaction.

"What did they do when you said you'd go to the police?" she asked. "Promise to stop beating you?"

"No, but they let me do what I wanted. I didn't want to go to the police and be stuck in a foster home, I never figgered on *that*. But there was this old guy—well, I guess he wasn't so old, but he'd lived hard. He was a haker, and I wanted to go with him. We lived in a back alley where the rats killed the cats, but I could get across Main Street down onto the waterfront. You know where that fancy marina is today?" She nodded. "Well, it was far from fancy then, but it was salt water and there was the whole harbor and the break-water, and the big bay outside. . . ." He watched it on the ceiling. "Seems like it was always blue, never rough. He taught me how to bait trawl. Gave me a dime sometimes. I used to hate to go back across the street. I'd fool around down there till the other kids would be coming home from school. Christ, those afternoons. It was coming summer, and the alley stunk worse than the city dump, and there were those two to come home to." He laughed and shook his head. "Well, I asked Mick if he'd hire me to bait trawl and wash down the decks, and cook, and he laughed and said sure. He never expected me to show up, but I did, and they left town."

"Was it a good summer?" she asked.

"You better believe it. It might not've been like life in the TV commercials, Mick wasn't much of a mother as far as making me drink milk and brush my teeth, but he was a damn sight better than the one I had. . . . Turned out sometimes I was tending *him*, when he had a skinful. But we made out." His voice faded. He was seeing it all on the ceiling again. "We made out."

"For how long? What about school?"

He shrugged. "He had this little shack, that's about all it was, down at the South End. He'd get chewing on how I ought to go to school, but I convinced him that as long as I didn't turn up they'd think I'd left town with my so-called folks." He pronounced the last word with loathing. "But if I did go, they'd find out where I was living and that I was an abandoned kid, kind of, and they'd say Mick wasn't any fit influence, and then where'd I be? Besides, who'd he get so cheap to be so useful to him? Well, by that time I could talk him around pretty good. I could think a lot faster than old Mick."

"I'll bet you could," Rosa said. She imagined the tough little boy, like pictures she'd seen of urchins on Italian streets. Velvet-eyed, twiggy arms and legs, cigarette hidden in a cupped, small-boy hand; wits sharp and feral.

"Hell, I was going on twelve, I could read anything, I could write better than Mick, I could do arithmetic. I considered I was educated enough. Besides, I was going to be a fisherman. Dammit, I *was* a fisherman. A haker, anyway. I figger I've baited about a thousand miles of trawl in my lifetime."

They laughed together. In the middle of it she remembered Jamie. He rose up on one elbow and leaned toward her, saying, "What's the matter?"

She started to say *nothing* but gave it up for a shake of the head, turning away from the bright inquisitive eyes.

"You're thinking about *him*, aren't you?" he accused her.

227

"I'm thinking about him too. That's why I talk so much. Look, you always so alone up here? Don't anybody neighbor? It's like you're miles from everything."

"Isn't that what you want? Yes, they neighbor. Sometimes the kids come. But they're mostly all related to *him*." She couldn't say the name. She couldn't even think it, she saw only pictures, and that was worse. "So nobody's thinking much of me today, and I can't blame them. Let's just hope everybody stays away till your friend Danny's been and got you."

They wouldn't, though; somebody would be around collecting for flowers. For the first time she thought of the cemetery where she had walked with Edwin. The deaths had all been so long ago, it had been a pretty, peaceful place. But no more. Not with Jamie in it. She got up quickly.

"You'd better stay there," she managed to say, and took the tray and went downstairs. She left the tray by the sink and went out. A boat was coming in fast, then the engine stopped. A Bennett coming home from the mainland, maybe. She bowed her face into her hands.

So she'd had Con and lost him; so what? At least there'd been the first of it, and never mind what they said, she could believe in his early good intentions if she wanted to; it was her own affair. Maybe, with a good childhood like hers, she'd had a little trouble coming to her, it was like saying you have to eat a peck of dirt before you die. But God alone knew the reason for giving some babies trouble as soon as they're born. Like that one upstairs. Abused as far back as he could remember, surviving in spite of it, the way the rats in the alley survived. Why bring God into it? "God is dead," Edwin wrote to her once, "if there ever was a God, which I doubt."

He's right, she thought fiercely. I never did want to believe in God who saw the sparrow fall but didn't do anything to save it.

27

He was both restless and reckless, for all his fear. When she went back into the house she could hear him moving around upstairs, and she didn't want him coming down. She took up an armful of paperbacks and a lamp. "Stay," he said eagerly, but she refused.

She longed to get away from the house just for a walk to the back shore, but she went only as far as the well, after dark, for two buckets of fresh water. After that she made up her own bed, and then went in to check on his lamp. He had fallen asleep. He reminded her of Con who, when something was bothering him, slept in the same tormented way, never still a moment, arms and legs flung about in spasmodic gestures.

"No, no," he muttered, then on a rising note, "*Look out! Grab him!*" He sat up straight in bed, staring at her in horror; her heart beat hard, it took her a moment to realize he didn't see her. He fell back on the pillows and slept so quietly that for a moment she wondered if he were dead, until she heard his breathing.

She took the lamp to her own room, so he couldn't knock it over in the next spasm, and undressed and went to bed. The sheets felt good to her body. She felt as if she'd been beaten, even her skin was sore. Her arms were bruised from the maniacal strength of his fingers last night. She wondered achingly how Nils and Joanna were resting tonight, and Linnie. Her eyes filled. She sighed heavily and longed for sleep. For a week of sleep.

As a child she had lain in bed listening to crickets. She made herself listen now, and they comforted her by the very sameness of the sound.

Once she woke in the night and heard him sobbing again. She sat up, hugging her knees, wondering if this time she should wake him, or just let it go on and wear itself out. When it seemed to subside she slept again, thankfully.

She woke suddenly because someone's hand was feeling delicately for her face in the dark. She was paralyzed with fear; he's going to strangle me, she thought. He really is a maniac.

"Rosa," he whispered hoarsely. "I'm afraid to sleep. I keep dreaming about it. You stopped it last night. Let me in, please."

He was already in, burrowing and pressing, whispering, "You're so warm. Put your arms around me, please." His flesh was very cold.

"No, no," she protested. "I'll make you something hot. I'll get you some flannel pajamas." But the words were so much babble, and she knew it. While she was saying them she was taking his icy body in her arms. She wrapped him in both arms and legs. He kept whispering, "That's good. You're so warm. Hold me tight. Keep it away. I keep dreaming I'm the one who's drowning and it's so cold . . . so cold. *He* shoves me down under. He's dead, and his eyes are like some blue glass aggies I once had. He's pushing me under." He shuddered violently and she embraced him harder. "Christ, the way his hands feel."

"Don't think about it," she said. You could tell his hair was black. Con's hair felt red even in the dark.

They lay tightly entwined for a time. He was quiet, and she heard the crickets again. There was a familiarity about this contact and the drugged comfort of it. When she knew what was happening she was not surprised. He began gently to kiss her cheek and neck. With his lips at the hollow of her throat he began to pull at her pajamas, and she thought with a great burst of joy, *Why not?*

That night he didn't dream again of dead men's hands trying to drown him; at least not that she knew of, her own sleep was so profound. She woke toward daylight, turning blindly toward a cooling and empty place, and thought Con had gotten up early to go haul. Then Quint came into the room, naked as he'd left her bed. "Where've you been?" she asked drowsily.

"Out back."

"Like *that?*"

He laughed. "Who'd see me? Besides, a quick jog in the cool dew sets a guy up. As you can see." He dived into the bed again and laid his body against hers. "Ah, feel that. You're like satin, you know? What am I like?" He rose up on one elbow to look down at her.

"I can't tell you, you're too vain already."

"Just for that, I'll torture the truth out of you. Hey, do you have to go?"

"I never have to go," said Rosa grandly.

"Then you're the kind of woman I've always wanted. One that doesn't have to go pee every five minutes." He gathered her into his arms, and made love to her again, not as desperately as last night, but with delight and mischief.

Afterwards he said in a slow, wondering way, "I feel *safe* with you. That sound crazy? Saying that about somebody you're making love to? But I do. It's not only the way you hauled me ashore that night and practically lugged me through the woods and into this house, and you keeping me here, feeding me, and—uh—tending out on me, you might call it, but it's the way you *are*. I knew it that night, crazy as I was. As long as I could see you and hang onto you, I felt safe. . . . You know something? I never slept so sound in my life as I slept with you. . . . Like if you were holding me

231

I could dare to let myself go, because nothing could touch me. You wouldn't let it."

She didn't know what to say. He went on. "I never felt so safe in my life, that I can remember. Because the earliest thing I remember is being so scared I messed and puked, both at once and they rolled me in it."

She groaned at that, and tried to hold him even closer; like an actual attempt to rescue that child. "But you must have felt safe with Mick," she said, "except for worrying about the truant officer."

"Sure," he said. She felt the vibrations of his laughter against her throat and under her hands, rather than heard it. "Except when I got to be thirteen or so, and Mick started chasing me around the place."

"To *beat* you?"

"Not exactly. Seemed Mick liked pretty boys. But only when he was drunk. He fought hard against it. I'm sure as hell not forgetting that he took me in and hid me. And those first two years haking were all that a kid could ask, a kid who was crazy about salt water and boats, and been knocked around enough to addle his brains. Then when I began getting some size on me, and Mick had those long winter evenings to sit around getting drunk—well, we began a losing battle. Scared hell out of me. I'd run out and stay till I thought he'd gone to sleep. Next day sometimes he didn't even remember, and that was good, because if he did remember and try to apologize it was awful."

He was silent, his face hidden from her, heavy with the weight of memory.

"I couldn't keep running out in snowstorms or in zero cold, there wasn't anybody near I could go sit with. We never mixed, anyway, because of the police and the welfare and everything. So I got a padlock and used to lock myself in my room. I had the loft, and he had the downstairs. . . . It was cold as hell up there with the door shut but it was— Well, sometimes hearing him trying to make it up the stairs I'd think, 'Oh hell, with all he's done for me I ought to . . . well, it wouldn't hurt me any, I mean it's not like being a girl and getting knocked up,' but—" Even now he flinched. "I just couldn't make myself unlock that door. I'd sit there staring at it and shaking and I couldn't make myself do it."

"No." She stroked his shoulders. "I'm glad you couldn't. . . . What happened? How long did you stay after that?"

"He fell backward down the stairs one night. What a noise, like a sack of old rocks tumbling down, and what a groan he fetched. It turned my stomach. But I waited, to be sure it wasn't a trick. He was so damn strong and he had no sense in him at all when he was drunk, you'd never know he could be so easy and gentle when he was sober. . . . When I still didn't hear anything after a long while, I snuck down and looked. He'd fetched up against the woodbox, and he must've had a hell of a thin skull because it was caved right in."

"Dead?" she whispered.

"Dead and cooling off. The fire'd gone out. I guess I was in shock. I remember covering him over, and then I went upstairs and locked my door again and crawled into the sack. At least I must have, because that's where I woke up. The window was the first thing I saw, all thick with frost and the sunrise shining through it orangey-gold, and I could see my breath like smoke, and I didn't remember what happened last night. I thought he was already up and out, but there'd be a fire downstairs and the coffee made, and some oatmeal. He was a great one for that, he called it his porridge, and he said growing boys needed plenty of porridge. See, that's how he was when he was sober."

"He couldn't help the other thing, Quint. He was sick. But he was strong too, if he could fight it when he was sober."

"Yeah, yeah. . . ." He was dreadfully intent on getting this over with, he couldn't stand interruptions. "I always slept in my clothes those cold nights. So did he. Made us kind of gamy, but what the hell, we weren't moving in the most refined circles, you might say.... Anyway, I grabbed my shoes and unlocked my padlock and started down. The cold met me first, and then I saw this—this *thing* down there, all covered up with this filthy old Hudson's Bay blanket. I didn't know what to do. It was like the end of the world. Crazy as he was when he was drunk, he was all the family I had. And where could I run to? It was the dead of winter. I couldn't even figure on living on clams and mussels in some empty cove somewhere. A kid's born a victim, you know that? He doesn't ask to be born, and he'd got nowhere to hide. Nowhere till now," he muttered, and began kissing her shoulders and breasts.

"Tell me what you did," she said. "Where did you go?"

"I don't want to talk about it any more. Later, maybe."

She expanded under his caresses like parched earth under rain. But it was full morning in the room now, and she had to get his letter mailed. Damn his letter. Why should the drought begin again? Oh well, she thought, her fingers on his cheekbones, palms cupping his jaw, nobody will come tomorrow anyway, and maybe there'll be a storm. . . . Let there be a storm, all day and all night, with the trees thrashing and the surf booming in, and nobody stepping outside their doors.

Except for the funeral.

"What's the matter?" he said against her mouth. "Had enough?"

"I have a terrible confession to make."

"You can't tell me you've been faking because, sweetie, I know better. You are one magnificent lay, and you love it."

"Of course I do," she said. "But I'm not a superwoman after all. I have to go."

"I'm disillusioned," he said, rolling over. "I'll never trust a woman again." She sat up and looked down at him, and he reached for her breasts. "What a pair of beauties. No wonder

234

I sleep so good with you. All right, you can go, but you'll have to climb out over me."

"No funny business," she warned him, "or I won't answer for the consequences."

"I never argue with a woman's bladder."

She slid out across his legs, watching him warily. He pretended to grab and she jumped away, they both burst out laughing. She didn't mind his watching her dress, she felt light and lithe in her motions as she had always felt after love and foolery with Con.

"What was your husband like?" he asked suddenly, as if he were reading her mind.

"Something like you." She took a clean blouse out of a drawer and put it on. In the mirror she saw him, black head and brown torso against the pillows and was incredulous all over again. Two days ago he had not existed for her and now she was as familiar with the weight of him upon her as she had been with Con's, and those hands punching a pillow into comfort behind his head had been where only Con's had been.

"How like him?" He was prepared to be entertained.

She said, "I've got to go, remember?" She escaped.

She wondered if the mailboat would bring Jamie back today, or the Coast Guard. A dreadful anticipation overwhelmed her until she heard Quint walking around overhead. Yes, he was somewhat like Con, but more vulnerable. Con had lost his parents young, but he'd had adoring relatives, to hear him tell it. She hadn't been a refuge for Con, she'd been just someone else to adore him and give him what he wanted.

She hadn't been able to refuse him anything, even Phyllis. But how far away it all seemed, the soreness was all worn off. Any immediate pain was connected with Jamie; she thought of him without a name, she could not say it even in her thoughts, and wondered how long it would be before she could say it. Would anyone notice if she didn't go to the cemetery? She had had a crawling dread of funerals since

235

her mother's, when she was fourteen; she had gotten through her father's by some form of self-hypnosis.

She tacked a couch cover over the stairway window looking toward the harbor, and carried a basin of wash water, with soap and towel, up to Quint. "I wish we could eat downstairs," she said, "but I don't dare take chances."

"Never mind, we'll go right back to bed."

"I have to mail your letter, remember. I want to get down there before the boat comes." So I won't have to see many people. So I won't see if they've brought him. . . . She made up the beds and went back down to fix a hearty breakfast.

The small bedroom was pleasant in the morning, with the misty sunlight coming in, and the scent of the woods stirred up by the wind. They were both hungry in spite of what haunted them, both shared and private.

When they'd finished he tried to coax her back onto the bed with him. "Just to be matey, that's all. . . . Come on, love." His eyes were shining with innocent greed.

She needed days of rain to end the drought. She stood in the doorway, her toes curled in her moccasins and her arms folded as if in defense against her own instincts; below her armpits her fingertips dug painfully into the tender area over her ribs.

"Your letter, remember."

"To hell with the letter."

"That's what you say *now*, but after the boat went you'd be saying Christ, I can't hide in this room forever, it's driving me up the wall now."

He slumped on the edge of the bed looking at his feet. "I forgot what I was hiding from."

I made you forget, she thought proudly. I brought you rest. She went over to him and he embraced her around her hips and put his face against her belly. "Don't be gone long."

"I won't," she promised. "And stay up here. There are children next door, and other children come there. They might run across into the yard after a ball or the dog, or something." She took his head in both her hands and tipped it back; he looked blindly up at her and she leaned down and kissed him.

28

Once she was out in the lane the atmosphere became staggeringly oppressive. Even the Percy house was unusually quiet for this hour of the morning, as if the children were being kept in because their noise would be disrespectful to the dead. The dead. THE DEAD. It couldn't be. *Just stick your head out the door and whistle.* I should've done that, she thought wildly. I'll bet he'd come. It had to be someone else Quint saw. But the yellow hair. Who else is that blond? Maybe that's what sticks in his mind, but it was someone else he hit.

With consternation she saw that she was almost at the wharf, and she wasn't yet prepared to look Mark Bennett in the eye. Should she say, "I'm sorry," or pretend she'd been at home sick and hadn't heard anything yet? How could she carry that off? She never could hide anything, good *or* bad.

"You young ones come up off that wharf *now!*" Maggie Dinsmore was hurrying down through the shed, Tiger rushing ahead of her. She hadn't noticed Rosa, who stood by the railing over the water and looked out across the windy gray-gold harbor without seeing it, trying to get up the strength to walk into the store, drop the letter in the slot under the post-office window, and walk out again.

Someone came out of the store behind her, talking. "That chopper won't be back today. It's breezing on all the time." It was Terence Campion. He was not speaking to Rosa. Someone had come out with him, who answered.

"They won't find him now anyway, poor bastard. He's on bottom somewhere.... Hi, Rosa! Where you been?"

She had no time to assimilate the familiarity of a voice which she had known she would never hear again. At the sound of her name she turned and looked into Jamie's face.

Campion nodded and smiled at her and went away. She seemed to see it without taking her eyes off Jamie. She knew her mouth was open, her chin shaking.

Jamie gripped her upper arm, where Quint had gripped, and it hurt. "Are you all right? You look sick."

She had a dizzying sense of mixed-up time, as if it were happening again, the day she heard from her lawyer and stood out here with the letter. *Are you all right?* Jamie had asked her then. *You're feather-white.*

Today he had a scraped and bruised cheekbone. "I'm lightheaded," she said unsteadily. "I've been having summer complaint. I shouldn't have come out, I guess, but I—this letter—"

He took it from her without looking at it, and went inside to mail it. She leaned against the wall, feebly waiting. Her head wanted to fly off her shoulders. When he came out again he said, "Is there anything you want from the store?"

"No, I'll just go home and go back to bed." She laughed weakly.

"How about a bucket of fresh water? Have you got any aspirin?"

"Oh, I'm over the worst of it," she assured him. "I just n-need to sleep it off. So don't worry about me. I've got plenty of water keeping cold in the refrigerator, and juice, and stuff." Her voice rattled around in her head like dry peas in a pail.

"All right. But—" He braced his hand on the weathered

shingles by her shoulder and said in a low voice, "How about the other thing? I mean, you getting things kind of sorted out? Not feeling so upset?"

"I think so." God, if her legs didn't give way here and now. "I mean, what's the sense? It's not the end of my life."

She couldn't get a deep breath. Maybe she *was* sick. This could be the beginning. Heroines in the old stories used to have brain fever when life became too much for them. They passed into delirium and blissful comas, and woke up with everything solved for them, and their hair cut short and growing out curly even if it hadn't been curly before. A drunken mirth began deep down under her ribs somewhere. Jamie's smile was both agreeable and puzzled.

"Hey, is it that funny?"

"It's funny I fussed so long and now it's—" She waved her hands. "Just nothing. All the time I wasted and it doesn't amount to Hannah Cook. I couldn't keep it from happening, but now that it's happened I'm still alive. I've survived."

"That's great! That's the way you ought to feel. Can I come up by and by?"

"Not till I'm over this. I think I could sleep for about two days. . . . What was the helicopter around for, all day yesterday?"

"Oh, didn't you hear about the fracas the other night?" He explained, somberly. "Poor cuss, he wasn't even a regular, just somebody filling in for a guy who was sick. Probably thought if he could go a couple of weeks he'd make a bundle, the way they've been doing. Of course anybody can fall overboard any time, that's an occupational hazard, but usually somebody sees it happen and can grab him. But in the middle of the fight, and at night—the carrier was lit up like a liner but that made it just that blacker outside, and if you got the light in your eyes you were blinded. That's how somebody took a swipe at me and I never even saw it coming." He touched his scraped cheekbone. "Laid me low in the bottom of the boat and I was damn near tromped to death by Hugo

Bennett's boots.... Well, this kid could have been blinded like me and made a misstep, or lost his balance, and gone overboard without anybody seeing him. They say he's got no family to miss him, but that doesn't make it any better. His life must have meant something to *him*."

Oh, it does, it does! she thought. He's been fighting for his life since he was born. She couldn't look into Jamie's face, she watched the harbor while he was talking, at *Sea Star* swinging slowly in a half-arc at her mooring when the gusts came down over the village; then swinging slowly back. She became aware that he was silent. She roused herself.

"That's who you were talking about when you came out of the store."

"Yup. We were looking for him all day yesterday. We're going along the shores today on foot. I don't think we'll find him, but some think he may show up rolled up in a mess of kelp. In that case the crows and the gulls will point him out." He was grim. "We're in everybody's bad books for trying to drive them out that night. Nobody was meant to get hurt, for Pete's sake, we just wanted to make it impossible for them to get that seine overboard. But they called our bluff and went ahead with it. Anybody could see we were firing high. And we went out there and started raising hell to keep the water so roiled up it would drive any herring away. Well, that's when the battle was joined, as the man said." He had become much older since the last time she'd seen him.

"No knowing what'll happen when things like that get going," she said. "Well, I'm going home to bed. I'm sorry for what happened. I'm just glad it wasn't somebody from here."

She pushed away from the shingles. "See you later," she said, and walked away. *He was alive.* Her whole face felt loose and trembly now, not just her chin.

On the path she met the Percy boys galloping toward the store, slapping their flanks and whinnying realistically. Marjorie came behind them. "Hi!" she said. "Where've you been? I never saw hide nor hair all day yesterday, and not much before that. I started over once yesterday, but Kathy Campion showed up."

Bless Kathy Campion. —It was easy to sound limp and wobbly, she felt it. "Oh, I've got some bug or other, I'm just lying around and sleeping it off."

"Oh, hey, do you need anything? I've got stuff for upset stomach, backdoor trot, anything you can mention."

"Thanks, but all I need now is sleep, I guess."

"I'll keep the tribe from playing Indian under your windows."

"Don't be too hard on them."

"Oh, did you hear about that poor kid?"

"Jamie just told me. It's terrible."

Once her spruces closed in behind her and the village was hidden, she had the sensation of returning to a reality so concentrated that her brief journey to the outside could have taken place in a dream or delirium.

When she went into the house Quint was sitting on the stairs by the covered window. "I've been looking through a hole," he said. "Makes it better than a movie. Those kids next door are cute little buggers, aren't they? Their mother's not bad either." He came down off the landing and as she stood looking at him, trying to think how to begin (why couldn't she simply say, "You didn't kill anybody") he put his arms around her and burrowed his face in her neck. "I missed you. Isn't that the damndest thing? Just that little while, and I thought you'd never come back, you were giving me away, and I'd—" He lifted his head. His eyes were wet.

"You'd go to jail."

"No. First thing I thought was I'd never sleep with us wrapped so close we can't tell where one begins and the other leaves off. Then I saw you coming. What it did to me! There's my woman, I thought. And it's the first time I ever thought that about any girl.... Surprised me, you know?"

"There'll be no more of it after your friend comes."

He was smiling. "Listen, I've been thinking. Come on." He tugged her over to the stairs and made her sit down, one arm around her, the hand in the neck of her blouse. "Just let me handle 'em a little.... Look, you're free, and I will be. As soon as I get somewhere safe, where I won't be likely to run into somebody who knows me, will you come?"

All she had to do was tell him that Jamie was alive, and it would be ended. She said desperately, "If you'll take your hand away—" She tried to move it. "It's distracting. I can't think."

"You're not intended to think about anything but how good we go together." His touch was delicately exacerbating. "You know what, you're my rock of ages." He sang in a light true voice. " 'Rock of ages, cleft for me, Let me hide myself in thee.' "

"That's practically blasphemy!"

"Why? It's not the Bible, it's just words some guy once wrote and put to music, like you."

"But he meant——"

"Never mind what he meant. I know what *I* mean.... And it's not all one-sided, is it, Rosa?" He dropped his voice, his warm breath played over her ear. "If you're great for me, I know I'm pretty damned good for you."

"Yes, you are," she said. Tell him now, and he'll be gone on today's boat.

"Well, don't sound so sad about it." He took his hand from her breast and put it under her chin, turning her face around to him. "What's wrong? Don't you think I mean it about you being my woman? Hey, you depressed about that guy? You must have known him. Did you run into sad faces down there? Talk about the funeral, maybe? Jesus, funerals are awful and it's kind of sickening to think I caused this one, even if I didn't mean it. Was he married? Have kids?"

242

He looked so worried her own ambivalence was swept away, and she put both arms around him. "He's single. . . . No talk of funerals. I didn't see anybody," she lied. "Nobody was in the store, I just mailed my letter and came away."

"You were long enough." The words were muffled in her shoulder.

"I looked around in the store for anything I needed. Then I waited, but nobody came. Mark Bennett was busy down on the wharf, I guess. . . . Anyway, I left." Tell him, *tell him.*

"Look, doesn't anybody speak to you around here?" He raised his head and looked indignantly at her. "Wouldn't somebody come around to tell you the news?"

"Marjorie Percy just did, in the path. And I told her I was getting over some bug or other and needed sleep. She'll pass that around and nobody'll come near." It was like the time when he'd come into her bed, and she'd known there was still time to stop, but she hadn't stopped; in fact, she'd made him welcome.

"But we'd better not take chances, just the same," she said. "Come on upstairs and tell me what happened after Mick died."

"Till we get tired of talking," he said, following her. The thought of sex always cheered him immensely. She thought, later I'll go out and come back and pretend I just heard about Jamie.

It was a strange day, without time or change; they moved freely through the upstairs rooms in the shadowless light behind the translucent shades. An hour felt like three or four hours, but, later, half a day felt like half an hour.

After Mick died, Quint couldn't make himself go to the police, so he had gone to the fish buyer who always bought Mick's fish. He called the police and the city buried Mick. The trouble was, the dealer wanted to take Quint home with him until arrangements could be made for his care; he thought Quint was Mick's nephew, and had no idea the boy hadn't been going to school. Quint felt everything closing in on him. In new panic, he hitchhiked out of town, but a truckdriver questioned him ruthlessly and turned him over to the State Police.

So the welfare people had got him after all, and he'd been made a ward of the state. "It wasn't so hellish," he said. "Not heaven, but they didn't beat me, nobody chased me around trying to de-virginate me, I got plenty to eat, and I was in a fisherman's family. I had to go to school, but I could be around the shore in my spare time—guy had plenty for me to do, that's why he took me—and summers I was his full-time helper."

He'd even managed to finish high school, though he hadn't showed up at the graduation exercises. At eighteen he was on his own, working at one thing or another, never staying very long at anything. "I guess I was born to be a drifter," he said. "But I've never been in real trouble. Until now."

"But it was accident, and you're not caught," Rosa said.

"I could be. You could still do it." He laughed at her expression, and seized her.

Later he said suddenly, when she thought he was asleep, "Hey, if Danny doesn't come—I mean if he can't come—I could get aboard your boat at night and in the morning you could go to the mainland. Nobody'd question that, would they?"

"No—"

"What's the matter? You scared of being caught transporting a criminal?"

"Thinking about this coming to an end." They were lying naked on his bed.

"Aw, listen, I want you with me, wherever I am! My woman."

"We'd never feel so free anywhere else."

"You feel free *here?*" he asked. "Right on the spot where the guy was killed, practically? His friends and relations all around?"

"But they think you're dead, remember? It makes you

invisible." She smiled at his angry, troubled face, and put her hand on him. Sex always diverted him; she didn't know if his ardor and staying power were natural gifts, or the fruit of his fear and desperation. But she could meet him, and did so with pride, at the same time recognizing the drive of her own desperation. He needed her, therefore she needed him. She understood that.

Now, stretching under his hands, she thought that maybe she wouldn't tell him this afternoon. What difference would tomorrow morning make? He couldn't get off the island tonight anyway. But once she told him, even though he would probably want to sleep with her again, nothing would be the same.

Unless, even though free from murder, he still needed her and not as a hiding place.... She couldn't think about that now. But later.

In late afternoon she slid out from under his flung arm and leg, not easy to do without waking him. But he was really tired now, enough to sleep without nightmares. He hated the dark, and the light made him feel safer.

Downstairs she sponged herself off at the sink, dressed, and went out. She felt as if she hadn't been outside for a week. The boisterous southwest wind bruised the woods and carried the smells of wild apples fallen and rotting on the ground, and the honeysuckle. She walked a little way into the restless woods and sat down on a boulder beside the path, where she could watch the house. At her feet shadows shook across the spills and mosses. Crossbills chattered in the swaying tops of the spruces.

Tomorrow at this time everything would be different. He'd either be foolish with relief and gratitude, and off the island as soon as he could find a way, leaving her his thanks to remember him by (and nothing else, if she'd been lucky enough); or there was the possibility that had come to her upstairs, that he needed her anyway. That he was still the child crouched in the freezing dawn not knowing where to run.

Looking up at the shade flapping gently against the screen of his room, knowing how his brown body looked sprawled in heavy sleep, she thought that no matter what she ever did to that room it would always be saturated with what had taken place there.

Even Con had never been so fierce. But then Con had what he wanted. He wasn't trying to forget that he'd killed somebody and was scared foolish of being caught. *Scared stiff*, Quint had said once today, laughing uproariously.

Maybe that was the secret; the body frantically declaring life in the presence of death.

Supposing Jamie *were* dead. Just one year of his life had been richer than all of Quint's twenty-five. But I could enrich it, she thought. Give him whatever he thinks it takes. Some kind of security, anyway. A home, the boat, money. . . . Or why else had he crawled ashore at her feet?

Her heart didn't leap like a fish or soar like a gull at the prospect. It was simply a statement of fact, that was all.

The children were there before she knew it, triumphantly led by Tiger, who took all the credit for the discovery. The Percy boys were trailed respectfully by the Dinsmore girls; they'd brought a string of small mackerel they'd caught in the harbor.

"Mum says freeze 'em if you don't feel like eating 'em right off," Young Ralph told her. They were all beaming. She felt surrounded by amiable elves. She scratched Tiger's back and he looked up at her with a melting gaze that reminded her of Quint satisfied.

She thanked the children, remembering not to glance up at Quint's window, hoping that he wouldn't wake up suddenly and make some quick, thoughtless move. The children wanted to talk about the whale Rob Dinsmore had seen. One of the boys said solemnly, "Hey, maybe he ate the drowned man," and the girls shuddered theatrically and rolled their eyes.

"Mama won't let us go round the shore till they find him. Just *in case*."

29

They left her on some mysterious signal, darting off the way schools of minnows suddenly changed direction. She cleaned the mackerel and broiled them for supper, with boiled new potatoes and a green salad. Quint ate a tremendous meal. Afterwards they played cribbage, and he skunked her, which pleased him enormously.

"See, women aren't equal. All that stuff about Woman's Lib is so much crap."

"I wasn't even trying," she said haughtily. He tipped back in his chair.

"That's no excuse. But don't feel bad if you're no good at cribbage. You got other advantages, and I don't mean just bed. You're a good cook, and you also own that boat out there."

"You still harping on that? You don't have much faith in your friend, do you?"

The front legs of his chair came down hard. "Now look, how's he going to row ashore and get me with that sea running out there? Hear that old bell?" He nodded his head toward the window. "You know as well as I do, this time of year it can keep on like this for a week. But you can get out of the harbor any time, if it's not a screeching gale. And Rosa, look..." He leaned across the table, and his eyes made her think of Tiger's, as the dog's had reminded her of Quint's. "We could head down east, from harbor to harbor. Or run straight from here to Isle au Haut, and gas up there and keep on going. There's a lot of space left down east, Rosa. Miles and miles of woods. Empty coves with old houses—"

"That somebody's hoping to sell to summer people for a hundred thousand," she said.

"Hell, there's still room for us somewhere. Get somebody to sell your Seal Point property. I'll make it up to you, Rosie, I swear." Eyes shining like Tiger's. "I'll really work and stick to it. Quint'll be dead off Bennett's Island somewhere, food for the fish and the crabs, and I'll be somebody else. I'll take a different name. Hey, let's think up a good name for me, Rosie. What's your favorite?"

She couldn't find words, there was just this overpowering incredulity at herself for actually listening; for having allowed it to reach this point. He squeezed her hands hard. "What about it, Rosie? Tell me you're crazy about me, right? And I'm crazy about you, right?" An even harder squeeze. His voice dropped to the familiar husky whisper that could brush her sensibilities like his fingertips on her body. "Let's go, love. You can gas up and pack up tonight, put me out aboard, and we can take off at daylight in the morning."

"Quint, Mark doesn't keep the store open in the evening. If I went and asked him to come down to the wharf tonight it would look pretty damn funny. It would look even funnier if I took off at daylight in the morning without a word to anyone, and headed northeast."

His shoulders slumped. He let go of her hands and began shuffling the cards. "Whichever way we go then, it'll look funny. If they notice every fart."

"Not if I headed for the mainland, and then changed course."

He came alive then, and dropped the cards. "Get ready tomorrow and take off the day after, then?"

"The day after." She didn't look at him, drawing the cards toward her. He was out of his chair and prowling, rubbing his hands, breaking into odd yelps of laughter. "Oh, Rosie, Rosie—hey, any charts here?"

"All aboard the boat." She began to lay out Canfield.

"I just wanted to dream a little." He was behind her, kissing her nape, pushing his hands down inside her blouse. While she went on laying out the cards, he pulled her shirt out of her slacks and unhooked her bra. "Come on to bed, Rosie love."

She tried to hold out, but she could not. In bed in the dusk, the world was this house, this room, and there was nothing to fear from the outside, because there was no outside, and there was no time either.

Morning came too soon. While he was still sleeping, she sat downstairs drinking fresh coffee. The day was clear and quiet. She wished that it were storming out there, so that she needn't go beyond plans. The plain fact, which she couldn't escape, was that she couldn't bear to lose Quint, she would have prolonged this forever if she thought she could get away with it. But she couldn't hide forever here, or hide him. By taking him to another place, couldn't she thus create another world as safe as the one she had made for him here?

Ah, but what was the substance of this world? He'd needed an instant shield from the consequences of his acts. Once outside it, how much would he need her? He was half-wild, after all.

She thought, I have to tell him. I have to know.

The return of the helicopter awoke Quint. He came down to go out back while she stood guard. He returned light-footed as the dancer or fighter he'd reminded her of, transfigured with mirth.

"Hey, you know how much it costs to keep that chopper going? The taxpayers are paying plenty to keep looking for me. Well, they owe me something! . . . Still, I'd rather have the cash." He talked and talked. What price could she get for the Seal Point property? What about rigging the boat for winter scalloping or shrimping? How much did she have in the bank?

It lacerated her nerves. *Tell him, tell him.* And see the joyous explosion of freedom? How much would the money mean to him after that? Plenty, if he'd never had much.

"Hey, shouldn't you be packing?" he asked.

"I haven't much to pack. How about a cake?"

"Great! Chocolate?"

"Go on upstairs out of sight, and I'll bring it up when it's done."

She covered it with a half-inch-thick frosting and carried it up to him with a quart of milk, hoping it would keep him quiet for a while. She returned to the kitchen and began passionately to clean the gas stove. Was sixty thousand for the Seal Point property too unrealistic? *Unrealistic!* Talk about the pot calling the kettle black. She said aloud, "Rosa, you're crazier than a goddam hoot owl."

"*Honest?*"

She turned so fast her head spun. Jamie stood in the doorway, looking pleased with himself. "Hi. I came up to see if you were dead of some mysterious tropical disease." He came into the kitchen, holding out a covered plastic container. "Home-made beef stew. My mother sent it up to you."

She tried not to act dazed and stupid. "Thank you very much. Thank *her* very much." When she took the container she almost dropped it.

"You're still shaky," Jamie said, catching it. "You look tired. Circles under your eyes."

"Yes, I guess I need another night's rest." Look square at him, you idiot. She was blushing so under her clothes that her back felt scalding hot, her face was burning and she couldn't hide it. Fumbling, she turned the stew into a saucepan and began rinsing the container. Jamie yawned and said, "I feel

250

thick today. I was up around three to see what the weather was, and I've been out since daylight looking for that guy. Gave up finally and came in for a mug-up."

She managed to give him a half-natural glance over her shoulder. "Where'd you look?"

"Oh, all around Sou'west Point to see if he'd been thrown up anywhere, and then I even went over to the southern end of Brigport. Tide might have carried him that way. But no sign."

She worked on the container as if it were really encrusted with years of soil. "Wouldn't the helicopter have seen him if he was at all visible?"

He yawned again. "Oh, most likely, unless he was buried under rockweed or wedged into a crack somewhere. Anyway, I went ashore on them to satisfy my own curiosity. I hate like hell to think of the poor guy left like that. Well, if he's carried away, the sea's as good a grave as any. I'd choose it for myself." His solemn eyes met hers. "But hung up somewhere like an old jacket or a piece of pot warp—nope."

She dried plastic as if it were porcelain. Jamie said, "The Coast Guard's calling off the search, so the chopper won't be back tomorrow. You know, if they'd just paid attention to us the first time we warned them off, he'd still be alive."

"Or if you hadn't used a gun."

"Look, we had a right. It's our island, after all. And we fired high. I hear they're saying we fired low, and Purvis'll swear to it. But they can't prove it. Anyway," he said defiantly, "we were bound to come to blows sooner or later, the guns had nothing to do with it. That was just to get their attention."

"Well, it seems to have done that all right." She fastened the lid on the container and handed it to him.

"Now listen, don't *you* go sour on me. We've got enough on our hands without our folks acting as if we're the local branch of the Mafia or something. We just happened to go into the store together this afternoon and some pillar of wit and wisdom said, 'How's things with Cosa Nostra, boys?'"

Rosa laughed. "Personally I don't think it's that funny," said Jamie, "but it wowed them in the store."

"It was your expression, that's all. . . . None of it's very funny, Jamie." She was wishing so vigorously for him to leave that he should have felt it. How could he be so stupid?

"That's why I need a little sympathetic companionship," Jamie said. "Can I come up tonight for an hour or so? Maybe we could walk over back and watch the sunset."

Out of the intensity of her desire to be rid of him, she was able to look him in the eye now. "Jamie, I'm going to take the boat over to gas up, and then I'm coming back here and fix up a sandwich and take it to bed, eat and read, and be asleep before dark. I plan to haul tomorrow."

"Tomorrow night, then," he said doggedly. "It's time you started living again, Rosa, the way I told you. Walking over to Barque Cove to look at the sunset isn't much, but it's a start."

"Tomorrow night," she repeated. "Yes, your lordship."

"All right. I'll gas up for you, so you can start resting up right now. And listen, if we're anywhere near each other when I stop for a coffee break tomorrow morning, I'm coming alongside. Understand?"

"Aye, aye, sir."

"*Dismissed!*" Jamie snapped, then laughed. "I feel better already. Well, I'll go tend to *Sea Star*."

"I'm much obliged, Jamie," she said, following him through the entry so he wouldn't delay.

"Think nothing of it." Swiftly he kissed her cheek and at the same time squeezed her shoulder. Then he left, waving without looking back. She felt shaky and tired enough to cry. She saw herself having coffee with Jamie, the two boats lying gently together in a lee spot; she also saw herself heading down east in *Sea Star*, with Quint out of hiding and at the wheel.

She went back into the kitchen, and Quint was there at

the front windows, hands braced on the window sill, trying to see past the spruces.

He twisted around. His color had turned worse than sallow. It was muddy. "Is there more than one guy with hair that yellow?" he demanded.

Without thinking she said, "His father, but he wasn't there that night."

"I didn't kill him, then."

"Not Jamie."

"Then *who?*" He came toward her, his eyes bulged in a frantic stare. "Listen, the way he talked, *I'm* the only one dead, and the way he said it I began to think I *was* dead, and hung up somewhere like he said, for the gulls to pick at." Sweat was running down his face. "Listen, was that it? Am I the only one?"

She nodded. He came closer, slowly, his thumbs in his belt. "How long have you known?"

She thought of saying, Since just now, when he came in. Her mouth was opening; she could have sworn on her life that was what she intended to say. But awed by the sweat-glazed mask she said, "Since yesterday morning, when I went to mail the letter."

"And you didn't tell me," he said in his husky whisper. "You came back here with a face like cream and you let me suffer."

"I didn't think you were suffering much," she said.

"I had to do *something* to keep from climbing the walls! I told you I can't stand being shut up, and this—this"— he took in the kitchen with a contempt that should have scarred the walls—"and woods practically right up to the windows, choking you to death. . . . Jesus, you knew, and you didn't tell me. You went through the whole stinking act. Are you some kind of a *nut?* You crazy because your old man walked out on you? Or did he walk out on you because you're crazy?"

He hooted savagely, and struck at her. Not able to take the gesture seriously, she dodged, and said, "Listen, Quint,

253

sure I should have told you. But leave that out of it, you'd still want to be smuggled off, you'd have no way to explain hiding out here while they all looked for you, the helicopter and everything—"

The back of his hand struck the words off her lips. She tasted blood. She was his height, and strong, but she had no defense against his speed, skill, and viciousness. He said things sometimes. Obscenities. She heard but they were just so many more blows to be warded off her face, her breasts, her belly. She tried backing toward the door, but he danced around there and fended her off. He was everywhere at once. Finally she dropped, crumpling forward as she fell and curling up like a sowbug to shield herself, head to knee.

He stood over her. His breathing was loud and rasping in the room, she could hear it over the thick throbbing in her ears. "Damn cow," he said. "Who do you think wanted *you?* All you were to me was a chance to hide out and get off this God-forsaken rock. And it turns out I didn't even need that!"

He kicked her in the side—with my moccasins! she thought as if that were the chief indignity—and walked out of the house.

She lay where she was, thinking with a calm hatred. If he comes back I'll meet him with a knife in each hand. But she needed the strength first. The shock and degradation of the attack were worse than the pain of the blows and the taste of blood in her mouth.

Gradually the pounding died down. She realized that quite a long time had gone by, and that probably he was not coming back.

She sat up carefully. Her side hurt from the kick, but not as if a rib was broken. She hurt in a number of places, especially around her cheekbones, and mouth. No teeth loosened; she'd dodged in time. Her head ached.

"Damn cow. Who do you think wanted *you?*"

She bowed her head into her arms and wept.

30

Someone was leaning over her, hands on her shoulders. If this is Jamie, she thought drearily, I wish anybody could die of shame. She tilted back her head and through swollen lids she saw Edwin.

She leaned her face against his knees. After a few minutes his hands began urging her up. His arm around her guided her to a chair at the table, then he went to the sink and came back with a basin of water. Absorbed and seemingly impersonal, he attended to her face, applying ointment where the skin was broken. She remembered doing this for Quint, and tried to think how long ago it was. The effort made her dizzy. She leaned her head on her hand. He got out ice cubes and wrapped them in a towel for her swollen mouth.

Without meeting his eyes she applied it, gingerly.

His notepad slid into her field of vision. "What happened?"

She took the pen and wrote, "Fell down stairs. Where did you come from, baby dear?"

"Lobster smack. Spur of the moment. —Did she fall or was she pushed?"

She turned her face away toward the windows and the spruces that hid the lane. Everybody disappeared beyond them eventually. Con, that day; Jamie, this afternoon, and he'd never come back once he found out about Quint. Quint—but had he gone that way?

255

She looked wildly around at Edwin, who nodded and began to write again.

"Drowned men rise up and become heroes. He just walked into the store and gave himself up. Performance straight out of TV western. Everybody's telling him he didn't kill anybody. He's smiling through tears and being the belle of the ball."

"Did he say where he's been hiding out?" Her handwriting was unsteady.

"In the woods at Sou'west Point. Living on mussels and periwinkles he cooked at night."

"His clothes could have dried out on him, but he had my moccasins. How explain them?"

Edwin smiled for the first time, and pointed across the room. Her moccasins sat neatly side by side just inside the door. "I found those in the path," he wrote. "He showed up in bare feet. They've given him someone's shoes.... Mark wants to feed him, but he claims his stomach's shrunk."

Rosa laughed scornfully, which caused excruciating pain in her lip. "The truth is, he's got a full gut. All I did was cook for him."

Well, almost all.

Edwin wrote, "Want me to claim he broke in here and attacked you? I'd be happy to wipe away that Gee-whiz grin."

She shook her head desolately. "I took him in and fed him. I can't get away from that."

"Why did he beat you up? Did he try to rob you?"

"I made him mad." She left it at that, and Edwin asked nothing more. He wrote that Quint was going ashore on the lobster smack. After that they sat there for a time. Edwin filled and lit his pipe. She was lost, not in thought, but in some chaotic limbo of words, broken phrases; the cold and heat, the light and dark of rushing cloud shadows. Grief almost that of bereavement; shame; rage; ridicule; grief returning, so chokingly bitter it was losing Con all over again.... She couldn't seem to settle on one thing before another swept it away.

All the time she sat immobile, leaning on her elbows, her hands cupped over her closed eyes. Edwin got up after a while and took his bag and his bedroll into his room. He came back, she heard the water pails clattering. He poured left-over water into the tea kettle and the wash basin, then went out with the two pails.

She roused herself to go upstairs and began methodically erasing any sign of Quint. She stripped the sheets off her bed and his; they'd used both. They would be boiled and bleached, and the blankets put out to air; in the meanwhile she tossed everything into the third upstairs bedroom. She opened the windows all around so that the afternoon wind could pour through like a tide. The books he had been reading, and the cards they'd played cribbage with, she would burn. She dropped them all into a pillowcase for the time being. She returned her sleeping bag to her room, and put fresh pillowcases on her pillows. . . . Half the chocolate cake was left, and Edwin could have it. It was too good for the gulls.

She carried the lamp downstairs and brought up the dry mop, though the place hardly needed it. If she'd had time and plenty of water on hand, she'd have scrubbed the floors. From the windows of the third room, she saw her water pails standing on the well curb, and Edwin was not in sight. In the late afternoon sunshine the village looked tranquilly ordinary. There was a ball game between the Percy, Dinsmore, and Campion children. A cluster of men stood talking by Philip Bennett's front porch, three of them Bennetts, she could tell even from this distance. Jamie came up by the Binnacle, hands in his pockets, heading home; the dog loped stiffly to meet him. The soft ball went wild and Jamie fielded it with an expert reach and tossed it back to a dandelion-headed girl.

The lobster smack was leaving. She didn't try for a glimpse of Quint.

257

Edwin had brought a box of green corn, tomatoes, cucumbers, and lettuce from his father's garden, as well as the usual steaks. Spur of the moment? she questioned. Just happened to be around the waterfront when the smack was leaving for the island? Just happened to have his bag packed, his bedroll ready, vegetables gathered, and steaks bought, and everything tucked handily under one arm?

The worst thing about Edwin's lies, or maybe the best thing, considering them from Edwin's standpoint, was that you had such a hard time challenging them.

It didn't matter, except that now he knew her disgrace, or part of it. Not the worst part. Even to obliquely refer to it, wordlessly, nauseated her because her body could still remember how it had been and would not repudiate its own rapture. How could you! How *could* you! she cried silently at herself as if at a child or sister who had disgraced her beyond tolerance.

She set the table and started heating water for the corn. Edwin returned with the two full pails, and she drank cold water thirstily, it was refreshing to her sore mouth. Meanwhile Edwin was writing. When she stopped drinking he handed her the pad.

"Gone. No change in story. Don't worry. He's got plenty to hide. Not just the beating. He can't brag he made a fool of you without admitting you made a fool of him."

"Thanks," she said bitterly. It was hard to shape words with her battered mouth. She wrote, "You sure know how to kill anybody's self-respect. What do you mean, a fool? I found him in the surf, half-frozen and scared senseless. I thought Jamie was dead but by accident, not murder. . . . I was trying to think what to do about him and he kept panicking." The pen slowed a little; damn Edwin's eyes, watching and assessing. What did he think he was, a lie detector? Bearing down on the pen she wrote, "When Jamie showed up here today I was surprised. *Glad*," she added. "I thought Quint would be too."

258

It was the first time she'd written his name. The shape of the words brought him before her eyes in a constantly changing series of images so that she was temporarily blinded, she didn't know what to write next.

Edwin got up suddenly and began fixing a drink for himself. Freed, she wrote, "Instead, he went off his head. If I was a fool, it was because I dragged him ashore that night. I should've left him there and told somebody else where he was."

She shoved the pad across to Edwin, and went back to getting supper. She cooked the corn and broiled steak for him and heated up the beef stew for herself. When they'd finished, he suggested going out to the cove and she went eagerly; it seemed months since she'd walked to the shore and tonight there was an almost supernatural beauty to the scene.

She wondered how long it would be before her eyes wouldn't go involuntarily to the place where Quint had been lying that night. She found she didn't want to be here after all, and pretended to slap fiercely at mosquitoes. Finally she told Edwin she was going back to the house, and left him climbing the rocks on the far side of the cove.

She sat on the stairs with her guitar. At least her hands weren't hurt, though she couldn't sing very well with her sore lips and lame jaw. She hummed safe songs that were talismans to return her to innocence. Nothing could do that, of course, but she might thus find a recognizable Rosa.

She went to bed when it was dusk, leaving a lamp lit in the kitchen. Listening to the crickets, she wondered again why Edwin had really come. He was through with the Parnell job. But with Laura Parnell? Whatever drove him, she was glad of it. She couldn't imagine, or didn't want to, what her frame of mind would have been tonight if he hadn't come.

31

She slept hard, and when she woke up it was like arousing from some nearly fatal illness. A crisis had passed, and she could feel only relief. She was very sore and lame, especially where she had been kicked, but she winced more at the debasement of it than at the pain.

The morning was clear, boats were already leaving, and the cry of a gull banking past her window, so close she could hear the soft rush of his wings, was like a summons to her, a message from the boat. She could hardly wait to get out there.

Edwin was already up. He poached eggs for her without consulting her, and served them with soft bread and butter. If he'd come to brood over lost opportunities, he didn't show it. Maybe he thought she was in worse shape than he was, she thought philosophically. Ah well, he didn't know the half of it.

The reflection of her bruised face in the mirror made her recoil.

"I wish I'd brought my paints," Edwin wrote. "You're sensational."

God, but it was good to have him there. She could even laugh, tender as her mouth was. "Look at *this!*" she bragged, pulling up her shirt. His eyelids flickered when he saw her ribs, he sucked in one cheek as if he were biting it.

When she was filling her thermos bottle, he wrote, "Fix more. I'm going too. Take that cake."

She made a face as if he'd suggested a drink before breakfast, but packed the cake carefully in the round cookie tin Jude had sent full of individually wrapped tomatoes.

Like the guitar, like Edwin, *Sea Star* was reality, and maybe all that she was meant to have. If Edwin should marry, or have a valid, absorbing love affair, she'd lose him, but for now he was here, and now was all one could count on.

They lay to for a coffee break in Bull Cove, and Jamie, seeing them from a little distance offshore, came speeding in. When he saw her face he went blank, as if he'd been slugged senseless. For once he was without words.

"I know it," she said at once. "I'm sensational. Fabulous. Edwin told me."

"What the hell *happened?*" He kept peering as if trying to discover her among the various purples and sick yellows.

"I tripped going downstairs. It's a wonder you didn't hear the crash. I was sure it would bring the Percys over, but maybe they thought it was a sonic boom. I did what you could call a bang-up job."

"Should you be out here?" He glanced accusingly at Edwin, who gave him a benign smile and went on sketching.

"Why not?" asked Rosa. Our motto, she thought. "I'm like a singed cat, a lot better than I look." She was so glad that neither of them knew about Quint that she felt almost drunk. A sore face was a helpful disguise while Jamie told her about Quint giving himself up.

"So now you aren't the Mafia any more," she said. "Have some cake."

"Hey, thanks. . . . No, now the line is, 'Take warning from this, it could really happen the next time.' I know one thing, that bunch won't be back, and nobody else will come that doesn't want a fight. We got the message across. But I was some glad when that little guy showed up. None of us wanted

261

him on our conscience, especially when they began saying he'd be full of buckshot when he surfaced." He laughed. "Know what? He thought he'd killed *me!* For a minute there I thought he was going to hug and kiss me like one of those French generals."

She laughed with him. Edwin, putting down his sketch-book to take some cake, didn't know what the joke was, but he looked genial. It was all fine. A happy ending for every-body, Quint gone, the story over. . . . She watched the two men eating the cake she'd baked for Con. No, for Quint. Edwin was showing Jamie the sketch he'd made of him, Jamie was amused and impressed. He was making an honest attempt to consider Edwin an ordinary man, neither fiend nor angel.

"How can I congratulate him for winning that award?" he asked Rosa.

"Say it to his face, or write it." She took the notepad and pen out of Edwin's shirt pocket and handed it to Jamie, who self-consciously wrote his message and showed it to Edwin. Edwin nodded, and held his knife over the cake, eyebrows questioning.

"Don't mind if I do," said Jamie, a little loudly, but visibly gratified at being able to communicate. Rosa sat on the engine box delicately sipping coffee through painful lips, her lids downcast so she could watch Jamie past her lashes. What grew between him and her—if she let it grow—would take time, but it would be sound and good. No doubt of that. Jamie wouldn't be coming to her for refuge; he was one of the most self-sufficient men she'd ever met. Jude had mentioned the solid silver dollar. Was that Jamie Sorensen?

It was only an insubstantial idea, almost as ungraspable as fog. She had bruises that nobody could see, and if she was glad that these two men couldn't know about her and Quint, she couldn't wipe out the fact that *she* knew.

The outer bruises should last forever, she thought bitterly. Too bad he couldn't have given me some real scars, to remind me every time I looked in the mirror. That's what I deserve.

Jamie said, "Thanks for the mug-up, friend." He untied the line that held the boats together. "I'll be up tonight, okay? I've got some nylon for my baitbags." He didn't wait for an answer, but went away fast, as he always did.

No matter what she did all afternoon, baiting up, washing sheets, going with Edwin to pick blackberries on the back shore, she was as conscious of Jamie as if he were there with her. She carried on long involved conversations with him which never reached any satisfactory conclusions; always there was the wall between. Transparent but unshatterable, not even to be scratched with a diamond, it was so hard.

You should hang on to him, you fool, she harshly addressed herself. You can take your time about it, but for God's sake—no, for your own—don't lose him. There are a thousand Cons, and *con* is right, but only one Jamie Sorensen. So what if there'll never be anything again like what you had with Con at the first of it? There's never another first: first pup, first grade, first boat. So you go on to the second, and that always has something the first didn't have.

But the wall remained, growing thicker as the evening came on. Edwin, though physically with her, was aloof, and she thought, We're not much help to each other. People *are* islands, and sometimes not even within shouting distance.

After supper he saw Jamie coming before she did, and went out. Apparently he too thought she should grapple Jamie to her with hoops of steel the way it said in the Bible about somebody or other.

At least Jamie wasn't asking for firm answers tonight. They talked quite a bit about the baitbags; he liked a good-sized one, and she knit a sample for him. He approved it, and after all this she asked leading questions about the fracas the other night. He was keeping his word about not applying pressure, and she was grateful for that. Her own doom-laden thoughts ran on and on beneath the surface; the house was

263

full of Quint, haunted by him. Jamie couldn't exorcise the presence, he only strengthened it. His very innocence gave it more and more substance.

I will never be free of it, she thought with chilling simplicity.

What kind of woman was she? The kind who would go to bed with any charming scoundrel who could make her feel sorry for him? Who could wheedle and blarney her into thinking she was needed? Or was that only her excuse? . . . Seal Point was right, whether it laughed or pitied. So she'd run away from the deserved result of her own behavior, only to smash her face upon the unyielding and undestructible truth out here.

Jamie thought Con had taken her in. Could he be that charitable about Quint? No. She could never tell him, and she couldn't live with it between them, not as he wanted her to live with him.

The unshatterable wall was the simple fact that she wasn't good enough for him.

"What are you thinking?" he asked all at once. "Or is it the bruises that give you that kind of melancholy look?"

"Like a sad clown," she said. "No, I'm aching in spots. I guess I'll take some aspirin."

She got up to go to the sink, eager to get away from his eyes. So this was over too, though he didn't know it yet, and pity made her throat ache. Pity for him or for herself, it didn't matter, it hurt just as much.

"You ought to be in bed," he said, pushing back his chair. "I'll be going."

"Looking for herring tonight?" she asked, shaking the tablets into her hand.

"I'll always be looking for herring," he said with a laugh. "It's not just a business, it's a calling." He came up behind her and put his hands lightly on her shoulders. She felt his lips on her nape. "Your poor mouth's too sore to kiss," he said.

When he had gone she stood in the dusky kitchen slowly stroking her throat, trying to drive out the pain. But I won't go away from here, she thought. I won't be driven. Anybody has to stop running sometime. . . .

Edwin came in while she was still standing there, he couldn't have been far away. He lighted a lamp and set it on the table, took down the cribbage board from the wall, went into his room and came out with an unopened bottle of Jim Beam.

The instant he put it on the table, she removed it and pushed it roughly into his hands.

"I don't know what in hell you're trying to forget," she told him. "But I know about *me*, and I've already rolled in the muck enough without getting drunk. And I'll be damned if I'll watch you doing it. Now if that's what you came out here for, you can just leave on the boat tomorrow."

He tipped back his chair, put his fingertips together, and nodded meditatively. She wanted to hit him. "And don't be so superior! If it's *love*"—she twisted her mouth on the word, and it hurt—"why don't you fall in love with somebody who'll love *you*? Or do you choose wrong on purpose, because otherwise there's no excitement?"

He shrugged.

"I know all about it," she said. She plucked the notepad from his pocket. "I slept with that little whoremaster," she wrote in a slashing hand. "Because he had nightmares, and he begged. He didn't have to beg very hard. I'd have done anything to hold on to him. Smuggled him off in the boat, sell my property to set him up down east somewhere. We talked about it. He had it all planned out and I never said No. I knew the second day that Jamie wasn't dead, but as long as Quint thought so, he needed me."

She laughed raucously, feeling tears in her eyes, and went on writing. "He beat me up when he found out. Everything else, all he said to me, was forgotten. He didn't even want my money. Now you know what I've got to get drunk about. What's your excuse?"

She shoved the pad at him. His cheekbones were flushed and his eyes in slits as if against too-bright light. He wrote, "Same as yours. I went back."

She saw everything behind the words. She saw the woman in the garden, with her hands up to her hair and then in the shadowy hall, smiling at Edwin with hungry uncertainty, her hand on his arm. Superimposed on this, clear in itself yet not draining vigor from the under-images, there was Con at the wheel of his boat, glancing around as if he'd heard his name, his eyes twinkling like the spots on the sea where wind and sun hit together; and there was Quint in her arms, and his husky whisper in her ear.

She looked again at the brief black words on the pad. "But that's not all," she said aloud. She went on with an effort, and the words fell desolately into the deep well of silence. "It's not the disgust that makes you ache. It's the b—"

She could not get out the word *beauty*. She felt her way up to her bed, blinded by both the dark and her tears.

32

The next day there was no overt strain between her and Edwin. He had not gone on drinking last night, and there was a morning freshness about him that made her feel haggard and ugly.

"You look like one of those sexy yachtsmen in the whiskey ads," she wrote to him across the table. "Getting some girl aboard to ply her with strong drink so you can seduce her."

"My name's a handicap. Whoever heard of a seducer named Edwin?"

"Change it then, create a new image. What's your middle name? I never knew." She heard herself with wonder; it was like watching herself walk a tightrope over a canyon, her gloom was so profound.

"Jerome. It's not much better." Maybe he was walking a tightrope too. After breakfast he went down to the store for pipe tobacco, and when he came back he wrote her an invitation to come out to Sou'west Point with him.

"The surf's building up. We're going to have a gale by nightfall."

"You go ahead and I'll fix us some lunch and come later."

"Right now," he insisted. "We don't need food. Pick up a couple of apples, and that cheese."

The very thought of hurrying made her sweat. "I feel as if I'd been sick. I've got to take my time."

He stood looking hard at her, and his lips moved as if he might actually speak, or attempt to. Finally he picked up his watercolor kit and went out. Disturbed by his odd behavior, she almost went after him, then she decided to take at least something to drink, some crackers for the cheese, a few tomatoes. She wouldn't mind staying away from the harbor all day. The more she thought of it the more eager she became.

She packed the thermos and the food in a plastic bucket, and went upstairs to get an extra sweater. From habit she went to her window and looked down at *Sea Star*. A strange boat was tied up at Mark's wharf, and there was a heart-stopping familiarity about her. Of course there can be more than one like that, Rosa told herself witheringly. But she couldn't stop looking.

Voices erupted from below, and she looked down and saw

267

the Campion children coming up from the direction of the store, on their way to the Percy house.

"What's the name of that boat at the wharf?" she called to them.

"*Phyllis*," Cindy Campion answered. She stood back the better to see up to where Rosa knelt behind the screen. "I think that's a pretty name. It means a green bough. I know what practically every name means. Mine means some Greek goddess." She preened and said her name lovingly. "Cyn-thia."

"That's nice," Rosa said. "Thanks, Cindy." She started to withdraw, but Johnny Campion called, "Hey, Mrs. Fleming, did you hear about the man hiding in the woods?"

"Yes, I heard. Wasn't that something, though?"

She ran downstairs and picked up the plastic pail. She felt sick to her stomach, yet incongruously she remembered they should have salt for the tomatoes, and she took the salt shaker off the table and unscrewed the cap and filled it. She wanted to run away, yet she knew why she was delaying.

Still, when Con went past the windows she began to tremble. He walked in without knocking, saying, "If I had a hat I'd throw it in.... Good God, Rosa, what *happened?*"

"I fell downstairs. It looks worse than it is." She was loud and brash. "You don't look so good yourself. Married life turning out to be kind of wearing?" Older, she was thinking. A lot older. Tired. Beat.... Money? Was he coming to her for *that?* Did he have the nerve? Of course he did. He had the nerve for anything.

"I'm not married," he said. "Rosie, I couldn't go through with it. When I knew the divorce was over, I was—I was—well, I can't describe how I felt, except it was awful."

"Yes, it was that," she agreed. "But for me, the awful part was long before the court part of it. Now that it's over, I'm—" she snapped her fingers. "Like that. Nothing to it. It's like going to the dentist. You come out walking on air." *I'm not married.* Had he really said that?

He dropped into a chair without taking his eyes off her.

"You put up a good front, Rosie. But look at you. Thin——"

"I find that a considerable improvement."

"But when you're off your feed, Rosie, there's something bothering you."

"It's just the other way around," she said crossly, "but I couldn't expect you to notice that. What do you want, Con? I've got things to do." She tucked the shaker in beside the tomatoes.

He came over to the counter, leaning his back against it so she couldn't avoid him. "I want you, Rosie," he said in a low voice.

Something seemed to shift in her head. It was happening as she had dreamed of it in those first agonizing days, and she could hardly believe what she was hearing. She put her hands swiftly in her pockets before they could give her away.

"Why now?" she asked. "You've had over two months to find it out. More than that, if you go back to before you got her pregnant. You knew when the divorce was coming off. Are you telling me that you didn't know you wanted me back until *now?*"

"Oh, God, Rosie," he said exhaustedly. "Everything was such a mess those last few weeks. Stuff didn't come, or got lost, the wiring was all bollixed up because we were hurrying to get her launched on schedule. The divorce crept up on me, Rosie, I swear. When I saw it in the paper, my God, I——"

"What about your unborn child? The little feller you got all teary about, who had to have a name? The son I couldn't give you?"

"It's not mine," he said.

Her mouth open, she stared into his face. He looked back with slightly reddened eyes, his mouth working as if trying for a jaunty grin that wouldn't come.

"Some joke, huh? She almost made it too. If it wasn't for some drunk throwing it at me, I'd be married now. The night I went into that bar was the luckiest night of my life.... I mean, after the night I met you."

"I don't get it," she said. "Whose child is it?"

"She told me finally. Nearly washed me out the door with hot tears. He's not a fisherman, he's some Limerock white-collar type who keeps his boat at Birch Harbor. He wouldn't break up his home to marry her, so she put the finger on me. After she told me *that*"—the grin finally came, weak but game—"I unshipped oars and rowed out of her life. Oh, Rosie, you don't know the half of it—it's like coming home—"

He reached for her, but she backed away. "What's she going to do now?"

"I don't know and I don't care. It's no skin off my nose."

"You could have been the father. You thought you were."

"You mean I should have stuck with her? Or *been* stuck with her?" He laughed. "You've got to be kidding!" He came toward her and she kept out of reach.

"If she'd been sleeping with the two of you, how could she be sure it was him? She was good enough for you to use, specially if she'd inherit a third of Adam Crowell's property. You could have accepted that child."

"With half the coast knowing it wasn't mine? Oh yeah, it had got around, all right. It's the kind of secret you can't keep. . . . This drunk had spilled his guts about it more than once, and he was the guy's cruising chum, so he knew where the body was buried. Hey, that's pretty good, isn't it?" Jauntiness had been attained at last; it took years off him while she watched.

"Ayuh, the prospective bridegroom was the last to know," he said. "Everybody's been snickering, but I don't care, I'm safe now."

She walked away from him into the sitting room and he followed. "Rosie," he said softly, "if anybody laughed at you on account of me, you're even now. But with us back together again, the way we should be, there'll be no more laughing, unless *we* do it at the rest of the world."

"Until when?" she asked. "The next time?" She turned on

him. "What you want is to save your face, that's it, isn't it? You'll tell how relieved you are, you were only marrying her to do the right thing, but you were having your suspicions and finally you bullied the truth out of her." By his weak protests she knew this was how he'd planned it, and she thought, At least I've learned to figure them out in advance. I never could, once.

"And as soon as you got the truth, you rushed straight back to the one love of your life, which is what you wanted all the time. Con Fleming's the winner again." She raised her clasped hands over her head. "The Winner!"

He was pale. "You *have* got hard."

"No. Up until a few weeks ago I thought I couldn't live without you, Con. It was so awful sometimes, like somebody getting a real case of smallpox from their vaccination. Which means you'll never need another one. It took. I'm not hard, Con, I'm just immune."

He looked so tired and so woebegone. He had come to her with his wounded pride, sure she would make it well again, and all her instincts were to do so. He searched her face in disbelief, and she turned away abruptly.

"You don't mean that, Rosie," he said behind her. "You *don't.*"

"Don't I? Look, Con, you want to shut everybody up, because you think they're laughing at you. But I'm willing to bet that even if Phyllis confessed to you that you weren't the baby's father, but you could be sure that nobody else knew it except the man, and he wouldn't tell it—well, you'd still be right there, Sunny Jim, because a third of Adam's property is quite a chunk. But I've got no more than my house, *Sea Star,* and what I stand in."

"What kind of a man do you think I am?"

"I think you're just the kind of a man you are."

"I can't believe—Rosie—" He tried to take her around the waist. She pushed him away with a thrust of her elbow.

271

"Look, Con," she said, "You've got the boat free and clear, and you're free and clear. So why don't you consider you're pretty well off and go on back? There's a blow coming up the coast, and you don't want to get caught in this harbor with a boat the size of yours."

"*Ours*." One last try.

She shook her head at him. "Yours. . . . They'll stop laughing after a while, Con," she said kindly. "They probably did at me. Of course I ran away. You might have to do that, but a change is as good as a rest, they say."

He wouldn't go and she wondered how much longer she could stand this. He stared wildly around the room, his blue eyes distraught, the new creases deepening. Suddenly he saw one of Edwin's small sketchpads. He pounced on it, snapped through the leaves, and threw it down.

"Is he out here?" he demanded. "The dummy?"

"*Edwin* is here," she said coldly.

His face went red. "To hell with both of you! You're two of a kind. A couple of nuts if I ever saw any. Well, if I don't have you, I don't have him for an in-law, and that's a bargain."

He walked out, almost taking the screen door off the hinges. This time she didn't watch him disappear beyond the spruces. I'm getting a fixation about them, she thought. I'll ask Edwin to cut down some and trim the others so I can see through to the field and the well . . . he's going he's going I can still call him back he came for me he wanted me we could start again and just take what there is not ask too much not think behind or ahead it would be something . . . it would be almost the way it was once I would take him on any terms . . . She stood blindly gazing, her fists in her pockets, until she knew he must be at the wharf.

Then she took the plastic bucket and went out. When she came to Barque Cove *Phyllis* was just emerging past the breakwater. After the first glance of recognition she wouldn't look again. From that glimpse, Rosa knew how sweetly she cut through the gray-green swells. That one glimpse would have to do her for the rest of her life.

Halfway across the beach she stopped and looked fixedly at a place where the water broke foaming and ran in miniature channels carved through a patch of sand among the rocks. Three nights ago Quint had crawled ashore there. —She stood as if between the two men and knew them for twins.

Not quite identical; Con's cruelty was worse than Quint's, which was at least direct. There was less indignity in the beating than in being so tenderly used or apologetically cast aside by Con whenever the occasion demanded. And at least Quint didn't require that his conscience be salved.

She climbed the far side of the cove, where the black rocks reflected heat from the diffused sunlight that glared over everything with a hazy pallor. She followed the track among the goldenrod, asters, and juniper down into the next cove, across its steep slope strewn with driftwood, and on to the next. The air was filled with the sound of surf and the rattle of the smooth stones in the undertow.

She came at last to Sou'west Point and looked for Edwin in the sea-burnt wilderness. Away from the wind the air was lifelessly warm. Sweating, she began to climb the final slope, and finally saw him on the granite prow, above the surf where she had seen him with Linnie that time. He was sitting cross-legged, the big watercolor tablet flat before him, and he was painting. Two gulls walked calmly around him.

She sat down at some distance from him. *The hell with both of you. You're two of a kind.* How right you are, Con, she thought, and I needed you to tell me. She glanced involuntarily toward Brigport. In the poor visibility the boat was no longer to be seen. She was fast, and he wouldn't favor her.

She got up again and went on toward Edwin. The gulls took off past his head, alerting him, and he looked around and saw her, waved his brush, and went on working. She sat down nearby and turned her face into the cold briny wind, letting it flow into her open eyes and assault them until she was forced to close them or turn away.

After a while Edwin reached a stopping place and got up and stretched. She pointed to his notepad and he handed it to her and then walked off away from her toward some scrub spruces. She wrote, "Con was here. Did you know it? Was that why you tried to get me to come with you? Did you know the news before you came?"

When he came back he took the pad, read it, and sat down beside her. She watched over his arm as he wrote, "I knew he was coming out. But not *when*. The story is out and all over the place like mumps. Was going to get you ready for it. But walked into this other—" The pen hesitated, and she took it and wrote firmly. "MESS."

"Then you saw the boat coming this morning and you tried to get me away," she said.

His hands moved fluently in a single question. "Are you going back?"

She answered him in kind. "To him—never."

As if one or the other of them had clapped a book shut at its finish, he stood up and reached for the bucket. She followed him down to the beach, and they began looking around for a clean board to use as a table. He found a crate door and kicked up loose stones until he'd made a level place. She set out the food. All right now, as long as you didn't see a blood-red jigger sail like a shout in the silvery day. Quickly she wrote, "You know what Con calls us? A couple of nuts. Two of a kind."

He laughed. "Could be right. Did it wound you to the quick?"

"If I could paint a picture of you," she said, "know what I'd call it?"

Cutting off cheese on the clean sea-bleached board, he shook his head.

"It just came to me, when I saw you all alone out here except for the gulls. I always wondered who he was, and now

I know he's you. The Man in the Wilderness, the one who goes around asking foolish questions of foolish people."

It wasn't a very good joke, but it would do, and Edwin appreciated it, or at least he appreciated her efforts. He lifted his coffee cup to her, and she lifted hers and repeated True's old toast: "Here's to us. Who's like us? Damn few!"

STRAWBERRIES IN THE SEA
by Elisabeth Ogilvie
About the author . . .

Where Elisabeth Ogilvie lives in Maine, nature makes a lot of the day-to-day news: care and feeding of a litter of raccoon kittens born too late in the fall to make it through the winter unaided; Canadian geese in the cove for the first time ever, resting on their way north; bobcat tracks after the first snow.

The author does most of her thinking and writing in the early morning when nobody and nothing else are up except her two cats who hold Olympic tryouts at dawn and manage to rout out the two resident Australian terriers with their decathlon performances. Much of her life has been concerned with children, those who have lived with her and those whom she has supported during her eighteen years as a member of Foster Parents Plan. She is now raising her sixth child through Plan, and hoping for her first to make her a grandmother.

OTHER BOOKS BY ELISABETH OGILVIE . . .

The Tide Trilogy

The first three volumes in the continuing narrative of Joanna Bennett of Bennett's Island, Maine.

High Tide at Noon (I)
Storm Tide (II)
The Ebbing Tide (III)

The Lovers Trilogy

Down East Books is pleased to reissue the second series featuring Joanna Bennett Sorensen and her family.

Dawning of the Day (IV)
The Seasons Hereafter (V)
Strawberries in the Sea (VI)

An Answer in the Tide (VII)

Following the fortunes of the third generation of Bennett's Islanders, *An Answer in the Tide* focuses on Joanna's son Jamie.

The Day Before Winter (IX)*

This long-awaited latest volume in Elisabeth Ogilvie's series of Bennett's Island novels rejoins Joanna Bennett Sorensen's family during the Vietnam era.

The Jennie Trilogy

Spanning eighteen years and ranging from Scotland to the Maine coast, the Jennie Glenroy saga offers vivid historic settings and unforgettable characters.

Jennie About to Be (I)
The World of Jennie G. (II)
Jennie Glenroy (III)*

My World Is an Island

Miss Ogilvie's entertaining autobiography of early days on Gay's Island back in the 1950s, updated with new photo-graphs and an epilogue by the author.

All titles are paperback unless otherwise noted.
*Also available in hardcover.

CHECK YOUR LOCAL BOOKSTORE, OR ORDER
FROM DOWN EAST BOOKS AT 1-800-685-7962